ALSO BY AMY HATVANY

Best Kept Secret

Outside the Lines

The Language of Sisters

Heart Like Mine

Safe with Me

somewhere out there

A NOVEL

AMY HATVANY

WASHINGTON SQUARE PRESS

New York London Toronto Sydney New Delhi

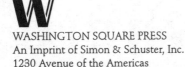

WASHINGTON SQUARE PRESS
An Imprint of Simon & Schuster, Inc.
1230 Avenue of the Americas
New York, NY 10020

First Washington Square Press trade paperback edition March 2016

WASHINGTON SQUARE PRESS and colophon are registered trademarks of Simon & Schuster, Inc.

For information about special discounts for bulk purchases, please contact Simon & Schuster Special Sales at 1-866-506-1949 or business@simonandschuster.com.

The Simon & Schuster Speakers Bureau can bring authors to your live event. For more information, or to book an event, contact the Simon & Schuster Speakers Bureau at 1-866-248-3049 or visit our website at www.simonspeakers.com.

Manufactured in the United States of America

10   9   8   7   6   5   4   3   2   1

Library of Congress Cataloging-in-Publication Data

Hatvany, Amy, date.
  Somewhere out there / by Amy Hatvany. — First Washington Square Press edition.
    pages ; cm
  1. Domestic fiction. I. Title.
  PS3608.A8658S66 2015
  813'.6--dc23   2015021661

ISBN 978-1-4767-0443-2
ISBN 978-1-4767-0444-9 (ebook)

*For Shane, and for the children
who have found a home in his heart*

For a seed to achieve its greatest expression, it must come completely undone.

The shell cracks, its insides come out, and everything changes.

To someone who doesn't understand growth, it would look like complete destruction.

—*Cynthia Occelli*

somewhere
out there

Jennifer

I wouldn't have done it if I hadn't been desperate.

I knew what the stakes were. I knew I might get caught. But it was well past midnight and both my babies were hungry and crying—Brooke, who had just turned four, and Natalie, only six months. A siren sound emanated from Natalie's tiny lungs, and Brooke's choppy, hiccuping sobs felt like sandpaper being rubbed against the tips of my nerves.

We had no place left to go. I was out of friends and money and favors I could call in. I didn't have enough gas to keep driving, so I turned in to a Safeway's deserted parking lot, dreading what I was about to do. My insides felt jittery and loose, as though all my organs had somehow detached. Every cell in my body told me to get out of this car and run. Disappear. Pretend the last five years never happened. But I couldn't. I had the girls. If it wasn't for them, I'd be free.

Shut up, I told myself. *Just shut the fuck up.* I parked the powder-blue, 1970 Toyota Crown station wagon that Brooke's father had given me before he kicked us out. The car was ten years old and had served as our home for most of the last three-plus years. The air inside it was stale and dry. I inhaled the sharp, bitter scent of ammonia, remembering the plastic bag full of Natalie's soiled diapers sitting near the rear hatch. I'd forgotten to throw it out.

I gripped the steering wheel as tightly as I could to keep my body from shaking. With the engine still running, the radio played on, and in the midst of my children's cries, Casey Kasem announced that Blondie's new number one hit, "Call Me," was coming up next on his weekly countdown. I yanked the keys from the ignition and shoved them into my purse, the same two sentences repeating over and over inside my head: *I can't do this anymore. I don't want to be here.*

The kinds of thoughts a good mother wouldn't think.

Natalie shrieked even louder. I closed my eyes, clenched my jaw, and tried not to scream right along with her.

"Mama, what are we doing?" Brooke whimpered.

Letting go of the wheel, I turned and saw her clutching her worn purple blanket, her fingers frantically rubbing its edging. Her "soft side," she called the silky, lavender trim. Whenever she was upset, she'd say, "Where's my soft side? I need my soft side!" and couldn't be comforted until I delivered her blanket and she could feel the satiny fabric against her skin. Now, her black curls shot out from her head in thick, wild corkscrews, and her violet-blue eyes shone with tears. With her lush-fringe lashes, porcelain complexion, and red-bow lips, people were always saying how much she resembled a young Elizabeth Taylor. Which I took as a compliment, too, because Brooke looked almost exactly like me.

"I just have to get us some food," I said, trying to swallow the sharp lump in my throat. "And then we're going to go camping."

At this point, Brooke had probably spent more nights of her life "camping" in our car than beneath an actual roof. I thought about the pale pink room where I'd slept my first fifteen years. It wasn't fancy, or big, but I remembered the comfy twin bed, the white bookshelves, and a closet filled with clothes. I felt sick knowing if something didn't change, I'd never be able to give my girls a room like that. I'd never be able to give them a home. I was only twenty. I didn't graduate high school. I couldn't work because I had no one to watch the girls. I did whatever I had to to survive. We bounced between staying at various friends' houses or cheap motels and sleeping in the car. Standing with them on street corners at busy traffic lights, I scrounged just enough cash for us to get by. I held a cardboard sign that said, MY CHILDREN ARE HUNGRY. CAN'T WORK. PLEASE HELP. Every time someone rolled down their window and handed me money, shame oozed through me like black, sticky tar.

"Nooo, Mama! I don't want to camp!" Brooke said. "I don't! I don't! I don't!" With each "don't," she kicked the back of the driver's seat.

"Please don't do that," I said, trying not to yell. I was already anxious; the last thing I needed was one of her tantrums to send me over the edge.

"No!" Brooke screamed, and kicked my seat again.

That was it. I lost it.

"Goddamn it, Brooke!" I growled. "Knock it off!" My molars ground against each other, fury spiking in my blood. I'd never experienced anything like that feeling before I had my girls; I loved them fiercely, but in my darker, more hopeless moments, I hated what they demanded of me just as much.

"Sorry," Brooke said. Her tiny voice trembled. There was just enough light from the store windows to see the flash of fear on my little girl's face before she buried her head in her blanket.

An aching remorse flooded my chest. "Oh, baby, I'm sorry," I said. "I shouldn't have yelled." She still wouldn't look at me. "Sweetie, please." I paused, waiting for her to peek up at me, which she did a moment later. "Want me to get you a treat?" I asked with what I hoped was a reassuring smile. "Maybe some cookies?"

Brooke nodded, still covering most of her face with her blanket.

"Oreos?" I smiled, knowing they were her favorites. She nodded again. "Okay," I said. "You stay right here with Natalie. I need you to be a good big sister and watch her for me."

Brooke dropped her blanket to her lap and shook her head. "I don't want to." She hated it when I left her alone. I tried not to do it very often, but sometimes, I didn't have a choice. There were certain things a little girl shouldn't see her mother do.

"I'll only be gone a few minutes," I told her, and my stomach clenched. I pointed to the store. "I'm just going to head inside, grab a few things, and I'll be right back."

"I wanna go with you."

I sighed. "Not this time. You need to stay here. Can you be my brave, big girl and watch your sister?"

Brooke looked to her right, lifted her blanket from her lap, and brushed its edge against her baby sister's cheek. Natalie, who had finally stopped crying, made a happy, gurgling sound; she loved her big sister so much. I'd hated being an only child; if I was grateful for anything, it was that they'd always have each other.

"Okay," Brooke squeaked, not looking at me.

"Thanks, sweetie. I promise to be quick." I slung my empty red backpack over my shoulder and got out of the car into the cold, dark night. *At least it's not the middle of summer,* I reasoned. *At least I'm not leaving them to swelter in the heat.* As though that distinction made any of this okay.

It was early October, and the air felt like it had teeth, nipping at my cheeks. Fat, cheerful-looking pumpkins rested in huge piles up against the building; scarlet leaves on the skinny maples lining the parking lot danced in each new gust of wind. I thought about what I might be doing if I was a normal twenty-year-old girl—I might be in college, planning what costume I would wear for Halloween. I might have a boyfriend who brought me flowers and took me to the movies; I might have a group of girlfriends I shopped with at the mall. I might be carefree and content instead of how I felt right now—how I almost always felt—tired, hungry, and scared.

Despite my apprehension, I waved and smiled at Brooke through the window. She waved back, tentatively, but as soon as I locked the doors, her bottom lip quivered, and I knew she was barely holding it together. When Natalie began to cry again, Brooke leaned over and patted her sister's small hand.

She'll be okay, I told myself as I spun around and walked away. *They both will. I have to do this. I'll be back as fast as I can.*

I jogged across the parking lot, trying to block out the sound of Natalie's cries as I entered the building. As the automatic doors shut with a *whoosh* behind me, I quickly surveyed the immediate area—there was no one else around. At this time of night I hoped there would only be a few employees—a couple of stockers and a cashier at most, a few other shoppers, and maybe a night manager working somewhere in the back. I had to be quick. Casual, but quick.

I strode past the enormous Halloween display, ignoring the bags of candy and decorative plastic skeletons. I grabbed a small cart, which I directed toward the produce section. I filled a clear plastic bag with six apples, carefully looking around before slipping four more into my backpack. I picked up two packages of baby carrots and put one in the cart, one in my bag.

So far, so good. I turned the corner, only to run right into a tall, skinny man with shaggy, shoulder-length blond hair and acne-pocked cheeks. He wore a white, short-sleeve shirt covered by a green apron and brown corduroy pants. He didn't look much older than me. A small, plastic tag pinned to his shirt said his name was Rick.

"Whoa," I said, giving him my best smile, even as my heart pounded against my rib cage. "Sorry. Wasn't looking where I was going."

Rick smiled, too, revealing slightly crooked, yellow teeth. "No worries." He surveyed the contents of my cart. "Finding everything all right?"

"Yep. Just picking up a few things I forgot to grab earlier."

"Let me know if you need anything. I'm over on aisle four."

"Thanks," I said again, then pushed my cart past him with as much confidence as I could muster, making sure to head in the opposite direction from where he was working.

Just keep going and get the hell out of here, I thought. Luckily, the Oreos were on an end cap I passed, so I put one package in my basket and another in my backpack, then moved on toward the baby aisle. I dumped a dozen jars of baby food for Natalie on top of the cookies, along with a box of teething biscuits. The last two things I needed were a loaf of bread and peanut butter, so I made my way to the bakery, keeping my eyes open for other employees as I snuck those into my bag, too.

I told myself I was only taking enough to last us a few days—that I'd make better money at a different intersection tomorrow. I tried to believe that stealing food for my children wasn't a crime. That it didn't make me a bad person, but a good one. Don't good mothers do anything necessary for their kids? If I'd had the cash, I would have paid for it all, but buying diapers and wipes and formula for Natalie had taken my last fifty bucks.

I was only a few feet away from the cash registers when I heard Rick call out behind me. "Hey!" His voice was hard. "Wait!"

Shit. I stopped and turned to face him. "Hey," I said, giving him what I hoped was a charming smile. My stomach churned. "So, you won't believe this, but I left my wallet at home." I gestured toward the half-full cart. "I'll have to come back." I looked in the direction of the same doors I'd entered and was about to walk toward them when Rick spoke again.

"No." He frowned at me and held out his hand. "I need to look in your backpack."

"What?" I said. I tried to sound offended, but my shaking voice gave me away. "Why?"

Rick kept his arm outstretched. "My manager has you on tape," he said with a stern look. "He saw everything."

I thought about arguing, pretending I didn't know what he

was talking about, but realized if there was a tape, denial would be pointless. "Please, you don't understand," I said, tears flooding my eyes. "I never do this . . . I just . . . My kids are hungry and I ran out of money. We're homeless. I didn't know what else to do." I glanced over his shoulder and saw a short, burly bald man striding toward us, his stubby arms swinging at his sides.

"Sorry," Rick said. His expression softened. "But you still need to give me the bag."

Reluctantly, I handed over my backpack, feeling the blood rush by my ears. All I could think about was the girls, outside, sitting alone and afraid in the dark. I would do anything it took to get back to them.

The manager approached us and snatched the backpack from Rick's grasp. "Someone's been busy," he said, with a hint of disgust. He had tiny blue eyes and small hands; his name tag said STEVE.

"Look, this was a huge mistake," I said, hoping I could plead my way out of this mess. I looked at Rick. "Seriously, I've never done anything like it." A lie, but one I hoped they might believe.

The manager stared at me. "Uh-huh."

I stepped forward and put my hand on his thick forearm. "It's the truth, I swear. I just needed to feed my kids. I couldn't let them starve. Please, just let me go and I swear I'll never come back."

Steve hesitated, and I thought I might have gotten through to him until I saw a brief flash of red and blue lights outside the glass doors.

My blood ran cold. "You called the police?" I'd only been in the store for ten minutes, at most. The manager must have been watching me the entire time.

"It's store policy," Rick said, sounding a little sorry to relay the information.

"Wait, please," I begged. "You can't do this."

"Yes, I can," Steve said, pulling away from my touch.

The *whoosh* of the doors opening silenced me, and two police officers came in to stand beside me. "This is her?" the younger one asked, taking me by the arm. He was almost as tall as Rick, but with a bigger build. His black hair was shorn into a buzz cut and his blue shirt was tight around his biceps. He smelled like cologne and stale coffee.

"Yep," Steven said. "Claims she was stealing to feed her kids." He unzipped my backpack and rummaged through its contents, coming up with a jar of pureed squash. "Might be true." He shrugged, like either way, it made no difference to him.

"It is true," I said. My voice broke on the words. "Please. They're still in my car."

The older officer finally spoke. "You left your kids alone out there?" He squinted, then looked toward the parking lot.

"I'll go check," the younger officer said, letting go of my arm. "Keys?"

"Please, let me go with you," I said, trying not to cry as I dug into my front pocket, then handed the keys to him. I imagined Brooke seeing the officer opening the car door, her screams as she realized it was anyone other than me. She had a real fear of strangers; for her own safety, living the way we did, I'd done my best to teach her not to trust anyone but me.

The young officer took off without a word, and I couldn't help it—the tears I'd been holding back began to fall. "Please," I said again, my entire body starting to shake. "Let me at least tell them it's going to be okay." Another lie, but one I hoped my little girl might believe.

"What's your name, young lady?" the older officer asked. His voice was stern, unyielding. His thick, gray mustache reminded me of my grandfather who'd died of a heart attack when I was ten. The way my grandma had cried at his funeral sounded like a howling wolf; my mother, a woman whose idea of showing emotion was a pat on the back, had been mortified. Three years later, when my grandma passed away, too, my mother didn't shed one tear.

My chin trembled. "Jennifer Walker."

"And what am I going to find when I punch your name into the system, Jennifer? Have you done this dance before?"

I held his gaze for a moment, thinking of all the decisions I'd made over the past four years, so many of them like tonight, knowing what the consequences might be, but still, thinking I knew best, deciding to take the risk.

"Yes," I told the officer, and then dropped my eyes to the floor. There was no sense trying to hide it; he would find out everything soon enough.

"This makes your fourth count of petty theft," my social worker, Gina Ortiz, said, looking at the thick file on the table between us. It was the morning after my arrest, and my public defender had left the small interview room in the police station just moments ago, after he informed me there was no way I was going to get out of spending at least a couple months in jail. "Up to two years," he'd said. "Maybe more, if things don't go your way."

But the girls, I wanted to scream. *What about my girls?* I'd been in trouble before; I'd even been put in a jail cell a time or two—only for a few hours, never overnight, and I'd always managed to get off with a warning or a fine. Now, here I was, contemplating the possibility that Natalie might learn to walk without me there to hold her hand.

The fact that I had children wasn't the lawyer's problem; it was Gina's. I'd met her two years ago, when CPS was called in after I'd been caught shoplifting for the first time, before I got pregnant with Natalie. She'd kept Brooke with her in the lobby while I went through processing at the police station, and then, when I was released with a warning because the store decided to not press charges, she told me I had to attend parenting classes, starting the following week. I'd blown them off, of course, and seeing her now, I felt a stinging pang of regret.

Gina was a heavier woman, thick around the middle with skinny legs, which I imagined probably made it difficult to find pants. Today, she wore a black pencil skirt and a red blouse with a big bow at the base of her neck. The color flattered her toffee-toned skin. "Not only that," she continued, "it's your second charge of child endangerment and neglect." She paused, and looked at me over the top of her glasses, which were perched on the tip of her slender nose. "Do you know what that means?"

I shook my head, pressing my lips together so I wouldn't cry. I dug the fingernails into my opposite arm until I drew blood; I'd already bitten my nails down to the quick. Could she really be talking about me, endangering my children? Sure, leaving them alone in the car wasn't the best decision I'd ever made, but it wasn't like I gave Brooke knives to play with while I was gone. I wasn't cooking crack in a kitchen while they sat on the floor.

"It means that while you go to jail, the girls go into foster care."

"No," I said. "Maybe the lawyer was wrong. Maybe the judge will understand I was just trying to feed them." A couple of fat tears rolled down my cheeks. I didn't bother wiping them away. "Please? Can you just wait and see what the judge says?"

Gina sighed, removed her glasses, and closed the folder in front of her. Her dark hair was pulled into a bun on top of her head with a few pieces hanging around her round face; she tucked the loose strands behind both her ears and looked at me. "It won't make a difference. It's almost certain you'll be convicted of theft and abuse. The girls are being removed from your care. When you get out, we can talk about a plan to get them back, but at this point, I'm sorry, Jennifer. There's nothing you can do."

"I don't abuse my children!" I cried, feeling as though she'd just hit my chest with a hammer; pain crackled along my ribs. "I've never even spanked Brooke! I just . . . made a mistake."

"Not just one mistake," Gina said. She gave me a pointed look. "And that doesn't count the times you didn't get caught."

My cheeks flamed, and I couldn't lift my eyes to hers. "I love them so much," I said, unsure of how I could prove this to the woman who held the fate of my girls in her hands. I could tell her how much I knew about them—how Brooke slept with one corner of her "soft side" stuck in her ear; how she giggled when I burped my ABCs, and how she sang "Row, Row, Row Your Goat," but I didn't have the heart to tell her she was wrong. I could tell her how Natalie smiled when I kissed her belly, how she rolled over for the first time when she was only three months old and then started to cry, she was so scared by what she'd just done. I longed to show Gina that despite all I'd done wrong, there were at least a few things as a mother I'd done right.

"I know you do," Gina said, gently. "But love isn't enough to be a good parent. There's so much more to it than that."

It was the kindness in her voice that broke me—I realized she wasn't judging me, she was only pointing out the situation for what it was. I let loose a low, keening cry from somewhere deep in my belly. The same two sentences from the previous night played on a constant track inside my head: *I can't do this anymore . . . I don't want to be here.*

"It's so hard!" I sputtered. "I love them, but it's so hard."

I leaned forward, face in my hands, and began to rock back and forth in tiny, measured movements. I thought about my mother, the look on her face when I told her I was pregnant with Brooke and I refused to do as she said and get an abortion. I thought about how her face held that same look when I informed her I was not only keeping my baby but dropping out of school and moving in with Michael, my eighteen-year-old boyfriend, who had his own apartment and a job at Radio Shack.

"You will not," she said, crossing her arms over her chest.

"You moved in with Dad when you were seventeen," I said, thinking this fact more than justified my decision. My parents had met their senior year of high school, and when my mom discovered she was pregnant with me, they got married. He'd left us twelve years later, becoming someone I heard from maybe once or twice a year, then eventually, not at all, but I was certain that Michael and I loved each other too much to share that same fate.

"And look how well that worked out," she said. Her eyes, the same color as mine, flashed. "I want something better for you, Jenny. Something more than I had."

"I will have something better," I assured her. "I'm just going to have it with Michael. We're not getting married right away. We're going to take it slow."

"Moving in with him and having a baby is not taking it slow." She shook her head and pressed her lips together before speaking again. "What kind of job do you think you can get without a diploma?"

"I don't have to work," I said. "Michael will take care of me."

"Like your father took care of us?" she shot back. "Trust me, you'll regret this. Even under the best of circumstances, being a mother is harder than it looks."

I hadn't cried then, the moment she told me if I left, I wouldn't be welcome back. I was so sure of myself, positive I was making the best choice for me and my baby. But now, sitting in the police station in a small room with Gina, I cried harder than I had in years. I cried because I'd been alone for so long. I cried because Michael had kicked us out when Brooke was only nine months old, telling me he never wanted to see either of us again. I cried because even knowing how hard it was raising Brooke on my own, I let myself get pregnant with Natalie. I cried because no matter how much I adored my babies, I was doing a shitty job taking care of them.

Mostly, though, I cried because my mother had been right.

"I know it's hard, honey," Gina said. She stood up and came around the table to put an arm around my shoulders. "It's the hardest job in the world."

I let her hug me and smooth my hair and rub circles on my back. I couldn't remember the last time someone had held me like that. It was always me, holding Brooke or Natalie. Or both of them at once. They were constantly on me, clinging to me, using my body for food or comfort, as though it was their property and not mine. And even though I was worried about them, even though I knew Brooke must be in full-on panic mode by now, surrounded by strangers, wondering why her mommy never came back like she'd promised she would, part of me was grateful to have a few hours where I wasn't responsible for feeding, washing, clothing, and entertaining them. I felt—right along with my guilt, terror, and shame—a tiny sliver of relief.

"I don't know what to do," I said, sniffling as I pulled away from Gina's touch. I looked up at her, distressed. "I just want what's best for them."

Gina squatted down next to me, staring me straight in the eye. "I believe you, Jennifer. I really do. I can hear how much you love them in your voice."

"Thank you," I whispered as I wiped both my cheeks with the bend of my wrist.

When Gina spoke again, it was with such tenderness, such compassion, it made me want to cry all over again. "I might be wrong," she began, "but it sounds like you might be saying that you're not sure if you can raise the girls on your own. That you're thinking of relinquishing custody." She paused, giving me a moment to digest what she'd said. "Is that right?"

"I don't know . . ." I said, the words stuttering out of me. Could I do that? Just hand my babies over to Gina and let her find them a good home? I remembered the vehemence with which I'd fought my mother against having an abortion or giving Brooke up for adoption. I remember believing in my bones that no one could do a better job of mothering my baby than me.

But that was before Michael kicked us out. Before I begged for money on a street corner; before I left Brooke alone in the car while I let a motel manager bend me over his dirty desk and use my body in exchange for two weeks' free rent in a dingy room.

Before I threw up right after he finished; before the moment four months later when I finally realized I'd missed my period and was pregnant again. Before I stumbled into an ER, about to give birth to Natalie, already imagining what lies I'd have to tell her about who her father had been.

If I gave my girls up, could I forget all of this ever happened? Could I forget that that wasn't the last man I'd let use me so I could give my girls a warm room for the night? During the cold winter months, when I ran out of money, having sex with a stranger was often the only way I could find us a place to stay. Could I erase everything, move on, and start a brand-new kind of life? Was signing away my rights the best thing for the girls, or just the easiest thing for me?

I looked at Gina through glassy, swollen eyes. "I don't know," I said again, with an edge of desperation. There was nothing easy about any of this. A battle raged inside of me, an agonizing tug-of-war between what I wanted and what I knew was right.

And then it dawned on me—this wasn't about me. It was about my babies. About giving them a good home, the kind of life I just couldn't provide. I'd done my best, and it wasn't good enough.

"I love them so much." I kept repeating these words as though they might somehow erase the damage I'd already done. As though they might make everything okay.

Gina was silent, waiting for me to say something different. Something more.

I sighed and glanced at my reflection in the window of the room. I had lost so much weight, I'd had to punch two extra holes in my worn leather belt so my jeans wouldn't fall down. My dark hair was thin, greasy, and matted; my face was puffy and red. I couldn't remember the last time I'd felt pretty, the last time I'd looked in the mirror and actually liked what I saw. Instead, I saw a failure—a stupid girl who kept making one bad choice after another. I saw a girl who could never do anything right.

Looking at Gina, I took in a deep breath and held it a moment before finally exhaling, then uttered the single most difficult sentence I'd ever said. "Maybe they'd be better off without me."

And the real tears came—hard, body-racking sobs that should have released my sorrow, but instead made me feel like I had only just begun to fall apart.

Natalie

Natalie Clark was running late.

She sat inside her car in the pickup line at Pine Wood Elementary on a Tuesday, waiting for Hailey to emerge from her second-grade classroom. Natalie drummed her fingers against the steering wheel, staring at the sign over the entrance that proclaimed in bright red letters: 2015 IS GOING TO BE OUR BEST YEAR YET! as she mentally tallied the number of red velvet cupcakes she had in the back of her car. The order had been for six dozen, but as always, on the off chance some of them didn't turn out flawless, she'd baked extra, and now was worried she'd spent so much time obsessing over getting the swirls of cream cheese frosting just so before filling the boxes, she might have set one on the counter at home.

"Damn it," she muttered as she unbuckled her seat belt, opened her car door, and jogged around to open the trunk. It was a gray and drizzly late-September afternoon, but instead of thinking about the damage the rain would do to her recent blowout, she counted the signature pale lavender boxes in which she delivered all of her company's, Just Desserts, products, and confirmed that yes, the entire order was there. Thank god. Natalie had wanted to pick up Hailey after she'd delivered the cupcakes to her client's house, then grab Henry from preschool on their way home, but now she would have to take her daughter along to drop off the order. It wouldn't be the first time her best-laid organizational plans were a victim of her culinary perfectionism.

The car behind her gave a quick honk, snapping her out of her thoughts, and Natalie looked up to see that all of the vehicles in front of her had already loaded their children and pulled away. Causing a backup was a major offense for parents who picked up their kids at the school; some people had been known to purposely rear-end a person not paying attention to the flow of the line.

"Unbelievable," her husband, Kyle, had said when Natalie told him about the deliberate fender bender she'd witnessed a couple of weeks ago. "The victim should threaten to sue for vehicular assault." Kyle was a defense attorney, and tended to notice potential legal threats the same way an electrician might point out bad wiring in another person's house.

Natalie was a lawyer, too, but after passing the bar and an unhappy three years at her father's firm, Bender & Beck, telling him that she wasn't going to return to work when Hailey was born had been one of the hardest conversations she'd ever had. But the truth was she wasn't passionate about the law—she'd only studied it to make her father happy—and something about becoming a mother had prioritized things for Natalie. It made her realize the days were too short, too precious, to waste spending them in a career that required insanely long hours and in general made her miserable. She and Kyle agreed that she would stay home until Hailey started school, and Natalie could use that time to figure out exactly what kind of work she wanted to do. Their son, Henry, came along two years after his big sister, and it wasn't until he started preschool that Natalie's favorite hobby began to morph into a job. She'd loved baking since she was seven years old, when a family friend gave her a hardcover cookbook filled with glossy, colorful pictures of perfectly round chocolate chip cookies and smoothly frosted cakes. She used to sit on the couch for hours, turning the book's pages, reading through each recipe as though it were a story, the ingredients its characters, dreaming of the bakery she might one day own.

She lost sight of that dream somewhere along the way and instead, ended up doing what her parents expected of her. She went to law school. Which in some ways was good for Natalie, who at her core was a little shy. It forced her to push through her insecurities and interact—to argue case law with her classmates and become, at least on the surface, a well-spoken professional. But it wasn't until she worked up the courage to leave her father's firm that Natalie started to follow her true passion. She became known among the other mothers in her mommy and me classes as the baker of the best cookies and other sweet treats, and was often called upon to provide the dessert for any group function. For Natalie, baking offered a way to connect. She lived for the looks on people's faces when they bit into one of her lemon drop cupcakes or caramel honey-pot pecan bars. Expressing their love of a sugary treat was a language everyone knew how to speak.

Soon, she started receiving offers to be paid for her talent. Encouraged by her customers' overwhelming positive response, she took several classes at the local community college to hone her skills and started Just Desserts catering company last year, when Hailey began first grade and Henry started a full-day preschool program, which, because of his later birthday and the fact that he didn't seem quite ready to make the transition into kindergarten, Natalie and Kyle had decided to keep him in for one more year. She relied mostly on word of mouth to gather new clientele, and wasn't making a fortune, but she loved the flexibility running her own business allowed. "You went from torts to tarts," Kyle liked to say, which always made Natalie roll her eyes.

Now, Natalie waved and smiled at the man in the blue Honda Accord behind her, hoping he wasn't about to ram her for her lapse in attention, which would undoubtedly ruin the cupcakes. "Sorry!" she said as she shut the trunk and rushed back behind the wheel. Throwing the car into gear, she pulled forward as far as she could, then glanced at the clock. Two forty-five, and she had to have the order delivered by three. "Where are you, munchkin?" she murmured, and then, as though Hailey had somehow heard her question, Natalie heard her daughter's voice.

"Mommy!" Hailey yelled. Natalie turned to her right and smiled at her little girl, who at seven, was not so little anymore. Her long curls bounced as she ran toward the car; Natalie couldn't bring herself to cut them more than an inch or two, so they looked like a mass of slender, brown Slinkys coiled down Hailey's back. Her hair color she got from Kyle—Natalie was blond—but Hailey was petite, like Natalie, with delicate features and startling violet-blue eyes that weren't a gift from either of her parents. Both Kyle's and Natalie's eyes were brown. At five, Henry's previously light mop of hair was beginning to darken to match his eyes, as well. He was looking more and more like his father.

"Mommy!" Hailey said again as she jerked open the car door and swung like a monkey into the backseat, dropping her backpack beside her. She quickly fastened her belt. "Guess what!"

"What?" Natalie asked, still smiling as she pulled away from the curb and onto the street. "Guess what" had recently become the preface to everything Hailey told her. "Guess what, Mom? I saw a bug!" and "Guess what? My socks don't even match!" Kyle found it a little annoying, but it amused Natalie, especially when Hailey and Henry got going on the "Guess what" game together. "Guess what?" Henry would ask his big sister. "My feet smell like farts!" Hailey would giggle, then reply, "Guess what? Your *face* smells like farts!" Basically, any mention of farts sent her children into hysterics, but regardless, it filled Natalie's heart with unspeakable joy when the two of them laughed and played. As an only child who tended to keep to herself, Natalie had always wished for a sibling; she'd promised herself that if she ever had babies, she would have more than one.

"I got an A on my spelling test!" Hailey said now. "I didn't even miss one!"

"That's great, sweetie," Natalie said, glancing in the rearview mirror at her daughter. "You studied hard with Daddy. Good job."

"Um, Mommy?" Hailey said. "I think you're going the wrong way." She peered out the window at the stores lining California Avenue. "Did you forget where we live? Are you getting Olds-heimer's?"

Natalie laughed. "No. I need to drop off a cupcake order before we pick up Henry. I'm running a little late." She pushed down on the accelerator, keeping a watchful eye out for cops.

"Ohhhh," Hailey said. Natalie heard the rustling of paper, and then her daughter spoke again. "Guess what else?"

"What?" Natalie came to a slow stop at a light, pumping her brakes, not wanting to jostle the boxes in the back and risk smashing the frosting she'd spent hours perfecting. She bit her lower lip, silently willing the light to turn green again. Her wipers squeaked across the windshield, sending goose bumps across her skin. Natalie was always the person who showed up fifteen minutes early to appointments or events. Being late went against everything her parents had taught her about respecting other people's time as much as her own. Kyle, who had a tendency toward tardiness—except to court—didn't always appreciate her persistent prodding to get him out the front door.

"Mrs. Benson says we have to do a family tree this week! I have to make a big poster and draw a tree on it and the names of all the people in my family!"

"Oh," Natalie said. "That should be fun." She attempted to sound enthusiastic, but her words came out stilted.

"Yeah," Hailey said, seeming not to notice her mother's reaction. "But I need to get some new markers so I can do it."

"What happened to your old ones?"

"Henry left the caps off. He's always messing up my stuff."

A block past Hiawatha Park, Natalie took a left turn onto Admiral Way, deciding that now was not the time to get in a debate with her daughter over who was at fault for the dried-out markers. She remembered how she'd had to complete a similar family tree assignment once. It hadn't gone well. She felt a sharp twinge in her gut, as she always did when she was reminded that there was a woman out there somewhere in the world who had given birth to her, and then had given her up.

Natalie hadn't known that she was adopted until she turned ten. She wasn't aware of it at the time, but what had spurred her parents' decision to finally tell her about her lineage was an article that her mother had read in *Parenting* magazine. The author, a child psychologist, suggested that in the long run, adopted children ended up emotionally better adjusted if they were told about their adoption—if they understood that someone else had given birth to them, but they had been chosen by their parents.

Natalie's mind still held the vivid memory of the night her parents sat her down in the living room and told her the truth. She remembered that the greasy smell of the Chinese food her mother had ordered for dinner hung in the air; she recalled the peach-and-blue–swirled pattern of the couch upon which she sat. She saw her father's black suit, his broad shoulders and dark, wavy hair; she remembered the long jean skirt and blue oversize cardigan her mother wore. She could still hear the way her mother's voice shook. "We need to tell you something, honey," her mother said. "Something important."

Natalie kept her hands folded tightly in her lap. She thought about the stash of candy she had hidden beneath her bed and wondered if her mother had found it. But before she could say anything, her father spoke.

"You know how much we love you," he began, and Natalie nodded, wondering what loving her had to do with Laffy Taffy and Jolly Ranchers.

"We loved you so much," her mother said, "that when you

were a baby, we adopted you. Out of all the other babies in the world, you were so special, we chose *you* to be our daughter."

"I'm . . . adopted?" Natalie said. She didn't know how to feel. Her eyelids fluttered, and she wondered if she might start to cry. She looked back and forth between her parents, not for the first time struck that she didn't look like either of them. They both had dark hair, while she was blond. Her eyes were brown when theirs were both blue. Natalie was petite, with a birdlike frame, and her father was muscular and six foot three; her mother was five foot seven with a tendency to bemoan her less than slender waistline and thick thighs.

"Yes," her mother said. Her blue eyes were glossy with tears. "You are. The girl who carried you in her belly was too young to take care of you. You lived your first six months with her inside a car." Her mother's tone reflected her deep dismay. "That girl did the best thing for you, honey. She gave you up. She gave you to us."

"She didn't want me?" Natalie asked in a small voice. She felt as though something in her chest had cracked open. Like a thousand hammers were banging around inside her head.

"*We* wanted you," her father said, coming over to sit next to her. He wrapped one of his long arms around her shoulders and pulled Natalie to him. He smelled like Old Spice, the aftershave Natalie and her mother bought him every year for his birthday. "You were always meant to be our little girl."

"But I'm not your *real* daughter," Natalie said. The muscles in her throat ached.

"Yes," her father said. "You are. We are your parents. Your only parents."

Natalie nodded, slowly, but her mind raced. She wondered what her birth mom was doing, if she had more children, and if she would recognize Natalie if she saw her now. She wondered who her birth father was, if he was tall, and if he wore Old Spice aftershave, too.

Her chin trembled as she asked her parents another question. "If she gave me away," Natalie began, her words stiff and halting, "does that mean you could, too?" She assumed this was a valid concern; she didn't know how it all worked. What if her parents decided they were tired of her, or that they didn't really want her in the first place? What if they realized that adopting her had been a mistake?

"Oh, honey," her mother said, taking a step toward Natalie and her father. She sat down on the other side of her daughter on the couch. "No. Never. We would never let you go."

"Are you sure?" Natalie asked, unable to hold back her tears. She felt them wet her cheeks, and her father cupped her face in his hands and used his thick thumbs to wipe them away.

"We are more than sure," he said, emphatically. He pulled his hands away from her face and kissed the top of her head while her mother rubbed circles on Natalie's back.

After a moment, Natalie spoke again. "Can I meet her?" she asked, but when she saw the way her mother closed her eyes and jerked her head to one side, she immediately regretted the question.

"No, honey," her father said. "You can't. The adoption was closed, which means everyone keeps their privacy. You're ours. Nothing in the world can change that."

At that point, Natalie didn't tell anyone that she was adopted. Her parents had kept it a secret for so long, she assumed it was something she shouldn't talk about with anyone else. Then one day, not long after her parents told her the truth, her teacher issued an assignment to create a family tree. When Natalie got home from school that afternoon, she dropped into a chair at the kitchen table, pulled out the large white piece of paper her teacher had given her, and unfolded it, smoothing it as best she could. Gripping her pen hard so it wouldn't wiggle on the page, Natalie drew a brown trunk and then a long branch, outlining three green leaves for her mom, dad, and herself. Then, off to the side, she added an extra leaf right on the same branch.

"What's my birth mom's name?" Natalie asked her mother, who stood at the kitchen counter, cutting up an apple and some cheese for Natalie's snack.

"What?" her mother said, setting down the silver knife she held. Her voice was tight. Uneasy. "Why?"

Natalie explained the assignment in low tones, keeping her eyes on the table. Her mother wiped her hands on a dish towel, then came over to join her daughter. She looked at the tree on the paper, and then back at Natalie. "Family's a complicated thing, honey," she said. "It has more to do with who takes care of you, not who gave birth to you. That girl doesn't fit in that category."

"Oh," Natalie said, feeling the inside of her chest start to burn. She hated that her mom used the term "that girl" when she referred to Natalie's birth mom. It made Natalie feel dirty, as though the woman who had carried Natalie in her belly was someone of whom she should be ashamed. "Sorry." She wasn't sure what she was apologizing for, but she knew she was responsible for the strained look on her mother's face.

"It's fine," her mom replied. "You can just use that other leaf for Aunt Vicki . . . okay?" Vicki was Natalie's father's sister, who lived on a ranch in Montana. They saw her once a year, at Christmas, and the only thing Natalie knew about her was that she wasn't married and her clothes smelled like horses.

"Okay," Natalie said, even though she felt like it was wrong to exclude her birth mother from the assignment. She waited a moment before another question bubbled up inside her, escaping before Natalie could stop it. "Was I a terrible baby?" she asked. "Is that why my birth mom didn't want me?"

Her mother pressed her lips together and shook her head, looking like she was about to cry. "You were perfect," she said, giving her daughter a bright, false smile. "What should we have for dinner?" she asked, making it clear that the subject was closed.

But thoughts of her birth mother wouldn't leave her alone.

Natalie often fantasized that her "other" mom might just show up and whisk her away to an entirely different life. Natalie made up stories about the circumstances surrounding her adoption. *Maybe she works for the FBI,* she'd thought. *Maybe living in her car was part of her job and she had to travel so much catching bad guys that she couldn't take me with her.* Her parents said they had the paperwork that made Natalie's adoption legal, but they wouldn't let her see it. They swore there was nothing more detailed in it than what they had already told her.

Now, Natalie pulled up in front of her client's beautiful three-story, red-brick home with only three minutes to spare, and tried to erase thoughts of her adoption from her mind. "I'll be right back, okay?" Natalie told Hailey as she pulled the keys from the ignition and unfastened her seat belt. Her client, an older woman hosting a birthday party for a friend, stood on the front porch, waiting, thin arms crossed over her chest. "Just have to run the boxes into the house."

"I can help," Hailey said, momentarily distracted from the subject of her family tree project.

Natalie turned around to smile at her daughter. "I appreciate that, sweetie, but it's raining. You just sit tight." She ran around to the back of her car and opened the hatch, then carefully lifted two of the lavender boxes and carried them up to the house as quickly as she could. After two more trips, her client handed her a check and Natalie climbed back into her car, shaking droplets of rain from her head.

"See?" she said to Hailey. "Easy-peasy."

"Guess what?" Hailey said. "I hate peas."

Natalie laughed, flipped a U-turn in the middle of the street, and drove south toward Henry's preschool, which was only a few blocks from their house. She headed down the hill toward Alki Beach, planning to take the back way to Henry's school through residential streets instead of dealing with all the traffic and lights on California Avenue. She and Kyle had bought their two-story

Craftsman on Gatewood Hill after he made partner last year, and they were still in the process of tweaking its features to make it their own. So far, they'd painted every wall with warm, natural hues, replaced all the appliances, and pulled up the carpets to re-finish the original hardwood floors. Natalie had just received ap-proval on a small business loan for Just Desserts, which would be spent remodeling the stand-alone garage they weren't using for anything but storage into a professional kitchen so she could take on bigger jobs. She'd already found and purchased a barely used commercial convection oven, a triple sink, and an enormous stainless-steel, double-door refrigerator-freezer on Craigslist; all she needed was to hire a contractor to bring the wiring up to code, put down a tile floor, and Sheetrock the walls, and she'd be in busi-ness. She often wondered if she had inherited her love of baking from the woman who'd given her up; her adoptive mother's skills in the kitchen consisted mostly of being able to artfully arrange the takeout she'd ordered on their dinner plates. Natalie wondered if she would understand herself better if she met her birth mother. Would she know from whom Hailey had gotten her violet eyes?

"Are you okay, Mommy?" Hailey asked, snapping Natalie out of her thoughts.

"Of course," Natalie said, glancing in the rearview mirror to see her daughter's brows knitting together over the bridge of her pert nose. The last thing Natalie had expected she'd be thinking about that afternoon was her birth mother. "Just trying to figure out what I'm going to make us for dinner."

"Risotto!" Hailey said. She loved to watch cooking shows and had taken to making a list of all the different meals she'd like to try. After overhearing Gordon Ramsay say, "Very good, that ri-sotto!" on an episode of *Hell's Kitchen*—which Natalie had turned off as soon as she realized that the majority of the show con-sisted of censored expletives—Hailey was now obsessed with the idea of the dish. She'd also adopted the famous chef's phrase for her more general use—after eating dinner, she'd look at Natalie and say, "Very good, that macaroni!" or after a bath, "Very good, that shampoo!" Always wanting to emulate his big sister, Henry began copying her, too. The other night, when he refused to eat his vegetables, he'd thrown his fork on the table, screwed up his face, and said, "Very bad, that broccoli!"

"I think we'll just have spaghetti," Natalie told Hailey as they pulled up in front of Henry's preschool. It was three thirty, and she was right on time to pick him up. Hailey liked to accompany Natalie inside so she could say hello to her old teachers. "You can help me make the salad."

"Okay," Hailey consented, and a moment later she and Natalie got out of the car, and together ran through the rain toward the building, holding hands.

Later that night, after the kids were tucked in and Natalie and Kyle were in their own bedroom, Natalie told her husband about Hailey's family tree project. "It really made me think about my birth mom," she said, curling up to her husband, draping one of her legs over his.

At five foot nine, her husband was seven inches taller than she was, built like a wrestler with thick muscular limbs. Name a sport and Kyle had played it, but his personal favorite, the one he still made time for, was racquetball. Any day he wasn't in court, he'd spend his lunch hour with his friend John at the gym, sweating out the stress from his job. While Natalie supported her husband's devotion to this activity, the only competition she wanted to participate in was being a contestant on *Cupcake Wars*; the only workout she enjoyed was speed-rolling hundreds of molasses cookies in crunchy, sparkling sugar for the PTA bake sale at Hailey's school. Unlike her mother, Natalie was blessed with a metabolism that allowed her to eat whatever she wanted and didn't require her to exercise in order to maintain her weight—another characteristic she wondered if she had inherited from the woman who'd given her up.

Kyle kissed the top of her head, then ran his fingers up and down her bare arm, giving her goose bumps. There was no place she felt safer than being tucked up against him. "I'll bet," he said. "You okay?"

"Sort of," she said. Kyle knew any discussions of her birth mother dredged up emotions Natalie would rather not feel, and questions she'd probably never have answered. She turned her head to look at him. His eyes were a lighter shade of brown than hers, like copper, flecked with bits of green. Besides his big heart and great sense of humor, they were among the things Natalie loved most about him.

They had met nine years ago, when he was thirty and she was twenty-six. He'd joined her father's practice about four months after she had, but as they never were assigned to the same case, their interactions were limited to the passing-each-other-in-the-hallway, head-bobbing, hi-how-are-you variety. She knew her father liked Kyle—he'd even gone so far as to say that the younger man was one of the top up-and-coming lawyers in the firm. She'd witnessed more than one female in the office lingering around him, asking insipid questions, and laughing too loudly at his jokes. Like them, she couldn't help but notice his good looks—in contrast to the well-cut, buttoned-up suits he wore, he had longish, wavy, dark brown hair, full lips, and an easy smile—and while dating among associates wasn't strictly forbidden as long as it was reported to Human Resources, Natalie preferred to keep her relationships in the workplace on a professional level.

Her and Kyle's first substantive conversation occurred at the beginning of her second year at the firm, when she was asked to do some research for a first-degree murder case in which he was defending a woman accused of killing her husband.

"Do you have a minute?" she'd asked, standing in the doorway of his dark wood-paneled office, holding a file in her right hand. He sat at his desk, staring at a stack of photos in his hands.

Kyle lifted his eyes to hers when he heard her voice. His face held a haunted, haggard look. "Sorry . . . what?" he said, clearly distracted by whatever it was he'd been looking at.

"I penned an opinion for the case," she said, taking a few steps toward him. "Do you have time to review it with me? Make sure I didn't miss anything on what you wanted to say about PTSD-induced psychosis?" Kyle's argument was self-defense, based on the fact that the husband had been violently abusing his client for ten years and in the moment she'd shot him, she'd been under the influence of ongoing post-traumatic stress disorder.

"Sure," he said, dropping the pictures onto the blotter. He glanced at them again, then blinked rapidly, as though he were trying to erase the images he'd seen. He gestured toward one of the well-padded, black leather chairs on the opposite side of his large maple desk. "Have a seat."

Natalie sat down and was about to hand him the papers she held, but instead, concerned by his demeanor, she kept them. "I don't mean to pry," she said, feeling her cheeks warm, unsure whether or not she should continue. "But are you all right?"

"I don't know." He nodded toward the pictures in front of him. "The police took these when she filed her restraining order against him. Her *third* restraining order. He broke her collarbone and her arm, that time. And gave her two black eyes. The first time, he fractured a rib that ended up puncturing her lung."

Natalie stayed silent, watching him drum his fingers on the edge of his desk. She could see what had happened to his client pained him, and it made her think there might be more to this talented litigator than just his handsome face.

"I'd kill him again myself, if I could," Kyle said. "Fucking bastard."

Natalie waited a beat before speaking. "I'd help you hide the body," she said. He smiled, their gazes locked, and the air between them took on an electric, butterflies-in-the-stomach quality. Later, the two would agree that in that moment, it felt as though they were seeing each other for the first time.

That night over drinks and more conversation at a local bar, Natalie learned that despite Kyle's in-control, polished-lawyer demeanor when he was at work, he was a man who felt things on a deep level. He was just careful about to whom he revealed this part of himself. "My dad was big on not showing your opponents any weakness," he told her during a discussion of their families. "He drilled it into me and my brother to be tough, so I learned to push down any sign of how I might be feeling in order to come out on top." He paused and gave her a wry smile. "Unfortunately, that tendency hasn't worked well for me in my personal relationships."

"Are you telling me I should get out now?" Natalie asked with a playful edge, suspecting that she understood Kyle better than he might think. She'd dated over the years, of course, but none of her relationships lasted more than a few months, her partners typically calling things off before they got too serious. The comment she'd heard most often was "You're hard to get to know."

Kyle stared at her a long moment before answering. When he did, he reached over and took her hand in his. "Please don't," he said, and her heart skipped a beat inside her chest. Later, he walked her to her car, kissed her, and suddenly, all of Natalie's resolve to avoid romance on the job disappeared.

They reported their relationship to HR, and to Natalie's father, who was thrilled with the match. Only a few months after that, they got engaged. They'd been married just over a year when she got pregnant with Hailey and quit the firm, Natalie's father conceding that if he couldn't one day hand his legacy over to his daughter, his more than competent son-in-law was the next best choice.

Now, lying in bed with him, Natalie burrowed her face into her husband's chest, and her next words came out muffled. "Do you think I should try to find out more about her?"

"Your birth mother?" Natalie nodded, and felt her husband inhale before speaking again. "Do you want to?"

She hesitated only a moment before answering. "Yes." She paused, and then went on. "But my mom will freak."

"Your mom's the most insecure person I know."

"Yeah," Natalie agreed, but she drew out the word, hesitant, feeling a little protective of the woman who had raised her. "You know she just has a hard time dealing with any kind of loss." Kyle understood that a few years before his mother-in-law and Natalie's dad decided to adopt, Natalie's mom had suffered a life-endangering ectopic pregnancy that resulted in a full hysterectomy—something Natalie was aware of only because her father had told her. Her mother's health issues and the lost baby were other subjects she refused to discuss.

"That was more than thirty years ago, Nat," Kyle pointed out, pulling away from her. "And she wouldn't be losing you. She has mothered you, loved you, taken care of you, and now you're an adult, well within your rights to want to know more about the woman who gave birth to you."

Natalie sat up and looked at her husband. He'd sounded very lawyerly with that speech, as though he was giving emphatic closing arguments to sum up his case to a jury. "Guess what?" she said, teasing him with their children's much used phrase.

He shook his head and pretended to scowl. "What?"

"You're right," she told him. "Completely and totally right."

"Was that on the record, Counselor?" Kyle asked with a grin. Natalie gave him a playful push, and he grabbed her, tickling her ribs. She squealed, and he put his hand over her mouth to keep the noise from waking the kids, who both slept just across the hall.

"What are you going to do now, huh?" he said, as she wiggled inside the circle of his strong arms. This kind of roughhousing often led to a session of passionate lovemaking, but tonight, when he finally let her go, instead of climbing on top of him, Natalie fell back against her pillows with a heavy sigh.

"Now," she said, "I'll have to go talk with my mom."

Brooke

Standing beside a table tucked in the darkest corner of the bar, Brooke was certain she was about to be sick. She clutched her pen, pressing it into her pad as she tried to ignore the rolling, twisting queasiness in her gut. The symptoms had come out of nowhere, and her first thought was that she probably ate something that didn't agree with her. She thought about asking to go home, but couldn't afford to leave work—it was Friday night and the place was packed. It would be her best tip night of the week.

Located in Pioneer Square, the Market had opened a year ago. It wasn't the cleanest or fanciest place to work—it was dingy and dim, catering less to Seattle's rampant hipster population and more to the blue-collar, grease-under-their-fingernails crowd. But the owner was nice enough and didn't try to get Brooke to sleep with him, which in her experience, was an anomaly. In her twenties, she used to apply for jobs at more upscale bars and restaurants, but when she interviewed and the owners saw her list of experience at biker bars and intermittent stints at Applebee's, they always passed on hiring her. Now thirty-nine, Brooke had accepted a career as a cocktail waitress, taking pride in the fact that after aging out of the foster care system at eighteen, she'd never taken another penny from the state. At times, she worked two, sometimes three different jobs in order to stay afloat, which was fine by her. It could be worse, she always told herself. She could not have a job at all.

Brooke wove her way to the servers' station at the bar and quickly punched in a ticket for her newest table—two double Jack and Cokes. She turned around, ready to walk the floor and check on her other customers, but then the gorge rose in her throat and she ran to the women's bathroom, hand over her mouth, barely able to shut the stall door behind her before she was over the toilet and heaving.

What the hell? she thought as she was finally able to stand up, wiping her lips and chin with a handful of toilet paper. She mentally reviewed what she'd eaten that day: a bagel with the last of the cream cheese, and a double cheeseburger off the McDonald's dollar menu on the way to the bar. It was likely the burger that did it, and Brooke immediately vowed to never again eat a fast-food meal.

She exited the stall and then stood in front of the sink, cupping water in her hand and washing out her mouth as best she could. Smoothing her black curls, she wiped away the mascara smeared beneath her eyes and applied a fresh coat of red lipstick, then popped three Altoids. The door swung open, and her coworker Tanya entered.

"Hey," Tanya said. "I just delivered your order to table twelve."

"Thanks," Brooke said, turning to look at Tanya, a short black woman with a heart-shaped face, a multitude of shoulder-length slender braids, and an enormous rack. "Tits equal tips," she liked to claim, completely unashamed to exploit her sexuality to make money.

"No problem," Tanya said, taking a minute to glance in the mirror. She reached into her tight, blue V-necked T-shirt and adjusted her breasts for optimal cleavage exposure. She looked over at Brooke and frowned. "You okay? You look like hell."

"Think I ate a bad burger," Brooke said. "I'm fine, now." After making her ill, her nausea had vanished.

"Hopefully not the kind of burger where you wake up with a baby nine months later," Tanya said with a grin. Her teeth glowed white against her dark skin.

"Oh, god, no," Brooke said, but something inside her dropped a few floors at what Tanya's joke implied. A pregnancy scare was not what her relationship with Ryan needed. They'd met a year ago, when he was newly separated and living on his own, and twelve months later, he had yet to pull the trigger on making the end of his marriage legal. This bothered Brooke less than it might have someone else—when she'd told Tanya about his circumstances, her coworker shook her head and made clucking sounds to indicate her disapproval: "Girl, that man has more baggage than a European vacation. You need to cut him loose."

But the truth was, Brooke was happy with how things were. Ryan didn't push her to move in with him and she didn't ask him where their relationship might be headed. Instead, the two simply kept each other company. They went out for dinner a few times a week, always ending up at his beautifully furnished downtown apartment, which overlooked the glittering lights of Elliott Bay, where they had the kind of passionate, mind-numbing sex that felt as necessary to Brooke as taking a breath. They kept things simple. Uncomplicated. Which was exactly how Brooke liked her relationships to be.

On the days she didn't see Ryan, she'd read the books she checked out from the library or binge-watch *Scandal* or *House of Cards* on Netflix. She'd go to the grocery store, noting the other shoppers with their big carts piled high with family-size bags of chicken breasts, pot roasts, and bulk packages of hamburger and boxes of macaroni and cheese—purchases that promised loud and happy meals around a dining room table, parents bribing their children with the reward of ice cream if they ate at least three forkfuls of green beans. The kinds of meals Brooke had never had. She'd stand in the frozen food aisle, watching these scenes play out, finding herself wishing that she, too, had grown up with a mother to nag into buying Double Stuf Oreos, Doritos, and pouches of sugary juice. She wished for any kind of mother other than the one who'd given her away.

"See you out there," Tanya said.

Brooke watched as Tanya spun around and headed back out the door, then a moment later followed her. As she worked the rest of her shift that night, Brooke tried to forget what Tanya had suggested. But after the bar closed and she sat at a table, tallying up her tips, she couldn't help but count backward to the last time she'd had her period—five . . . six . . . seven . . . eight weeks. She was late. Panic flooded her body in a cold rush, causing her skin to sprout goose bumps.

Calm down, she told herself. It could be anything. It could be stress. It could just be her, being irregular.

But even so, after she said good-bye to Tanya and Fred, the bartender, she drove toward her studio apartment on Capitol Hill, a voice inside her head reminding her that she was never irregular. She was on the Pill, but there were a few times this summer when she'd forgotten to take it and had to double up the next morning. If she was carrying Ryan's baby, she had to know. And so, on her way home from the bar, she stopped at a twenty-four-hour Walgreens and bought two early-detection pregnancy tests, along with a box of saltine crackers and a six-pack of ginger ale, in case she started to feel queasy again.

As she made her way back to her car, Brooke thought about the night Ryan first came into the bar and sat down at one of her tables with a group of his employees. Brooke had found herself doing a double take when she saw him, appreciating the strong angles of his jaw—the ruddy, lined map of his face. He had light brown hair, brown eyes, and a mischievous smile that hinted at a good sense of humor. She was attracted to him immediately.

"Can I get you another drink?" she asked him after he'd already had two. She lifted her eyebrows and put one of her hands on her jutted-out hip.

"No, thanks," Ryan said. "But when can I buy one for you?" The line could have come off as cheesy, but he spoke the words with such confidence, she found herself laughing and giving him her number.

They went out the next night she had off from work. From the beginning, he was up front about the fact that he and Michelle were still married, but only in name. "Before I finally left, we hadn't slept in the same bed for five years," he told her on their first date. He took her to the Metropolitan Grill, a landmark restaurant where the steaks were legendary, and the bottle of wine Ryan ordered cost more than Brooke's monthly grocery budget.

"That's awful," Brooke said, wondering why people bothered to get married at all, if fifty percent of those couples ended up hating each other, fighting over who got to keep their CD collection.

"She wants everything," he continued. "Half of our retirement and half the business, plus child support and spousal maintenance. I'd have to pay her seven figures to buy her out, then close to ten thousand a month. I've worked too hard for too long to just hand it all over to her."

"I don't blame you." Brooke knew that other women might be bothered by Ryan discussing his almost-ex on their first date, feeling like it was in bad taste, but Brooke didn't mind. In fact, she appreciated knowing exactly where Ryan was coming from. It made her certain he wouldn't ask more of her than she was able to give.

As their dinner progressed, Brooke learned that Ryan was forty-five, and the owner of one of the largest contracting firms in Seattle, running multiple crews on various important construction projects around the city. She admired the fact that he was self-made—that he hadn't been handed his company, he'd built it on his own, from the ground up. He was driven and passionate. She told herself her attraction to him didn't have anything to do with his money—though as they began to spend more time together, she had to admit that she enjoyed the luxuries it afforded them. They never drank anything less than a hundred-dollar bottle of champagne, and he hired an Uber to drive her back to her apartment at the end of the night if she didn't have her own car there. She liked the way that he laughed; she liked his handsome face and strong body—musculature chiseled by long hours of physical labor. He told her he was mesmerized by the combination of her black hair and violet eyes; he said her pale skin felt like silk. "You're the most beautiful woman I've ever seen," he always whispered when he slowly stripped her clothes from her body, and Brooke let herself believe him. The way he kissed her felt like a form of worship, and the intensity of their lovemaking—the escape it gave her—surpassed anything she'd ever experienced before. She couldn't get enough.

Still, he was married, and his very expensive divorce lawyer advised him to keep their relationship on the down-low, and not to introduce Brooke to his sons, for fear that Michelle would find a way to use Brooke against him in court. All of this was fine with Brooke. She never planned anything for more than a few weeks ahead.

A pregnancy would change all of that. A baby would change everything.

Brooke found a parking spot on the street near her building and quickly made her way into the old brick house that had been converted into six small studios. Once inside, she headed down the dimly lit stairwell and unlocked the door to her basement unit. Clutching the Walgreens white plastic bag, she flicked on a lamp and kicked off her shoes, looking around the place she had lived in for the past five years. The room was a perfect square, painted the palest shade of yellow Brooke could find to help brighten it. Her bed, which was really just a queen-size mattress and box spring on the floor, rested against the wall opposite the door, and her tiny kitchenette was to her left. All her clothes were in an old dresser she'd found at Goodwill for ten bucks; she'd painted it periwinkle blue to match the blankets and fluffy pillows on her bed. Over in the corner was the bathroom, a space barely big enough to fit a stall shower, toilet, and sink, which was where Brooke immediately headed, taking one of the pregnancy tests with her.

She opened the box, carefully reading the instructions, which told her she should perform the test first thing in the morning. It was almost three a.m. *Does that count?* she wondered, and then decided she didn't care. She needed to know if she was pregnant, and she needed to know now.

She took the test, washed her hands, and left the bathroom, only to pace in the other room. *Please, please, please,* she begged God, or the Universe, or whatever powers were out there. *Let it be negative.* Brooke had promised herself that if she ever did get pregnant, it would be only when she was completely secure in her decision to bring a child into the world. Her baby would never think she wasn't wanted, which was the only conclusion Brooke had ever come to about herself. Why else, after four years spent raising her, would her mother have given her up?

Her gut clenched, as it always did when she allowed herself to think about the woman who brought her into the world. She remembered the musty scent in her mother's car, the pitch-black nights, and the cold, hungry mornings. She remembered crying. She remembered being scared and alone.

And there it was—her mother's voice inside her head, playing like a record with a needle stuck in a groove: *I'll be right back. You wait here.* Cloudy images of her mother's silhouette, walking away. Brooke, wanting to be good, but being scared enough that her teeth ached. Her heart thudded so hard inside her chest that she worried it might explode.

"Damn it," Brooke muttered, angrily wiping her cheeks with the tips of her fingers. She had more important things to worry about than some stupid girl who left her daughter alone in a car, then left her altogether. A person like that didn't deserve her tears.

Where had her father been all of that time? Why hadn't he taken better care of them? Was he someone her mother had loved, or was getting pregnant with Brooke an accident with a stranger, just the first of her many mistakes?

She told herself that none of that mattered now. There was no changing any of it. She returned to the bathroom and grabbed the test from where she'd left it on the edge of the sink. *Negative, negative, negative,* she chanted inside her head, as though she could somehow manifest her desired result. But when she looked down, all she saw was the bright blue plus sign in the middle of the white plastic stick.

Shit. Brooke's shoulders slumped as she fell back against the wall. After a moment, she straightened, then tossed the test into the garbage. She decided to take the other one, too, just to be sure the results were the same. That there hadn't been some kind of mistake.

Three minutes later, Brooke had her answer. There was no doubt about it. She was pregnant. And she had no idea what to do.

Jennifer

I promised myself I wouldn't cry.

I knew the girls would be there any minute, the first time I would see them since the night of my arrest the previous month. I'd never been that long without them, but there I was, about to say good-bye. I was giving them up, making them wards of the state. With Gina's help, I had made the decision quickly, the way you pull off a sticky bandage, reasoning that it might be less painful than if I dragged the process out, hemming and hawing about whether or not it was the right thing to do. I already knew it was the right thing. For Brooke's and Natalie's futures, there was no better choice to make.

As Gina had predicted, I was convicted of both the petty theft and child endangerment and neglect, then sentenced to fifteen months in a minimum-security facility. After that hearing, Gina told me that Brooke and Natalie had been placed in a home with a couple who had been foster parents for years. Knowing they were safe and together was the only thing that sustained me as I lay in my narrow, uncomfortable bunk at King County jail, listening to the thick, rough snores of my cellmates, unable to fall asleep. I felt hollow, as though my insides had all been scraped out. In signing away my parental rights, I was effectively saying that the state knew better what to do with my children than I did. I was admitting failure as a mother. I was saying that if I raised my own babies it would be a mistake.

"Are you sure your mother wouldn't take care of them until you get out?" Gina had asked me. Even after I told her no, she said that in situations like this, the state required her to call next of kin.

When I saw her the next day, I asked how it had gone. "Not well," she answered, not looking at me.

"What did she say?"

"That her husband doesn't like kids."

"Her husband?" I said, feeling stunned. I had no idea that she had gotten married again. My mother was only twenty-nine when my father left us, unaccustomed to being a sole provider and living alone, and she had been anxious to find another husband. "I miss having someone to curl up with at night," she said.

"You can curl up with me," I replied, and she shook her head, looking out the window.

"It's not the same thing."

For the next few years, until I got pregnant with Brooke, my mother was always dating someone. But none of her boyfriends stuck around for more than a couple of months. I wondered about the man who'd finally stayed with her, a man I'd never met. I wondered what she would have said if I had reached out to her earlier, before she'd married him, to ask for her help. If I'd admitted how wrong I'd been to move in with Michael; if I'd begged for her forgiveness. I'd thought about doing this a hundred times, but pride kept me from picking up the phone. Pride, and an intense, quiet fear that she'd want nothing to do with me or my daughters. Now, even though I'd been expecting it, I felt my mother's rejection of her grandchildren—her rejection of me—like a stab in the heart.

"How much longer?" I asked Gina now. She sat with me in the family visiting room at the jail, ready to supervise my last visit with my daughters. None of this seemed real to me yet. I'd signed the papers, answered the judge when he asked me if I understood what I was agreeing to do, and the entire time, I felt removed from my own body, as though I were floating toward the ceiling, watching someone who looked like me go through the appropriate motions and play my part.

"Any minute," Gina said, reaching over to squeeze my hand. Her fingers warmed my dry, icy skin. The orange industrial soap in the jail's shower was like sandpaper. "You okay?"

I pressed my lips together and shook my head. "I don't know if I can do this," I finally said, my voice barely a whisper.

"The judge already signed off on the order."

"No," I said. The tension in my chest was unbearable, my muscles braided themselves into excruciating knots. "I meant I don't know if I can see them." I leaned forward, pressing my upper body against my skinny thighs, and grabbed my ankles. Gina placed her hand on my back.

"If you don't," she said, "you'll regret it. Trust me. You need closure."

Closure, I thought, *is impossible.* I was convinced giving them up was the right thing, the best thing for them, but the agony I'd felt after making the decision had shattered into sharp metal shavings lodged under my skin. Every move I made, every breath I took hurt more than the last.

Righting myself, I glanced around the room, a small, square space with brick walls painted gray, the table at which we sat, and a sad pile of dirty-looking toys in a basket in the corner. A crooked poster of *Sesame Street* characters hung by the door; some asshole had drawn a pair of blue breasts on Big Bird.

"Do you think they'll ever forgive me?" I asked Gina, who paused and gave me a long, thoughtful look before responding.

"I think you're giving them the very best chance you can."

As though on cue, the door swung open, and a woman with long silver hair entered, carrying Natalie in a car seat and holding Brooke's small hand. "Mama!" my older daughter shrilled, racing toward me. "Mama, Mama, Mama!"

"Oh, honey," I said, opening my arms as she threw herself full force into them, clambering up into my lap. Tears blurred my vision and I buried my face in her dark curls. She was warm and smelled like green apple shampoo; she wore a green-and-blue plaid dress, brown saddle shoes, and clean, white tights. *I can't do it,* I thought as I hugged her, kissing her sweet face. *I can't. What the hell was I thinking, that I could give this up?* It felt as though I'd agreed to have two perfectly healthy and functional limbs lopped off. From that point on, I'd be an emotional amputee.

The silver-haired woman stepped inside and set Natalie's car seat on the floor next to me. "I'll be back in an hour," she said, and Gina thanked her, moving a chair to the corner. She had already told me she couldn't leave me alone with the girls, that this final visit needed to be supervised. Another reminder of just how unfit a mother I was.

"Where have you been?" Brooke asked, her voice muffled against me. Her small fingers dug into my back. "I missed you so much!"

"I missed you, too," I said, choking on the words. I looked down at Natalie, who had her big sister's lavender blanket tucked around her. She'd already changed so much, just in a month. She was bigger, and had more wisps of light blond hair. Her cheeks were rounder and more pink than I'd ever seen, and she had even sprouted two teeth along her lower gums. As soon as she saw me, she began to cry, wriggling under the constraints of the harness. I leaned over, still holding Brooke, and with one hand managed to unhook her and lift her up to my lap with her sister. *My girls,* I thought. *My sweet, innocent girls.*

"I want to leave," Brooke said when she finally looked up and around the room. She sniffled. "I don't want to stay here."

"It won't be for very long," I told her. "We just get to visit for a little while."

"And then we get to leave," Brooke said, her dark eyebrows scrunched together with determination.

"Yes," I said, hoping she wouldn't ask if we would go to the same place. I kissed the top of her head again, as well as Natalie's. "How are you, sweetheart? Are you okay? Is the house you're staying at nice?" Brooke shrugged, but didn't answer, so I tried again. "Why does Natalie have your blanket?"

"So she won't cry," Brooke whispered.

"Wow," I said, and my jaw trembled. "What a good big sister you are."

"I have my own bed at Rose and Walter's house," she said. "And Nat-ly has a real crib. With a mattress and everything." She had reverted to using her baby voice, transforming her little sister's name into two syllables instead of three, something she only did when she was truly upset.

"Oh," I said, hating that my daughter saw having a mattress as a luxury. "That must be so nice." I paused. "Do you like Rose and Walter?"

Brooke nodded, slowly, looking a bit unsure.

"It's okay, baby," I said, sensing she was worried she might be hurting my feelings. "I'm happy you like them. I want you to have good things."

Brooke visibly relaxed. "They have lots of toys. And food, too." She babbled on for a while about all the different things Rose cooked for them, and which ones she liked the most. I listened as best I could, jiggling Natalie with one arm while encircling Brooke with the other, but there was a siren blasting in my head, causing my thoughts to blur. *Someone else is feeding them. Someone else is picking out their clothes and kissing them good night. I will never get to do that again. I've lost them.* My eyes glossed with tears.

"Where have you been?" Brooke asked me, jerking me out of my thoughts. "Why haven't you come get us?"

I stole a glance at Gina, who gave me an encouraging nod. "Well," I began, then cleared my throat. "I've been here, sweetie. I can't come get you. Mama made some big mistakes."

"But I want you to. I don't even care if we have to go camping. I want to be with you."

"I want that, too," I said, wishing I knew the right thing to say. Wishing I could soothe her. "A judge said that Mama has to be in here while you stay with Rose and Walter."

"Like when I have to be in time-out?" Brooke asked, and I nodded. Gina had told me earlier that Brooke was too young to understand if I tried to explain what was really happening, that she'd do better if I just hugged her and kissed her and told her I loved her so much. "She'll adjust," Gina said. "She'll figure it out."

"Hey," I said, thinking distraction would be the best way to change the subject. "Want to read a story?" I nodded in the direction of the corner with the basket of toys, where a small stack of tattered books rested on the floor.

A few moments later, I had both girls in my lap as I read to them, cherishing the feeling of their small, warm bodies pressed against me. Brooke covered both herself and Natalie with her blanket, her fingers working the satin trim for comfort, as I knew they would. I read them all the silly, meaningless stories, and then we read them again. I asked Brooke to point out different colors and letters as we went and let Natalie pat the pages with her chubby starfish hands. *Will they remember this?* I wondered. *Will this moment be something that lives inside them the way I know it will live inside me?*

As the hour passed, I stared at my daughters, determined to etch every detail of them into my brain. I memorized where Brooke's hair parted—on the right, her shiny dark curls sprouting out of her scalp like springs. The exact shade of her eyes, the way her nose turned up, just at the end. The cinnamon freckles sprinkled across her cheeks. I kissed all of Natalie's fingers and toes, blowing raspberries into her belly to hear her giggle one last time. I looked into her brown eyes, seeing my own gaunt reflection there. *Don't forget me,* I thought. *Please. Don't forget how much I love you.*

All too soon, the door opened, and the silver-haired woman reappeared. "Hour's up," she said, and Gina and I both stood. Shaking, I held Natalie against the left side of my chest, feeling the rapid, sweet beat of her heart against mine. Brooke clung to my right leg, pressing her face into my thigh, away from the woman. Every cell inside my body screamed the word *no*.

"Time to say good-bye," Gina said, quietly.

I felt a thousand pinpricks inside my lungs. *Do it quick,* I thought. *Rip off the Band-Aid.* I squatted down to Brooke's level, which forced her to let go of my leg. "Hey, pumpkin," I said. "I'm so happy I got to see you."

"I don't wanna go," Brooke said, her eyes shiny with tears. "Please, Mama. I wanna stay with you."

My bottom lip quivered, and I bit it. "I know you do. But it's against the rules." I paused. "I love you more than anything. You know that, right?" She nodded, pushing her face into my neck. I could feel her tears.

"Here," the silver-haired woman said. "Let me take the baby." She took a step over toward us, and that's when Brooke screamed, lashing out her arm to hit the woman on the knee.

"Brooke!" I said, unable to keep back my own tears. "You know better than that. It's not okay to hit!" Natalie began to cry, too, and I held her tighter.

"It's fine," the woman said, holding out her arms for Natalie.

I stood up, and I couldn't help it—I took a step back, twisting at the waist so Natalie was out of the woman's reach. Even though I knew I'd agreed to all of this, I felt a fierce need to protect my baby. I wanted to grab both my daughters and run.

Gina appeared at my side. "Jennifer," she said. "Don't make this harder than it already is."

I looked at her, the pain I felt dripping down my cheeks, until I finally relented, first peppering Natalie's face with kisses before I handed her over. "It's time for you to go, honey," I said to Brooke, again dropping down to her level. I hugged her tightly, cupping the back of her head with my palm. "I'm so happy you came to see me. Be a good girl and take care of your sister." My heart felt ragged and torn—sawed in two.

"Come on, sweetie," Gina said, carefully extricating Brooke from my embrace. "Say good-bye to your mom."

"Noooo!" Brooke cried, squirming as violently as she could, the way I'd taught her to get away from a stranger.

"It's okay, baby," I said through my tears. "You're going to be fine, I promise. You're going to be okay." I tried to reassure her— and myself.

Brooke struggled against Gina as the other woman lifted the car seat, where she'd harnessed Natalie once again, even as my younger baby shrieked.

"I'll be right back," Gina said. "I'm just going to help them out to the car."

A male guard stood at the door, holding it open as they began to leave. A jagged sob ripped through me. "I love you both so much," I said. "Don't forget your mommy loves you!"

"Mama, please!" Brooke screamed as Gina took her into the hallway. Her voice echoed and bounced, shooting through me like arrows as I stood alone in the room. "I want my mama!" she cried, over and over again. Her tears were razors, slicing open my skin.

"Wait!" I said, rushing toward the door, only to have the guard grab me.

"Back up, inmate," he said, as I pushed against his strong arm, straining so I could see my girls one last time.

"Mama loves you!" I cried out again, but Brooke had stopped talking by then, dissolved into an indecipherable auditory tangle of screams and tears. I leaned hard against the guard's arm, staring at the backs of the silver-haired woman and Gina as they walked down the hall. The last thing I saw was the flash of Brooke's lavender blanket, and then my daughters turned a dark corner and were gone.

The next few days passed by in a blur.

I remembered Gina hugging me when she returned to the

room, murmuring words too dull and meaningless to help. I remembered stumbling back to my bunk, the other inmates calling out names like "pussy" and "fucking crybaby," none of them knowing the magnitude of what I'd just lost.

I remembered feeling like I wanted to die.

I spent my days curled fetal on top of the scratchy gray blanket on my bed, fists tucked up under my chin, my face shoved into the pillow. Sobs racked my body, and I wept what felt like an endless stream of tears. Every time it seemed like I might stop, that I could control my grief, my sharp, hiccupping breaths, it would rise back up, washing over me in a wave with a violent undertow, pulling me down, down, and down. My babies' faces haunted me. Their cries echoed through my bones.

The only relief I found was in the blissful, dark comfort of sleep. I fought waking as best I could, closing my eyes and attempting to force myself back into an unconscious world. A world where I wasn't in jail, where I hadn't just given up my children. Hours went by, then days. I didn't shower, I didn't eat. I used the bathroom only when I absolutely had to. The correctional officers on each shift tried to talk to me, tried to make me rise from my bed, but I swatted them away. "Please," I croaked. "Just leave me alone."

I wasn't sure how, but word of what I'd gone through made its way around to the other inmates, and I started to feel the occasional pat on my back, to hear a soft voice saying, "It's okay, girl. You did the right thing." The compassion in their voices only brought up a fresh round of tears, the desire to spiral deeper into despair.

"You need to get up," one of them said. She sat on the edge of my bunk, the weight of her causing me to roll over. "You need to eat."

"No," I said, opening my eyes just enough to see the woman trying to rouse me. She was tall and thin, with braided blond hair and ice-blue eyes. Her long, bony fingers squeezed my arm.

"You think you're the only one in here with a sad situation?" she said. "Please, mama. I know you feel like shit, but you need to get up."

"I can't," I whispered. The marrow in my bones felt as though it had hardened into lead, pinning me to my thin mattress. I tried to move away from her, but she pulled me over onto my back, forcing me to meet her steely gaze. Her skin was almost translucent; I could see the thin blue rivers of veins in her long neck.

"Yeah," she said, "you can." She sighed. "You want your girls finding out you let yourself die? That the story you want to give them to carry around the rest of their lives?"

Her words tore through me like a knife. I hadn't thought past the moment I was in, the sharply barbed agony I felt. I hadn't considered the possibility that someday, wherever they might end up, my girls might want to find out what happened to me.

"Come on," she said. "You can do this."

And so I let her put an arm around my shoulders, helping me to sit up. My head spun, and I had to close my eyes again so I wouldn't pass out. My tongue was dry as sand; it stuck like Velcro to the roof of my mouth. She handed me a Dixie cup full of water and told me to drink. After I complied, I looked at her again. "Thanks," I said.

"No problem." She smiled, revealing horribly crooked, crowded teeth. "I'm Peters."

"Walker," I said. I'd made the mistake of introducing myself as Jennifer the first night I was here, only to learn that inmates all called each other by their last names. Now, I swallowed the rest of the water in the cup and felt the shrunken, dried-out cells of my body beg for more.

"What they get you for?"

"Petty theft," I said, and then had to steady my voice before going on. "Child endangerment and neglect." I dropped my eyes to the cement floor. "What about you?"

"Armed robbery." She paused. "How long did you get?"

"Fifteen months," I said.

"Headed to Skagit after this?"

I nodded. My public defender had explained that I'd stay in county lockup until a bunk opened up at the minimum-security women's correctional facility in Mt. Vernon. With good behavior, he told me, I could be out in less than a year. *Out to do what?* I wondered. *Beg for enough money to survive?*

"Me, too," she said. "Seven years."

"Sorry," I said, fiddling with the hem of my bright orange shirt.

"Don't be," Peters said. "Ain't nobody's fault but my own. And the worthless asshole boyfriend who talked me into it." She stood, and then helped me get to my feet, too. "Here," she said, handing me a granola bar. "Eat this, then hit the shower. No offense, but you don't smell too good."

"Sorry," I said again.

"Stop apologizing. Jesus."

"Okay." Still feeling numb, I unwrapped the granola bar and forced myself to take a bite. It felt like dirt in my mouth, but I managed to swallow it, then finished the entire thing. My stomach rumbled in appreciation. Peters reached under my bunk and handed me a thin, white terry-cloth towel and a flimsy plastic comb.

"Good luck getting through that black rat's nest with this," she said. I lifted my hand to touch my hair, only to discover she was right—after days on my pillow, my curls had matted into a dreadlocked mess. Brooke's hair had often ended up like this when we slept in the car; it took half a bottle of detangler and over an hour with a wide-toothed comb to smooth it again. I'd tell her stories and sing her songs to distract her from the yanking at her scalp, and now, the thought of holding her so close made me want to climb right back into bed.

Peters spoke again. "I'll see if I can find you some conditioner."

"Thanks," I said, pushing down the urge I felt to collapse.

"You're welcome. Now do us all a favor and go wash off that stink."

As weak as I was, I managed to shuffle to the bathroom, unsure if once I was there, I'd have the energy or inclination to get myself clean. I supposed that I could. I could do it like I'd have to do everything from now on—forcing each movement, each breath into my lungs. Putting one foot in front of the other until someday, I'd find a way to be far, far away from this pain.

Natalie

In fifth grade, the year Natalie found out she was adopted, she began telling herself stories. Not just the stories about whom her birth mother might be, but ones involving people she saw every day. She would lie in her bed, whispering to herself, acting out the kinds of conversations she wished were real.

"Hi, Natalie," she would say in a high-pitched voice, pretending to be Sophia Jensen, who was friends with practically everyone in their class. Sophia had bright blue eyes and thick red hair, which her mother fashioned into a French braid almost every day, setting off a frenzy of other girls wearing the same style. She was the girl everyone wanted to sit next to at lunch; the person who always received more Valentine's Day cards than anyone else. She was also the girl Natalie wished most to have as a friend.

"Hi, Sophia," Natalie would say, lowering her voice again, back to being herself.

"You look so pretty today," Natalie said, switching to her Sophia voice.

"Really?" Natalie replied, as herself.

"Yes," Natalie answered, as Sophia. "Do you want to come over to my house this weekend? I'm having a party. A sleepover."

"Wow," Natalie said, as herself again. "That's so nice of you. I'd love to."

"I just know everyone will be so happy you're going to be there," Natalie said, pretending to be Sophia once more. "We all think you're so smart and like you so much."

But the truth was, instead of attending parties, Natalie spent most of her time alone, or with her mother, who stayed home to take care of Natalie while her father went to work at his law firm. They lived in a large, three-story Tudor on a bluff in West Seattle that overlooked the Puget Sound. The house was surrounded by a thick forest of western hemlocks, red alders, and Douglas firs, and Natalie's room was on the third floor and had wide, clear windows, making her feel as though she were flying. She often stared out at the water, dreaming about the places across the ocean she might someday go, wishing she had a sister or brother to play with, or the courage to invite one of the girls from school over to her house. She wanted a best friend. But Natalie was quiet, the student who knew the answers to her teachers' questions but never raised her hand. She had a tendency to speak only when spoken to. At recess, she sat on a bench outside and kept her nose in a book—she loved anything by Judy Blume or Beverly Cleary— watching the other girls play on the monkey bars or jump rope together, wondering how they made talking to each other look so easy. As she peeked at them, she tried not to look too anxious, waiting for someone to invite her to join in, but no one ever did.

There wasn't a day Natalie got off the bus that her mother wasn't on the corner, waiting. Now that she was ten, she wished her mom would at least wait for her inside the house—none of the other kids had parents that waited for them on the street—but every time she dropped a hint about being able to walk the three blocks from the bus stop on her own, her mother pretended not to hear.

One Friday afternoon in April, the last day of class before spring break, Natalie and her mother entered their house and closed the door behind them. Natalie hung up her jacket on the coat rack, as she knew her mother expected her to, and set her backpack on the floor in its designated spot. "Can I watch *Rugrats*?" she asked. The cartoon was Natalie's favorite show.

"You don't have any homework?" Natalie shook her head. "All right. But put your laundry away first, please. It's on your bed."

Obediently, Natalie nodded, and turned toward the stairs.

"Shoes, Natalie!" her mother called out, and Natalie turned around and went back to the entryway, where she'd forgotten to put the white Keds she'd kicked off her feet onto the shelf in the closet. As her mother looked on, Natalie set them in their appropriate place, next to her dark green galoshes and the black slippers her father liked to wear when he got home from work. There were certain ways her mother liked things done: freshly washed and folded clothes needed to be put away in their proper places, never randomly shoved in one of Natalie's drawers, or worse, left sitting around. Doors always needed to be shut, towels hung in the exact middle of the bar, lights turned off when you left a room. Shoes needed to be on the shoe rack.

"If your life is messy on the outside," her mother had told her for as long as Natalie could remember, "your insides feel messy, too."

Natalie didn't really understand what her mother meant by that statement—she felt just fine if her dirty clothes landed on the floor instead of in the hamper, or if she forgot to put her breakfast dishes in the sink. Sometimes, she wondered what would happen if her mother walked into Natalie's room to find her daughter's entire wardrobe strewn across the carpet. She imagined the look of shock on her mother's face, taking some small measure of satisfaction from the thought, followed immediately by a ripple of guilt. However overly stringent some of her mother's rules might be, Natalie loved her, and wanted to keep her happy. She tried to do what was expected of her, if only to keep the peace.

Twenty-five years later, after dropping Hailey off at her school and then saying good-bye to Henry in his classroom, Natalie made her way to the preschool's parking lot. Just as she reached into her purse for her car keys, she looked up to see Katie, whose son, Logan, was in Henry's class and had invited Henry over to play that afternoon. Katie was alone now, so Natalie assumed Logan was already inside, too. Katie wore gray sweats and her brown hair was twisted into a messy bun on top of her head. She had the kind of good skin and natural beauty that didn't require makeup, something Natalie envied. With her light complexion and fair lashes, if Natalie didn't put on a little mascara, she barely looked like she had a face.

"Can Henry still come over this afternoon?" Katie asked.

"Yes, thanks," Natalie said with a smile. "He's excited."

"Logan is, too. I'll bring Henry home around five, if that's okay?"

"Perfect." Luckily, Henry wasn't the only one with a playdate that day—Hailey was going to her friend Ruby's house, too—Natalie had planned it that way so she could work on a dessert order she needed to finish for a party the next night without the kids clamoring for her attention.

But first, she needed to go see her mother. Natalie had spoken to her mom earlier that morning, while she fed Hailey and Henry scrambled eggs, asking if she could come over for coffee around ten. Natalie thought about the guilt she had felt in her mother's presence that day all those years ago when while working on her family tree. The guilt she still felt, today, when she thought about bringing up the subject of finding her birth mother. When she turned eighteen, Natalie had thought about registering with an adoption reunion organization, so if her birth mother was looking for her, she'd be easier to find. This was in 1998, before the Internet had taken over as the only way to get things done, so the process would have been more involved than simply typing her name into an online system—she would have had to go to the registry's office and fill out hard copies of paperwork. But when she talked with her dad about the idea, he begged her to reconsider.

"You know how your mom is," he said, running one of his large hands through his salt-and-pepper hair. Natalie knew that no one would ever look at the two of them and suspect they were father and daughter. That was one of the disconcerting realities of being adopted—you look at your parents, your entire family, and see nothing of yourself reflected back.

"She takes everything so personally," her father continued. "She'll be devastated."

At the time, Natalie conceded that he was right, so she let the idea go, reasoning that there wasn't any urgency, any real logistical need for her to find her birth mother. It was more a general curiosity, a wondering about the past. So what if one day the previous summer she had chased after a woman walking in the Junction who resembled an older version of Natalie, only to catch up with her and find that other than being petite and having blond hair, the woman looked nothing like her at all. So what if Natalie sometimes felt a dull, strange sense of emptiness she didn't know how to explain to anyone else, but often wondered if that feeling was the reason she had a harder time opening up to other people—if after being abandoned by her birth mother, she couldn't help but be wary of letting other people in, showing them who she was, for fear that they'd leave her, too. Natalie had a good family—a family who loved and provided for her. She reminded herself that was more than a lot of people had; she told herself that would have to be enough.

But didn't she, as Kyle had said, have the right to know more about the woman who gave birth to her? Intellectually, her curiosity made perfect sense, but as she parked her car in her parents' driveway, she knew that what made sense to everyone else didn't always align with what made sense to her mother. She didn't like emotional messes any more than physical ones.

It was almost ten by the time Natalie grabbed the small box of currant and almond scones she'd baked before the kids had gotten up—she always kept a little something in the freezer, ready to be put in the oven at a moment's notice—climbed out of her car, and entered the house. "Mom?" she called as she took off her shoes and put them on the rack in the closet. "Where are you?"

"In the kitchen," her mother answered.

Natalie walked down the hall and through the family room into the large, square kitchen her parents had recently updated with new maple cabinets and restaurant-quality, stainless-steel appliances. Her mother stood in front of the sink, wearing yellow rubber gloves, black yoga pants, and a blue hoodie. At sixty-eight, she wore her silver-streaked black hair in a stylish, chin-length bob. Natalie set the box she carried on the counter, then stepped over to give her mother a quick hug and kiss on the cheek.

"You know you have a dishwasher for that," she said, nodding her head toward the sink full of soapy water and what she assumed were the pans from the previous night's dinner.

"I know." Her mother shrugged. "But with just your father and me, it takes forever to fill the thing up. Besides, it's relaxing."

"Zen and the art of dishwashing?" Natalie said as she settled onto one of the stools lining the granite-topped island in the middle of the room, waiting for her mother to finish.

"Exactly," her mother said, turning to smile at Natalie as she set the last dish in the rack by the sink. She pulled off her gloves and set them on the counter. "Coffee?"

"Yes, thanks. I brought scones."

"My favorite." She grabbed two mugs from the cupboard and filled them with coffee from the pot she'd apparently already brewed. Natalie took one of the cups from her mother and set it in front of her so it could cool.

Her mother sat down next to her at the counter and held her coffee with both hands, as though warming them. Even their fingernails were different—her mother's long and elegant versus Natalie's short and square. "How are you?"

"I'm good." What Natalie actually felt was anxious, but she was trying not to show it.

Her mom reached inside the box and broke a piece off of one of the scones, then popped it inside her mouth. "Mmm," she murmured. "Fantastic. I love the almonds."

"Thanks," Natalie said, trying to find the right way to bring up the subject they needed to discuss. But first, she spent a while making small talk with her mom, inquiring about her volunteer work at the food bank and the European vacation she and Natalie's father were planning in the spring.

"And how are my gorgeous grandbabies?" her mother asked after they'd each finished eating a scone and decided to move to the more comfortable overstuffed couches in the family room.

"They're good, too," Natalie said. They settled into opposite ends of the same couch, and Natalie looked at her mom, who appeared about as relaxed as Natalie had ever seen her, and decided there was no sense waiting any longer. She dove into why she was there. "Hailey actually has a project for school that reminded me of one I had to do, too."

"Really?" her mom said. "What is she doing?"

"Our family tree." The muscles in her mother's face froze, as Natalie suspected they would, but she forged ahead anyway. "I know this is a touchy subject, but it reminded me of how I wanted to include my birth mother on mine and you didn't want me to. It made me think that it's time for me to at least know her name." She paused. "Kyle and I talked about it, and he thinks my knowing more about her might be a good idea, too." Her mom loved Kyle like he was her own son; Natalie brought him into the conversation because she wanted her mother to see that this idea wasn't just coming from her. She had her husband's full support.

Her mother pressed her thin lips together and looked out the large picture window, so Natalie did, too. The rain from the previous night had dissipated before dawn, and strong winds had blown away the steel-wool clouds. Now, the sky was an intense, brilliant shade of blue, as though the storm had scrubbed it clean.

After a minute of silence, Natalie spoke. "Mom?" she said. "What do you think?"

"Why," her mother asked, "do you think this would be a good idea?" Her voice was quiet but tense, and her fingers were linked tightly together in her lap.

"Because she's the only blood relative I have, other than the kids." Her mother closed her eyes and jerked her chin upward, as though Natalie had hit her. "Mom, please. I'm not trying to hurt you. I just think if I want to know my birth mother's name, I should be able to." Natalie grabbed a throw pillow and hugged it to her chest. "Honestly, I feel like I should already know it."

"You only want to know her name?"

Natalie shook her head. "I want to see my adoption file. I want to know more about where I came from."

Her mother's blue eyes glossed with tears. "You came from your dad and me. We raised you. We took care of you. Aren't we enough?"

Natalie gritted her teeth. "Of course you're enough. That's not the issue."

"Then what is? Tell me how I'm not supposed to feel like I haven't been a good enough mother to you when you want to go off and find another one?"

"Jesus, Mom." Natalie released the pillow she held, letting it fall to the floor.

Her mother stared hard at the fallen pillow. Natalie sighed, reaching down to return it to its rightful spot on the couch. Some things never changed. In her parent's house, if you dropped something, you picked it back up.

"Thank you," her mom said, looking at Natalie again.

"You're welcome," Natalie said. A deep pinpoint pain began to pound below her right eye. Oddly enough, her sinuses were often the barometers of her emotional state—the more stressed she became, the more they swelled. Her doctor told her it was likely an autoimmune response, her body's reaction to too much adrenaline. She pinched the bridge of her nose, trying to relieve the pressure, not knowing why she had thought this conversation would be any different than the others she and her mother had had about this subject. They always ended this way, her mother in tears and Natalie with the kind of headache that comes from banging your head against an impenetrable maternal brick wall.

"It would be harder," Natalie finally said, "but you know I can look for her without your help. I could hire a private investigator." She and Kyle had discussed that possibility the night before, in case her mother refused to cooperate. Now, Natalie kept her voice gentle, filled with as much compassion as it could hold. "But I came to you first, because I didn't want to hide anything. I wanted you to know that this isn't about you or Dad." She felt a barb of tears in her throat, and she had to swallow them down before she went on. "You are my mother. You will always be my mother. The one who held me and took care of me and made sure I had everything I could ever possibly need. You and Daddy both did that. And I'm not looking to replace you. You could never lose me . . . you have me. I'm already yours."

Her mother's chin trembled, and before Natalie could say anything else, her mom stood up and without a word, strode out of the room.

"Shit," Natalie muttered, pushing on the sore spot of her cheekbone with her thumb. She didn't know why she'd even bothered coming. She should have just found her birth mom on her own and told her mother about it after the fact. After Natalie could show her mother that the other woman wasn't any kind of threat—she was simply a part of Natalie's history, a history she was entitled to know.

Her phone buzzed in her purse, which she'd left on the counter next to the half-eaten box of scones, so she rose to get it. "On a quick recess," Kyle's text message read. "How's it going?"

"She just walked out on me," Natalie responded, grateful that her husband had remembered what she was going to do that morning.

"Not surprising."

Natalie's gratitude was quickly replaced by a flash of irritation at her husband's seemingly flippant remark, but she did her best to push it down, telling herself that he was in work mode, focused solely on pointing out the facts of a situation. She reminded herself that there were two parts of her husband—lawyer-Kyle and family-Kyle. Sometimes, when she needed one, she got the other. "No," she typed, "but that doesn't make it any easier."

"Sorry," he said, and she knew that her conclusion about his current mind-set was spot-on. "Be home as soon as I can tonight, OK?"

Natalie thanked him and shoved her phone back in her purse, trying to think about what else she could possibly say to her mother in order to get through to her. But before she could land on anything that might work, she heard footsteps behind her on the hardwood floor and spun around. "Look, Mom," she began. "I'm sorry." But then Natalie saw the box in her mother's hands, and she froze where she stood. The box was white, its edges slightly torn and yellowed with age. "What's that?" she asked, feeling her heartbeat quicken.

"It's what you wanted," her mother said. Her face was pale. "All we know. Everything before you were ours." She held the box out to Natalie, who took it from her. It was lighter than she'd expected; it seemed like something as significant as what her parents had kept from her all these years should have more heft. She fought the urge to rip the box open right then and there, but she didn't want to hurt her mother any more than she knew she already had.

"It's okay," her mom said, as though she had read Natalie's

thoughts. "I just called your dad. He agreed it was time for you to see it."

"Are you sure?" Natalie asked.

"No. But one of us should be here when you do."

Natalie cocked her head and furrowed her eyebrows, wondering what, exactly, she was about to see that her mother thought she needed to witness. But then it didn't matter, because she set the box down on the kitchen island and lifted its lid.

The first thing she saw was a purple blanket with a silky but threadbare trim. "I remember this," she said. Her voice quavered. "I used to sleep with it."

Her mother nodded, pressing a closed fist against her mouth. "Until you were Hailey's age," she said when she dropped her arm back to her side.

"It's the same color as my delivery boxes," Natalie said, a bit dazed by the realization. She remembered the day she'd chosen the lavender boxes for her business over white ones, something about the color appealing to her in a way she couldn't explain. She looked at her mother through glassy eyes. "Did my birth mother give it to me?"

"I don't know," her mom admitted. "Maybe. You had it the day we came to get you from the social worker. You wouldn't go to sleep without it."

Natalie lifted the blanket out of the box and set it on the counter. Her birth mother might have wrapped this around her. Natalie swallowed hard, then looked inside the box again. There was a single manila file folder with no label on the tab. She reached for it, but her mother's voice stopped her.

"Honey, wait. I need you to understand something, first."

Natalie looked at her mom, then back at the folder. Her pulse raced. "What?"

Her mom shifted her feet, her eyes darting to the floor, then back up to Natalie. "Your father and I did what we thought was best at the time."

An alarm began to sound inside Natalie's head, screaming in sync with the pounding beneath her eye. "What are you talking about?"

Her mother took a step toward her and placed a single hand on Natalie's forearm. She stared at her daughter's face as though trying to memorize something. "You said you want to know more about the girl who gave birth to you," she said. "When you open that folder you're going to see something I hope doesn't upset you too much."

"Mom, please. Just tell me." Natalie's thoughts spun with worst-case scenarios. Was her birth mom a prostitute? A victim of rape? Did she already know her? Natalie's mom didn't have any siblings, but her father did. Did her aunt Vicki get pregnant and then let Natalie's parents adopt her? Was this some big family secret they'd been keeping all these years?

Her mom reached into the box and picked up the folder, holding it out for Natalie. "You already know she gave you up because she couldn't take care of you," she said. She held very still, a muscle twitching just under her right eye. "But what you don't know . . . what your dad and I never told you . . . is that she gave up your sister, too."

Brooke

The Hillcrest Home for Girls was located on the outskirts of Georgetown, an industrial area in South Seattle. The four-story, blue square box of a building was set against a steep hillside; its locked windows, worn linoleum floors, and buzzing fluorescent lights screamed the word "institution" the instant someone walked through the front doors. It was the place where Brooke and Natalie were first separated; babies were kept in a different part of the building than the older kids.

Gina tried to explain what was happening. She dropped down, squatting next to Brooke, and looked her straight in the eye. "I know it's hard, sweetie. But believe me, I'm going to do everything I can to help you two find another home to be in together. Right now, though, you have to be away from each other a bit. You still can see her every day while you're here. Okay?"

Brooke bit her bottom lip and nodded, slowly. Gina was nice, even if she was the one who took her from her mom. Thoughts of her mother stung like tiny splinters trapped beneath Brooke's skin. Sometimes she picked at them, trying to dislodge the pain of missing her. Brooke didn't understand why her mom hadn't come to get them yet, why her time-out was lasting so long.

Gina led her around the building, and Brooke was relieved to see the cafeteria, where other children sat at long rectangular tables, eating from trays filled with spaghetti and green beans. It seemed like eating was the only thing Brooke could think about since she'd begun having regular meals with Rose and Walter. Now that she was somewhere new, she had worried it might be like living in her mom's car again, and the gnawing ache in her belly would come back. One of the first things she had done at Rose and Walter's house was to stand in the middle of the pantry, touching all the boxes and cans of food, counting them. "This is for us?" she asked Rose, her voice edged with wonder. "Pineapple and spaghetti? We get to eat it?"

"Yes," Rose had said, gently. But after they'd stayed there a few weeks and she discovered that, not for the first time, Brooke had hidden a jar of peaches and packages of cookies and crackers under her bed, Rose got angry. "We feed you more than enough. You don't have to take it."

Brooke didn't know how to explain why she took the food— she only knew that she found herself sneaking into the pantry every night, stealing away bits of anything she could save for later, just in case. After that, when Gina came to get Brooke and Natalie from the house, Brooke knew it was her fault, even though Gina told her it was because Walter's boss had unexpectedly transferred his job to another state.

She thought it was her fault, too, when two weeks later, Gina had returned to Hillcrest to inform her that her baby sister was being adopted. "We are?" Brooke asked, confused by the way Gina shook her head and frowned.

"She is," Gina said. "Only Natalie. I'm sorry, honey. For now, you're going to stay here."

Thirty-five years later, Brooke recalled the cloudy, fractured moments of that morning at Hillcrest. If she wanted to—if she let them escape—she could still feel the rough sobs that tore at her chest when Gina told her she wouldn't get to see Natalie anymore. Back then, she didn't understand that most couples looking to adopt only wanted babies, not older children, like Brooke, who were more likely to have behavioral issues. It was only 1980, and the system was less likely to take into account how important sibling bonds were for healthy development. She remembered the last time she saw her baby sister, in a room not much different from the one where they'd last seen their mother. She remembered Natalie's big, brown eyes and wispy blond curls, her chubby pink cheeks and the way she grabbed Brooke by the ears and gave her gummy and wet, openmouthed kisses.

"I love you," Brooke said, just before Gina took Natalie away. Brooke tucked her treasured purple blanket snug around her sister and then, just like their mother, Natalie disappeared.

Thinking of that moment now, Brooke tried to distract herself by heading into the bathroom to shower. She had an appointment at the women's health clinic at eleven, and it was already nine thirty. As she let the warm water rush over her, she considered her options. It had been a week since she realized she was late, which meant she had plenty of time to figure out her next step, but so far, the only thing she had decided to do was make this appointment to confirm the results of the home tests.

Two hours later, after taking yet another test at the clinic, Brooke sat in a small office with a woman named Jill, who couldn't have been more than a day over twenty-five.

"So," Jill said. "You're definitely pregnant." Her bright eyes and positive, bubbly demeanor made Brooke think she probably had been a cheerleader. Jill glanced down at the chart in front of her. "About eight weeks along, according to when you had your last period?"

"I think so, yes," Brooke said, holding her hands together tightly in her lap. Her stomach growled; she'd been too queasy to eat before she came. Now she was ravenous. She wished she'd thought to bring along a snack.

"Have you informed the father?" Jill held a pen with her right hand, poising it over the paper in front of her.

"No." Brooke purposely hadn't seen Ryan that week, telling him she had a stomach bug and didn't want him to get sick, too. Wrapped up in finishing a big job on a high-rise condo project, he hadn't pushed the issue. "Call me when you're feeling better," he said, and later that night, when she came home from an office-cleaning job, he'd had her favorite hot and sour soup delivered from a Thai restaurant down the street. A sweet gesture, to be sure, but a small part of Brooke couldn't help but wish he'd shown up to deliver it himself. She couldn't help but feel that if he really cared about her, her germs wouldn't matter. Having this thought surprised her—she'd never been a needy girlfriend—but something about the idea of carrying Ryan's baby made her wish that they were closer—that the minute she'd taken those tests, she could have called him and told him the news. She wished she had it in her to admit to how scared she was—to ask him to comfort her and help her make the right decision. Instead, she kept silent, clenching her jaw as she made the appointment at the clinic.

"Do you know who he is?" Jill asked. She kept her eyes pointed down, at her desk.

"Yes," Brooke said, feeling embarrassed to be having this discussion with a girl fifteen years her junior. Her hair was in a side-pony, for Christ's sake. She had perfect skin and cherry-pit dimples. She couldn't possibly know anything about making this kind of life-changing decision.

Jill set her pen down and looked at Brooke. "Well, there are three options. Parenting, adoption, or termination. We can assist with any of them." She paused. "Have you thought about which you'd like to pursue?"

"I'm not sure." Brooke shifted in her seat, crossed her legs, and began to bob her right foot as it hung in the air. "I'm thirty-nine, so this could be my last chance to have a baby."

"That's true," Jill said. She waited for Brooke to continue.

"The father is going through a divorce," Brooke said, quickly. She maintained strong eye contact with the younger woman to show she was not ashamed of her situation.

"Okay," Jill said, leaning back against her chair.

"And I definitely won't give it up for adoption."

"You're not comfortable with that idea?" Jill asked, with a slight tilt of her head.

"No," Brooke said. Her voice was hard. "I'm not." She wasn't against adoption, per se. Under normal circumstances, she knew it was an incredibly generous act, an amazing gift given to a couple or individual in need. But in her particular situation, with her particular past, it was something she just couldn't do.

Jill remained silent, waiting for Brooke to say more.

"I can't keep it," Brooke said, and her voice broke on the words. Tears stung the backs of her eyes, and she attempted to blink them away. Goddamn it. She didn't cry in front of other people, especially not strangers.

"Okay," Jill said, again, pushing a box of tissues across her desk.

Brooke grabbed one and wiped her eyes. "Can I take care of it now, while I'm here?" she asked even as her bottom lip trembled. "Or is there some kind of waiting period?" Her stomach folded in on itself, and without thinking, she placed a hand over her abdomen. Oh, god. What was she doing?

"Not in Washington State," Jill said. "Let me check the schedule." She kept her voice soft, her tone neutral. Brooke held her breath as the younger woman typed and clicked her mouse a few times, all the while looking at her computer. "We actually could fit you in this afternoon," she said, moving her eyes from the screen to Brooke's face. "Does that work?"

Brooke nodded, pressing a closed fist against her mouth. It was the easiest option, the one least likely to make waves in her life. She wouldn't have to tell Ryan. She could just get it over with. Nothing would have to change.

Jill eyed her, carefully. "There's no rush," she said. "You have some time to think about it, if you want to take a few days."

"No," Brooke said. "I want to do it now."

"Okay," Jill said, and then turned to type on her keyboard once again. "Do you have any questions for me about the procedure?"

"No," Brooke said. The less she knew, the better. She just wanted it done.

"There's someone to drive you home?" Brooke nodded, even though it was a lie. But Jill didn't have to know that. "You'll need to get some labs done, and an ultrasound, so I'll take you to a room and a technician will handle all of that." She flipped through a few pages from Brooke's file and raised her eyebrows. "You've listed 'unknown' for your family medical history."

"Yes." Brooke's pulse pounded inside her head; there was no subject she hated more than that of family. She had told Ryan that she was an only child, that her parents lived in Florida, and they were estranged. Lying to him—to everyone, really—was so much less painful than speaking the truth. She had wondered what it would be like to open up, to tell Ryan about her mother and the sister she'd lost along the way, about the foster homes she'd lived in, and the life she'd learned to tolerate at Hillcrest. She imagined saying the words "My mother decided she didn't want me when I was four years old, so she gave me away," and the physical reaction she had—her head spun and her throat closed as though she were choking on something hard and sharp—was so violent, she knew it was better to keep her mouth shut.

But now, sitting across from Jill, she decided to be honest, in the hope that it might put a quick end to the discussion. "My mother gave custody of me to the state when I was four. I have no clue about my father." Brooke's cheeks flamed, as though her past was something to be ashamed of. She hated that she had this reaction; if anyone should be plagued by that particular emotion, it should be the woman who'd discarded her as though she were nothing.

"I understand," Jill said, even though Brooke knew there was no way the younger woman understood anything of what Brooke had been through. "I understand" was just something people said to fill in a blank, when nothing else made sense.

"I have some more forms for you to read over," Jill said. She pulled open a file drawer in her desk and riffled through it, setting a small stack of paper in front of Brooke. "I'll give you a bit to review everything, then come take you back to an exam room." She stood up, pressing her fingertips into her desk. "It's going to be fine, Brooke. We'll take good care of you."

"Thanks," Brooke said. Jill might have been young, but at least she was kind.

Brooke spent the next twenty minutes filling out the forms that described the procedure and then signed them to give her consent. She also read the detailed aftercare instructions, relieved to note that if she opted not to have the sedative, she should be okay to drive home. She wouldn't even have to call in sick to work that night, if all went well. She'd pop some Advil and pretend the whole thing never happened.

She tried to relax the tight knot that had settled beneath her sternum with controlled breaths, only to have it spring claws and dig in deeper. She'd be fine, she thought, mentally repeating what Jill had said. It wouldn't be easy, but she'd made it this far on her own. She'd make it through this, too.

As promised, Jill returned to her office and then led Brooke down a long, well-lit hall to an exam room. She put her hand on Brooke's arm and gave it a short squeeze. "Feel free to give us a call any time, after," she said. "We're here to help."

Brooke nodded as she bit the inside of her cheek, hard enough to taste a coppery drop of blood. After Jill left and she was alone, Brooke changed into a gown and sat on the edge of the exam table, her bare legs swinging. A woman came to take her blood, and after she had left, another woman entered and introduced herself as the ultrasound technician. She was significantly older than Brooke, a little top-heavy, wore no makeup, and her gray hair was cut in a sensible, short bob.

"I'm Linda," the woman said in the crackling voice of a heavy-duty smoker. She confirmed Brooke's name and date of birth. "This won't take long. Can you lie back, with your head on the pillow, please?"

"Why do I need an ultrasound?" Brooke asked, as she complied with Linda's request. "If I'm just . . . if I'm not . . ." She clamped her lips together, unable to finish the sentence.

Linda stood next to her and placed a reassuring hand on Brooke's shoulder. "We need to confirm the gestational age," she said. "Make sure everything's where it's supposed to be, and that it's not an ectopic pregnancy."

"Oh," Brooke said. "Okay." She settled back against the pillow and turned her head toward the wall, where a poster of a tropical, sandy beach hung directly across from her. To let women imagine being there instead of on the exam table, Brooke supposed. To imagine being anywhere but here.

Linda helped Brooke get her heels in the hard plastic stirrups, put a warm blanket over her legs, and then pushed up her gown to expose her stomach. "Sorry, this is going to be a little cold," she said as she squeezed a clear gel from a white bottle. But even with the warning, Brooke startled when the substance hit her skin. Linda grabbed a wand from the white and gray machine that sat on a cart next to the table. The screen was turned away from Brooke's view. Linda pressed the end of the wand against Brooke's abdomen. She was silent as she typed with one hand, maneuvering the wand from one of Brooke's hip bones to the other.

"What are you doing?" Brooke asked. Her voice trembled, even though she tried to keep it steady. Had her mother thought about doing this when she got pregnant with her daughters? Did she lie in a room like this, and then change her mind, only to ultimately decide to dispose of them anyway? If she had this baby, was she destined to do the same?

"Just taking some measurements."

The knot in Brooke's chest pulsed. "Can I hear the heartbeat?" she asked.

Linda didn't answer, but Brooke saw her flip a switch on the machine next to the table, and a moment later, after Linda moved the wand and pushed it harder into Brooke's belly, the echoing *whoosh, whoosh, whoosh* of her baby's heart filled the air.

"Oh," Brooke said. Her hands clutched the crinkly white paper between her body and the table. Her eyes flooded with tears. "It's so fast." She paused, then turned to look at Linda. "Is that normal?"

"Yes," Linda said, holding the wand steady. She didn't say anything else, waiting, it seemed, for Brooke to tell her what to do next.

A whirlwind of indecision spun in Brooke's mind. This was the best thing to do. She wasn't equipped to raise a baby on her own. Her health insurance was shit. She didn't make enough money. Ryan would think she was trying to trap him into finally divorcing Michelle. He'd leave Brooke. And then what would she be? Alone like she'd always been, with no idea how to be a good mother because she'd never had one herself.

"You okay, sweetie?" Linda asked, breaking into Brooke's thoughts.

"I'm not sure," Brooke said, much more comforted by the older woman's presence than she had been by Jill's. If she had had a grandmother, Brooke would have wanted her to be someone like Linda.

"You're not sure if you're okay, or if you still want to go ahead with the procedure?" Linda pulled the wand off Brooke's belly, and the sudden silence that filled the room poured over Brooke like liquid lead. She found herself wanting to hear the baby's heartbeat again and again.

"Both." A few errant tears slipped down Brooke's cheeks, and Linda reached for a box of tissues. "Thanks," Brooke said as she took one and wiped her face.

"Of course," Linda replied, setting the box back on the counter. "Women cry in here all the time. They change their minds, too. It's one hundred percent your decision."

Brooke nodded, keeping her eyes locked on Linda's. "I know," she said, feeling a tornado buzzing around the knot in her chest. Her own heart pounded, and she suddenly realized the link between her baby's heartbeat and hers. They were already connected. This thought shot through her in an electric bolt, and shivers raced across her skin. What she'd mentioned to Jill earlier—that at Brooke's age this was likely the last chance she'd have to become a mother—seemed even more poignant now. This was her chance to break the cycle her own mother had started. This child wasn't disposable. It needed a mother. It needed Brooke. Whatever it took, however much she might have to sacrifice, she could have this baby and be the kind of parent it deserved. She could give it everything her own mother never gave to her.

Fifteen minutes later, Brooke was dressed and had climbed into her car. It was raining again, a slow and steady drizzle, but the changing leaves on the trees surrounding the lot looked like they had been dipped in fire, their roots plugged in and their volume turned up. Her head still spinning, she grabbed her phone from her purse and called Ryan.

"Hey," she said. It was the middle of day, and Brooke knew he was on a job site; she heard the banging of hammers and the buzz of electric saws in the background. She tried to think of what to say next, but the words logjammed in her throat. She couldn't do it on the phone. She needed to see his face.

"Hey, babe," Ryan said. "Everything okay? You sound stressed."

To say the least, she thought, then forged ahead with the reason she'd called. "Can I see you tonight? Or do you have the boys?"

"Not until the weekend. I'd love to see you. Are you working? Should I bring the crew by for a beer?"

"Not tonight, okay?" Her voice wavered. "But I'm off around eleven, so I'll come to your place after that."

"Can't wait, gorgeous."

They hung up, and Brooke started her car, skipping between feelings of terror, exhilaration, and panic from one breath to the next. And then she drove toward home, trying to figure out the right words to tell Ryan she was going to have his baby, wondering if she'd just made the biggest mistake of her life.

Jennifer

In August 1981, I was ten months into my sentence at Skagit Valley Correctional. When I woke up each morning, if I tried hard enough, I could forget where I was. I could pretend my thin mattress and gray, scratchy blanket were actually luxurious, that the funky, earthy smell of too many bodies sleeping in one place didn't exist. I could tell myself there wasn't a woman who had sold painkillers on a downtown Seattle street corner in a bed less than six feet from me, or guards posted at every door. I could believe that the early-morning light hitting my face streamed in through a beveled glass window instead of one secured with padlocks and wire mesh.

I could, if only for a moment, forget that I'd given my children away.

And then, when my eyes fluttered open, the truth came, slamming into my chest like a wrecking ball, and I wept, missing my girls. I imagined Brooke, holding her sister's hand, helping to teach her how to walk. I pictured Natalie, gripping her older sister's fingers, her chubby, slightly bowed legs taking one shaky step after the other. I remembered their sweet, little-girl scents and the way their belly giggles always made me laugh, too. I remembered the way they felt tucked up next to me in the back of our car, the three of us cuddled beneath an unzipped sleeping bag and several more blankets, keeping each other warm. I remembered all of this, and then tried to force myself to forget it. To instead focus on the task in front of me. Get up. Stand in line for the bathroom. Shower. Brush my teeth. One thing at a time, trying not to let my thoughts stray too far beyond the next indicated step.

Still, faced with long hours with nothing to do, I found myself writing little notes to my daughters whenever they came to mind. I used a yellow-and-brown–striped spiral notebook I'd found in the common room, jotting down a sentence or two at a time on the blue-lined pages, my lips twitching the way they always did when I was trying not to cry. *Mama loves you so much,* I wrote to Brooke. *You have such a big, tender heart. You cried the first time you stepped on an ant and accidentally squished it; you asked if we could take it to the doctor. I hope you're with people who know this about you. I hope you are tucked into bed every night with a story; I hope you're in school now, and have lots of friends. I hope you never go to bed hungry.* For Natalie, I recorded everything I remembered about her first six months: *You slept through the night when you were only three weeks old, sweet girl,* and *I swear you smiled at me the very first time I held you.* I wasn't sure what I planned to do with these notes, but each time I wrote one, I experienced an infinitesimal flash of relief.

This morning, I stood in the kitchen at five thirty, wondering if my daughters would ever read the notes I'd written them, bleary-eyed as I mixed together enough pancake batter to feed three hundred inmates.

"Get those cakes on the griddle, Walker," the kitchen manager, O'Brien, barked from across the room. She was an imposing woman of Native American and Irish descent, almost six feet tall and lithe. Her thick, black hair was lopped off just beneath her jawline, and her green eyes were set like emeralds above sharply drawn cheekbones. In another life, she might have been a model. In this one, she was a convicted cocaine dealer serving twenty years. She was also my boss.

"I'm on it," I said, turning off the industrial mixer. I unhooked the large bowl and hefted it to the counter next to the stove, where I began spooning half-cup portions onto the already greased and hot griddle. We had less than an hour to get breakfast done; the first wave of inmates would line up at six, expecting to be fed by six fifteen, ready to threaten us with bodily harm if they weren't. I'd been useless in the kitchen at first, having never used more than a toaster, but O'Brien believed in baptism by fire. My first week on breakfast duty she made me solely responsible for the production of scrambled eggs and banana muffins, and within a few hours, even with her screaming at me about everything I was doing wrong, I'd all but mastered the stove and the ill-tempered oven. I found I actually liked cooking; it was one of the few things that forced me to focus on something other than where Brooke and Natalie might be, and if they'd ever find a way to forgive me for letting them go. *They're better off without me,* I told myself, so often that it became my mantra. *They won't even remember me. They deserve so much more than I could give them.*

"Walker!" a man's rough-edged voice called, yanking me out of my thoughts, surprising me enough to cause me to drop the ladle I held into the vat of batter.

"Shit," I muttered, reaching into the sticky mixture to fish out the utensil. Once I'd grabbed it and set it on the counter, I turned toward where the voice came. One of the guards, a large black man with a belly that hung well over his belt, stood in the kitchen's entryway with his thick arms crossed over his chest. I raised my hand and waved. "Here," I said, keeping one eye on the pancakes already on the stove. If I couldn't flip them, they'd burn, and we'd have to serve them anyway. There was not enough time or enough supplies to make more.

"Report to Myer's office as soon as you're done with your shift," he instructed. "Eleven o'clock. Don't make me come find you."

"I won't." I grabbed a spatula and started flipping the pancakes, relieved they were only just on the cusp of turning black. Donald Myer was my assigned counselor, who was supposedly part of my rehabilitation process, but in reality, I'd only seen a couple of times. I doubted he could match my face with my name.

As I continued to cook, O'Brien sidled up next to me. "What the hell was that about?" she asked. Her breath was stale and laced with the instant coffee she purchased at the commissary and drank almost constantly. A few months before, she had broken a woman's nose when she caught her trying to steal her stash of Folgers, a stunt that had landed her in solitary confinement for two weeks.

I shrugged. "No idea." I was lucky, I knew, to work with O'Brien, and that she liked me. Most of the other inmates respected her, and as long as I was part of her crew, they left me alone. I quickly learned who the most dangerous women were, and made it a point to serve them extra-large portions and two desserts whenever I could. Food was a powerful presence inside the prison's walls, and I used it to my advantage.

"You do anything wrong?"

"Not that I know of," I said, though I knew that didn't necessarily matter. I'd seen other women punished, their privileges taken away, for so much as looking at one of the guards in what was interpreted as a disrespectful manner, so it was possible I'd screwed up and didn't know it. Other than my work in the kitchen, I made it a point to keep to myself; to not get in anyone else's way. My belly clenched, wondering why he wanted to see me. Was I being assigned to another job? The laundry or, even worse, custodial?

"You keeping anything illegal in your bunk?"

"No," I said. "Now let me get these goddamn pancakes cooked." I shoved my hip against her in a playful movement, and she swatted my butt as she walked away.

"Make sure you get your lunch prep done before you leave," she said, looking back at me over her shoulder.

"Yeah, yeah," I said, waving her off. After I finished serving breakfast and cleaning the stove, I spent the next few hours mixing together canned tuna and cold, already-boiled noodles with cream of celery soup and shredded cheese, then poured the casseroles into shallow baking pans. I popped them into the oven to warm, and the next shift, responsible for serving lunch and prepping dinner, showed up a little before eleven. I headed out of the kitchen, down a long hallway to Myer's office. I thought about showering first, so I wouldn't smell like grease and tuna fish, but was too afraid of being late.

I smoothed my dark curls as best I could as I walked; they'd grown halfway down my back, and most days, I pulled them into a ponytail just to keep them out of the way while I worked. I readjusted it now, before knocking on Myer's door.

"Come in," he said. The words traveled on a weary voice. I entered the room and closed the door behind me. He was a slight man, probably in his late forties, with a bald patch on top of his head that reminded me of a flesh-colored yarmulke. He kept his eyes on his desk. "Can I help you?"

"I'm Walker. One of the guards told me to report here when I was done with my shift in the kitchen?" I stood with my hands behind my back, in an at-ease position. It was a small room, and I was less than six feet away from him.

He finally looked up, peering at me over black-framed bifocals that rested halfway down his nose. "Ah, right. Walker." He shuffled through the stack of files on his desk. "Please," he said, gesturing to the metal chair across from him. "Sit."

I complied and carefully folded my hands in my lap, waiting for him to speak. The sun beat in through the window, creating a stifling heat. My heart pounded, and my forehead beaded with sweat.

"So," he said. "You're probably wondering why I called you in." I nodded and again waited for him to continue. He skimmed the paper he held in his right hand, then looked back at me. "You're getting out," he said. "Early release."

"Really?" I blinked fast, unsure I'd heard him correctly. "Why?"

He shrugged. "You're a lightweight. Nothing violent on your record. No disciplinary actions while you've been here. You'll be processed on Friday and the bus will take you back to Seattle to meet with your probation officer." He paused. "Any questions?"

I shook my head, thoughts whirling. *What will I do? How will I survive? Should I visit my mom?* A dull ache formed in my chest at the thought of seeing her again. "Thank you," I said. I perched on the edge of my seat, waiting to see if he would have anything else to say.

He stared at me a moment, then leaned back in his chair, drumming his fingers on the tops of his thighs. "Can I give you some advice?"

"Sure," I said, which I figured was the only right answer.

"You seem like a nice girl. You still have plenty of time to start over." He waited a beat. "You know what I'm saying?"

I nodded, still clutching my fingers together in my lap.

"You've made good choices in here. You've kept your head down and done your job. Keep it up on the outside and you'll be okay."

"I will," I said. "Thanks."

He dismissed me, and I hurried back to the kitchen, where O'Brien was overseeing the lunch crew as they pulled the tuna casseroles from the oven. "Hey," I said, and she strode over to the entryway, where I stood.

"Don't you have a meeting with Myer?" she asked.

"I already went," I said, a little breathless. "I'm getting out on Friday. Early release."

"No shit," O'Brien said, with a slow smile. "Congrats."

I shrugged, shifting my weight from one foot to the other, and ran a hand up and down my opposite arm.

O'Brien raised a single eyebrow. "Let me guess. You're worried how you're going to make it?"

"Yeah," I said, relieved she understood. This wasn't her first stretch in prison; she'd done five years at a women's facility in Tacoma two years before she came here. She could have shortened her sentence this time if she'd been willing to turn in dealers higher up on the chain, but she "wasn't no snitch," she told me. She'd be rewarded for her loyalty, she said, when she got out. The world she lived in was one I'd only witnessed in movies and on TV. I took her word that everything she said about it was true.

Before answering me, she glanced around the room and then lowered her voice. "You're quiet. You know how to fly under the radar. My boss is always looking for people like you."

My eyes widened when it hit me what she meant. "You want me to be a dealer?" I whispered.

"Fuck no," she said, laughing. "Delivery girl. My boss will set you up with an apartment and put you to work. You'll have pay stubs to show your PO and everything. It pays for shit, but then there's the cash he gives you on the side. A thousand a week."

I was quiet for a minute, processing what that kind of money would do for me. But I didn't really want to be connected to a coke dealer.

"Listen," O'Brien said, putting her hand on my arm. "It's not like it would be forever, you know? Just long enough to get you on your feet."

"I don't know . . ." I thought about seeing my mother again, what I would tell her about myself, where I was living, what I was doing for work. Maybe she would be willing to let me stay with her now, even though she had remarried. I could get a real job and start all over again.

"Think about it, Walker. You can go back to school. Get a degree. Buy a house. I don't know. You could do whatever the hell you want." When I still didn't answer, she grabbed the notepad she kept tucked in her waistband, set it on the counter, and wrote something down. Tearing off a piece of paper, she handed it to me. "Here," she said. "If you decide you're interested, call the number and tell whoever answers that I sent you."

"Thanks." I took the paper, knowing I would throw it away as soon as I could. If I was going to change my life, delivering drugs was no way to make it happen.

"You're welcome." She put a hand on my shoulder. "Maybe you could use the money to get your girls back."

My eyes prickled with tears. I'd thought every day about regaining custody of Natalie and Brooke, but was unsure of my rights. The way Gina had explained it to me made it sound as though once I'd signed the papers, there was no turning back. Still, I couldn't help but harbor a bit of hope. *Maybe there's a chance,* I thought. *Maybe I can find a way to be their mother again.*

Friday came, and once I was back in Seattle, I gave my probation officer my mother's address on Beacon Hill when he asked where I'd be living. He handed me a piece of paper with a list of places where I could apply for work, mostly jobs at fast-food joints flipping burgers or washing dishes in a diner, which I stuck in the backpack that carried my few belongings: my spiral notebook and an extra pair of jeans.

"Don't fuck up," he told me, and sent me on my way. I had a little cash in my pocket, "gate money," they called it, so I waited for the bus at the downtown Metro station that would take me to my childhood home. Even though I'd been away from the city less than a year, things looked so different—buildings seemed bigger and taller somehow, crosswalks filled with more people, and the streets busy with more cars. After months of having to follow a precise schedule, of daily head counts and bunk inspections, I marveled at the freedom of being able to board the bus, drop in my fifty-five cents, and ride wherever I wanted. A few times I found myself glancing over my shoulder, looking for a guard.

When my bus came, I sat in the very back, staring up at the advertising posters glued near the ceiling, including one with a picture of Harrison Ford for a movie called *Raiders of the Lost Ark*. I

couldn't remember the last time I'd been to a theater; it was probably when I was still with Michael and pregnant with Brooke.
Another poster immediately caught my eye: it was a picture of
a red-haired little girl with long braids who wore denim overalls
and held a structure built out of Legos. The white lettering on the
ad proclaimed, WHAT IT IS IS BEAUTIFUL. Before I knew it, I had tears in
my eyes, wondering if Brooke liked to play with Legos, or if she
preferred the company of dolls. Perhaps she enjoyed both . . . or
neither. There was no way for me to know.

At least they're together, I told myself. *At least they have each other.*
I kept my eyes down for the rest of the ride, and after I got off
the bus at the appropriate stop, my stomach twisted as I walked
the two blocks to the house I'd grown up in—a two-bedroom,
dark brown, rectangular box of a 1950s rambler. The August sun
beat down on my skin; drops of sweat beaded at the nape of my
neck and dripped down my back. It was almost four o'clock, and
I figured my mother would be home. That was, if she was still
working the early shift as a pharmacy clerk at Pay 'n Save. She
had a new husband—I supposed it was possible she had a new
job. She could have moved somewhere else entirely.

But then I saw her car parked in the driveway—a dark green,
two-door VW Rabbit—and I knew she was there. I ran over the
things I thought I should say, the words I hoped would help her
forgive me. I was her daughter, for god's sake. She had to forgive
me—isn't that what mothers are programmed to do? I imagined
if my father hadn't left us, he would have fought for me to stay
when I got pregnant with Brooke. He would have been on my
side. He would have helped make everything okay. That was the
story I told myself. The way I wished things might have been.

With my pulse racing, I stood on the front porch and knocked,
wondering what I would say if my mother's new husband appeared. I had to assume she'd told him about me, but I didn't know
if his distaste for children extended to after they'd become adults.

Fortunately, my mother was the one who opened the door.

When she did, her eyes widened and her jaw dropped. "Jenny," she said, still gripping the knob. Her dark curly hair was pulled back from her face with a white plastic banana clip, and she wore a puffy-shouldered blue blouse with a high, ruffled collar tucked into black stirrup pants. At thirty-eight, except for a few more lines across her forehead and around her mouth, she looked almost exactly the same as she had when I was growing up—short and curvy, with the same violet eyes she passed on to me. If she and I stood in a room together with a hundred other people, there would be no doubt that we were related.

"Hi, Mom," I said. My voice shook as I tried to smile.

"What are you doing here?" she asked. She glanced behind her and then looked back at me, moving the door a few inches toward shut.

"I need to talk with you," I said. "So much has happened and I just—"

"I know what happened," she said, cutting me off. "The woman from Social Services told me you were going to jail and wanted me to take care of your kids."

"I didn't ask her to do that. She was required to. I told her what your answer would be." She didn't respond, so I continued. "She said you got married again."

"I did."

"What's his name?" I asked, shifting my feet, unsure what I should do with my hands. It felt awkward, standing on the front porch of the house I'd lived in for so many years, wondering if she was going to invite me inside.

"Derek."

"I'd love to meet him."

"He's asleep." She glanced behind her into the house, again, then looked back at me. "He works the swing shift at Boeing."

"Did you tell him about me?"

"Of course," she said. "I tell him everything. He's the best thing that's ever happened to me."

I kept silent, feeling a sharp pain in my chest as I remembered that before I got pregnant with Brooke, my mother used those exact same words to describe me.

She looked behind me, toward the street. "Where are they?"

"Who?"

"Your kids, Jenny."

"Oh," I whispered, dropping my eyes to the porch. "I don't know."

"You don't know?" she repeated, leaning heavily on the last word.

"I gave them up. Signed away my rights." I looked back up at her, my words trembling.

"Really?" she said, raising both of her dark eyebrows.

I nodded. "I want to try and get them back, but I just got out and I don't have a place to stay . . ." I let my words trail off and kept my eyes on her face, trying to read her response before she spoke. I couldn't decipher the cloudy look in her eyes, so I rambled on. "I know it's a lot to ask, but it wouldn't be for very long, I promise. Just until I get back on my feet. I can help out. Clean or cook . . . I actually worked in the prison kitchen . . ."

She stared at me, as though she was trying to decide how to respond. "Hold on," she finally said. She disappeared from the doorway, then returned less than a minute later with a thin stack of cash in her right hand. "Here," she said, holding out the money to me.

I dropped my eyes to the bills and then lifted them back to hers. "I can't stay?"

She pressed her lips together and shook her head. "I'm sorry, but Derek just wouldn't be okay with it. He's very . . . structured." With her free hand, she reached out and grabbed my arm, pressing the cash into my palm. "Take it, okay? I know it's not much, but it's all I had in my purse. I can try to get you more later this week."

"But, Mom," I said, blinking back my tears. "I'm trying to fix things. I want to go back to school. Make a fresh start. Please. I just need a little help." I hated how desperate I sounded.

"I'm sorry," she said again. "I wish things were different, but that's all I can do." For the second time, she threw a glance nervously toward the back of the house, where her new husband was sleeping, and I wondered to what extent his "structured" personality might go.

"Mom, please!" I whispered.

"Take care of yourself, Jenny," she said. "I'm sure you'll be fine." And then she slowly shut the door in my face.

Dazed, I turned around and walked away from the house, shoving the money she'd given me into one of my front pockets. I felt numb, barely able to process what had just happened. I'd told my probation officer I'd be staying with her. I worried I might go straight back to jail if he came looking for me and I wasn't there. My car had been auctioned off and the proceeds used to pay the fines that went along with my sentence, so all I had was the money my mother had just given me, and the aching desire to find my children.

I need a place to stay. I need to figure out what I'm going to do. I trudged back toward the bus stop and checked the schedule when I got there, deciding that I should head back downtown, where I knew of a few cheap motels, places I'd stayed with my daughters.

An hour and a half later, I found myself in a small, dingy room with a full bed and a television that the manager told me only had three channels. The walls were covered in dark wood paneling, and the well-worn bedspread was a print of large orange and brown flowers. I'd used a few dollars to buy a ham sandwich and a Snickers bar at the corner gas station, so I sat on the bed and wolfed them down, then drank metallic-tasting water using a smudged glass next to the sink. The room smelled of body odor and mildewed, sour towels, but I was too exhausted to care. All I wanted to do was sleep.

I lay down on top of the covers and stared up at the ceiling,

counting the muddy brown spots that stained the white tiles, replaying the events of the day, sorting out everything I'd have to
do in the morning. I'd need to call my probation officer and let
him know where I was. I'd need to find Gina's phone number
and call her, too. I needed her to tell me that even without my
mother's help, I could get my daughters back.

Natalie

Holding the tattered white box in her hands, Natalie left her mother's house in a daze and climbed into her car. She had a sister. The sentence felt foreign, so apart from her normal lexicon that she had to keep repeating it in her mind to try to absorb it as the truth. She reached over to the box and pulled out the manila folder that held all the paperwork from her adoption. Flipping through it, she found the page indicating that her unnamed birth mother had relinquished all of her parental rights, both to six-month-old Natalie and to her four-year-old sister, Brooke. Their father was listed as unknown.

"We thought it would be easier for you this way," her mom had said, just moments ago, when Natalie was still inside. "Your dad and I only wanted what was best for you. The social worker said it was up to us, how much information we gave you. You were only six months old. It wasn't like you'd remember her."

"Did you meet her?" Natalie asked, still clutching her lavender blanket. "Did you even think about adopting her, too?"

Her mom stared at Natalie for a moment, then shook her head. "We really only wanted a baby, and were advised that older children tended to have behavioral problems. I didn't think I could handle something like that. Your father and I thought it would be better for her if she was adopted by someone more experienced. Someone better equipped than us."

"I don't know what to say." Natalie leaned against the kitchen wall, thinking about her mother's distaste for anything messy, shocked to hear that this predilection had extended to the possible emotional issues of a four-year-old girl. She could have grown up with a sister. She had a *sister*. Her muscles buzzed; her skin felt too tight for her body. Her mom was silent, her fingers laced together in front of her, waiting for Natalie to continue. When she did, it was with tears in her eyes. "I don't think I can be here right now."

"Sweetie, please," her mother said, reaching out and touching Natalie's hand.

Natalie jerked away. "I need some time to think. I'll call you." She grabbed her purse and headed out the door. She knew what her mother had told her was the truth—her parents had only done what they always did—what seemed best for her at the time. In her mother's mind, Natalie could see how the decision made sense. Chaos upset her, so choosing not to tell Natalie about Brooke likely seemed the right thing to do. Her father tended to go along with whatever kept the peace, whatever kept his wife happy, so he wouldn't have argued the point.

But then Natalie thought about Brooke, her sister, who was left alone, separated from the only family she had, and Natalie's heart squeezed inside her chest. She remembered Hailey at that age, only a few years before, Henry just last year. How vulnerable her children were then, with their delicate feelings and fragile, birdlike bones—how they still needed Natalie so much. What had happened to Brooke? Was she adopted, too? Did she wish she could find Natalie? Did she wonder why Natalie never tried to find her?

As she sat in her car in front of her parents' house after having left her mother inside, Natalie's stomach ached and her thoughts zipped through her brain so quickly she felt dizzy. She wanted to talk with Kyle, to process everything she'd just learned, but she knew he was still in court and a brief recess wouldn't be enough time for the kind of detailed conversation she needed to have. This wasn't the sort of news to break to her husband via text. Instead, she decided the best thing she could do was head home and sort out her next steps.

Once there, Natalie did her best to steady the turmoil she felt and let the skills she'd learned as a lawyer take over. Having a breakdown wasn't going to help her find her birth mother. She told herself that if Kyle could focus on the facts of a situation, she could, too. She'd just pretend she was researching a case.

Feeling determined—hungry for more information—she sat down at the kitchen table and lifted the folder out of the box, flipping through it again. There really wasn't much detail on the pages, mostly legal terminology and discussion of fees paid to the state for the adoption. Her birth mom was referred to as the "surrendering party." Is that what she had done? Natalie wondered. Surrendered her daughters? Did she surrender her feelings, right along with her rights?

A moment later, her eyes landed on the name of a social worker, Gina Ortiz. Natalie wondered if this woman could help—if she knew more about the situation than the file held. She got up and grabbed her laptop from the coffee table in the living room. Back at the kitchen table, she turned on the machine, and after it had booted up, she opened the browser, then typed, "Gina Ortiz Washington State social worker" into the search engine. She had no idea how old this woman might be, if she was working or if she'd retired long ago. For all Natalie knew, Gina Ortiz could be dead. But if her days as a lawyer had taught her anything, it was that almost every person left a paper trail. All she would have to do was find Gina's.

Natalie scanned the results on the screen. A link to the Washington State Department of Health's website was the first to come up, so she clicked on it, wondering if there was a list of individual social workers on the site. She found none, so she navigated back to the results page, where she clicked on another link—an association for social workers who were accredited to provide supervision to those new in the profession. But Gina Ortiz was nowhere to be found on the alphabetized list.

Discouraged, Natalie opened another page and brought up the Department of Health website again, deciding she would just pick up the phone and call them. She pulled her cell phone from her purse, punching in the appropriate numbers. An automated system answered, so Natalie pressed 0, knowing that would at least give her a real person with whom to speak. "I'm looking for a current, or possibly former, social worker," she explained to the operator. "Her name is Gina Ortiz. I need her address and cell phone, if possible."

"I'm sorry," the woman said. "I don't have access to that information."

Natalie hung up, frustrated, and drummed her fingers on the table next to her computer, staring at the screen until another idea struck her. She hit redial on her phone, and waited for the operator to answer again. "Hello," she said, in a much louder, more nasal voice than the one she'd used on her initial call. "Can you connect me with Shelly Philips, please?" Natalie used a name she had seen on the top of the association of social workers list, where Shelly Philips's title included lead caseworker at the Department of Health. She would have asked to speak with Human Resources, but Natalie worried privacy laws might prevent them from giving out an employee's personal information; Gina's supervisor wouldn't be held back by the same restrictions.

"Of course," the operator said. "I'll transfer you."

"This is Shelly," a woman's voice answered.

"I'm wondering if you can help me," Natalie said, switching back to her normal voice. "I'm a family law attorney who worked with Gina Ortiz on a custody case, and I've lost her contact information. Do you know how I can reach her?"

"I'm sorry, but Gina retired several years ago."

"Oh," Natalie said. "I didn't realize. Do you happen to have her forwarding information? I need to touch base with her on some specifics of the case. It's being revisited by the court."

"Are you sure I can't help you?"

"I'm sure," Natalie said. "She was well acquainted with the guardian ad litem, so I really need to speak directly with her."

"Let me see what I have on file," Shelly said. Natalie heard the clacking of the other woman's fingers on her keyboard, and before she knew it, Shelly was reciting Gina Ortiz's phone number.

"Thank you so much," Natalie said as she read back the ten digits, to make sure she'd gotten it right. "I appreciate it. Have a great day." She hung up, feeling more than a little pleased with herself. Then, after opening another page on her browser, Natalie punched Gina's name and phone number into a reverse directory and came up with her current address, which she jotted down, as well.

Staring at the numbers, she debated whether or not she should call Gina, or if she should just show up at the woman's front door. What if she slammed the door in her face? Natalie wondered.

But then again, what if she didn't?

Natalie's cell phone buzzed just as she pulled into the parking lot of the Shady Palms apartment complex in Des Moines, where Gina Ortiz lived. It was an older collection of buildings, likely built in the seventies, with cedar roofing and painted like a cake—chocolate siding with chocolate trim. "Hey, babe," she said when she answered the call, after seeing Kyle's name and picture pop up on her screen.

"Hey," her husband said. "I only have a few minutes, but I wanted to check in. Are you and your mom okay?"

Even though Natalie would have preferred to have this conversation in person, she gave her husband an abbreviated account of the morning's revelations along with her current whereabouts.

"Holy shit," he said when she'd finished. "You have a sister."

"I know," Natalie said, feeling like she might cry. "I can't believe they kept it from me."

"I can."

"Kyle," Natalie said, feeling another flash of irritation. His negative thoughts about her parents' behavior were the last thing she needed right now; she was having enough difficulty dealing with her own.

"Sorry," he said. "It just doesn't seem right that they waited so long to tell you."

"I know," Natalie repeated. "But we can talk about that later? I want to find out what I can from the social worker."

"Are you sure that's a good idea? Maybe you should take more than a minute to digest all of this."

"I'm not sure about anything," Natalie said. "But I do know I'll drive myself crazy if I wait. Hailey's going to Ruby's house for a playdate and Henry's going to Logan's. I've got until five o'clock." Natalie's plan to spend the afternoon working had evaporated; par-baking mini–chocolate lava cakes and making fresh lemon curd to fill bite-size tarts didn't seem important. She'd stay up all night finishing the order if she had to.

"The woman might not even be here," Natalie told Kyle. She had thought of this possibility on the drive over, but banked on the likelihood that since the social worker was retired, she'd be home.

"Okay," Kyle said. "I have to get back to work. Text me and let me know what happens, okay? I love you."

"Love you, too," Natalie said. They hung up, and Natalie's belly twisted. She wondered what she would do if Gina didn't remember anything about the situation. It had been thirty-five years, after all.

"Only one way to find out," Natalie muttered as she yanked the keys from the ignition and opened the driver's side door. She locked the car, glancing at the letters on the buildings, eventually landing on the large letter D painted on a sign. She strode across the lot, entered the building, and even though there was an elevator, used the stairs to reach the third floor. Standing in front of the unit labeled D-302, Natalie hesitated, then raised her hand and knocked.

"Coming!" a woman's voice called out. A second later, the door swung open and Gina Ortiz stood before Natalie. She was a heavy woman, and had wavy, shoulder-length hair that looked as though it had once been black but was now a peppery shade of gray. Her caramel skin was etched with a map of deep-cut lines, and she wore a colorful, bold-print caftan that skimmed the round shape of her upper body. "Can I help you?" she asked, appraising Natalie with a skeptical look.

"Are you Gina Ortiz?" Natalie said, in a rush.

The older woman's eyes narrowed. "Yes," she said, in a manner that made it clear she was wary. "You're not trying to sell me something, are you? There's a 'no soliciting' sign downstairs."

"No, no," Natalie said. "Not at all." She gave the woman what she hoped was a friendly smile. "I'm so sorry to bother you at home, and I'm not even sure where to start, exactly, but I literally just discovered that you were the social worker on my adoption. I also found out I have a sister I didn't know existed. I'm here to see if you can help me find some answers."

"I don't know," Ms. Ortiz said, drawing out the words.

"Please," Natalie said, and her eyes filled with tears. She hoped the woman wouldn't turn her away—that it would be obvious how much Natalie needed her help.

Ms. Ortiz's expression relaxed. She stood to the side, pulled the door farther open, and gestured for Natalie to enter.

"Thank you," Natalie said, and then introduced herself. Stepping inside the apartment, she was instantly reminded of Christmas—

the air was scented with cinnamon and the living room decorated in bold shades of red and green. The walls were covered with ornate gold picture frames, filled with images of laughing children and family gatherings. It made Natalie feel better, somehow, that Gina had had children of her own. That she might fully understand what it was Natalie's birth mother had chosen to give away.

"Have a seat," Ms. Ortiz said. She settled her body into a large, worn-in leather recliner, and Natalie sat on the red velour couch on the other side of the coffee table, perching on its edge, keeping her posture ramrod straight.

"I really appreciate this," she said. "I'm still in shock over the whole thing, to tell you the truth." Her hands shook, so she clutched her fingers together in her lap.

"Please, call me Gina," she said. "And you're in shock over being adopted or finding out you have a sister?" Natalie quickly clarified. "I see. Why don't you tell me a little about what you do know, and I'll see if I can help."

Natalie nodded, wondering where, exactly, she should begin. "I know I was adopted when I was six months old, in November of 1980, after my birth mother surrendered her parental rights to the state. I know we lived in her car before she gave me—I mean, *us*—up. My sister was four."

A shadow passed over Gina's face. "What did you say your name was?"

"Natalie." This was it. She was talking to the right person. Gina would tell her what she needed to know.

"Do you know your sister's name?"

Natalie's heart fluttered in her chest. "It's Brooke. Or at least it was. I suppose her adoptive parents could have changed it."

"She was never adopted," Gina said. Her voice was quiet. "Poor girl."

"You remember us?" Natalie's pulse quickened and a few tears escaped her eyes, rolling down her cheeks. She felt as though she was teetering on the edge of a precipice, about to dive off.

"I do," Gina said. "Your sister ended up staying at Hillcrest more often than in foster homes." She shook her head. "I just couldn't find her the right fit."

"Hillcrest?" Natalie asked.

"It's a state-run facility in South Seattle," Gina explained. "Temporary for some kids, a permanent home for others. You were there almost a month before your parents adopted you." She folded her hands over the expanse of her belly. "But Brooke was there for the better part of fourteen years. I was her case manager."

"Oh my god." Natalie's jaw dropped as she tried to imagine what that kind of existence would be like—what damage it could have done to a child. "Was she . . . what happened?"

"Well, she got into a bit of trouble when she was younger. She had a hard time accepting her circumstances. For a few years, she was certain her mother would come back to get her, and that, along with her behavioral issues, made it difficult to find her an adoptive family or even a foster home that would keep her very long."

"How awful," Natalie said, feeling as though *awful* was too weak a word to describe what her sister had gone through. Again, her mind flew to Hailey and Henry, how they might have reacted if they lost the only family they knew—if Hailey had spent four years living in a car and then was sent to live with strangers, wondering where her mother had gone. The idea of her daughter being a victim of a situation like that—picturing her curled up in a narrow bed of a group home with no one there to comfort her— made Natalie feel as though she might be ill.

All of those years Natalie thought she was an only child. All of those times she wished she had someone to talk to, someone to play with, and Brooke was somewhere out there, alone, like Natalie. Having read every child development book she could get her hands on when she was pregnant with Hailey, Natalie knew that infants under six months old can recognize their mother's smell and their family members' voices and faces. It was a significantly different kind of memory than recalling specific events or conversations—something that happened in the deep, primal part of a person's brain—but Natalie couldn't help but wonder if perhaps her psyche had been imprinted with her sister's shadow. Maybe her subconscious knew the feeling of her sister well enough to miss her after she was gone.

"She had a tough time of it for a while," Gina said, interrupting the thoughts crowding Natalie's mind. "But as she got a little older and learned how the system worked, she did her best to follow the rules. I think she believed if she did everything right, she'd find a family, too. Unfortunately, most foster parents who are looking to adopt prefer babies or younger children." She frowned. "It broke her heart when you two were separated, but she refused to talk about it with anyone. Even me. She internalized everything, and mostly tended to keep to herself."

Natalie thought about how shy she'd been as a child, wondering briefly if she and Brooke shared this trait because of their genes, or the way each of them was raised. "Do you know what happened to her?" Natalie asked. "After she left Hillcrest?"

"I'm sorry, I don't," Gina said. "But her last name was Walker."

"The same as my birth mother's?" Natalie asked.

"I can't tell you that," Gina said. "The records are sealed, so disclosing any part of your birth mother's name would require a court order. The same restriction doesn't apply in the case of siblings."

Natalie took a moment to digest this bit of information. She'd visited Gina in order to gather the kinds of details that might help her find her birth mother, but now it was clear that Brooke was the one Natalie should try to locate first. "What about our father?" she asked. "The paperwork listed him as unknown, but can you tell me anything about him?"

Gina looked at her a moment before responding. "You and Brooke had different fathers," she finally said.

"Oh." Natalie felt a little disappointed. *We're half sisters, then,* she thought. *But sisters, nonetheless.* "Do you know anything about mine?"

"Only that your mother didn't know his name," Gina said, not unkindly, but the words still stung. Natalie's father was some random stranger, a person she'd never know anything about. She wasn't planned, she wasn't wanted. No wonder her birth mother gave her up. Natalie swallowed hard and tried to focus.

"Do you have any suggestions of where I should look for my sister?" she asked, after she'd had a moment to compose her thoughts.

"Online adoption registries are your best bet. Social media, too. Facebook and the like. You could petition the court to open the files to your case, but that could take years and would be very expensive."

Natalie thought back to when she was eighteen, when she let her father talk her out of putting her name on an adoption registry list in case her birth mother came looking for her. If she had defied him and done it anyway, maybe she could have found her sister almost twenty years ago. They could have found their birth mother together after that. The frustration she'd felt toward her mother earlier that morning melted into something harder, something with teeth, gnawing at Natalie's insides. She knew her mother had been traumatized by the ectopic pregnancy and subsequent hysterectomy, but keeping a secret as significant as Natalie having a sister seemed extreme. Natalie wondered if there was more behind her parents' decision than they'd said.

"Did you know our birth mother very well?" Natalie asked, unable to keep the tremor from her voice. Integrating this new information about her past into the person she'd always believed herself to be felt as though she were trying to knit a ball of yarn into an already perfectly stitched blanket. There were suddenly gaping holes in the fabric of who she was. The world she was living in now was not the one she had woken up to that morning.

Gina stared at her a moment, then nodded.

"Is there anything you can tell me about her? Anything at all?" A few more tears escaped Natalie's eyes.

"She loved you," Gina said, softly. "Both of you."

"Then why didn't she keep us?" Natalie asked, unable to keep the aching desperation from her words.

"I'm sorry," Gina said, and Natalie knew there was nothing more the older woman could tell her. The only thing left to do was find Brooke, and see if her sister could fill in the blanks.

Brooke

"No! I won't go!" Brooke insisted as Gina took her hand and attempted to pull her from the car. It was 1984 and Brooke was eight years old. This was the fourth foster home Gina had taken her to in as many years.

"Come on now," Gina said, wrapping her arm around Brooke's shoulders. "The Martins are expecting you. They already have a daughter about your age. Her name is Lily. I promise, you're going to like it here."

"No!" Brooke yelled, literally digging her heels into the grassy parking strip. "Take me back! I need to be where my mom can find me!"

"Sweetie, we've talked about this . . ."

"She's coming to get me!" Brooke said, trying to keep from crying. Since she'd been brought to live at Hillcrest, her head had been filled with all sorts of stories about what kept her mother away—a long illness. A car accident that had put her in a coma. Maybe she had amnesia. Maybe she didn't remember who she was. Brooke felt as though she were trapped inside a bubble, holding her breath, waiting for her mother to return. Each time she was called to the front office, Brooke would rush down the hall, positive that this time, her mother would be there. When she wasn't, it was as though Brooke had lost her all over again.

Now, undeterred by Brooke's resistance, Gina managed to get her and the black plastic bag filled with the few changes of clothes she owned inside the Martins' house, where she introduced Brooke to a blond woman with bangs that stood straight like a wall from her forehead. The rest of her hair was crimped, and she wore a pair of acid-wash jeans and a light pink polo shirt with the collar turned up around her neck. Her lipstick matched her shirt.

"This is Jessica," Gina told her.

"Hello!" Jessica said with a big smile, revealing tiny teeth that reminded Brooke of white Tic Tacs. "You must be Brooke. We're so happy you're here. Lily can't wait to meet you."

Brooke dropped her eyes to the floor and didn't respond. Gina could make her live here, but she couldn't make her talk. She looked around the living room as Jessica and Gina excused themselves to the kitchen. The walls were painted a pale blue, and the trim was white. All the furniture looked as though it had been taken from a magazine and plopped down in just the right place—a couch the color of peaches, two navy-blue armchairs, and a wrought-iron coffee table with a glass top. There was a tan brick fireplace and pictures on its mantel—Brooke took a few steps over to them and peered at the couple, Jessica in her mermaid-style white dress with huge, puffy sleeves and her husband looking movie-star handsome in a tuxedo with his hair feathered perfectly on each side of his head. He was blond, too, his hair cut shorter on the sides and left longer in the back, almost to his shoulders. He had a strong jaw and bright green eyes. There were pictures of a girl with blond hair, whom Brooke assumed was their daughter, Lily. She looked mostly like her mother, with the exception of having her father's large teeth, which, with her oval face, Brooke thought made her look a bit like a horse.

Brooke smoothed her hand over her unruly black curls and

looked at the pictures again. However much she hated the idea of living with this family instead of her mother, she caught herself wishing that she looked more like them—that people might easily mistake her for a member of their family. It was a game she played, spotting physical traits she shared with other people, wondering if she could pass as one of their relatives. Everyone commented on her violet-blue irises, a color she had yet to see in another person's eyes. "Your mom had them," Gina had once told Brooke, thinking, Brooke was sure, that this piece of information might make her feel better, when in fact it only made her feel worse.

Gina soon left, and Jessica showed Brooke the rest of the house. There were two bedrooms, one at the front of the house, where Jessica and Scott slept, and the other, down the hall, which Brooke had to share with Lily, Jessica and Scott's nine-year-old daughter. When Brooke met Lily later that afternoon, the older girl announced that since it was her house, first, she was in charge of their room. At this, Brooke rolled her eyes, but at the time, kept her mouth shut.

Over the next several weeks, as she tried to get used to another new school and living in a house with three strangers, Brooke stayed on her best behavior, which wasn't the easiest thing to do with Lily around. The older girl talked incessantly, and it drove Brooke crazy.

"I love my teacher," Lily said. "She has the nicest smile and always gives me the papers to hand out to the rest of the class. Mrs. Pearson wasn't like that last year. She was cranky all the time. We used to laugh at the stupid glasses she wore, but then I felt bad about it and told the other kids they should stop, which Mom said I was brave to do and I think she was right. Do you think that was brave?"

"I think you should shut up," Brooke said, sounding as nasty as she could. She was already sick of the sound of Lily's yammering. And then, she couldn't help it, Brooke threw her math book at Lily's head. Lily ran to her mother and tattled, of course, and as punishment, Jessica told Brooke that she had to stay alone in her room for the rest of the night, missing out on the pizza they were going to order and the video they had rented—*Mr. Mom.*

"You can eat in here and think about what you've done," Jessica said. She brought a sandwich and a glass of milk, then left again, closing the door behind her. Brooke pulled the sandwich apart and smeared mayonnaise, turkey, and cheddar cheese across the cheery yellow paint on the wall. *I hate you,* she thought as she poured the milk on Lily's pillow.

A while later, Scott came to check on her. When he discovered what she had done, his eyes darkened as he took a couple of steps over to where she lay on her bed, her arms crossed over her chest. "Get up," he growled.

Brooke glared at him, her chin raised, but didn't move.

"Fine," he said. He grabbed her, lifted her up, and managed, despite how she flailed against him, to sit and then lay her facedown, over the tops of his thighs.

"Let me go!" Brooke yelled, but he didn't listen. The next thing she felt was the smack of his open palm on her rear end. "Oww!" she cried, feeling the tears spring up in her eyes almost immediately after his hand had landed. She'd never been spanked before. She squirmed and wiggled, trying to get away, but Scott used one of his strong arms to hold her in place. His hand smacked her again.

Tears still ran down Brooke's cheeks, but instead of crying out, she pressed her lips together as hard as she could and tried not to make a sound, not wanting to give him the satisfaction of knowing he had hurt her. She kept her eyes squeezed shut, and her fingers curled into tight fists, wondering if her real father would have spanked her, if she had ever spent time with him.

When Scott stopped after swatting her twice, Brooke felt numb, despite the way the skin on her rear end throbbed. It was as though something had snapped inside her, and in that moment, she didn't care about the consequences Jessica and Scott might dole out. As the weeks progressed and her behavior didn't improve, they tried different ways to discipline her. When she purposely clogged the toilet with Kleenex, they took away her TV-watching privileges. When she refused to help wash the dishes, they didn't let her have dessert. When she called Lily a bitch—a word she'd heard other kids say at Hillcrest—they put her in time-out. Scott spanked her again after he caught Brooke purposely tripping Lily as they entered the kitchen to eat breakfast. But no punishment worked, because Brooke had already decided that there wasn't a thing they could do that would hurt her more than her mother already had.

One morning, after Brooke had been living there a couple of months, Lily returned to their room after taking a shower to find Brooke still in bed. "You have to get up," Lily said, in a snotty tone that made Brooke want to smack her.

"You're not the boss of me," Brooke mumbled, burrowing her head under her pillow. "I don't feel good." Since losing her mother and Natalie, Brooke rarely felt good. It seemed like there was something heavy growing under her skin—something thick and black, like an infection. Her stomach often burned like there was a fire crackling inside it; acid rose up into her throat when she lay down to try to sleep. The night before, her dreams had been filled with the feeling of chasing her mother, running around corners and up hills, but never finding her. When she woke up, her chest ached and her pillow was wet. She knew her eyes would be swollen and red, and she felt as though she hadn't slept at all. She didn't think she could go to school.

"Faker," Lily said, with contempt. A moment later, Brooke felt her covers being stripped off her body. She slept in a tank top and a pair of underwear; the cold air in the room pinched at her exposed skin.

"Hey!" Brooke yelled, and she leapt up, tackling Lily by pushing her shoulder into the other girl's waist. They both ended up on the hardwood floor, wrestling, until Brooke grabbed Lily's thin, wet hair, yanking it as hard as she could.

Lily screamed, and Jessica appeared almost instantly, attempting to tear the two of them apart. "What's going on?" Jessica demanded when she was finally able to separate them. She stood between the two girls, staring at Brooke as she spoke, making it clear who she assumed was the instigator.

Brooke's chest heaved, and she watched as Lily's usually pale pink complexion turned tomato red while she told Jessica that Brooke had tackled her for no reason. "She pushed me over! And pulled my hair!"

"Did you do that, Brooke?" Jessica asked.

"She pulled my covers off first!" Brooke said, shooting a hateful look at Lily. "I told her I didn't feel good! I might have pneumonia!"

"You're a liar!" Lily whimpered through her tears.

"I don't care if you felt bad or not," Jessica said. "This is unacceptable behavior. Do you understand me, Brooke? I won't have it."

"I don't have to do anything you say!" Brooke screeched.

"Oh, yes you do," Jessica said. "As long as you're living here, you'll follow our rules."

"I don't even *want* to live here!" Brooke yelled. "I want my mom!"

"Too bad!" Lily taunted. "Your mom doesn't want *you*!"

As soon as Lily spoke the words, Brooke felt as though her heart had exploded, breaking up into a million pieces. She wanted to tear Lily into shreds. A hot, primal feeling took her over, and she bent her fingers, clawing at Jessica to get away.

Jessica cringed and cried out, letting go of her hold on Brooke's wrist, then pressed a hand over the spot where Brooke had scratched her arm. Brooke looked at her fingernails and saw that she had drawn blood. Jessica lifted her hand and saw this, too, and as she stared at Brooke, her jaw dropped.

Brooke trembled, wanting to cry. She wanted to tell Jessica and Lily that she didn't know what was wrong with her—that she was sorry for all the bad things she'd done. But instead, she crawled back into bed, creating a tent with the covers, where she stayed as Lily got dressed and left for school. Not long after she was gone, through the thin walls, Brooke heard Jessica talking on the phone, but she couldn't really hear what was being said or to whom she was speaking. After she hung up, Jessica came back into the bedroom. "Are you hungry?" she asked, but Brooke stayed silent. She felt the mattress sink as Jessica sat down and attempted to pull the blankets off.

"Just leave me alone!" Brooke screamed, holding the covers down around her head. "Stop touching me! I don't want you to touch me!" Her skin hurt, worse than the times Scott had spanked her.

Jessica didn't say another word. Instead, she simply left the room. Brooke felt bad for being so rude. Jessica was way better than some of the foster mothers Brooke had heard stories about from the other children at Hillcrest—mothers who put locks on the refrigerator and cupboards so the kids wouldn't eat too much food. She was better than the single woman Brooke had lived with for six months the previous year, who told Brooke that it was her job to clean the cat box and do all the laundry as part of her "rent"; better than the older couple who'd taken her in right after Natalie was adopted and ended up sending her back to Hillcrest after only a few weeks, saying that they'd made a mistake in taking on another foster child when they already had three. Jessica might have punished her, Scott might have spanked her, but hadn't she deserved it, every time?

If Brooke was honest with herself, there were moments when she liked living with Jessica and Scott. She liked playing Uno with them on Friday nights and having chocolate chip pancakes every Sunday morning. She even liked lounging on the couch and watching *Scooby-Doo* or *Bugs Bunny* with Lily after they got home from school. But as soon as she found herself feeling the tiniest bit content, she was overwhelmed with guilt. She worried it would make her mother feel bad if she knew that Brooke was happy living with other people.

Still, Brooke stayed in her room that entire morning, rising only when she had to use the bathroom. She didn't eat, she didn't say another word to Jessica, who again had been talking on the phone in a low voice. The only thing Brooke heard her say was "She's a total hellion!" and she knew that Jessica could only be talking about her.

Scott came home from work early, around noon, and a couple of hours after that, before Lily got back from school, Gina arrived and told Brooke in a quiet tone that it was time to pack her things. Brooke thought about Lily discovering that she was gone, and she wondered if the older girl might miss her. Probably not, with how horrible Brooke had been to her most of the time. She wondered if Jessica and Scott would find another little girl to foster and maybe adopt—a girl who didn't scream and yell and hurt other people.

"What are we going to do with you?" Gina said as they drove away from Jessica and Scott's house. She looked in the rearview mirror at Brooke, who was staring out the window. "Did you hear me, honey? What can I do to help you?"

Brooke shrugged, not looking at Gina, too afraid if she did, she might start to cry. She'd gotten what she wanted—she was going back to Hillcrest—so why did she feel so awful? She bit the inside of her cheek, and tasted pennies.

"She's never coming back," Brooke finally whispered. "Is she?" She kept her eyes on the side of the road as she spoke, counting each of the trees as they drove along. Her mother was out there somewhere in the world, living her own life, pretending that Brooke and Natalie didn't exist.

"No," Gina said quietly, knowing without having to ask who Brooke meant. "She's not."

When Brooke remained silent, Gina spoke again. "It'll be okay. Maybe not today, and maybe not tomorrow. But eventually, I promise, you're going to be fine."

Brooke nodded, knowing that her social worker was just doing her job, telling Brooke what she needed to hear. She knew that adults made promises they couldn't keep all the time—the kinds of promises that simply never came true.

Just before midnight on the day she'd gone to the clinic and decided to keep the baby, Brooke stood in the hallway of Ryan's apartment, trying to work up the courage to knock. She'd been distracted all night at the bar, mixing up orders and spilling drinks like a newbie waitress; she ended her shift having earned less than a hundred bucks. She kept playing out different scenarios of the conversation she had to have with Ryan in her head: one where he dropped to his knees and placed an ear against her belly; another where he screamed at her to leave. Not knowing which reaction he'd have was torture. She was so accustomed to keeping her lovers at a distance; she didn't know how to manage these new feelings—the ache of need she felt in her gut. Suddenly, she wanted Ryan to need her, to want a relationship with her, to be the father of her baby. She wanted him to say, "We'll take care of this child together." It reminded her too much of how she had felt growing up, every time Gina took her to meet yet another foster family, wondering if this one would finally be the last. When Brooke would walk through a new house, touching the furniture, the pillows, the pictures on the walls, whispering only to herself, trying out the word "home," to see if it fit.

And now, there she stood with a bright wedge of hope in her chest, about to tell Ryan the truth. She told herself that how she grew up didn't matter. She'd have this baby, and then maybe, she and Ryan could build a family all their own.

Just do it, she thought, and finally, she lifted her hand and rapped on the door lightly, three times. She'd never asked for a key to his place, and he had never offered one.

Ryan opened the door and grabbed Brooke, hugging her close. He buried his face in her neck. "I missed you, babe," he said.

"I missed you, too," she said, clinging to him. She relished the hard lines of his body, the safety she felt in his embrace. He moved his head so he could kiss her, and she let him, feeling his hands roam up and down her sides, over her ass, cupping her to him. He gave a little groan and scooped her up, carrying her down the hall toward his bedroom. She wanted to stop him—she knew that what she needed to tell him should come first. But still, she let him lay her on the bed and slip off her clothes. She let him kiss her and touch her and take her to the edge. "You're so beautiful," he murmured as he entered her.

At least she couldn't get pregnant, Brooke thought, and then she turned her head, stuffing the heel of her palm in her mouth, resisting a half-hysterical urge to laugh.

It was over quickly, quicker than usual, and when Ryan rolled off of her, they both lay on their backs on his king-size bed, fingers laced together. "God, I needed that," Ryan said, trying to catch his breath. He moved his hand to rub the curve of her hip. "You okay? You seem quiet."

She curled to her side and faced him, tucking one bent arm under her face. "Just a lot on my mind," she said.

"Oh yeah?" he said. His tone was light, which Brooke took to mean that he couldn't fathom that she, with her small apartment and simple job, could have anything too worrisome with which to deal.

"Yeah," she said. She swallowed and reached out her free hand to caress the length of his arm. "I need to talk to you about something."

"Okay," Ryan said, with more than a hint of wariness. Brooke sat up and leaned against the pillows. With a puzzled, slightly apprehensive look, Ryan did the same. "What's up?"

Brooke decided that the best option was just to get the truth out as quickly as possible. It was only two words. "I'm pregnant," she said, staring at the now-wrinkled steel-gray comforter. "I didn't have the flu. It was morning sickness."

Ryan was silent, and Brooke made herself look at him. "Ryan?" she said, after a moment. "Can you say something? Please?"

"You're sure it's mine?" he asked. He didn't look at her.

She gasped, and her eyes filled with tears. "Of course it's yours. Jesus." She pulled at the comforter, covering her naked-ness, and swung her legs over the side of the bed. She felt his eyes on her back.

"I'm sorry," he said. "I had to ask."

She whipped her head around and shot him an angry look over her shoulder. "You had to? You think I've been sleeping with someone else?" A thought struck her then, and what felt like a hard stone sank inside her belly. "Are *you*?"

"No," Ryan said. "I just . . . I'm sorry. I shouldn't have said that." He sighed and put one of his callused hands on her back. She jerked away. "Brooke, don't. I said I'm sorry. You surprised me, that's all. I thought you had all of that taken care of."

"All of what?" she asked, and he shrugged. "Birth control, you mean?"

He nodded. "I mean, we've been sleeping together for a year, and this is just happening now?"

"So this is my fault," she said, unable to keep the hostility from her words.

"I didn't say that."

"Yeah. You did." Brooke stood up and yanked on her under-wear and jeans, which Ryan had tossed on the floor. He didn't want this, she thought. He didn't want her. She should have known he'd react this way. She'd been a fool to think anything else. She bent over, looking for her bra, and when she found it, she put it on, followed by her white T-shirt.

"Brooke, stop. Let's talk about this." Ryan rose from the

bed, pulled on his boxers, and came around to where she stood. He grabbed her arm, and again, she tugged away. He stared at her with dark clouds in his eyes. "Please. Tell me the truth. Did you . . . was this . . . something you planned?"

"No! I'm on the Pill, but apparently, it didn't work. No birth control is a hundred percent." She shook her head in disbelief. "You think I would do that?"

"I don't know." He raked his thick fingers through his hair and looked away, out the window to the sparkling lights of downtown. "I've seen it happen. A friend of mine got divorced, and his mistress poked holes in her diaphragm to trap him into marrying her."

"I'm not your fucking mistress," Brooke said, hoping he could hear the disgust in her tone. Even though technically speaking, since he was still married, she was his mistress, she hated the dark underbelly indications of the word. "And I'm not trying to trap you into anything. If you don't know me well enough by now to know I would never do something like that, then maybe you don't know me at all."

He was silent for another moment, still staring out the window. "I do know you," he finally said.

Brooke hesitated, his words serving as a temporary balm. Maybe she was being too hard on him. She'd had a week to get used to the idea of carrying his child; she should give him more than two minutes to do the same. She reached out and took both of his hands in hers. "I promise, I don't have an agenda here. I just needed to tell you. That's all. I needed you to know."

"Of course," Ryan said. "And I'm not going to leave you alone to deal with it. I'll help."

"Really?" she said, softening her voice. She allowed herself to feel another brief spark of hope, a softening around the edges of her heart, a place that had been hardened for years.

"Of course," he said. He gathered her into his arms again. "I'll pay for everything. Go with you to the appointment."

The muscles surrounding Brooke's stomach seized. The

whoosh, whoosh, whoosh of her baby's heartbeat played inside her head. "You want me to get rid of it," she said, quietly.

"What else can we do? You know my situation. If Michelle found out I knocked you up—if she found out about you at all—she'd have the exact ammunition she needs to take everything she wants from me in court. I can't have that, Brooke. I can't have anything more involved than what we already have."

Brooke cringed at his use of the phrase "knocked you up." The crudeness of it; the total lack of heart. She broke out of his embrace and took a couple of steps back. He sounded like a selfish, irresponsible teenage boy, terrified of telling his parents what he'd done, focused only on how the situation affected him.

"And what do we have, exactly?" she asked him, lifting her trembling chin. She crossed her thin arms over her chest, curling her shoulders forward.

"We have this," he said, gesturing toward the bed. "We have fun together. We laugh. We don't take anything too seriously."

"No responsibility, no commitment," Brooke said, keeping her voice low. This was what she always had with men. What she wanted. And yet, with a baby on the way, couldn't she want something more? Wasn't she entitled to it?

"Yes," Ryan said. "Which doesn't mean I don't care about you. But I thought you understood it. I thought you knew what not telling Michelle or the boys about you meant."

"What does it mean?"

"It means you can't get pregnant!" Ryan said, throwing his hands up in the air, and then letting them drop back to his sides. "It means you can't keep it. I'm sorry, but why would you want to ruin a perfectly good thing?"

Brooke blinked back her tears and focused on saying her next words without crying. "I already made the appointment," she said, but before she could continue, he cut her off.

"Oh." The relief in his voice was tangible. "Good. You probably should have led with that."

"No," Brooke said, raising her eyes to meet his. She wondered if their baby would have her violet eyes or his brown—if they'd have a girl or a boy. "You don't understand." She kept her voice as calm and steady as she could. "I went to the appointment today. But I couldn't go through with it. I want to keep the baby."

Ryan put his hands on his hips, shifted his stance, and glared at her. "It's not just up to you."

"Yes," Brooke said, feeling a grief so profound, so heavy, she worried it might sink her to the floor. "It is."

And with that, she spun around and walked down the hall, making sure her car keys were still in her front pocket. *Screw him,* she thought as she waited for the elevator. It didn't matter. Nothing had changed. She'd do this like she'd done everything else in her life. She'd find her way through it on her own.

Jennifer

Five days after getting out of jail, after seeing my mother, I was almost out of money. She had given me just over two hundred dollars, but the cost of the motel room alone took more than half of that, and I spent most of the rest on food and a few pairs of much-needed clean underwear and socks. I thought about her offer to get me more money if she could, but then rejected the idea, the same way my mother had rejected me. I didn't think I could handle reaching out, only to have her turn me away again. I'd have to find a different way to make some cash.

I passed the hours sleeping and watching TV—shows I'd never seen before, like *Greatest American Hero* and *Dynasty,* and others I remembered watching with my mother before I moved out, like *The Waltons* and *M*A*S*H.* I lost myself in the silly plots and overdramatic dialogue, trying not to think about the way my mother had closed the door on me. How she'd chosen a man over helping her only child.

I'd left Gina three messages, and she hadn't called me back. It wasn't until Thursday—my sixth morning in the motel—that the black phone on the nightstand next to the bed finally rang. I'd been half-asleep, so the shrill sound startled me, and as I reached to answer it, I accidentally knocked the phone to the floor.

"Jennifer?" I heard Gina's muffled voice say as I lunged over the side of the bed.

"Yes!" I called out, snatching up the receiver and putting it to my ear. "I'm here." I struggled to right myself again, sitting up against the headboard. Sunlight edged the tattered curtains in a golden halo, and the red numbers on the clock radio told me it was almost ten. I was due to check out at noon, and I had no idea where I would go after that.

"I'm sorry it took me so long to call you back," Gina said. "I've been busy with home visits this week."

"That's okay," I said. Gina didn't say more, so I forged ahead with the reason I'd called her. "They released me early from Skagit," I said. "For good behavior. And I just . . . I can't stop thinking about my girls."

"I'm sure," Gina said.

"I miss them so much," I continued. "I was wondering . . . now that I'm out . . . is there any chance . . . any way I can get them back?"

"I'm sorry, Jennifer," Gina said in a low, steady voice. "You signed away your rights. The girls are wards of the state now."

"I know," I said. A single tear rolled down my cheek, but I didn't wipe it away. "I just feel like I made the wrong choice."

"I understand that," Gina said. "But the fact is, the decision was made. Papers were signed. If you wanted to regain custody, you'd have to hire a lawyer and file a petition with the court. It could take years, and you'd have to prove you were capable of taking care of them." She paused. "Have your circumstances changed? Do you have a job? A place to live? Appropriate child-care?"

I glanced around the dark, dingy room where I'd spent the last several days. The only change to my circumstances was that they'd gotten worse. Not only did I not have a job or a place to live but I was a felon. "No," I whispered into the phone, feeling stupid that I'd called. "Not yet."

"Then there's nothing you can do," Gina said, softly.

"Can you at least tell me how they are . . . or who they're with?"

"I'm sorry," Gina said again. "I can't. The terms of the arrangement are closed. You agreed to that, remember? To protect your anonymity and give your girls the freshest start you could?"

"I remember," I said. "I just didn't know it would feel like this."

"Like what?"

"Like I tore out two big chunks of my heart." My voice shook, and I tried to steady it. "I feel like I'm broken."

"I'm sorry, Jennifer. I really am," she said, and a few moments later, we hung up. I curled fetal under the covers, my back to the window, and I began to cry. It was final. There was no way I could have my daughters with me again. I didn't have money for a lawyer, and even if I did, considering my current situation, there was no way a judge would rule in my favor. I was no better off than I'd been the day I gave them up. Who knew how long it would take me to find a decent job and a place to live? It could take years, and by then, the girls would have been with their new family long enough that my trying to regain custody would only disrupt their lives. It would only cause them pain.

Rolling over, I wiped away my tears and grabbed my notebook and a pen from the nightstand next to the bed, flipping to the next blank page. *I wanted to get you back,* I wrote. *I swear I did. But when I tried, I was told it was better this way. Better for you both to have a new life with a new family instead of with me. I wish things were different. I wish I were a better mother to you both.*

I wanted to say more. I wanted to come up with some reasonable explanation for the choices I'd made. Instead, I shut the notebook and pulled the covers over my head, escaping into a troubled sleep, dreaming of my daughters, dreaming that I heard them crying in another room, and I was unable to get to them. I pounded on the walls, desperate to reach my girls, and then woke to realize the hammering I heard was the motel manager's fist on my room door.

"Check out was an hour ago!" he yelled.

"Okay, sorry!" I said, blinking my swollen and scratchy eyes, wondering if I had it in me to invite him in and do whatever I had to to keep the room for another week. My stomach lurched at the thought, so I splashed some water on my face, got dressed, grabbed my backpack, shoving what was mine inside it before heading out into the warm August afternoon. The bright sunlight made me squint. *Maybe I can find a good street corner and hold up a "will work for food" sign,* I thought. *Or maybe I should just find a park where I can camp out.* The weather was warm enough that I could get away with it, as long as the cops didn't show up and tell me I had to leave.

I counted the few bills I had left in my pocket—fifteen dollars and some change. Enough to take the bus to a nice suburban area where it was less likely a park would be patrolled at night. During the summer months, before I'd had Natalie, I used to take Brooke to Lincoln Park in West Seattle—we'd spend the afternoons playing on the jungle gym and splashing around in the wading pool, eating peanut butter sandwiches, and then spend the nights in our car. It was as good a destination as any, so I left the motel parking lot and hiked over to Third Avenue and Pike Street, where I knew the number 118 bus had a stop that would take me where I wanted to go.

A little over an hour later, I was there. The park was off Fauntleroy Way, near the Vashon ferry dock. It was heavily wooded but also had a large, brightly hued jungle gym, several sets of tall swings, and picnic tables scattered across the lush, vibrant lawns. I made my way to one of the empty benches that surrounded the playground and dropped down on it, my shoulders hunched. I felt lost. *No one knows where I am. No one cares if I live or die. My daughters will grow up without me. I'm only twenty-one, and I've already ruined my life. I should have kept the phone number O'Brien gave me. At least then I'd have a way to make money.*

A little girl's voice jerked me out of my thoughts. "Mama!" she cried, and every hair on my body stood on end. I'd been so preoccupied, I had barely registered the other people in the park.

Oh my god. Brooke. My eyes shot like pinballs around the immediate area, looking for my daughter. For her mass of black curls.

"Mama, look!" the girl's voice said, and I stood up, my heart thumping loudly enough that it echoed inside my head. I performed a frantic search of the children's faces around me. It sounded just like her. *Could she really be here?*

"I see you, honey!" I looked over toward the swings and noticed a tall, dirty-blond-haired woman standing with a group of other mothers, and then back in the direction that she waved. A young girl with long, brown hair waved back, jumping up and down on the curved bridge that connected one part of the jungle gym to the other. She wore yellow Salt Water sandals and a black-and-white polka-dot sundress.

"Mama! I'm on the bridge! Do you see me?" She did a little dance, causing the bridge to jiggle. She looked to be about five years old.

"I do!" her mother called out. The woman made her way over to the climbing structure, and as she approached it, her daughter ran across the bridge to a platform, where she stood with her arms outstretched, bent at the knees, bouncing up and down.

"Catch me, Mama!" she cried, and her mother stood close to the platform's edge. The little girl leapt with assurance, locking her tiny legs around her mother's waist and her arms around her mother's neck, the same way Brooke had often done with me.

My eyes blurred and my stomach heaved. I put my face in my palms, chest burning and shoulders shaking. *Oh, god. My girls. Where are my girls?* I hadn't considered what it would feel like, seeing other children out in the world. In jail, I'd been protected from this particular brand of torture. What I felt in that moment was a prison all its own, with walls built out of shame, self-loathing, and blistering regret.

When I looked up again, I saw the blond-haired woman set her child on the ground and make her way back toward the group of parents she had been talking with at the swings. I watched as the little girl spun in circles, her head down, giggling as her dress whirled out from her body. She gave a small jump, and then did it again, spinning and spinning and spinning, only to finally stumble and fall over. Her head bounced on the black rubber mat of the playground.

I raced over next to her and squatted down. "Are you okay, honey?" I asked, pushing back the fine hair of her bangs from her sweet face. She was whimpering and tearful, though not loudly. I glanced over at her mother, and saw that her back was to us; she was busy talking with her friends. She hadn't seen the fall. "Did you hurt yourself?" I asked the girl, and she nodded, pushing out her tiny and pink, chubby lower lip.

I gathered her into my arms and lifted her up. Her skin was warmed by the sun. She smelled sweet, like strawberries, tinged with just a touch of summer sweat. I squeezed her to my body, then started to feel dizzy, and my heart began to race. I closed my eyes and felt as though I'd been sucked through the dark vacuum of a black hole, back to that small room with my babies, holding them for the last time.

No, I thought. *No, no, no.*

The child struggled against my embrace, pushing at my chest with her small hands, but not with enough strength to break free. I held her tighter. "Shh," I murmured. "It's okay, baby. I've got you."

This time, when the little girl cried out the word "Mama!" all I could hear was Brooke's voice. All I could think of was getting away, saving my daughter, not letting anyone take her. Blinking fast, I shifted my eyes toward the blond-haired woman, and at the same moment, she turned and saw me. "Hey!" she called out.

She strode in my direction, arms swinging at her sides. "Hey!" she said again, louder this time, and with more urgency.

A river of discordant noises raged inside my head—a jarring, crashing cacophony of sound. *I can't let them take her. I can't.*

Before I knew what I was doing, I spun around, the little girl still safe in my arms, and headed toward the woods, running as fast as I could.

"Mama, Mama, Mama!"

"Shh, honey, shh," I said. I had one arm wrapped around her body, holding her to me. With my other hand, I cupped her head, pushing her face into the curve of my neck as I ran, trying to protect it from the whip-sharp sting of the branches that scratched at my bare arms. I felt the heat of her tears on my skin, her tiny rib cage heaving against mine.

We'll be okay. We just have to get away. Then no one can take her.

Each step I took crunched atop the pine needles covering the ground. There was no path. No easy way to snake through the trees. But I didn't think. I didn't stop. I had no idea where I was going or how far I'd already gone. The only thing I could do was run.

"I want my mama!" the girl cried, and a chunk of her straight brown hair flew up and blinded me.

Wait. Brooke's hair is curly, like mine.

I wasn't carrying my daughter. The realization reverberated through me, like a church bell being struck inside my head.

It took only this brief moment of distraction for the tip of my toe to catch on a thick root. My foot twisted, sending a sharp spike of pain from my ankle, up my shin, and into my knee. Both of us tumbled, and the girl flew out of my arms, landing hard against the trunk of a tall evergreen a couple of yards away.

Her cries got louder then, and despite having the air knocked out of me from hitting the ground, I managed to crawl over to her. She had a large cut on her forehead; it gushed bright red blood down the left side of her face. *Oh, god,* I thought as I took in her unfamiliar features. *What did I do?*

"It's okay, sweetie," I said, managing to sit up. I ripped off the bottom of my shirt and pressed it as hard as I could over the wound on her head. I heard people shouting behind me, though I couldn't make out what they said. "I'm so sorry," I told her. "Let me take you to your mama, okay?"

She was hysterical, screeching so loudly I couldn't be sure that she'd heard what I said. I stood up, and the piercing agony in my right ankle almost took me down again. Ignoring my own injuries, I helped her stand so I could inspect hers. Her hair was a mess, and her legs and arms looked as though they'd been attacked by an angry cat; no matter how much I'd tried to protect her skin, the razor-tip ends of the tree branches had had their way with her, too. A river of tears ran through the mess of grime and blood on her face as I put more pressure on the cut on her head. Her eyes were squeezed shut, her mouth was open wide. Her sundress was dirty and torn.

Seeing all of this—knowing I was responsible for her injuries and her tears—I started to cry, too. I heard a dog bark and knew I had to get her back to her mother just as quickly as I could. I felt dizzy and sick, bells going off inside my head, but I picked her up, keeping the makeshift bandage pressed against her forehead as I limped in what I hoped was the direction of the play area. My ankle screamed at me with every step. After only a moment, I saw her mother and several other adults charging toward me.

The girl's mother sped up until she reached us. She yanked her daughter from my arms and held her close. "Shh, shh, baby," she said. "I've got you. You're all right. Everything's going to be fine." She gave me a fierce glare. "What the hell is wrong with you?"

I took a step backward, almost stumbling again because of the pain in my ankle. "I don't know," I said. "I'm so, so sorry." My eyes widened as two men—fathers who had been playing with their children at the park—pushed past the woman. Each of them grabbed one of my arms and squeezed them, tightly. "It's okay," I said. "I'm so sorry, but she's okay. We fell. I don't know what happened."

"My wife called the police," one of them said to the woman.

"Wait," I said, feeling panic rise in a wave inside my chest. "You don't understand. It was a mistake. I thought . . . I saw her fall and heard her crying and I thought she was mine." A sob tore at my throat. "I'm sorry," I said again. "Please. I'm so sorry."

The woman said nothing. She simply held on to her daughter, whipped around, and walked away. The men who held me led me back through the woods, never letting up on their grip.

The gravity of what I'd just done sank down deep in my body, melting into a dark, rancid ink, staining my insides black. Before I knew it, my stomach heaved and emptied its contents on the ground. I straightened and tried to wipe my mouth as the two men still moved us forward.

I saw the red and blue flash of police lights as we exited the woods. The woman and her daughter were already with the paramedics, and when the officers saw the two men holding me, they marched in our direction. When they reached us, the two men finally let go, only to have one of the officers tell me to put my hands behind my back.

"Wait, please," I begged. "Let me explain."

The officer took my arms and forced them behind my back, securing my wrists together with handcuffs. "There's nothing for you to explain," he said. He was a muscular black man with a strong jaw and a bald head. "We have multiple eyewitness accounts that describe how you grabbed the child from the playground and ran into the woods."

"I didn't mean to," I said, choking on my tears. "It was a mistake. I thought she was my daughter. I didn't realize what I was doing."

"Tell it to your lawyer," said the other officer, a stocky woman with pale skin and black hair, shorn short against her head. "Right now, you're being placed under arrest for attempted kidnapping."

"You have the right to remain silent," the male officer began, and as he continued reading me my rights, my mind went blank, and I didn't hear anything else. I couldn't take my eyes away from the mother as she stood next to her little girl, who the paramedics had now placed on a gurney. The mother had her hand on top of her daughter's head as she also held one of her small hands. She only glanced up at me once, and it was with so much bitterness, so much hate in her eyes, I looked at the ground. I wondered if there was something really wrong with me. There had to be, for me to do something so unthinkable. Why else would I have grabbed that little girl and run? Why else would I have thought I was holding Brooke?

After the officer finished speaking, he asked if I had any identification. "In my back pocket," I said, and he reached for my wallet, pulling out my driver's license, which had expired two years before. He took it and walked over to his vehicle, then climbed inside the driver's seat. A couple of minutes later he returned and spoke to the female officer as though I wasn't standing right there.

"Jennifer Walker," he said. "Just out last week from Skagit Correctional."

"Really," the female officer replied. "What was she in for?"

"Several counts of petty theft and child endangerment and neglect." The officer looked at me and frowned. "Guess they let you go too soon."

I didn't respond. To him, I was just a criminal. A repeat offender. Nothing else. *Maybe that's the truth,* I thought. *Maybe I'll be better off in jail. I'll never get my daughters back anyway, so what does it matter?*

The female officer held me by my elbow and led me to the police car. I was still limping— my ankle felt like it was on fire—but I didn't care. I deserved whatever pain I was in. The officer opened the back door and helped me turn so I could get inside. She kept her hand on top of my head so I wouldn't knock it into the roof as I sat down.

Once the door was closed, I looked over one final time and saw the little girl sit up and hug her mother. She had finally stopped crying and had a clean white bandage on her forehead. I leaned my own head against the window, trying not to be sick again, hoping she would be okay. I hoped I hadn't traumatized her too much.

I waited a long while for the officers to finish taking more statements from the other people in the park, and when they both finally climbed into the seats in front of me, I was more than ready to leave. *At least I know where I'm going,* I thought as we drove out of the parking lot and onto the street. *At least now, I have a place to stay.*

The next day, after hearing my side of what happened, my public defender, a short, heavy man with dark pouches of skin under his brown eyes and a thick, Tom Selleck–style mustache, suggested I enter a not-guilty plea. "You had just found out you can't get your children back," he said, as we sat together in a small room in the King County jail. "The judge might feel sorry for you."

"No," I said. I'd picked up the girl and run away with her into the woods. I was guilty. There was no point in trying to make excuses.

"Suit yourself," he said with a shrug.

Later that afternoon at my hearing, I pleaded guilty to attempted kidnapping and reckless endangerment of a child, for which the judge issued me a sentence of ten years. It could have been much worse, he told me, if I'd used a weapon or tried to put the little girl in a car and drive away. He cited my past offenses of theft and neglecting my children as adding weight to his decision to put me away for as long as he did. I didn't argue. I simply stood in the courtroom and listened to the litany of things I'd done wrong. Each word was like a jagged nail pounded into my body, confirmation of how broken and useless I was.

After the sentencing, I spent four weeks in King County jail, waiting to be assigned to a prison. It was only dumb luck that returned me to the women's facility in Mt. Vernon and the regimented life to which I'd become accustomed over the previous year.

"Well, well, look who's back!" O'Brien said as she walked into the small space on the cellblock that held my bed and one other. "What happened, Walker? You miss us or something?"

"Something like that," I said, not wanting to relive what I'd done in the park. I'd tried several times to write my daughters another note after the few sentences I'd written my last morning in the motel, but was only able to get down two words: *I'm sorry.* I wrote them over and over again, filling page after page, knowing that tiny sentence would never be enough to express just how deeply the roots of my regret were planted inside my heart.

"You get your work assignment yet?" O'Brien asked as she dropped down to sit on my bunk with me. She smelled like grease and bleach.

"No," I said. "I just got here this morning." It was late afternoon, and I'd spent the entire day lying in my bed, staring at the ceiling tiles, counting them, trying not to think about anything at all.

She put a hand on top of my thigh. "I'll see what I can do about getting you back in the kitchen, okay?" She smiled. "It'll be like old times."

"Thanks," I said, grateful she wasn't pushing me to tell her what I'd done to land back there so quickly. The old hollow sensation had returned and taken over my body, ever since the moment in the woods when I saw the blood rushing down that little girl's face. It felt as though I were hovering just outside of my skin—me, but not me. There, but not part of anything going on around me. My soul tethered to my body by only a thin wisp of thread.

The next morning after breakfast, my counselor, Myer, called me into his office. I sat down in the same metal chair I'd been in just a month before and folded my hands together in my lap. I stared at the floor.

"So," he said, leaning back in his own chair. "I guess you didn't listen to my advice." I kept my eyes cast downward and didn't respond, so he sighed, then continued. "You're being assigned to the vet program. You'll need to report to the community room for orientation this afternoon at two o'clock."

"Vet?" I said. "As in war vets?"

"No, Walker. You'll be working with dogs. Learning how to train them to be guides for people with disabilities. It's a pilot program, led by a local veterinarian."

"But I don't know anything about dogs," I said. "I've never even had one." Of course, I'd wanted a puppy when I was a little girl. My dad had even brought one home as a surprise for my seventh birthday, but after three nights of the sweet little mutt whining and chewing up the edges of my mother's couch, she insisted that my father take it back to the pound.

"He'll teach you," Myer said. "That's the point. Now go on. And don't give me any flak over this. I know your friend in the kitchen wants you there, but the warden's on my ass to get more inmates into the antirecidivism programs." He pushed a brochure across his desk. "Take this, too."

"What is it?" I asked as I stood up and reached for what he was giving me.

"Information on getting your GED. Now that you're here a while longer, you should do it."

A "while" longer, I thought. As in ten times longer. I'll be thirty-one when I get out. I took the brochure and thanked him before I left his office and headed toward the kitchen, where I told O'Brien about my new assignment.

"That fucker," she said, pressing the bottom edge of a clipboard against her stomach. "What the hell do you know about dogs?"

"Not much," I said. "But I guess I'm going to learn."

"Hey," O'Brien said, reaching out one of her long arms to pull me into a side hug. "Glad you're back, bitch."

I nodded and gave her a perfunctory smile before I went back to my bunk to wait until I needed to be at the orientation. At noon, I went to the cafeteria, but only because not showing up at meals was against the rules unless you were in the infirmary. I didn't eat, though. Since the day in the park, I seemed to have lost my taste buds. Everything I put in my mouth had the texture of sawdust. It took a huge amount of effort to chew, and the only way I managed to eat anything at all was to wash down each bite with large swallows of water.

After an hour of sitting alone at a table with an untouched tray of mushy spaghetti and limp, slightly browning iceberg lettuce in front of me, I returned to my bunk until the clock read a quarter to two. I didn't want to go learn about this stupid program; I didn't want to go anywhere. I only wanted to stay in my bed, counting my breaths, counting each minute until a decade was done. But not wanting to incur Myer's wrath, which could include ending up in solitary for refusing to follow an order, I forced myself to wander toward the community room. Looking through the windows, I saw a short, stocky man with a bright shock of thick, red hair sitting at one of the tables. He wore blue slacks and a long-sleeve, pink button-down, which I couldn't help but think was an unfortunate choice with his coloring. It made him look like an overripe strawberry.

I opened the door and entered the room. There was no one else there; it was just the two of us. Myer must have made it off-limits to anyone else during this meeting. The man looked up and smiled, then rose from the table. "Jennifer?" he asked, and I nodded, then made my way to the table, as well.

He held out his hand, and I took it in my own limp grasp for less than a second. His fingers were warm and a little sweaty. *Is he nervous?*

"I'm Randy Stewart," he said. "And this is Bella."

I glanced down next to his feet, noticing for the first time there was a dog in the room. It looked like a yellow Lab, and its snout rested on top of its outstretched front legs. It wore a red-and-black harness over its back, which had some kind of writing on the side, but I couldn't read it from where I stood. I'd never encountered a dog who didn't freak out the minute someone new entered the room, demanding to be petted, but this one hadn't even raised its head.

"Have a seat," Randy said, gesturing to the chair across the table from him. He sat down, and I joined him. "So," he continued. "How much do you know about our program?"

"Nothing," I said.

"Okay, then!" he said, with so much cheer it raised the hairs on the back of my neck. *You're inside a prison, you idiot,* I thought. *What the hell is there to be so happy about?* Then it hit me. He got to leave. He had a life outside of these walls. I looked at his left hand and saw a gold band. He probably had a family, too. Kids, even. He wasn't anything like me.

He reached down inside a black leather bag next to his chair and pulled out a large blue binder, then pushed it toward me on the table. "This will be your bible," he said. "Everything you need to know about how to raise and train a guide dog, like Bella here."

"How am I supposed to do that?" I asked. "I don't know anything about dogs."

"That's what the bible is for. And me." He looked at me expectantly, but when I didn't speak, he went on, ignoring my disinterest. "I own a vet practice in town. We train guide dogs as a community service, as well as providing free obedience training for local rescue shelters. Part of this program, after you've worked with me here and earn approval for work release, is to come to the clinic and get some basic, hands-on training as a vet tech. You can even start working toward a two-year degree in veterinary sciences, if you want." He glanced down at a folder in front of him. "I understand you need to get your GED, but as soon as you do, if you want, you can start taking college courses."

I scowled, wondering what else that file had to say about me. "Is this supposed to be some kind of fucking rehabilitation bullshit?" I wanted to shock him, but my foul language didn't make a dent in Randy's jovial demeanor.

"Only if you let it," he said. "What you get out of this is entirely up to you. If you don't buy into learning all you can, doing all you can do with the dogs, I'd be happy to tell Mr. Myer that you're not suited for the program."

I stood up, pushing my chair away from the table with a loud screech. "You can tell him that now," I said. I wasn't interested in being rehabilitated. This man was crazy if he thought working with dogs would fix whatever was wrong with me. My head began to buzz again as I flashed back to the moment in the park, to running through the woods with another woman's child, thinking that child was mine.

"Jennifer, please," Randy said, as he stood up as well. He was only a few inches taller than me, and his stomach strained the buttons on his ridiculous pink shirt. He picked up the binder and held it out to me. "Just read through it. If you're still not interested, fine. I'll talk with Mr. Myer. But this is a new program here. You'd be the first inmate I'd get to work with. I'd hate to be a total failure right out of the gate."

I stared at the binder, then back at Randy. "Bella, door," he said, and the dog, who still hadn't moved, got to her feet and trotted over to the room's entrance. She jumped up and, using her front paws, pushed down on the silver handle and slowly walked on her hind legs until the door was fully open. She looked back at us, waiting, it seemed, for someone to come toward her.

"Holy shit," I muttered, and Randy smiled again.

"Impressive, right?" he said. "And that's only a basic skill. There's so much more to it than that." He shook the binder in the air. "So what do you think? Are you in?" he asked. "Will you give it a chance?"

I glanced over to Bella, who stood on her hind legs, motionless. I reached out and snatched the binder from Randy's grasp. "I'll read it," I said. "But I'm not making any promises."

"That's all I ask," he said, and then I walked out of the room, past Bella, reluctant to admit I just might be holding a tiny scrap of hope.

Natalie

By the time Natalie said good-bye to Gina at her apartment and made it home, it was four o'clock and she only had an hour before Hailey and Henry were due back from their playdates. She considered using the time to get started on the order prep for the party she was catering the next night, but after her conversation with Gina, she couldn't think of anything else but trying to find her sister. Work would have to wait.

She grabbed her laptop from her desk in the den, opened a search engine, and typed in her sister's name. The first link that came up was for Facebook, suggesting that Natalie search for Brooke Walker on the social media site. Natalie clicked on it and logged in to her personal Facebook account, which she really only used to post pictures of the things she baked, then typed in her sister's name again. A list of over three hundred women came up, all living in various cities across the United States. Natalie had no way to know where Brooke might be living. Had she stayed in Seattle, or did she flee the area when she turned eighteen? She scanned the list and then filtered it by adding the modifier "Seattle, WA" to the search field with her sister's name, and the results came up blank. Similar searches of

Instagram, Twitter, Pinterest, and Tumblr came back empty, too. If her sister was in the Seattle area, she certainly didn't spend any significant time online. *Of course, she could be married,* Natalie thought. She could have been adopted and have an entirely different last name. If that was the case, it was a pointless endeavor to search on social media platforms for the name her sister had had when she was four.

Frustrated, Natalie closed out the web page and opened a fresh tab. She remembered Gina's words about the various online adoption registries, so she did a search for the largest, most reputable one. Natalie clicked on the link at the top of the list and saw that it was a mutual consent registry, meaning that if her sister—or even her birth mother—was already registered on the site, Natalie could be contacted within a couple of days of when a data match was found. While the site didn't have access to court records and couldn't confirm a relationship as authentic, it could at least provide first contact with a possible blood relative. The FAQ page recommended that if necessary, once the two individuals connect, they could petition the court to open their records, or voluntary DNA testing could be done.

This could be it, she thought as she eagerly used her email address to create a log in and filled out her own profile with as much information as she could about herself. She listed her maiden name as Natalie Walker, thinking that would be the name Brooke might search for if she was, in fact, looking for her sister, too. She filled in her date of birth and the dates and details of her infancy as best she could, using the same story her mom had told her and Natalie had passed on to Hailey. She noted her brief stint at Hillcrest before she had been adopted, she described her physical characteristics, and then she went on to fill out the limited information she knew about her older sister. She entered her name, and all the information about how they had both lived in a car with their mother, how she had signed over her parental rights to the state. She entered the fourteen years Brooke had stayed at

Hillcrest, as well as Gina's name and contact information, in case Brooke had included that in her profile.

Natalie was just about to hit submit when there was a knock at the front door. "Mommy, I'm ho-ome!" Hailey called out from the porch. "Let me in!"

Natalie stood up and stared at the screen as she pressed her index finger down on the mouse, and then a box popped up informing her that her profile had been successfully posted to the site. *Please,* she thought. *Let this work.*

"Coming!" she said as she jogged toward the foyer and opened the door. Hailey hugged her legs as Natalie waved at Ruby's mom, who had stayed inside her car in the driveway, waiting until Hailey was safely in the house. Ruby's mom beeped the horn once before backing out and driving away. Another car pulled up in front of the house then, and Natalie recognized Katie at the wheel.

"Hey!" Katie said as she climbed out of the car and walked around to the other side. She opened the back door and helped Henry release his seat belt, and Natalie watched as her son raced up the walkway and into the house.

"Hi, Mama!" Henry said as he pushed past both her and Hailey, dropping his Buzz Lightyear backpack on the bench next to the door. Buzz was Henry's latest obsession; he'd watch all three of the *Toy Story* movies every day if Natalie let him. At night, he slept with a hard plastic, electronic Buzz doll, something she'd found at a consignment store for just a couple of bucks and sometimes regretted buying because of the toy's irritatingly loud mechanical voice. In the morning, Natalie knew Henry was awake and pushing buttons when she heard "To infinity . . . and beyond!" coming from his bedroom.

"Thanks for bringing him home," Natalie called out to Katie, who stood next to her car. "I'm happy to return the favor when Logan plays over here."

"Sounds good," Katie said, smiling. She gave Natalie a short wave and then climbed back in the driver's seat and drove away.

Natalie ushered Hailey inside and shut the door behind them. Henry was already lying on his stomach on the couch, propped up on his elbows and scissoring-kicking the cushions as he played with two small action figures, Buzz Lightyear and Woody. His head was bent down and his shoulders were hunched, intent on whatever story he had them acting out, narrating their conversation under his breath, first in Buzz's voice, "I've set my laser from stun to kill!" and then, in Woody's slow drawl, "Reach for the sky!"

"Guess what?" her daughter said as she pulled off her bright red jacket and dropped it to the floor. "Ruby has a new kitten! His name is Tux because he's black and has white fur shaped like a bow tie on his neck!"

"Hang that up, please," Natalie said. Hailey groaned as though she'd just been asked to carry a load of bricks across a desert, but then hung up her coat on one of the hooks by the door.

"But did you hear me?" Hailey said as they walked together into the kitchen. "The kitten's name is Tux! Like Tuxedo! Because of the bow tie. Get it?"

"I get it," Natalie said, waiting for her daughter's inevitable request.

"He is sooo cute," Hailey said. "I wish I had a kitten." She looked at Natalie sidelong and raised her eyebrows. "It's almost my birthday, you know." Her birthday was actually in March, five months away, so "almost" was a bit of a stretch.

"I'm sorry, honey, but you know with my baking I can't have animals in the house," Natalie said. Her kitchen was licensed commercial, and even though she'd soon be moving her work space out into the more spacious and fully remodeled garage, state regulations still forbade any animals on the premises.

"I know," Hailey sighed. "It's not fair."

Natalie glanced at her laptop, thinking she should shut it down, but then decided against it. What if a data match came back tonight? Unlikely, Natalie knew, but still, she kept her computer on.

"How about you work on your family tree while I work on my dessert order?" Natalie suggested as she opened up the refrigerator, pulled out six pounds of butter, two dozen eggs, and a bag of lemons, and set them on the counter. She'd get the lemon curd going first, and then make the truffle filling for the chocolate lava cakes.

"I already finished it at Ruby's," Hailey said.

"Wow," Natalie said. "Can I see it?"

"Okay!" Hailey pushed her chair back and raced to the foyer, where she'd hung up her backpack along with her coat.

Henry wandered into the kitchen then and attached himself to one of Natalie's legs, sitting on her foot. His arms held tight around her knee while she unwrapped cubes of butter and plopped them into a pan on the stove.

"I'm back!" Hailey announced when she returned, holding a large piece of white construction paper than had been folded in half, which she opened and delivered to Natalie. "It's kinda bad," she said. "The leaves are all crooked."

"Very bad, that picture!" Henry said, letting go of his mother's leg.

"Very stupid, my brother!" Hailey shot back.

"Hey. No name-calling," Natalie said, immediately wondering if she and Brooke would have quarreled like this, if they had been raised together. Would they have been close? Would they have stayed up all night giggling about the boys they liked or gossiping about their friends? Would they have fought over clothes and makeup and whose turn it was to clean the bathroom? Would Brooke have fed her ice cream when Natalie cried over her first broken heart? There was no way she'd ever know the answers to these questions, and the thought of that, being victim of that kind of loss, made Natalie's heart ache.

Still holding the paper Hailey had delivered, Natalie smoothed it onto the counter. Her daughter had drawn a picture of herself at the base of the tree, under the ground. Her curls were drawn in brown springs shooting out from her head, directly linked to the tree's squiggly roots, which Natalie thought was a creative touch. There was a branch and leaves right above her for Natalie and Kyle, as well as for Kyle's older brother, Sean, who lived in Los Angeles with his wife, Isabelle, and their two boys, Carter and Cody. Hailey had given both of her cousins their own leaves, too. Her parents' branch was above them all, along with a branch and two leaves for Kyle's parents, who lived in South Carolina and rarely came to visit.

"You did a beautiful job, honey," Natalie said, and for what felt like the countless time that day, her eyes filled with tears.

"Are you crying?" Hailey asked, incredulous. "It's so good it made you cry?"

Natalie laughed. "Yes," she told her daughter, even though that wasn't the reason for her tears. However much she might like to, she couldn't tell Hailey that the project wasn't complete. In order to be an accurate picture, a true account of their family history, the drawing needed another branch and two more leaves.

Natalie did her best to keep busy the next couple of days, trying not to think too much about Brooke or check her email too often to see if the adoption registry had found a match. Instead, she focused on work, fulfilling her weekly orders for the three local espresso stands who had hired her to provide them the baked goods they offered their customers. Since it was fall, she made a selection of seasonally themed muffins: cranberry-orange corn-meal, pumpkin streusel, and eggnog spiced with a hint of fresh ground nutmeg, as well as tender almond croissants and a variety of bite-size, melt-in-your-mouth scones. She met with three different contractors who gave her bids on the remodel of the garage and hired her first choice, excited that the work would soon begin.

But after a week of trying to be patient, Natalie decided she couldn't take the waiting any longer—she needed to do something more, take some kind of action to try to find her sister. It struck her that she could visit Hillcrest, the state home where she and Brooke had stayed after their mother gave them up—where Brooke had ultimately spent most of her childhood—and see if they had anything in their records that might lead Natalie to where her sister was today. It was a long shot, but Natalie was anxious enough to do it anyway.

"Do you want me to go with you?" Kyle asked when she told him her plan. They were in the kitchen after the kids were asleep.

"I don't think so," Natalie said as she wiped down the counter. "But thanks for offering." She appreciated her husband's support, but she also felt like this was something she wanted to do alone.

The next morning, after she had dropped off both kids at school, Natalie used the map function on her iPhone to find the address for Hillcrest, then followed the GPS instructions that led her to the facility in a residential neighborhood on the outskirts of Georgetown. Her heart thumped hard behind her rib cage as she parked in the lot next to the three-story, gray-brick building and climbed out of her car, clutching her purse in a tight grip. It was a little strange, knowing that she had stayed inside these walls for a month when she was a baby; the vision she'd had of her adoption process didn't include a place that looked as stark as this. She'd imagined something along the lines of a daycare center, a cheerful yellow building with lots of flowers in its yard, rooms filled with chubby babies waiting for their new parents to bring them home. But visiting Hillcrest wasn't about her, it was about finding out more about Brooke.

It was another drizzly day, typical of Seattle in early October, so Natalie held her coat over her head as she made her way up the front steps and pushed open the glass door to where a heavyset man with broad shoulders and a shaved head sat at a desk to her right. He wore a black uniform, which she assumed meant he was a security guard. Two metal detectors stood in front of her, similar to those found at airport checkpoints, as well as a machine with a black conveyor belt that looked like the ones travelers had to put their carry-on luggage through.

"Can I help you?" the man asked. In contrast to his substantial build, his voice was high pitched and nasal. He sported a closely shorn, black goatee.

"I hope so," Natalie replied, readjusting her jacket so it hung correctly. "My sister and I stayed here when we were kids. We were separated thirty years ago, and I'm trying to find her."

"Do you have an appointment?"

"Um . . . no, actually. I wasn't sure if I'd need one. I was just hoping to talk to an administrator."

The man looked her over, as though trying to decide something. "Let me see if anyone's available." Natalie thanked him, and he grabbed for the phone on his desk. "Hey, Lizzie. I've got a woman here needing to talk to someone about the time she and her sister stayed here." He paused, listening for a moment. "Yeah. Okay, thanks. I'll let her know." He hung up and looked back at Natalie. "You're in luck. One of our case managers is free. She'll be down in a minute."

"Thanks so much," Natalie said, relieved.

"No problem. Can you sign in here, please?" He pointed to a clipboard on his desk, and Natalie took a couple of steps over so she could comply. After she had, he nodded in the direction of the metal detector. "Go ahead and walk through now, and put your purse on the conveyor belt."

Natalie did as he asked, feeling a bit like she was entering a prison. She wondered if the kids who stayed here felt the same way, having to be checked for weapons every time they entered the building, being treated like criminals in a place they were supposed to call home. After picking up her purse, she waited for the case manager, taking in her surroundings. The floor was dingy white linoleum with several cracks and missing chunks along its surface, and the air had a stale, locker-room quality. The walls were gray cinder block, which Natalie thought only added to the jail-like feel of the building. There was nothing soft or inviting about the space; she could only imagine what spending the majority of her childhood here might have done to Brooke. What kind of person it might have turned her into.

"Hello," a voice said, interrupting Natalie's thoughts. She turned to see a blond woman coming toward her. The woman looked to be in her mid- to late twenties and wore jeans, a blue-and-white–striped sweater, and black Converse sneakers. Her long hair was pulled into a simple, sleek ponytail at the base of her neck. "I'm Melissa Locke." She held out her hand, and Natalie shook it.

"Natalie Clark," she said. "Thanks for seeing me."

"You caught me at a rare slow moment," Melissa said, with a smile. "How can I help you?" Natalie took a moment to explain why she was there, and when she finished, Melissa spoke again. "Hmm. Well, we can check our files, but it's unlikely we'd know where your sister went after she aged out, unless she kept in contact with someone here. What year did you say she left us?"

"I'm pretty sure it was 1994," Natalie said. "That's the year she would have turned eighteen."

"Okay," Melissa said. "Let's go see what we can find."

Natalie followed the younger woman to her office, a cramped, cube-shaped room without a window but with three walls lined with tall black filing cabinets. Melissa gestured for Natalie to sit in the chair on the other side of her desk while Melissa sat in front of her computer. "Most of our records are digitized, so we should have something on her," she said as she typed. "Here we go. Brooke Walker." Her eyes moved over the screen, reading aloud what she saw on it. "Brought in with her six-month-old sister, Natalie, in October of 1980." She paused, reading more, silently. "You were right. Looks like she did age out in 1994, but we don't have anything on her after that. Nothing official, anyway."

"Would there be something unofficial?" Despite having known that the odds were against there being anything substantive here about her sister's whereabouts, Natalie couldn't help but feel disappointed.

"We actually have one employee who worked here back then. Miss Dottie, our kitchen manager. She was only twenty when she was hired, and has been here almost forty years. The kids love her, and she's got a great memory. A real knack for names. Maybe she knew Brooke."

"Is she here?" Natalie asked, feeling a surge of hope.

"She should be. Let me check." Melissa reached for the phone on her desk, and after a quick conversation, she hung up and looked at Natalie. "She's in the middle of overseeing lunch prep, but we can head down to the cafeteria and wait for her, if you like."

"That would be great," Natalie said, fingering the edge of her leather purse strap. "I was wondering, though . . . if it's not an inconvenience, is there any way I can see a bit of the building? Where Brooke might have stayed?"

"Sure," Melissa said. "I'd offer to show you where you were for the brief time you were here, too, but we don't house babies anymore. They're kept in a different facility altogether. The infant room has been remodeled into a study hall."

"Oh, that's okay," Natalie said. She'd been so focused on finding out more about Brooke, it hadn't even crossed her mind that she might want to see where she had spent a month of her own life—she wouldn't have remembered it anyway.

Melissa moved her eyes back to the computer. After a moment of scrolling, she smiled at Natalie. "Found it." She stood up and headed out the door, Natalie following right behind her.

They walked down a long, narrow hallway that was lit by buzzing, yellow-tinged fluorescent lights and then went up a flight of stairs. The walls there were plaster instead of cement, painted the same dingy white as the linoleum, and were covered in brightly colored posters with inspirational sayings on them, including one that said, "The struggle is part of the story." As she walked by it, Natalie noticed that beneath that statement someone had written "Fuck you and your story" in thick black ink. She winced, practically able to feel the anger coming off the resident who had penned those words.

When they got to the second floor, Melissa led Natalie down another hallway, this one lined with several gray doors. Melissa stopped at the third one on the right and gestured for Natalie to enter. "This is it," Melissa said as they each stepped inside. "She stayed in a lot of different rooms before she hit ninth grade, a new one every time she came back from another foster home, but this is where she spent her last four years."

Natalie moved her eyes around the room, which was about the same size as Hailey's bedroom at home, but rather than her daughter's frilly canopy bed covered in a lime-green comforter and lavender pillows, the space had four black metal, twin-size bunk beds squeezed along its perimeter. There were no windows, no other furniture besides the beds, and nothing hung on the walls. The space was blank, industrial. There were dented cardboard boxes with handles under the bunks, which Natalie assumed served as makeshift dressers. There was nothing about the room that said home.

Natalie took a step over to one of the bunks and sat down on the thin mattress, resting the heels of her palms on the scratchy gray blanket. She thought of her children, how they might react to being relegated to a room like this—how they might survive knowing their mother had given them up—and she had to fight back an ache in her chest. She thought about the room that she had grown up in, with its big windows and comfy, full-size bed. She remembered wanting to redecorate it when she turned thirteen, abandoning the pink and white frills for blue paint and posters of Luke Perry and Jason Priestley. She thought about how lucky she was to have been adopted, that her parents had saved her from living in a place as sterile as this.

Natalie moved her eyes upward and noticed that the plywood beneath the top bunk mattress was etched with so many names, it was difficult to decipher one from the other. "Julie Peterson was here, 1987," Natalie read aloud.

"The kids like to leave their mark," Melissa said.

Natalie slowly scanned the wooden board above her again, and without a word Melissa, seeming to sense what Natalie was trying to do, stepped over to another bunk, checking the plywood on that bed for Brooke's name. When neither of them found it, each moved to a different bunk. Natalie was just about to give up when Melissa spoke. "Here she is." She pointed to a spot above where she sat, and Natalie quickly joined her. Melissa stood up, leaving Natalie to look at the spot where the younger woman had pointed. It took her a minute to find her sister's name, but when she did, she reached up and slowly traced her index finger over the gouged wood, the muscles in her throat thickening. "Brooke Walker," her sister had carved in jagged letters. "Here too fucking long."

"Wow," Natalie said, and her eyes blurred with tears. The fact that her sister had sat in that exact spot—that she'd taken the time to make sure there was evidence of her existence in that space— hit Natalie hard. She couldn't imagine the life of a young girl in these surroundings: sharing a room with seven likely revolving-door strangers, sleeping on a thin mattress with a flat pillow and a stiff, scratchy blanket. Having no one to tuck her in at night. Nothing to make her feel treasured and safe.

"Miss Dottie should be free by now," Melissa said. "And I have a meeting I need to attend pretty soon . . ."

"Oh," Natalie said, standing up and wiping her cheeks with the back of her bent wrist. "Of course. Sorry."

"No need," Melissa said. "I'm happy to help." She led Natalie to the end of the hallway and down another set of stairs, then turned a corner and pushed open a pair of black swinging doors. The room was set up with multiple rectangular tables and metal benches. To their right was a large, square open space in the wall, and through it, Natalie could see four women working in the kitchen. One of them stood off to the side with a clipboard in her hand. She was a tall woman with a sturdy-looking build and olive skin. Her silvery black hair was pushed down beneath a net, and she wore a bright red chef's coat, white sneakers, and jeans.

"Miss Dottie!" Melissa called out, and the woman left the kitchen and came to stand in front of Natalie. "This is Natalie Clark," she said, and quickly explained why Natalie was there.

The older woman listened with her head cocked to one side, still holding her clipboard, and then looked at Natalie. "What did you say your sister's name was?"

"Brooke Walker," Natalie said. "Melissa said you might remember her?"

"I'll let you two have a chat," Melissa said. "Thanks, Dottie. And good luck, Natalie. I hope you find what you're looking for." Natalie thanked her, and Melissa turned and left the room.

"Let's sit," Miss Dottie said, gesturing toward one of the tables. "I'm just about ready to retire, so I have to practice not being on my feet all damn day." She cackled, and Natalie smiled politely. The two of them sat and Miss Dottie set her clipboard down. "Now. Brooke Walker . . . Brooke Walker." She squinted her eyes and repeated Natalie's sister's name a few more times, as though she were fingering her way through a cabinet in her head, looking for the right file. "When you say she aged out, again?"

"Nineteen ninety-four," Natalie repeated, wondering if there was any point in having this conversation. She imagined thousands of children coming and going from this facility over the past thirty-some years. How could Miss Dottie remember a single face? "She stopped being sent to foster homes when she turned fourteen and stayed here all four years of high school."

"Ah!" Miss Dottie said, loudly enough that it startled Natalie. "I remember. Dark curls, pretty eyes. So blue they almost look purple."

Just like Hailey's, Natalie thought. Her pulse quickened.

"If I recall," Miss Dottie continued, "her and that wild girl, Zora Herzog, talked about getting a place together when they left. They were the same age, but Zora'd only been here two years before she turned eighteen."

"She and Brooke were friends?" Natalie asked, feeling excited but a little wary at Miss Dottie's use of the adjective "wild" to describe Zora.

"I wouldn't say friends, exactly," Miss Dottie said. "More like they happened to be leaving at the same time and needed someone to split rent with."

Natalie considered this before speaking again. "You said Zora was wild. How so?"

"Oh, you know," Miss Dottie said, waving a dismissive hand around in front of her face. "The kind of girl that they'd probably put on some kind of drug now. She was a hyper little thing. Loud, too."

"Was Brooke the same way?"

"Hmm," Miss Dottie said, pressing her lips together and making them pooch out a little, like she was about to give someone a kiss. "Not that I recall. Pretty sure she was a quiet one. Kept her head down." She shrugged. "That's all I remember. Does it help?"

"I think it will," Natalie said, thinking that Miss Dottie's description of Brooke matched what Gina had said about her. "Thank you." She stood, and Miss Dottie joined her.

"My pleasure, honey," she said. "Your life turn out all right, after being here?"

Natalie smiled, thinking of her parents, of Kyle and the kids and the home they shared. "I was only here a month when I was a baby," she said, "but yes. It did."

"Glad to hear it," Miss Dottie said, bobbing her head and then repeating the phrase. She gave Natalie a wave and then headed back into the kitchen.

Five minutes later, Natalie sat in her car, doing an online search for "Zora Herzog, Seattle," on her phone, relieved that the girl Brooke might have moved in with after leaving Hillcrest had such a unique name. It would make finding her all that much easier. She could have waited until she got home and done the search on her laptop, but she was too excited about what she'd learned. Maybe Zora and Brooke were still friends. Maybe their shared background at Hillcrest had created a bond that linked them. Maybe once Natalie found Zora, she'd find Brooke, too.

It didn't take long for Zora's name and contact information to come up on the search engine, and Natalie was grateful the other woman hadn't chosen to keep her address and phone number un-listed. She glanced at the clock and saw she still had plenty of time before the kids got out of school, and a quick check on the map told Natalie that Zora lived in White Center, which was on the south side of West Seattle and only a fifteen-minute drive from Hillcrest. Again, she thought about calling first, but she couldn't contain her enthusiasm and decided to head right over to Zora's house. Even if she wasn't home, Natalie could leave her a note. She put her phone on the passenger seat, started her car, and went exactly where her GPS told her to go.

Brooke

When Brooke's cell phone rang about a week after her argument with Ryan, she almost didn't answer. But when she saw his face on her screen, she decided it was only fair to hear whatever else he might have to say. A small voice in her head even went so far as to suggest that he might have changed his mind and would support her in her decision to keep the baby, and though she was hard-pressed to admit it, this possibility was what made her pick up the phone.

"Brooke, please," Ryan said. From the horns beeping in the background, she could tell that he was in his car, on his headset, likely on the freeway on his way to a job site. "I know you're upset, but we need to talk about this."

"I don't really see what else there is to say," she said. She tried to sound strong, unshakable, but she worried that he could still hear the tremor beneath her words.

"You can't just make a unilateral decision," he said. "It's my child, too. I have a say in how we handle it."

"It's not an 'it,'" Brooke snapped. "It's a baby." She had lain in bed just that morning, running her hand over her stomach again and again, marveling at the fact that there was a *human being* growing inside her. She'd gone online and discovered that at nine weeks, her baby was about the size of a peanut and already had earlobes, which seemed to Brooke like such a random thing for her to know. But it also made what was happening seem more real. "It's my body," she told Ryan now. "So it's my decision. I don't need anything from you except to be left alone. You're off the hook."

"It's not that simple!"

"Actually," Brooke said, "it is." She hung up the phone, steeling herself against the rush of conflicting emotions she felt. One part of her, the part she had honed over the years to keep the men in her life at an emotionally safe distance, was determined that cutting Ryan out of her life completely was the right call. She didn't need him, that part told her. She could do this. She'd be fine. But another part of her, the more exposed, needy part that had risen to the surface as soon as she found out she was pregnant, screamed at her to call him back, to ask him to support her, even if he didn't agree with her decision to keep the baby. But the idea of this, the idea of admitting her weakness, made Brooke squirm. She'd learned a long time ago that it was safer never to show anyone that kind of vulnerability.

By the time Brooke was twelve, she had been in and out of ten foster homes and had been sent back to Hillcrest every time. But at the start of seventh grade, Gina took her to live in a two-bedroom apartment in North Seattle, near Green Lake. Claire, the woman who was to be her new foster parent, was different from the other people with whom Brooke had stayed. She was in her late thirties and had never been married or had any children, something she told Brooke over a dinner of grilled cheese and tomato soup a few hours after Gina left the apartment. "I never thought I'd do something like this," Claire said.

"Why did you, then?" Brooke asked in a guarded voice, looking over the main living area, where they sat at a two-person table. The room was highly feminine, decorated in pale pastels with plush furniture, silky sheer curtains, and lots of pillows. There was a big bowl of Hershey's Kisses on the coffee table, along with a stack of fashion magazines like *Glamour* and *Cosmopolitan*. Claire was a short, curvy woman with wide hips and a big smile. Her hair was brown and straight, and that day, she wore a stretchy polka-dot headband to pull it back from her round face.

"Because I don't have a mother," Claire said in a quiet voice. "And I thought it would be a good thing to help take care of someone who doesn't, either."

Brooke wasn't accustomed to grown-ups telling her private information about themselves—usually they just lectured her about everything they thought was wrong with her—so she blinked a few times before responding. "What happened to her?"

"She died when I was two," Claire explained. "I was raised by my grandparents, because my father couldn't handle taking care of me on his own." She gave Brooke a long look. "I understand that you lost your mother, as well."

Brooke bit her bottom lip, feeling a swell of emotion in her chest that she normally was able to keep pressed deep down inside. "I didn't lose her," she finally said, hoping that in taking this risk, telling Claire the truth, she wasn't making a huge mistake. "She gave me away." Her voice cracked on the last few words, and she dropped her eyes to the floor, unable to make eye contact. "I was only four."

"I'm sorry," Claire said. "That must have hurt you so much."

Brooke nodded, feeling a few errant tears slip down her cheeks. She never talked about her mother with anyone, and suddenly, here she was, discussing her with Claire. Maybe it was the fact that Claire hadn't pushed her to talk; she'd simply shared a bit of her own story and made Brooke feel safe in sharing the basics of hers. And as the weeks passed by, Brooke found herself opening up more and more to Claire, and bit by bit, the weight she normally carried under her skin began to melt away. "I didn't know how to stop myself from being bad," she said after telling Claire about living with Jessica and Lily and how Scott had spanked her.

"Oh, honey, you're not bad," Claire said, pushing Brooke's dark curls back from her face. Brooke was in bed, and Claire sat on the edge of her mattress. The only light in the room was that of the small lamp with the pink floral shade on the nightstand. "You were hurting, and sometimes, when we hurt, we lash out at other people so they will hurt, too. It doesn't feel like that should make sense, but everyone does it at some point. Most of the time, we don't even realize we're doing it."

"Really?" Brooke sniffed, allowing herself to feel a little bit better. "Have you?"

"Of course. I get lonely sometimes. And I get really sad, too. But the trick is not letting those feelings control you."

"How do you do that?"

Claire thought for a moment, and then spoke. "Well, you know that saying 'every cloud has a silver lining'?"

"Yeah . . ."

"Okay, good. So when I'm feeling sad or angry or lonely, I try to find something positive to think about, instead."

"The silver lining?"

"Exactly." Claire smiled and gave Brooke's arm a quick rub. "I sit down and make a list of everything that I'm grateful for. All the good things I can think of. And pretty soon, before I know it, I feel better."

Brooke pondered this. "What kinds of things?"

"That depends," Claire said. "Sometimes it's bigger stuff, like I'm grateful I have a job and a place to live. Other times I have to dig deeper and write down littler things, things I have to really think about to notice, like the way the sun sparkling on the lake makes me feel or how a bowl of ripe strawberries smells." When Brooke didn't respond, Claire screwed up her face into a funny expression. "That probably sounds weird, right? How smelly strawberries make me feel better?"

Brooke smiled and nodded. She liked how Claire wasn't always so serious, like most of the other adults Brooke had known.

"I guess the point is forcing myself to focus on how there are so many good things in the world, even when I'm having a hard time," Claire said. "I've found that the more I do it, the easier it gets, and the less often I feel bad." She paused. "Tell me something. If you had to make a list like that right now, what would it have on it?"

"I don't know," Brooke said with a shrug.

"Come on. There has to be something you're grateful for. Ice cream? Puppies? John Stamos?" Claire smiled at her, clearly teasing. She knew how much Brooke liked to watch *Full House*.

"I like ice cream . . . and puppies," Brooke said, feeling her heart beating a little faster as she thought about what she wanted to say next. She looked at Claire, taking in her foster mother's full, pink cheeks and sweet, loving smile, and suddenly, her eyes filled with tears. "But what I'm really grateful for right now is you."

"Oh, sweetie, thank you," Claire said, leaning down to hug Brooke. She pressed her mouth against Brooke's ear, whispering the words "I'm grateful for you, too."

After that conversation, Brooke felt like maybe the sad and lonely part of her life was over. Maybe Claire was the mother she was truly meant to have. Her foster mother worked as a medical transcriptionist for several different doctors, which meant she didn't have to go to an office and was there every day when Brooke came home from school. They didn't have a lot of money, but on Saturdays, they liked to take walks around Green Lake and feed the ducks bits of old bread; they spent their evenings playing Scrabble or watching shows like *Who's the Boss?, Growing Pains,* and *Cheers*. Once in a while, Claire would surprise her with a copy of *Tiger Beat* magazine, and the two of them would spend a Friday night painting each other's toenails and debating over who was cuter, Johnny Depp or Rob Lowe. Except for the time she'd spent with the lady who had made her clean the cat box, Brooke had always lived with at least one other kid, and she found that she liked being the only child in the house. She'd never had a grown-up's undivided attention the way she had Claire's. She absorbed it like a thirsty sponge. She'd learned from other kids at Hillcrest that most foster parents liked to have as many kids as they could because it meant the state gave them more money every month. Claire wasn't like that. She was content having Brooke around, and never mentioned the possibility of taking on another child. She seemed happy.

There were times, though, when Brooke came home to find that Claire had never gotten out of bed. "I don't feel well," Claire told her when Brooke would sit on the side of the bed in her dark room.

"I'll bring you some soup," Brooke offered, but Claire refused it.

"I just need to sleep," she said, and Brooke would leave her alone, spending the evening alone, warming up a frozen dinner, doing her homework and watching TV, worry aching in her gut. The morning after one of those days, Claire almost always was up and showered before Brooke, having made breakfast and packed Brooke a lunch, so Brooke told herself the episodes meant nothing. She told herself that everybody had bad days. Claire probably just hadn't made a silver lining list for a while, and once she did, she'd feel better.

Brooke spent over a year with Claire, wondering when the older woman would tell her that she wanted to adopt her. "I love you," Claire said each night when she'd tuck Brooke into bed. It took Brooke almost six months before she could tell Claire that she loved her, too. Brooke felt as though her future had been decided. She finally had the one thing she'd always wanted—a family.

Then one afternoon when Brooke was thirteen and returned to the apartment after school, excited to tell Claire that she'd gotten an A on her algebra test, she opened their front door to find the living room empty and dark, and instantly, she was concerned.

"Claire?" Brooke called out as she set down her backpack and took off her coat. The desk where Claire normally spent her days looked as though it hadn't been touched. Brooke hurried down the hallway to Claire's bedroom and threw open the door. The lights were off, and her foster mother was under the covers, not moving. There was a pungent, sour scent in the room, as though someone had recently been sick.

"Claire," Brooke repeated as she took a few steps to the side of the bed. There was vomit on Claire's pillow. "Hey," Brooke said, reaching out her right hand to shake Claire's shoulder. "Wake up!"

Claire didn't open her eyes. She didn't move. Her skin was white.

"Claire!" Brooke said, feeling her heartbeat thudding inside her head as she climbed into bed, kneeling next to the older woman. "Please! You have to wake up!" Again, Claire didn't respond. "Claire!" Brooke shrieked, feeling the noise she made tearing at her vocal cords. "Help! Somebody . . . I need help!" She put both hands on her foster mother's body and rolled her over onto her back. Claire's jaw was slack, her mouth open, her tongue lolled partway out, a sight that made Brooke's stomach turn.

Just then, their neighbor, Mrs. Connelly, an older woman whom Claire sometimes invited to join them for dinner, appeared in the bedroom doorway wearing one of her brightly colored housecoats and fuzzy pink slippers. "What in the world are you screaming about, child?" she said as she entered. Her eyes landed on the two of them in Claire's bed. "Oh no. What happened?"

"She won't wake up!" Brooke cried. Hot tears wet her cheeks as she shook Claire again.

Mrs. Connelly took a few steps across the room and reached for the cordless phone.

"Please, Claire!" Brooke sobbed. She could barely hear Mrs. Connelly talking over her tears, but it sounded as though the older woman had called 911. Brooke smothered her face against Claire's ample chest, the smell of sweat and vomit mixed in with her foster mother's favorite lavender body wash. Brooke liked the soap so much, Claire had bought her her own bottle.

"Help's on the way," Mrs. Connelly said, placing a hand on Brooke's back and then pulling it away. "They'll be here any minute."

"She has to be okay!" Brooke said. "She just has to!" She didn't know what she would do if Claire died. "Where's her list?" Brooke asked, looking up at Mrs. Connelly with stinging and swollen eyes.

"What list?" Mrs. Connelly said. Her white, finely spun hair was thin enough for her pink scalp to show through, and her face looked like tissue paper that had been crumpled and unsuccessfully smoothed back out.

"Her list!"

"Honey," Mrs. Connelly said, "I don't know what you're talking about." She reached out to Brooke again, but Brooke batted her hand away.

"Don't touch me!" she screamed, feeling as though something fragile inside her had shattered. Her heart was beating so fast, she could barely catch her breath. She wrapped herself around Claire's body again, burying her face into Claire's neck. This couldn't be happening. She'd practically just found Claire; she couldn't lose her already.

A few minutes later, the medics arrived and two men had to pry Brooke from the bed. "No!" she cried. "I won't leave her!" She fought them, kicking and scratching and doing anything she could to stay next to Claire. In the end, one of the paramedics had to stand with his thick, muscled arms holding Brooke with her back to his chest, her arms restrained while the other medic examined Claire.

"Is she all right?" Mrs. Connelly asked in a tight, worried voice. "Is she going to be okay?"

"We need to take her to the ER," the medic who was examining Claire said. "Can you stay with the girl?"

"Yes," Mrs. Connelly said.

"No!" Brooke said. "I want to go with her!"

"I'm sorry, but you can't," the man who was holding her said. "And I need to help my partner, so if I let you go, will you promise to let us do our work?"

"Yes," Brooke whimpered, forcing her body to relax. She would do anything, anything at all, if it meant that Claire would be okay. The man released her, and Brooke watched as the medics lifted Claire onto a yellow backboard and transferred her to the gurney they'd brought with them. One of her arms fell off to the side, looking as though she were reaching out for help, and Brooke rushed over to squeeze her hand. "I love you, Claire," she whispered. "I love you so much."

"Let them go," Mrs. Connelly urged her, and Brooke released Claire's hand, stepping aside so the medics could wheel the gurney out of the bedroom, down the hall, and out the front door. Brooke stood in the living room, feeling helpless, the tears still running down her cheeks.

"Why don't you come sit down?" Mrs. Connelly said as she lowered herself onto the couch. When she patted the cushion next to her, the sagging jowl beneath her chin jiggled. "We need to call your social worker."

"No, we don't!" Brooke said, shooting the older woman a hateful look. Her throat felt raw from crying; she thought about how the last time she had a cold, Claire had made her lemon tea with lots of honey and fed her cinnamon-sugar toast until Brooke felt better.

"She needs to know what's happening," Mrs. Connelly said. She reached for the yellow pages Claire kept on the end table. Brooke had to fight the urge to run over, take the thick book from her, and toss it out the window. Instead, she shut the front door and shuffled to the couch, slumping down in the corner farthest away from her neighbor. She held a pillow to her chest, gripping it tightly, waiting as Mrs. Connelly looked up the number for Social Services and eventually spoke with Gina, relaying what had happened. After Mrs. Connelly hung up, she picked up the remote control and turned on the TV. "Just for distraction," she said as Bob Barker appeared on the screen, asking if the contestant on *The Price Is Right* wanted what was behind door number one or door number two.

But Brooke was already distracted enough. All she could think about was Claire, the way her skin had gone from white to gray in the time it took the medics to arrive. All she wanted was for her foster mother to be okay.

Two hours later, Gina knocked on the apartment door. When she entered, she had dark half-moons bruised under her eyes and her flowered, black gunnysack dress with the white lace collar was rumpled.

"I'm not leaving!" Brooke said as she took in her social worker's unkempt appearance. Her entire body went rigid, bracing itself for whatever Gina might say or do. "You can't make me!"

Gina glanced at Mrs. Connelly. "Thanks for staying with her. Can you give us a minute?"

"Of course," the older woman said. She rose from the couch and headed toward the door, pausing before she went through it. "I'm in Two-B, if you need me."

Gina thanked her again, and then joined Brooke on the couch. "I just came from the hospital," she said.

"Is she awake?" Brooke said.

"No, honey, she's not. She's stable, for now, but still unconscious."

"Why?" Brooke's bottom lip trembled.

"Because she took too many pills."

"Maybe it was an accident . . ."

"It wasn't an accident, Brooke. The doctors had to pump her stomach. It was a suicide attempt."

"She did it on purpose?" Brooke began crying again. If Claire had felt bad enough to try to kill herself, then she'd been lying to

Brooke. Writing a list couldn't make anything better; focusing on a silver lining didn't do a damn thing to help. "Why? Was it . . . me?"

"Oh, honey," Gina said. "You didn't have anything to do with it. The truth is she has a history of depression that we didn't know about, and now she needs to work on getting better. She won't be coming home for a while."

"But I can help her when she does!" Brooke said. Her nose began to run, and she swiped at it with the back of her hand. "I'll take care of her! We take care of each other!"

Gina reached out a hand toward her, and Brooke pulled back. She didn't want the other woman to touch her. The pity in Gina's eyes only made Brooke feel worse. "That's not how it works," Gina said. "I have to take you back to Hillcrest. You need to pack your things."

Brooke shook her head, pressing her lips together as hard as she could. She balled her fingers into tight fists, trying to fight off the wave of sadness that rushed over her. *No,* she thought. *No, no, no.* She couldn't leave. Claire was the only person who ever understood her. She was the only one Brooke needed. Brooke would write silver lining lists for them both and then stand next to Claire's hospital bed, reading them to her until she woke up.

"Come on, honey," Gina said, reaching out for her again, and this time, feeling defeated, Brooke didn't pull away. She knew it was pointless to resist. She let Gina put an arm around her, stand her up from the couch, and lead her to her room, where her social worker put as many clothes as she could in a black plastic bag, because Brooke still didn't have a suitcase. Brooke stood by, numbly watching, tears rolling down her cheeks.

"Can I at least go see her?" Brooke asked after they'd grabbed her backpack along with her clothes and left the apartment. Her eyes stung and were swollen.

"I'm sorry," Gina said again. "But no."

As they drove away from the place Brooke had thought she'd

forever call home, something closed down inside her. A heavy door slammed shut. Her tears ebbed, and she felt hollow and numb. And the only thing Brooke knew for sure was that she would never put her heart at risk like that again.

Twenty-six years later, Brooke thought about that moment in Gina's car the morning Ryan called her and she hung up on him. She reminded herself that emotional neediness was not a quality she wanted to possess. No matter what Ryan thought, she had decided to have this baby, and letting herself fall victim to pregnancy hormones and god-knew-whatever else that was causing her to feel weak toward him was the absolute last thing she wanted. Opening herself up, allowing someone else to see her messy insides, was just not something she did.

She was done with silver linings; she had learned to live with the clouds.

Jennifer

I turned twenty-seven in March of 1987, almost six years after my first meeting with Randy in the community room. In that amount of time, despite my initial doubt about participating in the program, I managed to earn my GED, as well as my certification as a dog trainer, for both basic obedience and service animals. The previous spring, I'd begun an online program for prisoners sponsored by a local vocational college, and combining that with my work experience at Randy's clinic, I now had an associate's degree as a veterinary technician. I was just over four years away from being released. With good behavior, it might be sooner. I had a parole hearing coming up in August, and this time, if I was let out early, I swore I wouldn't screw it up. This time, I promised myself I'd have a plan—a place to live and a job—so I wouldn't end up right back behind bars.

Unlike during the first year I'd spent in prison, my days were full, but no matter how much I kept myself busy working and studying, my girls were constantly on my mind. Brooke would be eleven soon, and Natalie would turn seven. The ache I felt for them was a wound that wouldn't heal—if I allowed my thoughts to pick at its edges too much, it began to bleed.

Still, I wrote to them, gradually filling up the pages of five spiral notebooks that I kept on the shelf next to my bunk. They were nothing profound, just thoughts I had about them, things I wanted them to know about me. They were too young, yet, for me to write about the things that mattered, the things I really needed to say.

I wonder what your favorite subject is, I wrote to Brooke. *Which you love more, words or numbers. If you are finished playing with dolls or if you still hide one or two of them in your closet, the same way I did when I was ten years old, bringing them out, hoping I didn't get caught, unsure if I was ready to let go of that little girl part of me. Do you fight with your sister, or do you still take care of her, the way you always did when she was a baby? I wonder if you'd recognize me if you saw me on the street, with our same black hair and violet eyes. Do you look in the mirror and see me, the same way I see you?*

You have my lips, I told Natalie. *The top one a bit thinner than the bottom. I'd hold you in my arms, feeding you a bottle because from the moment you were born you refused to nurse, and you'd rest one of your soft, perfect hands on my chest, on top of my heart. When you looked up and smiled, I saw in your round, brown eyes the kind of mother I wanted to be.*

On their birthdays every year, I wrote each of them a longer letter, filling it with as many memories of my own childhood as I could. *I fell down the cement stairs at school in the first grade,* I'd written Natalie last year, when she turned six. *I broke my arm and I knocked out my two front teeth. Have you lost any teeth yet? I hope you believe in the Tooth Fairy . . . and in Santa Claus and the Easter Bunny. I hope you believe in magic. And that the people who are taking care of you love you as much as I do. I hope you love reading as much as I did when I was your age. I hope you have lots of friends and a room full of toys. I hope you have everything I couldn't give you.*

I tried not to think about the fact that it was doubtful they'd ever have the chance to read any of what I wrote them. On a warm, sunny morning in May, four months away from my parole hearing, I climbed into the back of the gray prison van and reminded myself that I was writing the letters more for me than for them. I wrote them to help ease my own pain.

"Ready?" Mendez asked, glancing at me in the rearview mirror. A broadly built, stoic guard from the Dominican Republic, Mendez accompanied me into town three times a week for my participation in work release at Randy's clinic. He was required to be in the same room with me while I worked, or at least very nearby.

"Yep," I said. Most of our conversations went like this, monosyllabic statements and replies. I was anxious to get to work that day. After two weeks of intravenous antibiotics for a systemic infection, Winston, one of the dogs I'd been helping care for, was still struggling. I wanted to see if the new round of meds Randy had prescribed had taken effect. I put on my seat belt and settled in for the thirty-minute ride.

As we drove along the back roads from the prison into town, I eyed the landscape that had become so familiar to me during this commute. At its heart, most of Skagit County was farm country, and over the past couple of weeks, the plowed fields had begun to sprout green with the promise of bountiful summer crops. Ancient houses alongside red, rickety barns were scattered across the hillsides. The Mt. Vernon Animal Clinic was located just on the edge of downtown. Not quite the city, but not the country, either. It was a sprawling, one-story building with lots of large, square windows and an enormous fenced area that we used for exercising and training the dogs. There was an indoor-outdoor kennel in the back of the building as well, and that was where I spent the majority of my time.

Mendez pulled into the driveway, taking the van to the farthest spot in the corner of the parking lot, near the doors where we typically entered. The scrubs I wore for work were similar to the ones I wore on the inside—they were blue, and lacked only the large block lettering announcing I was an inmate at the Department of Corrections. Here, I got to wear white sneakers instead of plastic, slip-on sandals; I kept them in my cellblock and always put them on during the drive. Both Mendez and I climbed out of the van and walked in through the double glass doors that led to the office within the kennel.

"Hey, Jenny," Chandi, the office manager, said as we entered. Only here was I referred to as Jenny or Jennifer; the rest of the time, I was like any other inmate, known by my last name alone. There were two reception areas in the clinic, one out front for veterinary patients, and this one, in the back, for animals being groomed and/or boarded in the kennel. Since I'd completed my certification, Randy had decided to offer a monthlong, intensive, in-house obedience training program for owners who had dogs but didn't necessarily have the time to attend weekly classes. Part of my job was to spend several hours during my shift with each of these dogs, working with them on basic instructions and tasks; the other part was to keep the kennels clean and assist with whatever additional duties Randy required. Sometimes that included helping conduct an exam, and others it put me cleaning out kennels, or on the floor with a terminally ill animal, holding it close, scratching its head as Randy gently put it to sleep.

"Hey," I said to Chandi, who was an East Indian woman about my age. She had thick, black hair and flawless light brown skin. Under different circumstances, we might have been the kinds of friends who went to parties together or shopped at the mall. Instead, we were the kinds of friends who only saw each other when a prison guard escorted me through the door. "Busy morning?" I asked.

"Not really. But Randy asked to see you when you got in," she said, nodding in the direction of the hallway that led to the main building.

"Oh," I said. "Okay, thanks." I glanced at Mendez, who barely bobbed his head and then followed me to my employer's office.

When we got there, I peeked around the doorjamb and lightly rapped my knuckles on the wall. "Morning," I said.

Randy looked up from the pile of papers on his desk and smiled. He wore his white doctor's coat and a lime-green polo with the collar turned up, channeling a chubby Don Johnson. As usual, his thick shock of red hair was a mess and his cheeks were pink—from exertion or excitement, I couldn't decipher.

"Jenny! Good morning!" he said. *Excitement it was, then,* I thought as he gestured for me to enter. "Have a seat."

Mendez dropped into a wooden bench outside Randy's door as I complied, setting my elbows on the arms of the chair and linking my fingers together in front of me. "What's up?"

"Good news! Myer approved my request for you to bring a dog into the facility." Randy never called where I lived a "prison," which at first I thought was ridiculous but now appreciated as a kind, humanizing gesture. He treated me with as much respect as he did any of his employees, and required those around him to do the same. I was incredibly grateful not only for his willingness to teach me but for the chance doing this kind of work gave me to feel like a normal, decent person again.

"No way," I said. Randy had been trying for the past year to get Myer to allow me to keep a service-dog-in-training with me at all times. This was how other service animals were effectively conditioned—living with their trainers for up to two years after they'd been properly socialized and had mastered all other basic obedience commands, working with them tirelessly to learn to ignore their natural instincts in favor of giving their masters what they needed. Until now, I'd only been able to work with a dog when I was at the clinic.

"Way," Randy said with a grin. "It took some doing, but he agreed to it, as long as I'm willing to sign a waiver for any damage the dog might do to the facility or the other residents."

I smiled, too. Despite his doctorate and almost two decades as an esteemed professional in the veterinary field, I'd come to understand that, in many ways, Randy was still just a little boy who'd grown up on a local farm, loving animals. His passion and enthusiasm for his work had proved impossible for me to resist. "Do you have a dog in mind?"

"Actually, I do," he said, handing me a piece of paper. "It won't be a service animal."

"What?" I asked, taking the paper from him, but not looking at what it said. "Why not?" Training service animals was what I'd studied so hard to do. I loved the idea of a dog changing the life of a person with special needs. I loved the thought—after everything I'd done wrong, all the damage I'd done—of contributing something so pure and good to the world. It was the one tiny spot of brightness that shone inside me, a living amends for my sin of taking that child in the park from her mother. For the decision I made to give away my girls.

"Well, you know I've been working with a local no-kill shelter, trying to help find homes for strays," Randy said, snapping me out of my thoughts. I nodded and waited for him to go on. He shifted forward at his desk and leaned toward me as he spoke again. "One of our biggest obstacles has been behavioral issues with the animals. Most of them have had no training, or they've been mistreated or violently abused, so they're exceptionally difficult to work with."

"Right." I already knew all of this. I drummed my fingers on the tops of my thighs, anxious for him to get to the point.

"So, what I'm thinking is that you could take these unskilled and wounded animals and teach them how to behave so they'll have a much better chance of finding a home. You'd be providing an amazing service."

"But what about the service dogs I'm working with? What happens to them?" There were currently two dogs living with Randy and his wife that he brought in to the clinic on the days I worked so I could further their training to be guide dogs. I'd just finished teaching them obstacle avoidance, the most important safety skill dogs must learn in order to lead their masters along the safest route. Over the next several months, I needed to reinforce this skill in them by using repetition and reward. I wasn't sure I could do this and work with a dog from the shelter.

"You'll continue with their training when you're here. Myer also approved you to come to the clinic four days a week instead of three." Randy grinned, leaned back in his chair, and crossed his arms over his chest. "Not too shabby, huh?"

I shook my head, wondering how the other inmates would react not only to my having a dog with me at all times but to my getting the freedom to leave the prison four days a week. There were other work-release programs in which the women took part—things like highway cleanup and grounds maintenance—but I was the only prisoner who worked for Randy. He'd tried to add another inmate to the program but decided that was too demanding for him and asked that Myer allow me to be the single participant for the term of my incarceration. And because Randy offered to pay for the cost of transporting me to and from the clinic, Myer agreed, as long as I didn't cause either of the men any problems.

"Come on," Randy said, standing up from his desk and heading out of his office. "I brought in your first pup this morning. She's a sweetie, but she's had a rough time of things. You're exactly what she needs."

I followed him as he walked toward the kennel, and Mendez followed me. From the linoleum-lined hallway, I could hear the echoes of the dogs barking, excited as the other vet techs took them out of their pens for their midmorning play sessions in the fenced yard. When we entered the room that housed the animals, Mendez, as he always did, sat down in the chair next to the door, and Randy went directly to the last pen on the right-hand side of the first row. I went with him.

"Here she is," he said, and I crouched down and looked through the chain-link gate.

The dog was curled up in the far corner, her fluffy, tan tail wrapped around the front of her body like a blanket. She looked to be about forty pounds, and her nose was tucked beneath her hind leg. She was shaking. "Hey, sweetie," I said, glancing at the tag on the gate to see if she had been given a name, but the space was blank. I made a kissing sound, and she looked up at me, the fear she felt obvious in her big, brown eyes. "It's okay, baby," I murmured. "It's all right, sweet girl."

"The people at the shelter called her Wendy," Randy said, "but I thought you might come up with something better. She's about nine months old." He handed me the key to the kennel. "I've got other clients to see, so why don't you spend the day with her? Get to know each other a bit. Chandi has everything you need to take with you tonight at the front desk. Food, a bowl, et cetera."

"You don't need me to do anything else today?" I asked, straightening back up to look at him face-to-face. "I wanted to check on Winston." Randy's face fell, and my stomach heaved.

"He didn't make it through the night," Randy said. "I'm sorry, but the infection damaged his heart. He went in his sleep."

I bit my lower lip as a few tears rolled down my cheeks. Losing animals, bearing witness to their deaths, was part of this job, and yet every time I went through the process, the sorrow I'd worked so hard to push down came rushing back. It never got any easier.

Randy set a comforting hand on my shoulder, gave it a squeeze, and then a moment later, was gone. I put the key in the lock on the gate, and slowly opened it. Again, the dog lifted her head, gazing at me with a worried intensity. Her tail lifted once, twice, wagging a nervous warning. That was something I'd learned early on working with dogs, that when they wagged their tails, it could mean any number of things: fear, excitement, or hesitance. It could also mean they were about to attack.

"Hey there, puppy," I said in a low, soothing voice. How you spoke to a dog was just as important as what you said. She needed to know I wasn't a threat, so after I locked the gate behind me, I got down on my hands and knees, to be at her level. "It's okay," I said. "It's all right, sweet girl."

She tensed, and tucked her tail between her back legs, eyeing me. I was just a couple of feet away, so I lifted one arm, holding my hand out, fingers curled under so she could sniff me. In six years, I'd never been bitten, and I didn't want to start now. Randy wouldn't have given me a vicious animal, nor would Myer have approved it.

The dog lifted her head and stood up, tail still tucked between her legs as she took one hesitant step, then two, toward me. "That's it," I said, in a singsong tone. "Good girl. That's a good girl. Come here, you sweet thing." I kept completely still, allowing her to make the decision to come to me.

Finally, she stretched out her neck and sniffed my hand. She took another step, moving her wet nose to my arm, allowing my fingers access to her neck. When I scratched her, she startled but didn't pull away, allowing me to move my hand up and over her head, down her back and side to her belly. There wasn't a dog I'd met who didn't succumb to a good belly rub, and this girl was no exception. As my hand touched her there, her body softened, and she rolled to the ground, over onto her back to give me better access.

"Good girl," I said again, looking her over as I loved her up. She was tan with black markings, likely some kind of shepherd mix. Her fur lay flat against her body, and though her tail was full, it had a wiry texture that reminded me of a Labrador retriever.

"What should I name you?" I asked her as I ran my fingers through her fur, giving her a full-body massage. She grunted and wiggled on her back, encouraging me to continue. "Wendy doesn't work, does it?" I paused, thinking. "What about Jazz? Or Trixie?"

Her ears perked at the sound of the second name, so that's what I decided to call her. With the long "e" sound at the end, it was similar enough to the name she'd been given by the shelter that she would still respond to it, but Trixie had more personality. More pizzazz.

I smiled until my fingers hit something raised and rough along her rib cage. "What's this?" I said, using two hands to move her fur out of the way so I could see what I had only felt, and my eyes landed on several thick red scars that ran the length of her left side. My bottom lip quivered, and then I leaned down to rest my face on her warm body. Someone had beaten this poor pup, with something big and hard enough to break her skin.

"It's okay," I crooned as I righted myself and looked her straight in the eye. "I'll take care of you now. No one will hurt you again."

She looked at me like she'd understood exactly what I'd said, as though she knew that promise was as important for me to make as it was for her to hear. Then she climbed into my lap, sitting on the tops of my thighs while resting her head on my chest. She let loose a low, contented groan, melting her body against mine. I wrapped my arms around her, continuing to pet her, hoping she knew that whatever had happened to her in the past was over, and from this moment on, a new kind of life had begun.

Within two months of my having Trixie with me twenty-four hours a day, she had lost all signs of quivering shyness and blossomed into a confident, sweet animal who curled up in my bunk with me each night. She took to obedience training as though she'd been waiting for it all of her life. She was a quick study, picking up on the basic training I provided, and even showed signs of having the qualities of a good service animal candidate, something I planned to discuss with Randy later that week.

It was a Tuesday evening in early July, and I was walking with Trixie down the long hall toward my bunk when a voice I didn't recognize called out to me. "Hey!"

I kept walking, keeping a firm grip on Trixie's leash. "Heel," I said in a low tone when she started to trot past me. I gave her collar a quick, gentle tug to the right, and she responded by bringing her pace back in sync with mine.

"Hey!" the woman said again, and I glanced over my shoulder, seeing her lumber toward me. I only knew this woman by reputation—she was serving time for being the getaway driver when her boyfriend robbed a corner store. Since she'd entered the prison a few weeks ago, she'd gotten into two fistfights in the cafeteria and threatened to beat up anyone who came near her in the showers. I'd done my best to stay out of her way, but there I was with her in a side hallway, having just returned from my shift at the clinic with Mendez. There was no one else around.

"I'm talking to you, bitch!"

My heart began to pound, and I took a deep breath in an attempt to calm it. Though my instinct was to run, I stopped, knowing it would be stupid to try to get away from her. Better to try to be friendly—maybe even get on her good side using my connections in the kitchen. If I'd learned anything during my time in a correctional facility, it was to keep my head down and avoid making enemies. O'Brien and I were still friends, and the threat of her wrath kept most of the harder, more violent criminals in our midst away from me, but this woman was new to the prison. She had no idea who O'Brien was or my relationship with her. Even if she did, she likely wouldn't care.

"Sit," I instructed Trixie as the woman approached us. "Wait." Trixie did as I asked, and posed silently by my side, awaiting my further instruction.

"What the fuck is that animal doing in here?" the woman asked, huffing and puffing a bit. She was at least ten years older than me, almost as round as she was tall, likely outweighing me by a good sixty pounds. She had dirty blond, short hair and a mouthful of yellow, uneven teeth. Her blue scrubs were flat against her large breasts and stretched at the seams; blurry, black tattoos traveled up the skin of her thick neck.

"It's part of my work-release program," I said with a smile, trying not to display the anxiety I felt. "I train her and do other work with animals at a vet clinic in town."

"Is that so?" the woman said, crossing her arms over her chest. She stared at me with tiny, round blue eyes, then looked at Trixie.

"It is," I said, keeping my voice as steady as possible. I glanced around the hallway to see if anyone I knew might step in and discourage this woman from harassing me, but we were alone. *Where's a guard when I need one?* "What's your name?"

"Blake," she said. She lifted her eyes back to mine, scowling.

"I'm Walker," I said, keeping my eyes locked on hers. I'd never found myself in this kind of confrontation, but I'd witnessed many of them, and as with dogs, in prison, only the weaker animal looked away.

"Yeah," she said, and she took a step toward me, putting her face only inches from mine. "You must be pretty special to get this kind of gig." Her breath was rotten, full of decay; I tried not to flinch. "Tell me. How am I going to get me a gig like that? Leave this shithole a few days a week, just like you?"

"I don't know," I said, and I couldn't keep the tremor from the words. My entire body tensed, and picking up on this, Trixie bared her teeth and growled, a low and deep, gurgling, threatening sound.

Blake's leg shot out from her body and connected with Trixie before I knew what was happening. The dog yelped, and I screamed, "No!" and then I pushed at Blake's chest as hard as I could. Trixie strained at the end of her leash, snarling at the woman who had just kicked her.

Blake stumbled backward, and then something dark flashed in her eyes. "Now you're fucked, little girl," she said, and she came at me again, her thick fists clenched, and the last thing I remember was Trixie barking and the bright sparkle of pain exploding inside my skull as Blake jumped on top of me, grabbed me by the ears, and banged my head against the floor.

Natalie

"Your destination is on the right," Natalie's GPS announced as she turned off the main road and onto a side street. It was an older neighborhood, one she'd driven through but never stopped in before, filled with rows of small houses with overgrown lawns. Zora's house looked as though it had once been painted blue but now, after years of the sun bleaching the siding, it was more of a washed-out shade of gray. The roof was carpeted in thick green moss and sagged in the middle; the square window next to the front door had a large crack running diagonally across it. All the shades were drawn, so Natalie worried that the woman she'd come to speak to wasn't there—probably at work for the day. But then, she saw one of the dingy yellow shades lift up at its corner, and a child's face peeked out at her, only to quickly disappear again.

Natalie grabbed her purse and got out of her car, heading toward Zora's porch, which was actually just a couple of crumbling cement steps. The yard, like the ones around hers, was overgrown with weeds and littered with brightly colored but heavily weathered children's toys. Three full garbage bins sat along the edge of the fence, and one of them had tipped over, littering the grass with paper and other bits of trash. Natalie raised a hand to knock, but the door opened before she could. She looked down to see a dark-haired little boy who looked to be about three years old standing in front of her, wearing only a baggy black T-shirt that hung on his skinny frame like a dress, its hem reaching just above his knobby knees. He had smears of jelly on his cheek, and he looked as though he hadn't bathed in days.

"Hi," she said to the boy. "Is your mommy home?" The boy nodded, staying silent but opening the door wide enough for Natalie to step inside. She hesitated, leaning her head in but not crossing the threshold. "Hello?" she called out. "Is anyone here?" She looked to her left, into a tiny living room where a television was playing loudly, set on the Cartoon Network. She saw a rail-thin woman sitting on one end of the couch, her head lolled back, eyes closed, and mouth open.

Worried that Zora was unconscious, Natalie disregarded her uncertainty about entering uninvited and stepped inside. The air held a ripened, moldy scent, like fruit left too long in a warm place, and the coffee table and floor were littered with plates that still had bits of food on them—an apple core, pizza crusts, and half-eaten pieces of toast with jelly. When she saw a clear plastic baggie with a few white capsules in it peeking out from under a tattered trashy magazine, a sinking feeling pulled at Natalie's stomach.

"Hey!" she said, reaching out to shake Zora's shoulder.

"What!" Zora said. Her eyes snapped open, and she looked at Natalie, blinking rapidly. "Who the fuck are you?" she mumbled, shoving off Natalie's touch. "What the hell are you doing in my house?"

Natalie straightened and took a couple of steps back, away from Zora's rancid breath. "I'm sorry, but your son opened the door and it looked like you were unconscious. I was just making sure you were okay."

"I was sleeping, for Christ's sake!" Zora said. She stood up, and Natalie took in her appearance. Zora wore black leggings and a tight, thin-strapped purple tank top without a bra. Not that she needed one; her chest was nonexistent, and her clavicle looked like a sharp piece of jewelry at the base of her neck. Her dark brown hair was a stringy mess around her pockmarked face, and she reached up to push it back.

"I'm sorry," Natalie said again. After seeing the baggie full of pills, she was pretty sure that in Zora's world, "sleeping" was another way to say "passing out after taking some kind of narcotic." The little boy had climbed up on the couch and grabbed a blanket that had what looked to be coffee stains on it, and then glued his eyes to the cartoons on the television screen. "You are Zora Herzog . . . right?"

"Who wants to know?" Zora demanded.

"I got your name from Miss Dottie at Hillcrest," Natalie said, and went on to explain her search for Brooke.

"Huh . . . Brooke Walker," Zora said as she grabbed a pack of cigarettes from the table and shook one out and lit it. She took a long puff and then blew out a white plume of smoke through her nose and tilted her head, peering at Natalie through half-lidded, mascara-smeared eyes. "Yeah, I know her."

Natalie's pulse quickened at Zora's use of the present tense. "Is she still in Seattle? Do you know how I can reach her?"

"Maybe." Zora took another drag on her cigarette and looked Natalie up and down. "That depends."

"On what?" Natalie asked. A sense of dread filled her as she waited for what Zora might say next.

"You know how it is. Not everyone wants to give up information for free." She sucked on her cigarette again, turning her head to the right in order to blow out the smoke.

"Do you actually know where Brooke is?"

"Like I said, that depends." Zora lifted a single dark eyebrow. "How much cash you got on you?"

She was a liar, Natalie realized. Zora had no idea where

Brooke was, she was just an addict trying to work an angle for money. Whatever hopes Natalie had had in coming here vanished. "Sorry to have bothered you," she said quietly. She turned around and faced the front door, thinking she would report the little boy's living situation to Child Protective Services as soon as she got home.

"Wait," Zora said. "You have to have something. Please. My kid is hungry. You can see that. Every bit helps."

Natalie stopped, and even though she was fairly certain that whatever cash she handed over to Zora would be used for more drugs, on the off chance she was wrong, she reached into her purse, opened her wallet, and handed the other woman a handful of bills. "Please," she said. "Use it the right way."

"Yeah, of course," Zora said, snatching the money from Natalie's hand. Then she laughed, a dry, barking sound. "You know Brooke was a hooker, right? A total whore. I have no clue where she is now. Probably in a shitty hotel room waiting to suck her next dick."

Natalie cringed at Zora's vulgarity, and she raced out of the house with tears in her eyes, wondering if there was any truth to what the other woman had said. Even if Zora was a liar, it was within the realm of possibility that Brooke was a prostitute, or at least had been at one time. Natalie couldn't imagine bringing her sister into her world—introducing Brooke to her children—if she was, in fact, anything like Zora. Brooke could be a drug addict, a criminal . . . and yes, a prostitute. It might have been callous, but there was no way Natalie would want anything to do with her if she was any of those things.

"Maybe it's not such a bad thing that you're finding all this out now," Kyle said later that night when the kids were in the playroom enjoying their one hour of screen time while he and Natalie sat together on the living room couch. She'd filled him in on everything that had happened earlier in the day, including the phone call she made to CPS. Not surprisingly, the social worker who took the report indicated that Zora Herzog already had a file with the agency.

"Maybe," Natalie said. "It's just disappointing."

"I know." Kyle put his arm around her shoulders and kissed the top of her head as she leaned against his chest. "But what you saw today isn't exactly an uncommon result for kids who get stuck in the system. I've defended them as adults. Brooke had a very different upbringing than you, and I think it's important to take that into account."

"Lots of people have a difficult time growing up and turn out just fine."

"Of course they do."

Natalie appreciated her husband's attempt at neutrality, and his ability to comfort her, but the truth was that she believed people tend to do one of two things: either they break the patterns they experienced in their childhood or they perpetuate them. The odds were that Brooke had done the latter.

"Do you think I should just focus on my birth mom?" she said, tilting her head so she could look up at her husband. "And not worry about Brooke?"

Kyle nodded. "It might be better to leave well enough alone."

While she wasn't completely certain that was the right path, it was the stance Natalie took. For the next couple of weeks, she focused on work and taking care of her family, trying to make peace with the idea of not looking for her sister. In making impromptu visits to Gina, Hillcrest, and Zora, Natalie had been fueled by emotion rather than rationale. She'd simply gotten ahead of herself. After the remodel on the garage was complete, she would look into filing a motion to open her sealed adoption records and wait patiently for the legal system to find her birth mother. It was the least disruptive, most sensible thing to do.

In the meantime, Natalie knew she needed to speak to her parents more about why they'd kept Brooke's existence from her, so when her cell phone rang on Tuesday in the early evening, two weeks after she'd met Zora, she grabbed for it. The caller ID told her it was her father, and she hesitated only a moment before picking up.

"Hi, Dad," she said. She was certain her mother had already reported how Natalie had stormed out of her parents' house after getting the news about having a sister, so she braced herself for a reminder of how sensitive her mother could be.

"Natalie," her dad said in his usual low voice. Natalie used to think that James Earl Jones had nothing on her father's sonorous baritone. As an adult, she loved sitting in court, listening to him question a witness or present his passionate closing arguments to a jury. She had loved it less as a teenager, when he used that voice to yell at her for doing something to make her mother unhappy. "We haven't heard from you in a while. Are you all right?"

This was not the first question she had expected her father to ask, so it took her a moment to respond. "I don't know," she said, which was as honest an answer as she could give. "I'm confused. And hurt, I guess."

"Angry, too, I'd imagine."

"A little bit. Yes."

"I'm sorry we kept it from you so long," her dad said. "It really was what we thought would be easiest for you." He paused. "Perhaps we were wrong."

Natalie knew how much it took for her father, a dedicated debater not only in his professional life but in his personal one, to admit that he may have made a mistake. She decided to take that for the olive branch it was, and to save the story of meeting Gina and seeing Hillcrest for another time, when they were in person. "It's okay, Dad. I love you guys. I'll see you soon."

They hung up, and almost immediately, her phone chimed with a notification indicating that she had an email. When she saw who it was from, her heart literally skipped a beat and she strode into the den, where Kyle sat, working at his desk. The air smelled of the white bean and chicken chili Natalie had simmering on the stove, and the kids were in the backyard, playing on the jungle gym before the sky became too dark.

"What's wrong?" Kyle asked when he saw the look on her face. He scrunched his eyebrows together. "Is it the kids?"

Natalie shook her head. "You're not going to believe this," she said. "But the adoption registry I put my information on just sent me an email. They think they found Brooke."

"Wow." Kyle pulled his hands back from the keyboard and set them in his lap. He had taken off the jacket to his suit when he got home from work but only loosened his tie instead of removing it, so it rested halfway down his chest like a green silk noose against his white shirt. "What are you going to do?"

"I don't know," she said. "I was just starting to feel okay about letting the idea of meeting her go."

"You still don't know anything about her living situation."

"Right, but . . ." Natalie trailed off, unsure what else to say. She felt twin urges—one to call the adoption registry immediately and the other to delete the email and pretend she'd never seen it. She didn't want to find her sister—to meet her—only to discover that Brooke wasn't the kind of person she wanted to know. It would be easier to just let the situation go.

Kyle stared at her with assessing eyes. He knew how to read her, Natalie thought. She knew she couldn't hide how conflicted she felt.

"You don't have to decide right now," he finally said.

"You think I shouldn't talk to her."

"I think it might not even be her."

"What if it is?"

"Okay. Let's say it is. What if she's just like Zora? What if she's had trouble with the law, or a problem with drugs? What if she is a prostitute? Do you want to bring someone like that around the kids?"

Natalie realized he was using his careful, I'm-dealing-with-a-hostile-witness voice with her, and it made her jaw clench. She couldn't blame Kyle for being concerned at the prospect of inviting a total stranger into their lives; his lawyer-brain was trained to automatically highlight areas of concern. Seeing all angles of a situation, looking for red flags so he could better argue his points was part of who he was; it was what made him good at his job. It was also what made him occasionally infuriating to have as a husband. Natalie tended to look for the good in every situation, and Kyle had a habit of pointing out the bad.

Natalie sighed, feeling like they'd already had this conversation. But things were different now. There was a real chance that the adoption registry had found out exactly where Brooke was. If Natalie didn't at least talk to the woman who could be her sister, she knew she'd regret it for the rest of her life. Despite the apprehension she felt, she knew what she had to do.

"I need to call her," she told Kyle. "I need to know if it's her."

He bobbed his head, once, and then stood up, coming to stand in front of her. "I just don't want you to get hurt," he said as he slipped his strong arms around her waist, pulling her to him.

"I'm not saying I'll meet her," Natalie said. Adrenaline pumped through her body, and her cheeks flushed pink. "We'll just talk. I'll be careful."

"That's all I ask," her husband said. And then Natalie pulled away from him, eager to reread the email from the adoption registry and take the next step.

Brooke

The Friday morning before Halloween, Brooke was about to jump in the shower when her cell phone sounded. She grabbed for it, half-expecting to see Ryan's face and number—he'd sent her a couple of texts since they last spoke, despite her having asked him to stop—but instead, an unfamiliar number popped up on the screen. Brooke swiped her finger and said hello.

"Is this Brooke Walker?" an older woman's voice inquired.

"It is," Brooke said, cautiously, hoping she didn't just get caught by a telemarketer.

"My name is Sarah," the woman said, "and I'm with the National Adoption Registry. I'm calling about your sister, Natalie."

"What?" Brooke said, squeezing her cell phone and pressing it hard up against her ear. Shivers shot across her skin. "What did you say?"

"Ms. Walker, were you surrendered to the state by your mother in October of 1980?"

"Yes," Brooke said, hesitantly. On impulse, she had filled out a profile with the adoption registry in 1994, when she was eighteen. She had just left Hillcrest and thought her sister or mother—or both—might be looking for her, too. But the last time she had updated her contact information on the site was almost ten years ago, when she switched to her current cell phone number. As months passed, and then years, without receiving a single notification of a possible match, Brooke gave up hope.

"Did you have an infant sister named Natalie Walker, also surrendered, but adopted in November of 1980?"

"I did," Brooke said, feeling the tingle of impending tears behind her eyes. Was this really happening?

"Well, then, Ms. Walker," Sarah said, "I'm happy to tell you that your sister recently completed a profile on our website and our search engine made a match with the data you both provided." She paused. "Of course, as we are only a not-for-profit organization and not a legal entity, we cannot guarantee that this woman is, in fact, your sister."

Brooke's heart sank. "But you just said . . ."

"I know," Sarah said. "The data looks very much like a match, but I'm required to tell you that any official verification of relationship, if you so choose it, would be your responsibility." She waited a moment, and when Brooke was quiet, Sarah spoke again. "I understand this is an overwhelming moment for you. I went through something similar when I received the call about the son I'd given up for adoption. He came looking for me here, and after we found each other, I started volunteering for the organization."

"Oh," Brooke said, "that's nice." It felt like a lame response, but it was the only one she could come up with in the midst of her stupor. *Natalie wants to see me,* she thought. After thirty-five years. Or seventeen, if Brooke counted from the moment Natalie turned eighteen and didn't need her adoptive parents' permission to search Brooke out. Brooke's stomach twisted, wondering why her sister had waited so long. Was she sick? Does she need something only Brooke could give her, like bone marrow or a lung? Was she reaching out not because she wanted to, but because she had to?

"Natalie has asked for permission to call you," Sarah said, interrupting the questions eddying in Brooke's mind. "I can't give out your contact information without your approval. She also offered to email first, if that would be more comfortable for you."

"No," Brooke said, looking around her tiny studio, wondering what her sister would think of how she lived. And of the fact that, in seven months, she would be an aunt. Brooke swallowed back an itch in her throat. "It's okay. She can call me."

"I can give you her number, too," Sarah said, "if you'd like to call her, instead. She indicated she's fine with whatever you want to do."

"Have you already spoken with her?" Brooke asked.

"No, but we've emailed. She seems like a lovely person. At least, her emails were lovely."

The muscles in Brooke's belly relaxed. "That's good to know. Thank you."

"You're welcome," Sarah said. "Let me give you her number and I'll pass yours along to her. Do you want me to set up a time for the call, so you'll know when it's coming?"

"I don't think so," Brooke said. "I'll probably just call her right now."

Sarah laughed. "I said the same thing about calling my son. I couldn't dial fast enough." She gave Brooke Natalie's number, and wished her luck. "Call us if you need anything," she said. "We're here to help."

After they hung up, Brooke stared at the number she'd written down for a good, long time. It was local, with a 206 area code, which likely meant that her sister still lived in Seattle proper. That she, like Brooke, had grown up here. Close, but not together. Brooke wondered what Natalie's life had been like, if she had other siblings that had taken Brooke's place and made her presence in Natalie's life unnecessary. How would she feel, meeting them? Or meeting the couple that had wanted to adopt Natalie but not Brooke? And what if this woman wasn't her sister? What if the registry had gotten it wrong? If Brooke did decide to meet her, she could be setting herself up for disappointment, like she had with Claire. Brooke was certain she couldn't go through something like that again.

But what if it was Natalie who'd found her? What if she didn't have to be alone anymore? This thought made tears spring to Brooke's eyes, and she wished she had someone to talk with, but the person she'd been closest to was Ryan, and for all intents and purposes, their relationship was over. And it wasn't like he knew anything about her past.

Her phone beeped, indicating she had a text, and she quickly checked it, thinking perhaps Natalie had decided that text messaging would be an easier way to connect than having an actual conversation. Her pulse sped up as she read another note from Ryan. "Please call me," it said. "We have to figure this out."

Brooke tapped on the reply box and typed in a short reply: "There's nothing to figure out. I'm having the baby. You don't want to be involved. The end." She pressed send, and then decided to say one more thing. "Stop calling me. Stop texting. It's over. I don't want to see you again." She sent that message, too, and when the phone rang in her hands only seconds later, she jerked and accidentally dropped it. It skittered across the hardwood floor.

"Shit," she mumbled as she crouched and fished it out from beneath the night table next to her bed. "I told you not to call," she said, assuming it was Ryan when she answered, not bothering to look at the screen.

"Oh," a woman's voice said. "I'm sorry . . . I thought . . ." Her voice caught on the words, and Brooke realized her mistake.

"Oh my god," she said, breathless. "Natalie?"

"Yes."

"Oh, god," Brooke said again. "I'm sorry. I thought you were someone else. I mean, I know you're you—the lady from the registry told me you're you—but I thought you were my boyfriend. Well, my ex-boyfriend. We just broke up." She paused. "Sorry, I'm babbling." Brooke gave a nervous laugh. "Can we start again?"

"Sure," Natalie said, sounding just as tense and edgy as Brooke felt, which oddly made Brooke feel better. It dawned on her that Natalie didn't know for sure that Brooke was actually her sister, either, and was likely struggling with all the same what-if scenarios that were spinning through Brooke's head.

Brooke sat back down on her bed, stretched her legs out on the mattress, and leaned against her many pillows, deciding that for the time being, she would go with the assumption that this woman was, in fact, her sister. "I can't believe this is happening."

"Me, either," Natalie said. "You have no idea."

Brooke picked up one of her fuzzy throw pillows and squeezed it to her chest with one arm. "Is this the first time you've looked for me?" she asked. "I mean, it's been a long time. I'm sure you don't even remember me."

"That's actually sort of complicated," Natalie said.

"How so?"

"I didn't know about you. Not until last month."

A shiver spider-crawled up Brooke's spine. "I don't understand."

"My mom . . . well, that is, my parents . . . my adoptive parents, didn't tell me that I had a sister. I always thought it was just me."

Tears welled up in Brooke's eyes. "How could they not tell you?" she asked, again wondering if this was actually her sister on the phone. Maybe this whole thing was a giant mistake.

"Like I said, it's complicated." It was quiet a moment until Natalie went on to explain how her parents had finally turned over her adoption file, and how she had gone to see Gina Ortiz.

"You saw Gina?"

"Yes," Natalie said. "She said she always wished she could have found you a family." She paused. "I also went back to Hillcrest and met Miss Dottie. She told me about a girl you were roommates with after the two of you aged out of the system. Zora Herzog. I went to see her, too."

"Oh," Brooke said, a little unsettled that this woman who could or could not be her sister had been digging around in her past. It made her feel exposed, a position she most decidedly did not enjoy.

"Did you live with her?"

"For a little while. Not long. Why?"

"Do you still see her?"

"No," Brooke said, feeling a bit like she was being accused of something. "Did she say that I do?"

It took Natalie a few seconds to respond, and when she did, it was in a quiet, measured voice. "She said that you were a hooker."

"What?" Brooke exclaimed. Her cheeks flushed hot and red. "That's a lie. She's out of her mind."

"Okay," Natalie said, but she didn't sound totally convinced.

"Look," Brooke began, "I did live with Zora for a couple of months after we left Hillcrest. We were both working at the same restaurant as hostesses and we knew we'd need to pool our money to find a decent place to live. But then she started dating this horrible guy who turned her on to drinking all the time and taking whatever pills they could get their hands on, so I moved out as soon as I could. I haven't seen her in twenty years. Okay?" She realized she was ranting, but she couldn't help it. She was furious that Zora had uttered such a nasty, blatant untruth.

"Okay," Natalie said again, and this time, it sounded as though she believed Brooke. "I'm sorry for asking, but I just . . . I needed to know before . . ." She trailed off, and Brooke filled in the rest of the sentence.

"Before you decided if you wanted to meet me?" She felt a pinch inside her chest, like she'd been found guilty of something she had never done, but she also understood why Natalie would ask the question. If Brooke had been in her shoes, she supposed she would have done the same thing.

"Yes," Natalie said. "I have kids, you know? I just needed—"

"It's okay," Brooke said, interrupting her. "I understand."

"Thanks."

An awkward silence fell between them, and Brooke flashed back to what it had felt like to hold her baby sister in her arms. She heard their mother's voice, telling her to be a good, brave big sister. "I'd like to see you," she said, and when Natalie didn't respond, Brooke continued. "Do you want to see me?" Her voice was small, a fragile thing.

"Yes," Natalie said. "I do. When do you want to meet?"

It was Natalie who suggested the Westside café as a good place for breakfast the next morning. Brooke had never been to the restaurant, so she left her apartment an hour early to make sure she wouldn't be late. She'd struggled over what to wear, wanting to make a good impression the first time Natalie saw her, and finally landed on a simple black skirt with an elastic waist—maybe she was imagining things, but at twelve weeks, her clothes were already starting to feel tight around her stomach—black tights and knee-high boots, and a purple sweater Ryan had bought her because he said it brought out the color of her eyes. She let her curls dry naturally to reduce their normal frizz, then swiped on a little mascara and lipstick before she walked out the door.

Twenty minutes later, Brooke was searching for a parking spot on the very narrow, heavily populated residential side streets that T-boned the main stretch of Alki Beach. She had already driven past the restaurant, so she knew where it was, but it took her another fifteen minutes to find a place to park. It was a cold but clear morning, and the sidewalk lining the beach was littered with people jogging, walking, or pushing strollers in their Columbia fleece outerwear. The blue water of the Puget Sound shimmered as though diamonds had been scattered across it, and after Brooke walked the four blocks back to the restaurant, she stood for a moment, looking out to the green islands across the way. One of them was likely Bainbridge, but Brooke couldn't have picked it out—local geography had never been her strong suit. Though the sun was shining, the breeze was icy coming off the water, so she tucked her hands into her coat pockets and pushed the restaurant door open with one of her shoulders.

"Good morning," the hostess said over the clang of pots and pans from the exposed kitchen and the noisy chatter of already-seated patrons. "Are you meeting someone?"

Brooke nodded. "A woman named Natalie." Her heart pounded an errant rhythm inside her chest, so she took a deep breath in an attempt to settle it. She looked over the small dining area, unsure if she'd recognize her sister after all these years.

The hostess smiled. "Right this way, please."

Apparently, Natalie had come early, too. With her hands still shoved in her pockets, Brooke followed the hostess through an archway and to the very back of the seating area, to the last table, where a woman with long, straight blond hair sat alone. When she saw the hostess bringing Brooke her way, the blond woman stood up, one hand gripping the edge of the table and the other splayed across her chest.

"Thanks," Brooke told the hostess when they were several tables away. "I see her." The hostess smiled, told Brooke their server would be with them soon, and then headed back toward the front. Brooke walked, the muscles in her legs quaking, the rest of the way to her sister.

"Hi," Natalie said, dropping her hand from her chest. She smiled at Brooke, and then took a step toward her. "I feel like we should hug?" She hesitated, waiting for Brooke to give the okay, and so Brooke bobbed her head, letting this petite woman with dark chocolate eyes put her arms around her. It was a short embrace, and an uncomfortable one, but when Natalie pulled away, Brooke's eyes immediately filled with tears.

Seeing this, Natalie ushered her into the seat opposite her at the table, then handed her a tissue. "I thought we might need these," Natalie said, using one to wipe beneath her own eyes.

Brooke didn't know what to say. *She might not even be my real sister,* Brooke reminded herself. *We don't look anything alike. Without DNA testing, there's no way to know for sure.*

But then Natalie reached for something in her black leather bag, which was sitting on the chair next to her, and pulled out a faded and worn lavender blanket. She held it carefully, as though it might fall apart, and suddenly Brooke felt as though she might, too.

"My soft side," she whispered, unable to hold back her tears. Oh, god. It was her. It was Natalie. Her sister.

"Your what?" Natalie asked with a puzzled look.

Brooke reached out for the blanket, and Natalie handed it to her. "That's what I called it," she said. "My soft side. I don't know why. I just . . . did." She clutched the worn fabric, her fingers rubbing the blanket's silky edges in what felt like an autonomic response, as natural and uncontrollable as the beat of her heart. "I haven't thought about this in years. I forgot I gave it to you."

"You?" Natalie asked. "Not my—I mean, our—birth mother?"

"She didn't give us anything," Brooke said in a flat voice, unable to lift her eyes from the blanket.

"Oh," Natalie said.

Brooke finally managed to look up, and took a moment to catalog her now grown-up baby sister's face. Her hair was a darker blond, parted on one side with fringed bangs, and fell in a smooth curtain just past her shoulders. She had large, dark brown eyes, arched brows, and bowed lips, similar in shape to Brooke's. Her skin was pale, but her cheeks glowed pink and the minimal makeup she wore accented her features. She wore jeans and a plum-hued cardigan with simple silver jewelry, including a twinkling diamond band on her left ring finger.

"You're married," Brooke said, and Natalie nodded.

"My husband's name is Kyle. We have two kids." She reached for her phone and tapped on the screen a few times, until she found what she was looking for. "Here," she said. "This is Hailey. She's seven."

Brooke took the phone and stared at the close-up head shot of Natalie's daughter. "Oh my god," she said, taking in the young girl's brown spiral curls and wide-mouthed grin.

"You two definitely have the same eyes," Natalie said, using the tips of her fingers to wipe at the tear that slipped down her cheek. "I never knew . . . I always wondered where they came from."

Brooke stared at the little girl, blown away by seeing her eyes in another person's face.

Natalie reached over and swiped the screen again, bringing up a different picture, of a little boy with light brown hair and an impish grin. He stood with his arms lifted and held out straight, like an airplane's wings. "That's Henry," Natalie said. "He's five, and currently obsessed with Buzz Lightyear. Last year, it was dinosaurs."

"They're adorable," Brooke said, sincerely. She had a family, she thought. The sealed door in her heart cracked open—just an inch—just far enough to make it easier for her to breathe.

Their server arrived then, saving her. He asked if either of them would like something to drink. "Mimosas?" Natalie said, giving Brooke an inquiring look.

Brooke almost nodded, then remembered she couldn't. Not with the baby. "Not for me, thanks," she said. "Just peppermint tea. And some dry wheat toast, please." She couldn't tell if the slight nausea she felt was due to morning sickness or her rocky emotions, but either way, she didn't want to get ill.

"I'll take coffee, then," Natalie said. "And the continental breakfast, with a blueberry muffin."

After the server left them, Brooke glanced down at the blanket, then tried to hand it back to Natalie. "No," Natalie said, holding up a single hand, her palm facing Brooke. "You keep it. It was yours."

Again, a million questions ran through Brooke's head. She didn't know where to start, so she decided to return to the subject they'd discussed on the phone. "I can't believe you never knew about me," she said. "Though I guess it explains why you didn't look for me before now."

"Did you ever try to find me?" Natalie asked.

"Other than putting my profile on that registry, no. I didn't. I'm sorry."

"It's okay," Natalie said. "You don't have to explain."

"But I should," Brooke said. "I want to." She fiddled with the satiny edge of the blanket, oddly comforted by this familiar movement. "I guess I thought that if you hadn't looked for me, you didn't want me to find you. I figured your life was good with your adopted family, and maybe you didn't think adding me to it was a good idea." So much for not opening up. But talking with Natalie felt different; Brooke sensed that no matter what she said, she'd be safe.

Natalie reached out and put her delicately boned hand on top of Brooke's. "If I had known about you, I would have tried to find you right away." Natalie's bottom lip trembled. "I wish . . ." She paused before trying again. "I wish my parents knew better than to let us be separated. I wish we could have been raised together."

"It wasn't just them," Brooke whispered, trying to control her own tears. She was not typically a crier—could it be her pregnancy hormones? "The state didn't know better. Neither did Gina."

"Still," Natalie said. "I know things must have been so hard for you. I'm sorry for that."

"It wasn't your fault." Brooke shrugged. "But thank you."

The server arrived then with their drinks, Brooke's toast, and Natalie's breakfast, and after confirming they didn't need anything else, he left them alone again.

Brooke took a few timid bites of her toast and washed them down with a sip of her tea. She watched Natalie pick at her muffin with her nose scrunched up with distaste. "Something wrong?" Brooke asked her, nodding toward the baked good.

"Not really," Natalie said; then she gave Brooke what seemed like a guilty look. "Well, actually, yes. It's dry. And overmixed. Possibly not made from scratch."

Brooke lifted her eyebrows and took another sip of hot water. "You can tell that with just your fingers?"

Natalie laughed and brushed off the crumbs from her hands on a napkin. "I can, actually. I bake for a living. I own a catering company called Just Desserts."

"Wow," Brooke said. "That's so cool."

"What do you do?"

"I'm a cocktail waitress," Brooke said. She waited to see a shadow of judgment fall across Natalie's face, but it never came.

"I used to be a lawyer," Natalie said, making a face like she had smelled something unpleasant, "but I hated it. I had Hailey and decided that staying home with her was more important. And after Henry came along, the baking thing just sort of happened."

For the next two hours, they shared little bits of themselves with each other, carefully feeling out what seemed safe to discuss. Brooke spoke mostly about work, the various places she'd been employed over the years, some of the men she'd dated, and a few vague details about her breakup with Ryan. She struggled with whether or not she should tell Natalie about being pregnant. The truth perched on the tip of her tongue their entire conversation, but each time she was about to speak, something inside made her hold back. Even though she felt certain Natalie was her sister, it seemed too soon to share something so personal with a woman she didn't really know. Not yet.

It wasn't until Natalie had finished her third cup of coffee that she brought up their mother again. "Did you ever try to find her?" she asked.

"No," Brooke said.

"And she never reached out to you?"

"No," Brooke said again. The question prodded at an angry, inflamed knot in her stomach—a wound that had been there since the day she last saw her mother.

"Do you know her name?"

"Jennifer Walker."

Natalie leaned forward, resting both hands in the crooks of her elbows. "Do you have any idea what happened? Why she gave us up?"

Brooke felt the heat rise in her cheeks, wrestling with how much she should say. If she should say anything at all. But then she decided her sister deserved to hear the truth. "She went to jail for child endangerment and neglect. And theft." She watched her sister's mouth drop open and then spoke again, keeping her voice as steady as she could. "I prefer not to think about her, really. Or talk about her. If you don't mind."

Natalie looked at her with big brown eyes, and Brooke flashed on the last time she saw them at Hillcrest, the morning Gina had taken her sister away. If she closed her own eyes, she could almost remember what it felt like to hold her baby sister in her arms.

"Oh," Natalie said. "Of course." But Brooke could sense her sister's list of unasked questions. They sat in uncomfortable silence for a few minutes until Brooke glanced around at the other busy tables. "We've probably taken up this space long enough this morning," she said. She raised her hand, indicating to the server they were ready for their check.

"This is on me," Natalie said, reaching into her purse and pulling out a black leather wallet. "Please."

Brooke pulled a couple of twenties out of her purse and set them on the table. "Thank you," she said. "But no. It's my treat."

Natalie began to protest, then seemed to think better of it and put her wallet away. "When can I see you again?" she asked.

Brooke hesitated, still struggling to comprehend that the woman sitting across from her was actually her sister. But she couldn't resist the eager look on Natalie's face. "How about we have coffee next week?" Brooke said. "There's a great little spot near my apartment on Capitol Hill."

"Perfect," Natalie said. "I'll text you, and we'll figure out a day that works for us both."

The two of them stood up and walked through the restaurant, back out into the bright glare of midday. Natalie hugged Brooke again, and this time, the embrace felt easier, more natural. Brooke let her sister hold her longer than she normally would another person.

"I'm happy I found you," Natalie said, and for the first time since finding out she was pregnant, Brooke allowed herself to feel a small and bright, perfect piece of happiness, too.

Natalie

Kyle was sitting at the kitchen table typing away on his laptop when Natalie got home from meeting with Brooke. He looked up when she walked in the room and lifted his fingers off the keyboard. "How'd it go?" he asked. Despite his obvious reservations about the situation—even after Natalie had explained that Zora had been lying about Brooke being a hooker—he hadn't tried to keep Natalie from going to meet Brooke. The only thing he said as she was about walk out the door was "Be careful," and reminding herself that he had her best interests in mind, she promised him that she would.

"Where are the kids?" she replied as she set her purse on the counter, then sat down at the table across from her husband. Both Hailey and Henry almost always came running when Natalie returned from being out; the fact that they hadn't, now, made it clear they weren't in the house.

"Your mom and dad offered to take them for a few hours," Kyle said. "I needed to get some work done on this brief, so I took them up on it."

"Oh," Natalie said, pushing down a small flicker of annoyance. "I thought you guys were going to hang out." Saturday mornings were supposed to be Kyle's alone time with their kids—a few hours a week for them to spend together, uninterrupted by work or anything else. Normally, Natalie used the time to go shopping for baking supplies or to get prep done on orders she might have upcoming for the week, but her meeting with Brooke had taken priority over any work Natalie needed to get done.

"We did," Kyle said. "For a bit." He drummed his long fingers on top of the table. "I just thought it might be easier for us to talk when you got back without them here."

"Oh," Natalie said, again. She knew the case he was working on was monopolizing his thoughts, so it made sense that he was working on it now, while he was waiting for her to return. And it actually was thoughtful of him, to give the two of them a little time alone to talk about her brunch with Brooke. Maybe she was being too sensitive.

"So," Kyle said, leaning back in his chair and crossing his arms over his chest. "Tell me everything."

And so Natalie did, recounting the details of her meeting with Brooke. She described her sister to Kyle, and told him about Hailey having her eyes. "You two must each have a recessive gene," their pediatrician had once told them. "But even with that, there's only a twenty-five percent chance of two brown-eyed people having a blue-eyed child. One of you has to have a relative somewhere with Hailey's eye color." At the time, hearing this had made Natalie's stomach ache, knowing that since no one in Kyle's immediate family had blue eyes, the color must have come from someone she would most likely never meet.

"Wow," Kyle said now. "You're absolutely sure it's her?"

Natalie nodded and then told him about the blanket, how Brooke had given it to Natalie when they were separated. "You should have seen her face when I showed it to her. It was like she was a little girl again. It broke my heart." Natalie didn't know how to describe what she felt when she saw this other woman— her sister!—sitting across the table, holding that blanket with tears in her eyes. There was something guarded about Brooke, yet something so fragile and vulnerable, too. Even though she was the younger sister, it made Natalie long to gather Brooke up in her arms and tell her everything was going to be all right. Any doubts she had harbored had quickly evaporated.

"Did you guys talk any more about her past?" Kyle asked, attempting to sound casual, but Natalie knew he was fishing for confirmation that some of his suspicions might be true.

"You mean did I ask her for proof that she's not a hooker?" The instant that barbed comment left her mouth, Natalie regretted it, but his continued skepticism felt unwarranted. Natalie had asked about Zora's accusation, and Brooke had offered a completely reasonable, believable explanation. She seemed normal, and after her initial hesitation, Natalie wanted to enjoy the fact that she'd met Brooke. She wanted to bask in the pleasure of knowing she was no longer an only child. She had a sister. All of those conversations she'd had lying alone in her bedroom, talking to imaginary playmates, maybe they weren't so imaginary. Maybe the entire time, she'd been talking to a subconscious memory of Brooke.

"Natalie—" Kyle began, but she cut him off.

"Can you hold off on the judgment until you meet her? Please?"

"I don't mean to judge," her husband said, carefully. "I'm just saying that we need to understand more about her."

"And I'm just saying the only way we're going to understand anything about her or what her life has been like is if we spend time with her. If I spend time with her, first. It's not like I asked her to come live with us. We're meeting for coffee next week, and maybe I'll see what I can find out about her criminal past then."

Kyle stared at her for a long minute before speaking. "I'm sorry," he said. "I don't mean to ruin this for you. I know how much it means." He stood up and walked over to her, pulling her up so they could stand face-to-face. He put his strong arms around her. "You just don't let a lot of people in close to you, honey. At least, not this quickly. I'm feeling protective. That's all."

Natalie's body stayed rigid for a moment, and then she relaxed into her husband's embrace. He was warm, and smelled like maple syrup. "I get it," she said against his chest. "But you have to trust me, okay? I'm a pretty good judge of character."

"Well, that's true. You did marry me."

Natalie laughed and shook her head, pulling back far enough that she could look up at his face. "Cocky bastard."

"Ah yes," Kyle said with a smile. "But I'm *your* cocky bastard." He rubbed a circle on Natalie's back with one hand while letting the other wander down to cup her ass.

She looked up at him, amused. "Oh, really?"

"Really." He pressed his hips against her and gave her a good, long kiss that warmed her blood and made her joints feel rubbery and loose. The irritation she'd felt just moments before vanished, and desire took over.

"The kids might be home any minute," Natalie whispered, snaking her arms up to link her wrists behind his neck.

"Then we'd better be quick," he said, grabbing her hand and pulling her down the hall to the stairs that led to their bedroom, and Natalie felt like she had when they first met, when they couldn't keep their hands off each other. Once inside their room, he laid her down, and with a firm grip, pinned her arms above her head. Natalie felt her pulse quicken as he stared at her as though he were trying to memorize all the details of her face. "I love you, Nat," he said, and then she let him take her, knowing that even when they disagreed, Kyle's honesty was part of what she loved about him. He was her husband. He would always be on her side.

The next morning, after Natalie had finished with her baking prep for the week's orders and Kyle got home from playing racquetball with John, she grabbed her cell phone from her purse, which was on the kitchen counter.

"I need to call my mom," she told her husband, who was in the living room with the kids, keeping them occupied with books and Legos and building forts so Natalie could work without interruption. Yesterday, when her parents had stood on the front porch to drop off the kids, they'd kept the conversation brief and casual, no one acknowledging the life-changing bomb that had been dropped the day Natalie's mother handed her her adoption file. Still, Natalie noted a muscle twitching beneath her mother's right eye, a telltale sign of the stress she felt, and she knew she needed to resolve things sooner rather than later.

"Okay," Kyle said.

"I won't be long," Natalie said, and she headed upstairs. She sat on the bed, which was unmade and still smelled faintly sexual after their passionate quickie the day before. She smiled a little to herself, remembering, and then shook her head as though to rid it of those images before she dialed her mother's phone number.

It only took a few rings for her mother to answer. "Hi, honey," she said, sounding guarded.

"Hi," Natalie replied. "Thanks again for taking the kids yesterday. They had a great time."

"Oh, good."

Natalie decided the best thing she could do was get right to the point. "So, finding out I have a sister sort of put me in a tailspin. I'm sorry I haven't called to talk about it."

"Sweetie—" her mother began, but Natalie interrupted her.

"The truth is, I can't pretend to understand all your reasons for not telling me about Brooke." She paused, trying to sort out exactly the right thing to say. "I know you're afraid of losing me, which you never will, but I guess it makes sense you might feel that way. And I don't really know how else to tell you this, but I found her. My sister." The word felt stiff and strange inside Natalie's mouth, as though it belonged to a foreign language. "I met the social worker who handled our case and it took a few weeks after that. Brooke still lives in Seattle. She grew up here. We talked on the phone Friday, and I met with her yesterday."

Her mother finally spoke. "Does she know where . . . did you find . . . your birth mother, too?"

"No," Natalie said, thinking about the way Brooke had shut down when Natalie asked her about their mother. "Not yet."

"So she . . . your sister," her mother said, "isn't in contact with her?"

"No. She grew up in and out of foster homes, but mostly lived at Hillcrest."

Her mom let out a tiny, surprised yip. "She was never adopted?"

"No." Natalie was quiet then, letting this bit of information settle in before she spoke again. "I just wanted to be honest with you about what's going on. I don't want to keep anything from you."

"The way we kept this from you," her mother said in a barely audible voice. She didn't wait for Natalie's reply. "I'm so sorry, honey. I wish . . ." Her mother sounded as though she were about to say more, but then allowed her words to trail off into nothing.

"I know," Natalie said, feeling a flash of suspicion that her parents might still be keeping something from her, but she decided she wasn't up to pushing the issue. "You did what you thought was best at the time. There's no way to change it now."

Jennifer

When I finally left the infirmary in late July of 1987, Blake had been transferred to a high-security prison and I hadn't been to the vet clinic for over a month. Her attack on me had resulted in a severe concussion, a broken cheekbone, and four cracked ribs. One of my lungs had collapsed, too, which was the reason I had to stay in the prison medical wing for so long—the doctors needed to make sure all of my ribs had healed so they wouldn't pierce my other lung when I got back up and around.

The only thing that kept Blake from beating me to death had been Trixie—when the guards found us in the hall, I was bloody and unconscious, but Blake was on her back with Trixie's snarling muzzle fixed directly over her jugular. She didn't bite the woman, but the threat she imposed was what saved me.

The morning I rejoined the rest of the inmates for breakfast, O'Brien handed me a special tray filled with French toast and bacon, which she knew was my favorite. "Missed you, girl," she said.

"Me, too." Other than Myer and Randy, I hadn't been allowed visitors in the infirmary. I never thought I'd be so happy to see my fellow prisoners.

"You headed back to the clinic today?" O'Brien asked.

"Nope," I said. "Meeting with Myer right after I eat."

"Maybe he'll put you back in the kitchen, where you belong." She winked at me, and I smiled, carrying my tray over to an empty table, where I ate slowly, taking small bites. My cheekbone had mostly healed, but chewing hurt if I wasn't careful. My ribs ached if I twisted too far in one direction or the other, so mostly, I stayed still. I wondered how my injuries would affect my ability to run and move while working with the dogs. I wondered if Trixie had been adopted while I couldn't take care of her. Randy told me several families had met with her, but as of a couple of weeks ago, she was still in the shelter. She hadn't been allowed to visit me in the prison's medical wing.

Several other inmates joined me at the table, and many issued their condolences, which I appreciated. I knew I'd been luckier than most during my internment; conflicts ending in a beating were common occurrences, and this had been my first. It was probably stupid of me to have pushed her, but seeing her kick Trixie had sparked a fury inside me I couldn't hold back. I was happy she'd been transferred. I don't know what I would have done if I'd had to see her again.

I finished my meal as quickly as I could, then made my way to Myer's office. The door was open, so I stuck my head inside, surprised to see Randy already sitting opposite Myer, who was at his desk.

"Sorry," I said. "Am I interrupting?"

"No, no," Randy said. "Come on in." He gestured for me to sit in the chair next to him, which I did, after closing the door.

"You're looking better," Myer said. "How do you feel?"

"Good," I said. "Not perfect, but yes. Definitely better."

"Glad to hear it," Myer said, and I gave Randy a questioning look.

"So, you wanted to see me?" I said, glancing back to Myer. Was he going to tell me I couldn't work with Randy anymore?

Would he say that Trixie was too dangerous to have on the premises? My heart fluttered at the thought of losing the one thing in my life that made me feel proud. The one thing that had helped me survive.

"I did," Myer said. "We did, actually." He nodded toward Randy, who sat there with a close-lipped, smug smile on his face.

"Okay . . ." I said, drawing out the word. "Is everything all right? Am I losing my work-release privileges?"

"Not exactly," Randy said, and again, I looked at him, confused.

"We brought your case in front of the parole board last week," Myer said. "And Randy testified on your behalf. As did a few of his employees."

"What?" I said. "But . . . my hearing isn't supposed to be until the end of August. Right?"

"Yes," Myer said, "but with what happened, and how well you've been doing overall since you started working with Randy, I decided to move it up."

"They approved your release," Randy said with a huge grin. He reached over and squeezed the top of my leg. "You're getting out today."

"What?" I said again. I dropped back against my chair, feeling like all the air had been pushed from my body. My mind immediately flashed back to the last time I'd been released, the bus ride into Seattle, my mother slamming the door in my face, blood running down that little girl's face. I felt my face flame red, the room began to spin, and I had to close my eyes. "No," I said, unsure if I'd spoken the word out loud or only in my head, until Randy replied.

"What do you mean, no?" he asked. "This is great news. You get to leave. You can come work for me full-time. My wife even found a tiny house for rent. We had to sign the lease for you, so we'll actually be your landlords. But it's already furnished. You can sleep there tonight. With Trixie. She's all yours."

I shook my head, unable to process what he was telling me. When I finally opened my eyes, both men were staring at me, waiting for me to issue some kind of appropriate response. "The parole board just . . . let me go?" I asked. "Without even talking to me?"

"With your clean track record in here, plus the testimony of Randy and his employees, you were a shoo-in," Myer told me. And then he did a rare thing—he smiled, too. "You've done great work since you came back, Walker. Hopefully you learned your lesson. I don't want you here again."

"I don't know what to say," I whispered. "I can't believe it." My head spun with a muddled mix of excitement and dread. Could I do this? Would I be okay on the outside this time around? I'd have a job. I'd have a place to live and people I worked with who knew and respected me. There'd be no reason to screw things up.

Still, a tiny sliver of doubt niggled beneath my skin. If I'd lost it the last time I encountered children, what was to keep me from losing it again? What if the only way for me to keep the past from destroying me was to stay locked up? What would I do the next time I encountered a child who reminded me of my girls?

"Well, believe it," Randy said. "I'm here to take you home."

And that's when the tears came, hearing that last word. I sniffed them back as best I could. "Thank you," I whispered. "You've done so much for me." I looked at Myer. "Both of you."

"I don't get too many success stories in here," Myer said. "Don't screw this up."

After my release, for the next five years, I led a quiet life, but a good one. It was 1992 and I was thirty-two years old, spending most of my days at the clinic working as a vet tech, assisting Randy with exams or treatment protocols. I was also a trainer for shelter dogs, as well as clients' animals who were boarded with us. Sometimes, I even brought home foster animals, but with my limited space and the long hours I worked, it was difficult to keep them long-term. I did manage to go back to school and get my bachelor's of science in animal biology; it took me three years, but fortunately, my time working for Randy counted toward the supervised clinical hours requirement. I had to take out a student loan, but with Randy and Myer's recommendation, I also received a decent scholarship reserved for former prison inmates.

I still lived in the small, one-bedroom house Randy and his wife had found. The house had a square living room with a fire-place and large, arched windows looking out into the yard. The kitchen was tiny but functional, and the bathroom was just down the hall from my bedroom. After a few years of building a little of my own credit, I had taken over the lease from Randy and Lisa, and with my landlord's permission, I'd painted all the rooms a creamy ivory and decorated with pieces of furniture I found at a local thrift store. It was perfect for me and Trixie, who had gradu-ally lost her puppy energy and grown into a mellow, extremely well-behaved, sweet girl that slept in my bed and barely lifted her head when my alarm went off at four a.m. to start our day. But by the time I was finished getting ready, she had gone outside through the dog door and sat patiently by her bowl in the kitchen, waiting to be fed.

After work, Trixie and I spent our evenings curled up together on the couch, watching television or reading. Sometimes, if I came across a particularly funny passage in a book or magazine, I'd read it aloud to her, and she'd stare at me with her dark, interested eyes, as though she could understand exactly what I was saying.

When I told Randy about this, he laughed and shook his head. "You need to get out more. To the movies or on a date."

I'd smiled, too, but waved him off. I liked things as they were. Simple. Uncomplicated. I had a routine and I kept to it. I avoided elementary schools and parks. When I did come in contact with children, with little girls, especially, I felt a little like I was watch-ing my interactions with them from above, policing my every word, ready to jump in and remove myself from the situation if I showed even a twinge of doing or saying something wrong.

Sometimes, I'd catch myself searching faces in a crowd, wondering if any of the young women I saw could be one of my girls. Brooke would be a teenager, now, a junior in high school, and Natalie would be twelve. I still wondered if my older daughter would recognize me if she saw me on the street. I wondered if she'd run the other way. I ached to know if they were okay, if their new family had given them everything I wished I could. The urge to search them out throbbed in my body, right along with my pulse. I went through bouts of wanting to find Gina Ortiz, to bang on her door and force her to tell me where my children were. Only I'd lost my right to know them. In fact, I had no more legal claim to them than a stranger. All I could do was write my letters to them on their birthdays, telling them everything I wished I could have said in person.

You're the age now that I was when I had you, I wrote Brooke back in August, when she turned sixteen. *I was so full of myself, so convinced that I knew exactly what was best for me and my life. I thought I was so mature, ready to take on the responsibilities of being your mother, when really, looking back, I realize I was still just a baby, myself.*

I hope you have people in your life who support you. I hope you have more common sense than I did back then, and parents and friends, teachers who you'd feel safe talking to about your problems. I always felt like my mother didn't have enough energy to deal with her own problems, let alone with mine, which is probably why I never talked with her about needing birth control. When I found out I was pregnant, all I could think about was holding you. I promised myself I'd do everything right. I'd have a happy marriage with Michael, the boy who was your father, and I'd take care of you the way you deserved. I made myself . . . and you . . . so many promises, Brooke. Promises I couldn't keep. I'm so sorry for that, honey. I'm sorry we lived in our car and that there were nights when you went to sleep still hungry and crying. I'm sorry I sometimes left you alone in the dark. I wish I'd had the strength to do better . . . to be better for you and your sister. I want you to know that even though I failed you, even though I couldn't give you the kind of life you deserved, I loved you so, so much. I love you, still.

Now, it was an early, icy-cold January morning, and as I thought about the letters I'd written, I reminded myself that I couldn't allow my thoughts to drift into the maudlin. That it was safer for me to focus on the life I led now instead of the one I'd ruined. I needed to get to work.

"Come on, girl," I said, after Trixie had eaten her breakfast and I'd poured myself a travel mug full of hot coffee. I pulled on my winter jacket and we headed out the door. Trixie followed voice commands well enough that she didn't need a leash, but since the law required it, I linked it to her collar and looped the other end loosely around my wrist.

Outside, it was still dark, but clear enough to see the sparkle of stars against the black sky. My right cheekbone and my ribs ached, as they always did when winter came. It was a painful reminder of the beating I'd taken. I had a car—a used, 1983 Nissan Stanza I was finally able to buy last year—but unless it was pouring down rain, I enjoyed walking the ten blocks to work, basking in the utter peace and silence of the early day before the rest of the world woke up.

Once inside the clinic, I locked the door behind me and made my rounds, turning on lights and greeting our patients who had stayed overnight. I issued their meds, loving them up as I did, inquiring as to their well-being. As usual, Trixie went straight to her spot on the dog bed in Randy's office, where she curled up and settled in for a nap. An hour later, at seven o'clock, Randy arrived. We'd grown to be even better friends since I left prison, and I'd gotten to know his wife, Lisa, too. They had me over to their house for holiday dinners, and celebrated my birthday by taking me out to my favorite Italian restaurant.

I'd asked Randy once, about a year after he spoke to the parole board and helped me get released, what it was that made him do this. Why he was so patient and generous to a woman who had clearly screwed up her life.

I'll never forget how he looked at me in that moment; I'll never forget what he said. "Why do you spend time working with rescue dogs? Why are you so patient and generous and kind to these mistreated animals, animals who made mistakes and were written off as worthless and broken?" He paused then, and smiled. "Sometimes, all we need is for someone to believe in us."

I'd hugged him then, for the first time since the day we met, and with as much gratitude as I could convey. After that, we never spoke of it again. I became just another one of his employees. A member of his family. It was more than I ever thought I'd have.

"We've got an emergency coming in," Randy told me now, as he shrugged off his thick parka and hung it on the hook by the front door. "Got the call about fifteen minutes ago."

"Anyone we know?" I asked. We had a host of frequent flier clients, owners who panicked the minute their pets showed any sign of unusual behavior. They'd call, freaking out that their dog or cat might have swallowed some kind of poison or sharp object, insisting they needed an emergency appointment. Most of the time, the animals were fine, and it was the owners whom we treated with soothing words and reassurances that their pets would be okay.

"No," Randy said. "Apparently, this guy just moved here and he saw our after-hours number in the yellow pages, so he called. His dog is lethargic and hot. Sounds like an infection."

I nodded. "I'll get the exam room ready."

"Thanks" he said. "Chandi should be in any minute, right?"

I glanced at the clock. Chandi was still our office manager and the person who opened the clinic each weekday at seven thirty. "If she's not here to let him in, I'll watch the door."

Randy nodded and headed into his office, where I knew he would try to catch up on a few emails or patient notes before meeting with this new client. I prepped the exam room, making sure there was a blood sample kit for Randy to use. Once I was finished, I returned to the front office, where through the glass door, I saw a tall man in a red ski jacket standing with one arm raised, about to knock.

I smiled and rushed to unlock the door, ushering him inside with his dog, a medium-size, black-haired mutt with white paws and a white patch on his chest. "Hi," I said. "I'm Jennifer. Come on back."

"Thank you," the man said, and I could hear the worried tension in his voice.

When we got to the room, I took the leash he held and shut the door behind us so the animal couldn't escape. The man shook off his coat, dropping it onto the orange, vinyl-covered bench next to the exam table, and looked at me with hazel eyes. His hair was dark blond and his skin was tan; I wondered if he'd come to Washington from some sunny locale, because Mt. Vernon hadn't seen blue skies or a temperature over fifty degrees since October.

"The doctor will be right in," I said, poising my fingers over the keyboard to the computer in the room. "Can I get your name and this little guy's so I can get a file started?"

"Evan Richmond," he said. "And this is Scout. He's never been sick like this before."

"You've brought him to the right place." I typed in their names, then got his address and phone number. "Dr. Stewart said you've just moved here. Where from?" I grabbed my thermometer and crouched down behind Scout, who had tucked his tail between his legs, making it difficult for me to take his temperature.

"Phoenix," he said. "My dad passed away last year. He was a mechanic, and left me his business. I came up here to sell it, but I grew up here, so I decided to move back and take it over instead. I'm a mechanic, too."

"I'm sorry to hear about your dad." I shifted on my tiptoes and looked up at him. "Can you help me, please? I need to get his temp." I nodded in the general direction of Scout's rump, and Evan dropped down on his knees, holding his dog's head while he lifted Scout's tail.

"It's okay, boy," he said. "She isn't going to hurt you."

"Thanks," I said, quickly taking care of one of my least glamorous responsibilities. *One hundred five,* I thought, cringing a bit. Evan was right. His dog was definitely ill.

Just then, Randy pushed open the door and entered the exam room. "Evan?" he said, holding out his hand. Evan shook it. "I'm Dr. Stewart." He looked down at the dog, who had curled up on the floor, lying on top of his master's black work boots. "And this must be Scout."

"Temp's one-oh-five," I murmured, and I felt Evan's eyes land back on me.

"That's high, right?" he asked.

Randy squatted on the floor and put his stethoscope against Scout's chest. The dog was panting, quietly but rapidly, clearly in distress. "We normally like to see it between one-oh-one and one-oh-three."

"Shit," Evan said, and I did something I never had with a client before. I reached out and put one of my hands on his arm. His tendons were pulled as tight as guitar strings.

"It'll be okay," I said. "You brought him in right away. We'll take good care of him." I thought back to Winston, the dog who had presented with the same symptoms all those years before. He hadn't responded to multiple rounds of antibiotics. If Scout indeed had an infection, I could only hope that what I'd just said to Evan would be true.

Evan bobbed his head, once, and then crossed his arms over his chest while Randy took a quick blood sample from Scout's back, right between his shoulder blades. He handed it to me, and I left the room and walked to the small lab down the hall, where I ran a few tests, waiting for Randy to join me and interpret the results. When he arrived a few minutes later, he checked the sample under the microscope and frowned. "High white blood cell count," he said. "Might be a systemic infection."

"I'll get a boarding kennel ready for him," I said, knowing Randy's next order without him having to ask. He would want Scout to stay at least for a few days on an IV so we could monitor the fever and figure out what was going on with him.

"Thanks," Randy said. "I'll go talk with Evan and then head back to my office."

A few minutes later, I returned to the exam room. Randy wasn't there, but Evan was sitting on the small orange bench. His head was in his hands, and the heels of his palms were pressed into his eyes. Scout was still curled up on his feet, panting.

I coughed, and Evan looked up. His cheeks were wet. "Sorry," I said. "I didn't mean to interrupt."

"That's okay," he said. He sniffed, seemingly unashamed of the fact that he was crying. He had to be at least in his early forties, ten years or so older than me. He was graying at the temples and had open fans of wrinkles at the corners of his eyes.

"Dr. Stewart told you Scout will need to stay with us a few days?"

"He did, thanks." Evan leaned down to scratch his dog's head. "Everything's going to be good, buddy. Jennifer's going to take care of you now."

At the sound of my name in his mouth, there was a small, rolling sensation in my belly. I hadn't felt anything like it since I'd met Michael our sophomore year of high school. I tried to shake the feeling off as I stepped across the room to pick up Scout's leash. Once I had, I straightened and looked at Evan, who stood up as well. "Chandi should be at the front desk by now," I said. "Or one of our receptionists. They'll go over the treatment protocol and let you know when you can visit."

"Okay," he said. "Is there a number I can call, just to check on him? See how he's doing?"

I hesitated only a moment before speaking again. "Sure. In

fact, let me give you my home number," I told him, feeling my face flush. "Just in case you want to call after hours."

He stared at me for a couple of seconds, and then he smiled, revealing a deep, single dimple in his right cheek. "I appreciate that," he said. "Thanks."

"Of course," I replied. I wrote down my number, and Evan stuck it back in his pocket. He squatted down next to his dog and scratched the animal's chest, whispering something I couldn't hear into Scout's furry ear.

"Come on, Scout," I said, giving the dog's leash a light tug. I felt Evan's eyes on my back, and I turned around to smile at him, too. "Try not to worry too much. It'll be okay," I said, and then I headed out the door.

Brooke

On the Tuesday morning following the brunch she'd had with her sister, Brooke waited at a table inside Crumble & Flake, the bakery at which she and Natalie had decided to meet. A large, golden-brown croissant sat on a plate before her, but she had a knot in her stomach, and even though she'd been hungry when she ordered it, she felt too nervous to eat. It was a little before ten o'clock, and the air was redolent with the scent of brewing coffee and warm, sugary treats.

Brooke wished she could have a cup of coffee instead of the herbal tea she'd ordered, but she'd read online that pregnant women should avoid caffeine. Which, considering how exhausted she was, felt like an unusually cruel punishment. Along with fatigue, her breasts were tender and her lower back was sore; she couldn't wait to be further into her second trimester, when most of these issues were supposed to subside. An online check for the size of her baby at thirteen-and-a-half weeks told her that it was approximately three inches long and now had the whorls of prints developing on its tiny fingertips. She still could hardly fathom that all of this was taking place inside her; she wondered when it would begin to feel real.

She realized that if she wanted, she could talk with Natalie about what it was like when her younger sister had been pregnant with Hailey and Henry. She could ask any question and Natalie would surely answer it. But it had been overwhelming enough, seeing Natalie on Saturday, knowing the woman who handed her that well-worn lavender blanket was the baby she'd said good-bye to all those years before. She was terrified of letting Natalie into her world, letting her sister see just how empty it was. She worried that Natalie would get to know her and hate her; that she'd ask about Brooke's friends and Brooke would have to tell her she didn't really have any. What if Brooke told her about the baby and Natalie thought she'd be a terrible mother?

Brooke glanced around the shop, trying to distract herself from her negative thoughts. The tables surrounding her were mostly filled with young mothers and their children, along with a few suit-and-tie businessmen typing away on their laptops. One of the latter, an older, dark-haired gentleman wearing horn-rimmed glasses, caught Brooke staring at him, and he raised one of his eyebrows as he smiled back. She immediately dropped her eyes to the floor, not wanting him to think that her look was an invitation to join her.

Fortunately, at that moment the bell on the bakery door sounded, and Natalie entered. She wore snug-fitting dark blue jeans, a double-breasted black wool swing coat, and knee-high black leather boots. Her blond hair was tucked behind her ear on one side, and her cheeks were pink from the cold October air. She waved at Brooke, then came over to join her.

"Hi," she said as she sat down at the table. "Am I late? I had a hard time finding parking."

"Not at all," Brooke said, watching her younger sister remove her coat, revealing the black, fitted turtleneck sweater she wore beneath. "You look nice."

"Really?" Natalie glanced down at her outfit. "Thanks. Pretty much everything I own is black, so I don't have to worry whether or not things match." She smiled again, then reached into the large bag she'd carried in, setting a small lavender box on the table between them. "I brought you a little something."

Brooke instantly recognized that the shade of purple matched the blanket Natalie had returned to her, loving that her sister had chosen it. She carefully opened up the box. Inside were nine pastel-hued, perfectly round macarons. She looked at Natalie. "Wow. You made them?"

Natalie nodded.

Brooke reached in and took one out, holding the delicate cookie between her thumb and index finger as she took a bite. "Oh my god," she said. The sweet meringue melted inside her mouth, filling it with the intense flavor combination of raspberry and lime. "It's amazing."

"Thanks," Natalie said again, looking pleased. She glanced toward the counter. "I should probably go buy something. I'm sure the owners wouldn't appreciate me bringing in my own dessert." She stood up and grabbed her purse. "Be right back."

Brooke waited for Natalie to return, sipping at the peppermint tea she had ordered, making sure she didn't make eye contact with the older gentleman with glasses, whose gaze she could still feel upon her. *You're the last thing I need, buddy,* she thought. Now that she was pregnant, she wouldn't be dating anyone for quite some time. So far, Ryan had respected her request to leave her alone, but it had been less than a week, and there was no guarantee that he wouldn't try to contact her again. She told herself that no matter how scared or needy she might feel as her pregnancy progressed, she would not be the one contacting him.

Natalie came back to their table, holding a large white mug and a plate with a croissant on it, just like the still-untouched one Brooke had in front of her. "So," Natalie said. "How're you doing?" She lowered herself into her seat and took a sip of what Brooke assumed was a latte from the white foam that stuck to Natalie's upper lip before she licked it clean.

"With us, you mean?" Brooke said.

"Yeah. It's a lot to take in, right? I'm trying to get used to hearing the word 'sister' rolling around inside my head. It's a little strange." She paused. "Wonderful, but strange."

"That's a good way to put it," Brooke said, allowing herself to relax a little bit. It was comforting to hear that she wasn't the only one having a hard time adjusting to the idea of having a sister in her life. "I'm happy you found me, but I guess I'd gotten used to the thought of never seeing you again. I'm still processing that it's really you."

"Do you have many memories of us when we were together?"

"A few," Brooke said. "I remember holding you a lot, helping to change your diapers and give you a bottle. I remember you always giggled when I stuck out my tongue." Natalie smiled and broke off an end piece of her croissant, then popped the pastry into her mouth. While her sister chewed, Brooke spoke again. "Did you always know you were adopted?"

"Not until I was ten," Natalie said, after she had swallowed. "And I always felt different from the other kids after I knew." She tilted her head, then spoke again. "Before then, too, if I'm being honest. I was a shy kid. I didn't really have any friends."

"I have a hard time believing that," Brooke said. Her sister seemed so warm and friendly. Over the weekend, Brooke had imagined Natalie with a large social circle, she and her husband going out with their couple friends for a date night each week, hosting holiday parties and summer barbecues in their backyard. The thought of trying to fit into a circle like that was intimidating.

"It's taken me a long time to get over it," Natalie said. "Law school taught me to fake confidence pretty well. But I'm still not especially close with anyone outside my immediate family."

Brooke smiled. Maybe she and Natalie were more alike than either of them knew.

"What about you?" Natalie asked.

Brooke was unsure how to convey the truth to her sister without it making Natalie feel sorry for her; the last thing she wanted was to feel pitied. "Well," she said, carefully choosing her words. "I didn't have a lot of friends, either. It was too hard, with all of us going into foster homes, and then back to Hillcrest when things didn't work out. There were always new kids, different kids, and it was rare to have the same people around me for very long."

"I can only imagine," Natalie said. She sipped her coffee, then set the mug back on the table. "What were your foster homes like?"

"Which ones?" Brooke asked, trying to keep the snap from her tone. But from the look on her sister's face, she'd failed.

"I'm sorry," Natalie said, looking chastised. "We don't have to talk about it."

"No," Brooke said. "*I'm* sorry. I'm just not used to discussing it. I tend to keep my past to myself." Natalie kept her eyes on Brooke but didn't respond, seemingly waiting to see if her sister would go on. "I don't have any particular horror stories," Brooke finally said. "No one beat me or burned me with cigarettes or locked me in a closet, which did happen to more than one of the kids I knew. I just didn't fit in anywhere. I didn't fit in with anyone. By the time I hit ninth grade, Gina stopped trying to place me in a foster home altogether, and I just lived at Hillcrest, going to school and biding my time until I aged out of the system. I started working in restaurants as a dishwasher and hostess when I was sixteen, then ended up cocktailing as soon as I turned twenty-one. I've been at it ever since." Brooke's muscles had been tense when she began to speak, but by the time she had finished, she felt lighter, and her body softer. The knot in her stomach had loosened. She hadn't spoken to anyone like this since she had lived with Claire. She had forgotten the relief that honesty could bring.

"You've never been married?" Natalie hadn't taken her eyes off Brooke, and appeared to be sincerely interested in her older sister's story. Brooke searched her face for any sign of pity but found none.

"Nope," she said. She imagined saying that she was pregnant, then immediately decided against it. At this point, there was only so much about herself she would reveal.

"Not the marrying kind?"

Brooke laughed, thinking how much more convoluted her reasons for not being able to fully commit to a relationship were. "I guess not," she said. "I like to keep things simple."

"I hope meeting me isn't too complicated," Natalie said, with a touch of worry.

"I don't think so," Brooke said. "At least, not so far." She hoped the lightness in her tone conveyed to Natalie that she was joking.

"What about meeting Kyle and the kids?" Natalie asked. "Would you be up for that?"

Brooke wondered if she had it in her to navigate interacting with Natalie's family. "I don't want to impose. Or make anyone uncomfortable."

"You won't," Natalie said. "It's a little over Henry's head, but I know Hailey would be thrilled to have a new aunt."

Her baby would have cousins, Brooke thought. An aunt and uncle of its own. "Are you sure?"

"Of course," Natalie said. "Why don't you come over to our house for dinner next week? Nothing fancy, just the five of us. We'll keep it casual. Is there a night that works best for you?"

"I usually have Wednesdays off," Brooke said.

"Perfect. I'll text you our address and we'll see you then. Seven o'clock?"

Brooke paused, trying to fight off the sense of apprehension brewing in her chest. What if Natalie's husband and the kids didn't like her? What if they met her and convinced Natalie that they shouldn't have a relationship? But the bright, optimistic look on her sister's face was too contagious to resist. "Seven o'clock," she repeated, and after that, she knew there was no excuse to be made.

Natalie

Monday night, a few days after Natalie's second meeting with Brooke, Natalie and Kyle lay in bed discussing the idea of telling their children that Natalie was adopted and about the sister she never knew she had.

"It's your news to tell," Kyle said, "but are you sure they're old enough to hear it?"

"I think so," Natalie said, appreciating Kyle's deference, especially considering his reservations about Brooke. "I know of one adopted kid in Hailey's class, so it's not like they haven't been exposed to it. It's treated so differently now than it was when I was growing up. It's out in the open. Talked about. Nothing to be ashamed of."

"I hate that you felt ashamed," he said, tenderly. He tangled his fingers with hers, and Natalie remembered the night when she'd first told him that she was adopted. It was their fourth date, and Kyle had taken her to a small French bistro on Lake Union, where they looked out over the water, sipping champagne and telling each other stories about how they'd grown up.

"I always wanted a sibling," Natalie said. "Being an only child can get pretty lonely."

"I wish my brother and I were closer," Kyle said.

"Why aren't you?" In all her childhood fantasies about having a brother or sister, Natalie never imagined anything but the two of them being the best of friends.

"A lot of reasons." Kyle set down his glass and linked his fingers together on the table, as though in prayer. "He's four years older than me, so he likes to boss me around. I put up with it when I was a kid, but when I hit junior high, I started challenging him and he didn't like it. We had some pretty epic fights. He broke my nose, twice, and I gave him more than one black eye."

"Oh my god," Natalie said. "That's terrible. I'm so sorry."

Kyle shrugged, but Natalie could see the emotion clouding his dark eyes and it made her long for a way to comfort him. "It is what it is," he said. "We get along on the surface now, but it's probably a good thing he moved to L.A." He cleared his throat, looked away for a moment, and then spoke again, returning his eyes to hers. "Most of the time, I feel like an only child, too."

Natalie reached across the table and took his hand in hers. "I was adopted when I was six months old," she said, surprised to hear the words coming out of her mouth. She hadn't specifically planned to share this piece of her past with him, but it seemed like the right thing to do, especially after he'd just related such a raw, honest aspect of his relationship with his brother. There was something about Kyle—something that made her feel like she could tell him anything. "I lived in a car with my birth mother until she decided to give me up. My parents didn't tell me anything about it until I was ten."

"Why not?" Kyle asked, giving her hand a gentle squeeze. His grip was warm and reassuring; Natalie felt like she never wanted him to let go.

"I don't really know. My mom hated whenever I brought it up after that, so I learned it was better to not talk about it at all. With anyone. I felt like it was something I needed to hide."

"But you're telling me."

Natalie pressed her lips together and bobbed her head, once.

"That must have been hard, keeping such a big fact about your life to yourself."

"It is what it is," Natalie said, repeating the statement Kyle had used about his situation with his brother. "I don't really think about it much."

"Have you ever tried to find your birth mother?"

"No. It would break my parents' hearts."

"What about your heart?" Kyle asked, and Natalie's eyes filled with tears, already sensing that the man sitting across from her was the one with whom she'd spend her life. He saw right through to the very core of her, and she saw into him, too. When he proposed a few months later, he took her back to that restaurant, got down on one knee, and said, "I want to build a family with you, Natalie. I want you to be the mother of my children, my partner in everything we do." He choked up then, but didn't bother to blink away the shine in his eyes. "I can't fathom choosing anyone else but you."

Now, remembering that moment nine years ago, Natalie felt an overwhelming surge of affection toward her husband. "That's part of why I want to tell the kids," she said. "I don't want to hide anything from them." She swallowed, hard, to keep the tears down. "We'll keep it simple. On a level they can understand. But I need to tell them. Okay? I don't want to lie to them about who Brooke is when she comes over for dinner this week."

"Okay." The next evening, after Kyle got home from work, he and Natalie sat down with the kids in the living room. Henry clambered up onto his father's lap, and Hailey settled right next to Natalie, who wasn't exactly sure how to start.

"So," she finally said, "your dad and I have something we need to talk with you about." She felt a strange sense of déjà vu, remembering how her parents had similarly sat her down in their living room to tell her that she was adopted.

"Are we getting a kitten?" Hailey said, her voice bright.

"I want a dog!" Henry said, wiggling excitedly on top of Kyle's legs.

"Hold still, buddy," Kyle said, clamping his arms around his son. "You're hurting Daddy's legs with your bony butt."

"Bony butt! Bony butt!" Henry chanted, and Natalie flashed Kyle an imploring look.

"That's enough, kiddo," Kyle said, nodding at Natalie, which she took as encouragement to continue.

"Mommy needs to tell you something about herself, actually," Natalie said.

"What?" Hailey asked, bouncing on the cushion, causing Natalie to jiggle, too. She put a hand on her daughter's shoulder, stopping the movement.

"Well," Natalie said, "you know how Azim was adopted by his parents?"

"Azim is E-thi-o-pian," Hailey said, carefully pronouncing the country's name. "That's in Africa."

"That's right," Kyle said. "But why don't we stop interrupting Mommy and let her finish. Okay?"

"Okay!" Henry shouted.

"So," Natalie said, "the first part of my news is that when Mommy was a baby, she was adopted, too. Gramma and Grampa chose me to be their little girl." Her throat closed around these last words, remembering how she'd felt the first time her parents had spoken them to her.

"But, Mommy, what happened to your *real* mom?" Hailey asked, looking up at Natalie with her big round eyes.

"Gramma is my real mom, honey," Natalie said. "She's the one who raised me. The woman who carried me in my tummy is called my 'birth mother.'"

Hailey pursed her lips. "Your birth mom didn't want to keep you?"

The question pinched the nerves in Natalie's throat. "Well," she began, coughing a little to hide the rush of emotion from her voice, "it wasn't that she didn't want to. It was more that she couldn't." *Is that true?* she wondered. *Or just the least painful version of the story?*

"How come?"

Natalie recited the same words that her mother had told her, almost verbatim. "She was young and all alone. She didn't have a job or enough money or any help to take care of me, so she decided that giving me up for adoption was the best thing. She wanted to give me a better life."

Hailey thought about this a moment, then spoke again. "If you and Daddy didn't have a job and couldn't take care of me, would you give me away?"

"Oh, honey, no. Never. Your dad and I love you and your brother so much. You know that."

"You love me to infinity and beyond!" Henry shouted, and both Natalie and Kyle couldn't help but laugh.

"We love you both that much, buddy," Kyle said.

Hailey twirled one of her long curls between two fingers, looking up at her mother with a thoughtful expression. "Are you ever sad that she gave you away?"

Oh, god, Natalie thought. This was dangerous territory, prodding at deep wounds, pushing on the tender, bruised spots of her heart. But Natalie had promised herself that she wouldn't be like her mom, shutting down conversations as soon as they led her to places she didn't want to go. She was going to tell her children the truth.

"Sometimes," she said quietly, as though uttering a secret she hadn't even told herself.

"I bet she's lonely," Hailey said. "I bet she gets sad, too."

Natalie couldn't speak. She felt her husband's eyes upon her, concerned.

"Your mom has something else to tell you, too," Kyle said. "Something a little bit exciting."

Natalie smiled at her husband, grateful for his support. She coughed, taking a moment to compose herself. "That's right," she said. "I do. I only just this week found out that I have an older sister that I didn't know about. Her name is Brooke. Isn't that pretty?"

Hailey nodded, digesting this, her violet eyes open wide. "Do *I* have a sister I don't know about?"

"No, honey," Kyle said. "You and Henry are our only kids."

"Are you sure?" Hailey asked, her voice a bit shaky, and Natalie thought about the previous night when she'd tucked her daughter into bed. Before Natalie turned off the bedroom light, she watched Hailey clutching the plush brown stuffed bunny she'd slept with since she was three, and had been reminded of Brooke's lavender blanket. How her sister had given up the one thing that brought her comfort so Natalie could have it instead. She felt herself begin to tear up, imagining that moment—a four-year-old Brooke wrapping a piece of herself around her baby sister. Finding the only way she could to say good-bye.

"Absolutely sure." Natalie leaned over and rubbed the tips of their noses together. "Want to know something cool?" Hailey nodded. "You and Brooke have the exact same color eyes!"

"We *do*?" Hailey spoke the words as though what her mother just said was the most amazing piece of news she'd ever heard.

"Yep," Natalie said. "I showed her your picture and she just couldn't believe it."

"Do I get to meet her?"

Natalie looked at Kyle, whose expression didn't reveal anything that he might be thinking, but that didn't mean Natalie couldn't sense it. "Yes," she told Hailey. "She's coming over for dinner tomorrow night. I thought maybe you could help me make the dessert."

"Okay," Hailey said, and then Kyle began tickling their son's ribs. "Oh no!" he said. "The Tickle Monster is attacking Buzz Lightyear!"

"Daddeee!" Henry howled, but he was giggling.

"I'm not Daddy," Kyle said. "I'm the Tickle Monster! And I'm going to get you! Moo-ha-ha!"

Hailey scrambled over Natalie's lap and attempted to insert herself in between her brother and her dad. "Get me, Daddy!" she said. "Get me, too!"

Kyle shot out one of his arms toward his daughter, so he could tickle them both. Their children squealed and laughed as their father played with them, and Natalie sat back with a smile on her face, so grateful for her husband. For the life they had built. Grateful, and also eager to know Brooke better, so their family could grow larger still.

Brooke

Despite a week spent coming up with reasons why she shouldn't go to her sister's house, Brooke found herself dressed and walking out to her car on Wednesday night, a little after six o'clock. She wanted to leave early, in order to give herself enough time to deal with evening commuter traffic headed into West Seattle from downtown. She was digging in her purse for her keys when she heard her name.

"Brooke," Ryan said, and she moved her line of sight, noticing that he was standing right next to her car.

She froze, her fingers curling around the bumpy metal edges of her keys. "What are you doing here?" Her pulse began to race. She could tell that he had come straight from a job site—his Carhartt jacket was dusted with a white, powdery substance, likely Sheetrock or cement. His hair and olive-toned skin were dusted with it, too, giving him a ghostly appearance—making him look significantly older than he was.

"I need to talk to you," he said, taking a couple of steps toward her so he was only a few feet away. If she wanted, she could reach out and pull him into an embrace.

"I told you we're done talking," she said, hoping she sounded more confident than she felt.

"No, you said *you're* done talking."

"I'm not interested in—"

"Brooke," he said. "Let me finish." He shoved his hands into his coat's pockets. "I know I can't make you end the pregnancy, whether or not I agree with your decision. That much is clear. I'm sorry our relationship is over. But that doesn't mean I'm the kind of man to just walk away from my responsibilities. I've always taken care of my boys, and I will help take care of this baby, too."

"I'm not asking you to," Brooke said, steeling herself against the urge she felt to weep. She imagined standing over their child together, Ryan's arm around her waist. She pictured him changing their baby's diaper, feeding it a bottle, but then forced those images down, knowing that that wasn't what he meant. He meant he would help financially. That he would treat their child as a monthly bill to pay.

"I know you're not," Ryan said. "It's not about that. It's about the right thing to do."

Brooke stared at him a moment, then pushed past him, toward her car. "I have to go," she said. She felt his eyes on her as she started the engine, and she spent the drive to her sister's house shoving down the temptation she felt to take Ryan up on his offer. But she'd told him she could do this on her own, and she would. She didn't need him.

Exactly three minutes before seven, Brooke pulled up to the address Natalie had texted, relieved that her brief interaction with Ryan hadn't caused her to be late. As she looked up the short walkway that led to a beautiful gray Craftsman-style house, her hands gripped the steering wheel in an attempt to steady the nervous tremors that shimmied through her body. She loved how the windows were trimmed in bright white paint and both the porch and chimney were built out of round river stones, giving the substantially sized home a more welcoming, cozy cottage look. The yard was full of well-manicured evergreens, and the long driveway leading up to the garage was littered with the signs of construction: piles of two-by-fours covered by a blue plastic tarp and a truck marked ELITE REMODELS along its side.

This is crazy, Brooke thought as she took in the outside of her sister's house. Everything about the place screamed "home." She didn't belong here.

She reached for the keys, which were still in the ignition, about to start the engine and drive away, when the front door of the house opened and Natalie appeared on the porch, waving. *Damn it,* Brooke thought. With a quiet sigh, she pulled the keys out and put them in her purse. She reached over to the passenger seat and grabbed the bouquet of yellow roses she'd brought, opened the driver's side door, and then, after locking the car, walked slowly up the front steps.

"Did you have any trouble getting here?" Natalie asked as Brooke made her way onto the porch.

"No," Brooke said, trying to smile as she handed over the flowers. She'd put them in a clear glass vase left over from the time Ryan had sent her a bouquet for her birthday. Her brief conversation with him had left her feeling even more jittery than she already did about meeting Natalie's family. "GPS brought me right to you."

"Oh, good." Natalie took the vase and smiled, ushering Brooke inside. "I don't know how I survived without that bossy little voice inside my phone telling me where to turn." Natalie set the flowers on an entry table. "These are beautiful. Thank you."

"My pleasure," Brooke said, letting her eyes wander over the high-vaulted ceilings in the living room, appreciating the thick, exposed wood beams and warm, earthy hues Natalie had chosen to paint the walls. Tall, cream-colored candles were lit on the mantel over the fireplace, and the air was redolent with herbs and roasting meat. Brooke's stomach growled; her appetite in the last week had grown exponentially, and she finally understood the real meaning of the phrase "eating for two." She took off her jacket and watched as Natalie hung it up in the closet.

"Is she here?" a little girl's voice called out, sounding as though she wasn't very far away.

"She is," Natalie said, just as the young girl Brooke had seen on Natalie's phone—her niece—came running around the corner from what looked to be a long hallway. "This is your aunt Brooke," Natalie said, and Brooke's heart skipped a beat.

"Hi!" Hailey said with an excited wave of her small hand. She rolled up on her toes and then brought her feet back down to the floor. She wore a red dress with blue-and-white–striped tights and black ballet flats. "I can't believe we didn't know about you!"

Brooke managed to smile, despite the fact that her chin quivered. "I know," she said. "It's crazy, right?"

Hailey nodded and peered up at Brooke's face with a squinty look. "Can I see your eyes?"

Natalie laughed. "Let's let her get away from the front door first, kiddo."

"It's okay," Brooke said, leaning down so her face was only a foot or so away from Hailey's. "I want to see yours, too."

Hailey smiled, and Brooke found herself staring at another set of her own violet-blue eyes. "Wow," she said. "Look at us!"

Hailey jumped up and wiggled a bit where she stood, which caused Brooke to pull back and straighten her stance so their heads wouldn't collide. "Yeah! It's like we're twins! You have curly hair, too! Just like mine!"

"Hailey," Natalie said, her voice full of gentle warning. Brooke appreciated that her sister was being protective of her, making sure Brooke wasn't getting overwhelmed. It was nice to feel cared for, even if it was by someone she was just beginning to know. Brooke smiled again, feeling more peaceful as the muscles in her body began to relax. *Maybe this won't be so bad,* she thought. Maybe she was worried about nothing.

Just then, a little boy raced into the living room to join them; Brooke assumed he had to be Henry. His hair was a tousled mop, darker than Natalie's blond, and he had almond-shaped brown eyes. "Mommy!" he said. "Is this the lady?"

"It is," Natalie said. "Henry, this is your aunt Brooke."

"Hi, Henry," Brooke said, still feeling like she might cry. This was her family, she thought. She had a family. The little boy had a smear of something red on his cheek, which she guessed was his mother's lipstick. The baby she carried would someday grow to be this age, and Brooke would be the only one responsible for its well-being. However many times she told herself she'd be fine, the thought still filled her with fear.

"Very pretty, that aunt Brooke!" Hailey said, in what Brooke guessed was supposed to be a British accent.

"Very stinky, my butt!" Henry said, and both he and his sister dissolved into laughter.

Brooke must have looked confused, because Natalie quickly explained the reference to Gordon Ramsay, and her children's obsession with the famous chef's well-known phrase. "Let's get you a glass of wine," Natalie said, gesturing for Brooke to follow her into the kitchen.

"Thanks, but I probably shouldn't drink since I'm driving home," Brooke said. She hoped she sounded natural; she'd thought of this excuse on the way over.

"Not even one?" Natalie asked, and Brooke shook her head.

"I'm kind of a lightweight."

"Ah. Got it," Natalie said. She led Brooke into the kitchen anyway, and invited her to sit at one of the barstools that lined one side of the granite-topped island. Hailey followed them, skipping along at Brooke's side, and Henry trailed behind, carrying a plastic toy that Brooke recognized from the *Toy Story* movies.

"Guess what?" Hailey asked, but before Brooke could answer, Natalie intervened.

"Honey, why don't you and Henry go hang out in the playroom for a bit so Brooke and Mommy can talk? You two could draw her a picture. I'll call you when dinner is ready."

"Okay!" Hailey said. "Come on, Henry! I'll race you!" The two of them ran out of the kitchen, and Henry's toy announced, "To infinity . . . and beyond!"

Natalie gave Brooke an amused look. "I wouldn't get a word in edgewise if they stayed." She reached into the cupboard and grabbed a wineglass, quickly filling it with sparkling water from a green bottle in the fridge. "Lemon?"

"No, thanks," Brooke said as she took the glass, grateful that it gave her something to do with her hands. "Is your husband here?"

A brief shadow passed over Natalie's face. "He's stuck at work. He'll be home soon, I'm sure." She pulled a small tray out of the oven and began placing what looked like puff pastry bites on a plate, which she then pushed toward Brooke. "Have one, please. Pastry with a little bit of goat cheese and fresh fig, and a drizzle of balsamic reduction."

"Wow," Brooke said, reaching for one. "So you're a baker *and* a chef." She popped the appetizer in her mouth, relishing the mix of toasted pastry, filled with a perfect combination of tang, salt, and sweet. She wished she could inhale all of them. She counted how many were left on the plate—six across and eight down, minus the one she'd eaten—and realized that being the guest who wolfed down forty-eight puff pastry bites was not the impression she wanted to leave with Natalie's family. She looked at her sister. "These are really tasty. The perfect bite."

Natalie smiled, clearly pleased. "Thank you. I like to dabble in the savory world. But my business is all about the sugar."

Brooke stood up from her seat. "Can I help with anything? It smells so good." Her stomach growled again, as though on cue.

"If you want to carry the potatoes to the table, that would be great," Natalie said, nodding in the direction of the stove top, where a large, cast-iron pot with a shiny lid rested. "The salad's already out there. I just need to slice the roast and we can eat."

"You don't want to wait for your husband?"

"No," Natalie said, looking away from Brooke for a moment. "I don't want the roast to get dry."

"Okay." Brooke walked to the other side of the kitchen and grabbed the potatoes, then made her way through a large, arched doorway to the dining room. Brooke set the pot down on a black iron trivet, and just as she was about to turn around, Hailey and Henry reappeared, each waving a white piece of paper in their small hands.

"Look at mine first!" Hailey said. "I'm the oldest!"

"No!" Henry protested. He shoved his sister, causing her to stumble, and then held his paper toward Brooke.

"Don't *push*!" Hailey said, jockeying to stand in front of her brother.

"Hey, you two," Natalie called out from the kitchen. "No fighting."

"Whoa," Brooke said. "How about I look at them at the same time? That seems fair, right?"

"Okay," Hailey relented, and handed her the paper she carried.

Brooke held the two pictures next to each other and looked them over. Hailey had drawn two stick figures under a rainbow, one with long black curly hair and one with brown, and Henry had scribbled with black crayon in the shape of what she assumed was supposed to be a fireman next to a pink building that had red flames shooting from the windows. She was about to compliment them both when there was the sound of a key in the front door. Hailey called out the word "Daddy!" and both she and Henry raced into the living room. Brooke glanced back into the kitchen, where Natalie stood slicing the roast. Her sister didn't look up at the sound of her husband's arrival.

"Hey, bug," Kyle said from the living room, and a moment later he came through the doorway, his daughter hitched on his left side with Henry trailing behind. Kyle had dark brown hair and wore a black suit with a white-and-blue pin-striped shirt and matching solid blue tie. "Sorry I'm late," he said. He set Hailey down and took a couple of steps toward her, holding out his right hand. "I'm Kyle. And you must be Brooke."

"That's me," she said, giving Natalie's husband what she hoped was a warm smile. "It's nice to meet you."

"Look at her eyes, Daddy!" Hailey said. "They're just like mine!"

Brooke's cheeks warmed as Kyle looked at her again. She held her body as steady as she could, maintaining a small, pleasant smile. If she'd had any doubt at all that Natalie was her baby sister, it had evaporated the moment she saw Hailey's violet-blue eyes. She hoped the similarity would have the same effect on Natalie's husband.

"You're right, they are," Kyle said. "Excuse me, for just a minute." He walked into the kitchen, where Brooke saw him take off his jacket, then slide up behind Natalie, who didn't turn to look at him. *She's pissed that he's late,* Brooke surmised. She looked away, then felt Hailey grab her hand.

"Come sit by me, Aunt Brooke," Hailey said, leading her toward the opposite side of the table. She climbed into a chair and patted the one next to her. Brooke smiled at Hailey, her heart warmed by being called an aunt, then sat down and put her glass to the top right of her plate. A moment later, Natalie and Kyle joined them, with Kyle carrying a large platter, which he set in the middle of the table.

"Can you get the kids something to drink, please?" Natalie asked her husband. Her voice was a little stiff, but Brooke didn't know her well enough yet to interpret to what degree her sister was irritated with her husband.

"Sure," he said, jogging back into the kitchen. Natalie took a seat at the head of the table with her back facing a pair of French doors. As soon as Kyle returned with two cups filled with milk, he lowered himself into the chair next to his son, setting their drinks next to their plates. He quickly poured some wine into his own glass. "All right, then," he said. "Let's eat."

"I'd like to make a toast first," Natalie said, looking at Brooke. "To the happy surprises in life. And to family."

Brooke raised her glass, but Kyle took an extra second or two to lift his. *Does he not want me here?* Brooke wondered.

Henry held up a hard plastic Buzz Lightyear instead of his glass and pushed a red button on its chest. "To infinity . . . and beyond!" the toy said, and everybody laughed.

"No Buzz at the table, kiddo," Kyle said, gently removing the toy from his son's grasp. Henry crossed his arms over his chest and pouted while Natalie picked up the serving tongs from the platter filled with perfectly cooked, fanned-out slices of roast and handed them to Brooke.

"So, Brooke," Kyle said, after she'd filled her plate and passed the platter over to Natalie. "Tell us a little about yourself."

"There's not much to tell," she replied as lightly as she could. "I grew up here in Seattle and I'm a waitress at a bar in Pioneer Square. That's about it. Nothing very exciting."

"Are you married?" Kyle asked.

"No," Brooke said. Didn't Natalie tell him any of what she and Brooke had already talked about?

"No children?" he said.

"No," Brooke said again, feeling a twist of queasiness in her gut. *Oh, lord. Don't let me get sick now.*

"Kyle," Natalie said. Her voice was full of warning. She gave Brooke an apologetic smile. "Sometimes he forgets he's not in court." She looked back at her husband. "Right, honey?"

Kyle hesitated only a moment before launching a relaxed smile. "Guilty as charged," he said. "I apologize. I'm happy you could join us tonight."

"I'm happy, too," Natalie said quietly, and Brooke nodded, despite harboring the distinct feeling that she wasn't quite ready to say the same thing.

Natalie

"Would anyone like coffee to go with dessert?" Natalie asked after they had all finished their dinner and moved into the living room. Brooke sat in the large recliner, while Kyle and the kids settled on the couch. Natalie stood in the archway that linked the kitchen to the front of the house, trying to figure out how the evening was going. On the one hand, Kyle had walked in almost two hours late—after promising to be there to help manage the kids and help her get dinner ready—and then practically interrogated her sister. On the other hand, after Natalie gently scolded Kyle for overwhelming Brooke with too many questions he already knew the answers to, he managed to keep the rest of the conversation polite and neutral, inquiring about the other places she'd worked and where she lived in the city, questions to which Brooke supplied very general answers.

"None for me, thanks," Brooke said, glancing at the clock on the mantel, which read eight fifteen. "In fact, I should probably get going."

"Oh no," Natalie said. "You can't miss dessert! It's my thing." Her eyes pleaded with Brooke. "Stay a bit longer?"

Hailey bounced on the couch and then climbed into Kyle's

lap. "Yeah! Mommy made a really yummy cake. It's lemon. With guess what? Raspberry filling! And I helped!"

"Me, too!" Henry said, holding on to one of his father's arms.

"Well," Brooke said. "In that case, I'd better stay." She crossed her legs and set her forearms over her abdomen. Natalie rushed into the kitchen and returned as quickly as she could with a tray covered in small dessert plates, which she set down on the coffee table. She'd found the table at an antiques store in the Junction, and while it was older and needed refinishing, Natalie loved its oval shape and elegant, curved legs. Once she got it home, she'd painted the table white, then used a wire brush to give its edges a slightly distressed, aged look. It was her favorite piece in the house.

"Here you go," Natalie said, handing Brooke a dessert plate.

"Thank you," Brooke said, stifling a yawn. "Sorry. I guess I'm more tired than I thought."

"A side effect of your job, I'd imagine," Kyle said. "You must work late."

"I do," Brooke said, carefully. She held on to her fork and the edge of her plate tightly.

"Have you ever worked outside the restaurant industry?" Kyle asked Brooke.

"No, actually," Brooke said, with a sharp edge. "I like what I do." As Natalie gave a plate to each of her children and then kept the last for herself, she was afraid her husband was pushing her older sister too far. Everything that came out of his mouth sounded like an accusation.

"That's great," Kyle said, overly enthusiastic.

Brooke took a small bite of her dessert, chewed it, and then set her plate on the small end table next to her chair.

"Is Mommy's birth mom your mom, too?" Hailey asked, breaking the bit of silence in the room.

Oh, god, Natalie thought, watching as Brooke folded her hands together in her lap. "Sweetie," Natalie said to her daughter. "Let's not talk about that right now."

"Why not?" Hailey asked, running a finger over her plate to swipe up a streak of raspberry filling.

"It's okay," Brooke said, and then looked at Hailey. "Your mom's birth mother is mine, too, but I didn't grow up with her. I lived in a state home."

"What's that?" Henry asked. His mouth was full of cake, and Kyle attempted to keep him from accidentally spitting it onto the couch by cupping his palm under Henry's chin.

"It's a place where children who don't have a family to take care of them can live," Brooke said.

"Ohh," Hailey said, looking back and forth between her mother and aunt, and Natalie gave Brooke the same apologetic look as she had earlier.

Brooke stood up. "The cake was so good," she said to Hailey and Henry, even though she'd only taken one bite. "You and your mom did a great job." Then she looked at Natalie and Kyle. "Thank you so much for having me, but I really am exhausted. I should head home."

Natalie set down her untouched dessert. This was not how she'd hoped the evening would end. "Are you sure?" Brooke gave a tight-lipped nod. "Okay," Natalie said. "Let me walk you out."

"Time for bed, you two," Kyle said. "It's way past your bedtime."

"Noooo," Hailey said, giving her legs a little kick, and Henry shook his head against his father's bicep, smearing it with raspberry sauce.

"Come on, kiddos," Kyle said, standing up and lifting a reluctant Henry from the couch. He looked over at Brooke and smiled. "I'm sure we'll get a chance to see each other again, soon."

Brooke nodded again, and Natalie accompanied her to the front door. She grabbed her older sister's coat and then her own, insisting on walking with her to her car.

"I'm sorry if Kyle said anything to upset you," Natalie said as they walked together in the cool evening air. They stood next to the driver's side door, lit only by the warm glow of the porch light and the streetlamp on the corner. "He's a little protective, and it just came out wrong."

"It's okay," Brooke said, but her voice broke on the words and she looked away, down the dark street.

Natalie reached out a hesitant hand and placed it on Brooke's forearm. "Oh, no. I'm going to kill him for making you feel like this."

Brooke sniffed and shook her head. "It's not him, really," she said, looking at Natalie with tears glossing her violet eyes. "It's me. I just . . . it's just . . . I'm not sure I fit in here."

"Of course you do," Natalie said. "This is new to all of us. It's going to take some time to adjust, but I promise, I want you to be here. I want to get to know you better." She swallowed hard, fighting back her own tears. "I always wanted a sister. And now I have one."

Brooke's shoulders shook, and she pressed a hand to her mouth. Tears rolled down her cheeks. "I've never had a family," she said after she'd dropped her arm back to her side. "I don't know how to do any of this. I don't know how I'm going to do anything."

Natalie tilted her head and stitched together her brows. There was a distinct, desperate edge to her sister's words. "How you're going to do what?" she asked. "Be my sister? We just . . . spend time together. We just get to know each other."

"No," Brooke said. "You don't understand. Seeing you tonight . . . seeing Hailey and Henry and Kyle, just reminded me how little I know . . . how I'm not . . . I can't . . ." She closed her eyes and began to sob quietly, and Natalie couldn't help herself, she pulled Brooke into her arms. She rubbed a circle on her sister's back, the same way she did for her children when they were upset.

"Hey," Natalie murmured, unsure exactly what it was about the night that had taken Brooke to this fragile point. "Everything's going to be fine."

"No," Brooke said again, breathing into Natalie's shoulder. "It's not. I don't know what the hell I'm doing. I might have made the worst decision of my life."

Natalie pulled back but kept her hands on Brooke's arms. "What decision? Coming here? Seeing me? Or is it something else?" She saw the fear in her sister's eyes, the tight muscles along her jaw. Whatever her sister was dealing with, it was big, and she was terrified. "It's okay," Natalie said. "You can tell me. I promise, I won't judge. I just want to help. Please. Let me help."

She watched Brooke glance off to the side and then down to the ground, as though she were uncertain what to do next. She seemed so small, so exposed, with her guard let down. She reminded Natalie of Hailey when her daughter's feelings were hurt, needing comfort. Needing reassurance. Needing to know she wasn't alone.

"I'm pregnant," Brooke finally whispered. "Ryan . . . my ex . . . is getting a divorce, but he's still married. He wants me to get rid of it and I basically told him to screw off."

Natalie was quiet a moment, letting this news sink in, Brooke's fatigue, refusal of wine, and her likely hormone-spurred tears suddenly making perfect sense. When Natalie was pregnant, she could cry over a burnt piece of toast. "What do *you* want?" she asked Brooke, who looked at her with wide, glassy eyes.

"I want to keep it," Brooke said after a moment. "I want to try and be the kind of mother I never had."

Natalie smiled, sensing this wasn't a decision her sister had come to lightly. "I'm so happy for you," she said. "Please, will you come back inside? We can talk. Just you and me."

When Brooke finally nodded, Natalie hugged her again. And this time, she wasn't so quick to let her go.

Brooke waited on the front porch while Natalie went back inside to talk with Kyle, who had already put the kids to bed. "She's still here," Natalie told him. "Can you give us some privacy? She needs to talk."

"What about?"

"She's pregnant," Natalie said, keeping her voice low. "She literally just told me. She's out there crying and scared and feeling like she doesn't fit in with us. Something you didn't help by treating her like she was in a deposition."

"I didn't mean—"

"Well, you did. And being late was great. Thanks for that." Natalie knew she was being harsh, but she didn't care. "Can we talk about this later, please? She's standing on the porch."

"Fine," Kyle said. And he turned and left the room.

Natalie rushed back to the front door and opened it. "Come in," she said, motioning for Brooke to reenter the house. Her sister's face was splotchy and red, streaked with mascara. She kept one hand placed over her stomach, as though protecting her baby; Natalie recognized the gesture from when she had been pregnant with her kids. Natalie hung up Brooke's coat again, and they returned to the living room, but this time, the two sat on the couch facing each other, just a few feet apart.

Brooke glanced around. "We're alone?"

"Yep. Kyle put the kids to bed, and he's gone upstairs, too."

"You sure he doesn't mind?"

"Of course not," Natalie said, hating that her husband had made Brooke feel that he might not be okay with her back in the house. Natalie shifted her position on the cushions until she was comfortable. "Okay. So, start from the beginning. Tell me everything."

She gave Brooke an encouraging nod, and then listened as her sister, in slow, halting sentences at first, described meeting Ryan and the months they'd spent together with Brooke staying in the shadows because of his impending divorce, and how that was fine with her because she never let the men in her life get too close to her anyway. As she became more comfortable telling the story, her voice relaxed, and she told Natalie how she'd discovered she was pregnant, her at-home tests and subsequent trip to the clinic, how she'd felt when she heard the baby's heartbeat. Finally, she detailed Ryan's reaction when she told him she planned to keep the baby.

"I just don't know what I should do," Brooke said. "If I can be a good mother."

"I think a lot of women feel like that with their first pregnancy," Natalie said. "I know I was terrified I'd screw Hailey up. Or at the very least, drop her on her head."

"Really?" Brooke asked as she sniffled and wiped her cheeks with a tissue from the box on the coffee table.

"Absolutely. It's totally normal to be afraid. I think it just shows how much you already care. When Henry came along I was much more at ease, because I knew what to expect. It's the unknown that's scary."

"But I don't have a clue about any of it. Being pregnant, childbirth, breast-feeding or bottles, or what kind of diapers I should use. Not to mention where I'm going to live. I can't keep a baby in my shitty little apartment."

"I highly doubt your place is shitty. I also don't think you have to decide all of that right now. Certainly not tonight." Natalie gave Brooke what she hoped was a comforting look. "How far along are you?"

"Almost fifteen weeks."

"Okay," Natalie said. "So, first thing, we need to find you a doctor. And get you on prenatal vitamins."

"I have a doctor. She scheduled an amniocentesis for me next week, since I'm over thirty-five."

"All right, good. I can go with you, if you want."

Brooke lifted her eyes back to Natalie's face, her chin trembling. "Why?"

"Why, what?"

"You don't even know me. Why do you want to help?"

"Because you're part of my family." Natalie felt her own jaw tremble then, and she had to struggle to keep back her tears. "That's what sisters do."

Brooke stared at her for a moment, unblinking. "You want to find her, don't you." It was more a statement than a question, spoken in a dull voice.

Natalie cocked her head to one side. "Find who?"

"Our mother. That's the whole reason you found out about me. You were looking for her."

"Well, yes. Sort of. I wanted to know more about her, but once I knew you existed, I started to look for you, too."

"And now that you've found me?"

Natalie searched Brooke's face, wondering just how much either of them resembled the woman they were discussing. Other than their petite builds, she and Brooke didn't look much like they were related. Now that she knew they'd had different fathers, Natalie had come to terms with the fact that she'd likely never meet hers. But her birth mother was different. It was she whom Natalie felt compelled to find. The woman who held her, took care of her for six months, and then just walked away.

"I do want to look for her," she finally replied, and Brooke closed her eyes. "I'm sorry if that upsets you, but I want to understand why she did what she did. Especially now, knowing you were already four when she gave us up. I want to know how a mother could do something like that. Why *she* did something like that."

"Does it matter?" Brooke said, opening her eyes again. "She did it. She neglected us. She left us in her car alone all of the time. I don't remember a lot, but I remember that. I remember going to find her because I was so scared and seeing her getting screwed over a desk in some strange man's office." She gripped her fingers together tightly in her lap. "That's the kind of mother we had, Natalie. And I don't want anything to do with her."

Natalie was quiet then, absorbing everything Brooke had just said. Did she really need to find this woman Brooke described?

Maybe having her sister in her life would be enough; they would have each other and why their mother gave them up wouldn't matter. But then something dawned on Natalie. "Maybe it will help you," she said. "Seeing her again. You could confront her, tell her how much she hurt you. Maybe it would be cathartic. Make you feel better about having this baby."

Brooke shook her head. "I doubt it."

It struck Natalie then that however empty she'd sometimes felt growing up as an adopted child—however many faces she'd compared her own to in a crowd, knowing she had a birth mother out there somewhere in the world—she'd never know the hollow existence Brooke must have had spending all those years fundamentally alone. Natalie's parents, whatever their mistakes, at least always made sure she knew how deeply she was wanted and loved. She couldn't imagine the rejection Brooke had faced as one foster home after another sent her back to the state. She couldn't fathom the kind of damage that had done to a little girl's heart. No wonder her sister was guarded; she was always poised for disaster, waiting for that next destructive wave to crash over her and pull her out to an uncertain sea.

"I understand," Natalie said, in a quiet voice. "And of course, I would never ask you to do anything you didn't want to do."

"But you're going to look for her."

"I think so. Yes."

They sat together in silence for a minute or two. Brooke kept her head down, and Natalie fiddled with the thick seam of a cushion. Natalie wondered if she should have lied to Brooke, but the last thing she wanted to do to her sister was what Natalie's parents had done to her. She wouldn't keep her search for their birth mother a secret, but she wouldn't broadcast it in front of Brooke, either. At the moment, her sister had bigger, more pressing concerns. And now that Natalie had found her, she resolved to be there for her, in any way that she could.

Jennifer

For our fifth date, Evan invited me to his house so he could cook me dinner. In the three weeks since the morning I'd boldly given him my number, we'd met for coffee two times, and he'd taken me out to lunch twice—all were limited, casual interactions that left me wanting to know him better. I had learned that he was forty-one, nine years older than me. I knew his father taught him everything about being a mechanic and that his mother had died when he was thirteen years old. I knew he moved to Phoenix when he was twenty-six, following a girl he ended up being married to for ten years, and then divorcing five years ago, about the same time I was released from prison. I knew he had a brother he wasn't close to and that losing both of his parents had left a black mark on his heart. I knew that Scout was his best friend.

As was my habit, I'd used broad strokes to paint the picture of my past. He knew that my father had left my mother and me when I was twelve, and that now, my mother had remarried and we were estranged. He knew I considered Randy and Lisa the family that I'd chosen, and that training service dogs and my work with animals in general was what fed my soul.

"Dogs are the best," he said. "Pure, unconditional love. You can't get that anywhere else." I told him I one hundred percent agreed.

Luckily, Scout had responded well to the first course of meds, and ended up only having to board at the clinic for three days. Randy guessed he'd eaten something rotten; sometimes food poisoning in dogs manifested with the same symptoms as an infection.

He showed no signs of it now, as he greeted me, barking and tail wagging in a circle when I climbed out of my car. I opened the rear door and let Trixie out, too. When Evan had invited me over, he'd insisted that I bring her along. The house his father had lived in and had left to Evan was about ten minutes from my place, and was located on several acres of flat, lush land. The house itself was a newer rambler with lots of windows and a porch that circled around the back. The enormous gray outbuilding that served as Richmond Automotive was about a hundred yards away from the house and had its own driveway. There were a variety of vehicles parked by what looked to be a rolling garage door; Evan had said since he'd taken over for his father, business was as strong as ever. His brother hadn't even come to their father's funeral; apparently, he was a financial adviser who worked on Wall Street and told Evan to ship whatever token his father might have left him. I found it comforting, actually, that Evan knew a little about dysfunction, that he didn't have some picture-perfect family. It made me a little less self-conscious about my own. I doubted that I could tell him about Brooke and Natalie—I hadn't even told Randy and Lisa about the daughters I'd given up. Just the thought of mentioning the loss of my children made me feel as though I were teetering on the edge of a dark abyss. Uttering a single word about them might cause me to plummet.

I made my way up the walk to the house, holding a plateful of brownies I'd baked for our dessert, trying to erase a twitchy sense of uneasiness. I hadn't told Evan about the years I spent in prison, either. I wasn't sure if there was a protocol for that kind of thing—was incarceration a fifth-date conversation or something that should come later? Should I have done it right away? I wasn't even sure what it was about Evan that had made me give him my number, let alone say yes when first he asked me out. All I knew was that from the minute I saw how he was with Scout, the unabashed tears he'd shed in worry over the animal he loved, I felt as though I'd met someone who might understand me.

I knocked on the door, both Scout and Trixie dancing excitedly at my feet, and a moment later, Evan answered. "You made it," he said, giving me a big smile that helped assuage my nerves. He stood back so I could enter, then took the plate I carried from me. "These look amazing. So do you."

My cheeks flushed and I dropped my eyes to the floor. "Thanks." I'd worn a short black skirt, black tights, and a purple sweater. I forced myself to look up at him again, taking in his casual outfit of jeans and a dark green pullover. "You look nice, too."

He closed the door behind me, leaving Scout and Trixie outside to play. The stereo was on, and Eric Clapton crooned the chorus of the heartbreaking "Tears in Heaven," a song that always made me think about my girls, because even though Eric Clapton's son had died and Brooke and Natalie were still alive—at least as far as I knew—I had lost them all the same. There was a large plaid cushion that rested in front of the fireplace—Scout's bed, I assumed. The living room wasn't huge, but it was filled with a comfortable-looking brown leather couch, a couple of recliners, and a standard coffee table, which was littered with newspapers, several automotive magazines, and a coffee mug.

"I hope you don't mind I didn't pick up," he said. "I actually think it's a good idea for people to see how the other really lives. I'm not a slob, but I don't exactly keep things neat."

"It's fine," I said. "Are the dogs going to be okay out there?"

"They should be," he replied. "Scout already knows this property like the back of his paw." He smiled, and so did I.

"Can I get you something to drink?" he asked as we made our way into his kitchen.

"A beer would be great," I said, eyeing what looked to be a simple but functional galley kitchen. The walls were painted light blue, the appliances were white, and the cupboards were oak. The air smelled of onions, garlic, and some kind of citrus.

Evan set the plate of brownies on the counter and then reached into the refrigerator to pull out a couple of Coronas. "Would you like a glass?" he asked, and I shook my head. He smiled again, popped off the caps on both, and then handed me one of the bottles. We clicked their long necks together as we both said, "Cheers."

I took a swig and then glanced at the stove top, which had a large pot on the front left burner. "What are we having?" I asked, grateful for the warm, soothing sensation that filled my body after that first swallow. I wasn't a big drinker, but I did enjoy a beer or glass of wine on occasion. Especially on nights like tonight, when my nerves were a little on edge.

"Tortilla lime chicken soup," Evan said. "I don't know why it's called that because there aren't any tortillas in it, but I think I remember you saying that Mexican food is your favorite, so I thought I'd give it a go."

I smiled, flattered that he'd remembered something I'd barely mentioned during one of our dates, then took another sip of my beer. "Do you like to cook?"

"I do." He paused to take a drink, then pushed a bowl of chips and another of salsa in my direction. "What about you?"

I nodded, embarrassed to tell Evan where it was that I'd learned to cook, and who had taught me. "But since I live alone, sometimes it feels like too much work, you know? It's easier to order takeout."

"I know exactly what you mean," he said, smiling.

We both grabbed for a chip, and then he motioned for me to taste the salsa first. It was a spicy explosion of sweet, fiery tomato, garlic, onion, jalapeños, and fresh cilantro. "Oh my god," I said, holding a hand in front of my mouth as I spoke so I wouldn't spit out any crumbs. "Did you make this?" He nodded again and tried some as well. "It's phenomenal," I said. "Seriously. You could bottle and sell it."

"Thanks," he said, clearly pleased. A few minutes later, after we'd talked about how our workdays had gone, he pulled a couple of soup bowls from the cupboard and used a ladle to fill them with the soup on the stove. There was no dining room, but there was a table in the kitchen, which I just then noticed had two small votive candles burning in its middle. "Let's eat," he said, carrying the bowls over. I picked up the chips and salsa and followed him, only to be interrupted by the sound of a dog whining and scratching at the back door.

"They must have sensed it was time to clean up anything we happen to drop," Evan said as he set the bowls down and took a couple of steps over to open the back door. Scout trotted inside with his white-tipped ears perked, still whining at his master. He was alone.

"Trixie!" I called out, hoping she was just outside, behind her playmate. I whistled, the short, sharp noise I used to call her in when we were at our own house. She didn't appear. "Oh, no," I murmured, dropping the two bowls I carried to the table. Salsa spilled out onto the light blue tablecloth, a fact I barely registered.

"I'm sure she's fine," Evan said, but we both ran out to the back deck. It was already dark and there was no moon. The sky was inked with heavy clouds.

"Trixie!" I yelled again. "Come here, girl!" I whistled again, but the sound broke. *She can't be gone.*

"Wait just a sec," Evan said. He turned around, went back into the house, and quickly returned with our jackets and a flashlight. He helped me on with my jacket, then put on his own. After closing the back door, we both headed into the yard, calling out Trixie's name.

"Where is she?" I asked, unable to keep the panic and desperation from my voice. My head began to spin. *Oh, god. Is it happening again?* I hadn't felt this way since the morning in the park with the little girl who fell down, all those years ago. Despite the icy air of the February evening, I started to sweat.

"She couldn't have gone far," Evan said. "Has she ever done this before?"

"No!" I said. I peered into the field, unable to see more than ten or fifteen feet in front of us, even with the flashlight. "I shouldn't have let her stay outside. We have a fence at home. Maybe she got confused. What if she's gone? What if she got hit by a car?" I began to feel as though I couldn't catch my breath. I bent over, my hands on my knees, my heartbeat pounding between my eardrums. "No!" I cried. "No, no, no! I can't lose her!" All I could think about was Brooke and Natalie, the last time I held them. The day the social worker carried them away.

Evan stepped over and crouched next to me, putting his long arm over my back. "Hey," he said. "It's okay. Come on now. We'll find her. I promise. You have her chipped, right? If she's lost, someone will take her to the shelter." His words were distorted, sounding as though they were traveling to me underwater.

I shook my head, squeezing my eyes shut, feeling as though my skin had been shrink-wrapped and was now too small for my body. *This is my fault,* I thought. *I shouldn't have stepped outside my routine. I never should have given him my number.*

And then, I heard a familiar bark. My head snapped up, looking with blurry eyes in the direction from where the sound had come. "Trixie!" I yelled, and less than a minute later, she appeared, racing toward us, tail wagging. I threw my arms around her, and she licked my face, trying to wriggle away. She was wet and smelled horrible, as though she'd found something foul in which to roll. "How dare you do this to me?" I whispered against her fur. "I couldn't bear to lose you."

After a moment, I managed to stand up. My face was hot and I was still shaking. Evan stood only a couple of feet from me. His brow was furrowed. "Let's go back inside," he said, and I shook my head.

"I think we should probably just go." I held on to Trixie's collar so she couldn't take off again. "I'm sorry. I don't think this is going to work for me."

"What isn't going to work? Dinner?"

I shook my head. "I'm sorry," I said again. I didn't know what to do or what to say. All I knew was I needed to leave. I needed to be back in my house.

"It's freezing out here," Evan said. He put his arm around my shoulders, and to my surprise, I didn't push him away. I let him lead us back to his deck and into the house, mostly because I wasn't sure I was in any shape to drive. Scout and Trixie wiggled around in the kitchen like they'd been apart for years. Evan removed our jackets and led me to the living room, where he sat me down on the couch. He pushed a blanket toward me, then turned to the fireplace, pressed a button on a remote control, and it roared to life. I stared at the clutter on his coffee table, feeling numb, as Evan grabbed a few old towels from his linen closet and dried off Trixie's fur. When he was finished, apparently exhausted by their outing, Trixie and Scout both lay down on the enormous dog bed in front of the fire, and Evan came over to sit by me.

He was quiet a moment, then finally spoke. "Can you tell me what happened out there?" When I didn't answer, when I simply pulled the warm blanket up under my chin, he sighed. "Are you mad at me? Do you think it's my fault that she ran off?"

This got my attention. "No," I said. "Of course not. It's just . . . it's me."

"What's you?" His voice was so gentle, so kind, it made me want to weep.

"I don't know how to explain it," I said, keeping my tone low and controlled. "I don't . . . I haven't talked about it with anyone. Ever." *Am I really going to do this? Am I going to tell him about my past?*

"You can talk to me," he said. "Maybe it would help."

I finally looked at him. His dark blond hair was slightly wavy and grew just over his ears; he needed a haircut. "I don't know if I can," I said.

"Try," he answered, and so along with my heart, I opened my mouth, and told him everything I'd done wrong. I told him about Michael, about my first pregnancy, how my mother pushed us away. I told him about living in my car, begging for money; about getting pregnant with Natalie and everything that came after the night I was arrested at the grocery store.

When it came to describing the decision I'd made about giving up custody of my girls, my voice took on a slightly robotic tone, as though a computer were dictating the details of the experience to Evan instead of me. I used the same tone to tell him the rest of my story, how I ended up back in prison, about the little girl in the park and how sure I'd been she was my older daughter. I explained how Randy took me under his wing and how Trixie basically saved my life when Blake beat me. I told him how I kept my life simple now, as a way to keep myself safe. I told him that when Trixie had disappeared tonight, I'd felt like I did the last day I'd seen my daughters—like my edges had worked loose and I was about to come undone.

Evan didn't say a word while I spoke. He didn't interrupt, he didn't ask questions. He kept his eyes on me the entire time. His face simply held an expression of concern, of interest in what I had to say. When I finally quieted, we both sat in silence for a few moments, and I waited for him to tell me that I should leave and not come back. That I clearly had issues I needed to deal with.

Instead, he reached out to pull down the blanket I'd tucked around me so he could hold my hand. "I'm so sorry," he said.

"For what?" I asked. The words came out strangled. *Sorry he met me? Sorry this wasn't going to work?*

"For everything you've been through," he said. He reached up with his free hand and cradled the side of my face. His skin was warm and callused, but I found myself closing my eyes and pushing my cheek into his palm.

"Quick," I said. "Tell me something horrible about yourself."
I was only half-joking; part of me really wanted to know Evan's ugliest mistake—that he, too, knew what it was to feel a brutal sense of shame.

He dropped his hand and sighed. "Well," he said, "I cheated on my ex-wife." He waited a moment. "With her best friend."

"Lots of people cheat," I said, thinking that his one transgression didn't even come close to matching all the things I'd done wrong.

"Yeah," he said. "But that doesn't make it any less shitty. I hate being that guy . . . the cheating asshole cliché. If I could go back and change it, I would. But since I can't, I had to learn to be okay with the fact that I fucked up, because at some point, everyone does. I think the key is to learn from what you've done wrong, and try to do better." He locked his eyes on mine. "Which it sounds like you've done. You've had to be so strong."

"I'm not strong," I whispered. "I'm a mess."

He didn't say anything. Instead, he leaned in toward me and put his lips on my own, kissing me until my entire body warmed and finally relaxed. When he stopped, he rested his forehead against mine. "Weren't you listening?" he asked, glancing toward the coffee table. "Messy is kind of my thing."

We were married seven months later, in late September, at Randy's house. It was a small ceremony, with only the clinic's employees and Evan's coworkers in attendance. I wore a fitted, simple white sheath and held a bouquet of pale pink roses, and Evan had on a pair of black slacks and a button-down that matched the flowers. Trixie and Scout sat next to us as we stood in front of the fireplace, and we laughingly referred to my girl as the mutt of honor and Scout as Evan's best dog. Randy and Lisa served as our witnesses. During the reception, as soon as the music started and after Evan and I had our first dance, Randy approached and asked if he could have the pleasure of the second.

"You've come such a long way," he said as we moved across their enormous deck. One end was covered in four round tables where people were eating and the other was empty to leave room to dance. It was a gorgeous, sunny fall day—the sky was a striking shade of blue and there wasn't a cloud in the sky. The trees that lined Randy and Lisa's backyard were a wild mix of gold, red, and green—a treasure trove of jewel tones. "It's been a pleasure to watch you come into your own."

"Stop it," I said. "You're going to ruin my makeup." I looked over to where Evan stood holding a beer as he chatted with a few friends from work. His smile was wide and his eyes were filled with the kind of love I still couldn't believe was meant for me.

Since that night when Trixie had run off, when I opened my soul to Evan and let all the pain in my life bleed out in front of him, I'd grown to feel lighter, more capable of moving around in the world without fearing I was, at any moment, about to fall apart. Evan saw who I was—he saw everything about me, good and bad—and loved me, still. And I saw everything about him. Because he understood what I'd gone through in letting go of my girls, knowing it would be too agonizing for me to revisit that loss as I would if I had another baby, it was easier for him to confess that he'd never really wanted children of his own. Like me, he was content with his work, happy to lavish his affections upon his dog, and now, me. Before I'd moved in with him in June, he had a huge parcel of the land around the house fenced in so I'd never have to worry about Trixie disappearing. Neither one of us was perfect, but we seemed to be perfect for each other.

"You picked a good one," Randy said, watching this silent, loving moment transpire between Evan and me. "We're so happy for you."

"Thank you," I said, standing up on my tiptoes so I could kiss his pink cheek. "For everything. I wouldn't be here without you."

"Aw, I just gave you a nudge in the right direction. You're the one who's done all the work." He paused, looking pensive. "As a matter of fact, I've been thinking—"

"Uh-oh," I said, fondly.

"No," he said, laughing. "This is actually one of my better ideas. Now that you've got your bachelor's, I think you should consider getting your doctorate. You already have more than enough undergraduate work credit hours. Someday Lisa's going to make me retire, and I'm going to want to sell my practice to someone I trust."

"Are you serious?" I'd been toying with the idea of going back to school to become an actual, accredited veterinary doctor instead of just a trainer and technician, but wasn't sure if I could handle the intense course work on top of having to work full-time. I also wasn't sure I could afford the tuition. But now that Evan and I were sharing expenses, it was possible I could make it happen.

"Of course," Randy said, spinning me around, "I can't think of anyone better suited for the job."

We continued to dance then, both of us quiet, as I considered how lucky I was that Myer had chosen me to meet with Randy in the prison's community room those many years before. Maybe I could learn to be okay without knowing what happened to my girls. I could continue writing them letters, even knowing they would never be read. Brooke and Natalie were the only people missing from this special day, and I couldn't help but feel an all-too familiar ache in my chest when I thought about them.

But then it struck me that if I hadn't let go of my children, I might not have the life I had now. I might not have found Evan. Maybe that decision, however heart-wrenching, was meant to be made. To shift the course of my life and put me right here, exactly where I belonged.

Brooke

After telling her sister about her pregnancy, Brooke left Natalie's house around nine thirty. Once home, she slept better than she had in weeks, and she couldn't help but correlate this with the fact that she'd been so honest with her sister about what she was going through. The only real hitch in the evening came from Kyle. From his behavior at dinner, Brooke suspected that he had concerns about inviting her into his family's life, which bothered her a little, although she was happy that Natalie had chosen a man who wanted to keep her safe. Brooke hoped that with a little time, he'd learn to trust her and she would learn to relax more around him.

The following week, Brooke arrived at her sister's house again, just before noon on Wednesday, thinking that they would eat and then head out for her appointment, which was at one thirty. She felt better knowing that her sister would be there with her, if only to sit quietly as Brooke listened to whatever the doctor might have to say. But when Natalie answered the door, she wore bright red oven mitts and a red-and-white polka-dot apron covered in flour.

"Did I get the time wrong?" Brooke asked as she took in the

rest of Natalie's appearance—there were smudges of chocolate on her face and in her hair, accompanied by a slightly manic look in her eyes. The air coming from the house was scented with yeast and toasted sugar.

"Not at all," Natalie said, gesturing for Brooke to enter. "I just screwed up the date on an order I took last month. I thought the party was next Thursday, but it's actually tonight. Desserts for a hundred. I'm swamped."

Brooke clutched her purse to her side. "Oh no," she said. "You should have called me. You don't have to come with me to the appointment."

"Of course I'm coming," Natalie said. "An extra set of hands is exactly what I need." She grabbed Brooke's purse and set it on the entry table. "Come on in."

"You want me to help?" Brooke said, hesitant. "Are you sure?"

"Absolutely," Natalie said. "Don't worry. I'll tell you what to do. And we'll be out of here in plenty of time to get to the clinic. I made sandwiches, if you want to eat. I've been sampling desserts all morning, so I'm already stuffed."

"I'm okay, too," Brooke said. She'd eaten a big breakfast, and wasn't hungry. She followed Natalie into the kitchen, where the counters were cluttered with bowls dripping chocolate batter down their sides, and piles of silver pans in the sink. The stainless-steel baker's rack against the wall near the back door was stacked with various kinds of miniature pastries—some had spun sugar on the top and others were covered in a shiny and thick chocolate glaze.

"It's not as bad as it looks, I promise," Natalie said. "Crazy is totally part of my process." She grinned and handed Brooke an apron. "Here. So you don't mess up your clothes."

Brooke wasn't wearing anything fancy—black leggings and a loose olive-green sweater—but she complied anyway, then washed her hands with hot water and soap. "I can see why you need to expand your work space," she said. She peeked out the kitchen window above the sink and noted that the lights were on in the garage. She could see the contractor's silver head through one of the building's windows. "How's it going?"

Natalie sighed as she stirred something on the stove. "I found out this morning that we're having a plumbing issue. Alex—that's my contractor—says his guy can't get to it until next week. Which means they can't finish the Sheetrock or painting this week, like he said they could."

Brooke almost offered to call Ryan and see if he could spare one of his plumbers to help, but she didn't want him to think that she was changing her mind about his offer of support for her baby. And the truth was, with the way things were between them, she wasn't sure he would do her that kind of favor. "I'm sorry," she said. "That sucks."

"Ah, well," Natalie said. "Par for the course with a project like this, I suppose." She nodded toward the white KitchenAid mixer on the counter. "If you could start that up on low, and then add twelve eggs, one at a time, letting each of them incorporate into the butter and sugar before adding the next, that would be great."

"Got it," Brooke said as she took a step over to the mixer, opened the gray cardboard carton labeled "organic farm-fresh eggs," and began to carry out Natalie's instructions.

"Are you nervous about the test?" Natalie asked over the loud whir of the machine.

"A little," Brooke admitted. "I just want everything to be okay. But the receptionist told me that I'll be able to find out the sex, too."

"Do you want to?" Natalie asked as she poured what looked to be molten caramel from a pan into a baking sheet. Brooke watched as she used a rubber spatula to expertly spread the hot substance around until it was smooth.

"Did you?" Brooke added the eighth egg, careful not to allow any shell to land in the batter. She couldn't believe how natural it felt to be with Natalie, working together in the kitchen, chatting as they did. It felt like they already knew each other, as though they hadn't been apart all those years. *Maybe this isn't the start of a new relationship,* she thought. *Maybe it's the remembering of the one we already had.*

"Absolutely," Natalie said with a grin. "I'm way too much of a control freak to have let it be a surprise. I needed to plan, especially with Hailey, since she was my first. To shop for clothes and paint the nursery. And once we knew, I read everything I could on how to be a good parent."

"Did that help with your nerves?" Brooke asked. Her self-doubt was a tiny, yipping dog inside her mind; she'd yet to find a way to fully silence it.

"A little," Natalie said. "But then she came out and I was terrified all over again that I'd screw her up."

"But you didn't," Brooke said. "She seems like a great kid. Henry, too."

"I hope so," Natalie said. "Time will tell, I suppose. If I've learned anything, it's that kids seem to be who they'll grow up to be pretty early in life. At least on a basic level. I think Kyle and I have helped teach them how to make good choices between what's right and what's wrong, but their personalities have been with them from the get-go."

Brooke thought about this as she finished adding the last egg, and when it was incorporated, she turned off the mixer.

"Sandwiches are in the fridge," Natalie said, "if you decide that you want one." But Brooke felt a wave of nausea rush over her, and whether it was due to her nerves or the baby, she didn't think she should eat. A rap on the back door interrupted her thoughts, and Natalie went to answer it.

An older man, whom Brooke assumed was the Alex that Natalie had mentioned, stepped into the mudroom and carefully wiped his feet on the doormat. He wore dark brown work boots, loose denim overalls, and a green plaid, flannel jacket.

"Hey," he said, lifting a hand in greeting at Brooke, who nodded in return.

"What's up?" Natalie asked.

"I just wanted to check and see what would be a good time for us to turn off the water so we can get some pipe work done in prep for the plumber." He glanced at the mess scattered across the room, the dirty dishes piled in the sink. "I'm guessing it isn't now."

Natalie laughed. "Why would you say that?"

"Just a hunch," Alex said, drily. "It looks like sugar Armageddon in here."

"Like Sara Lee exploded," Brooke added, and Natalie laughed. She grabbed a brown bag from the countertop, next to the toaster. "Here," she said, handing it to the man. "A little something for you and the crew. Do you have coffee out there? If not, I can make some."

She's a generous person, Brooke thought. *She has a good heart.* Brooke wondered if she had been adopted, like Natalie, raised in a family that loved her, would she be less guarded? Would she offer baked goods to mere acquaintances and invite her estranged sister into her life without so much as a hint of hesitation? There was no way for her to know.

"We're all set," the contractor said, taking the bag from her. "Thanks." He paused. "You should be careful, feeding us like this. We might start slowing down the work just so we can stick around longer." He winked, and then he was gone.

"Okay," Natalie said. "You can add the flour to the batter—it's right there, premeasured in the white plastic tub—then pour it into those pans." She nodded in the direction of four sheet pans on the center of the island, which looked as though they'd already been greased with butter and sprinkled with sugar.

"What is it I'm pouring?" Brooke asked.

"Almond sponge cake. They'll bake quickly, and I can finish them when I get back. Then the order will be ready to go for tonight."

"Are you sure you have time to go?" Brooke asked again, not wanting to inconvenience her sister. Accepting Natalie's offer to attend the appointment had felt uncomfortable, like Brooke was squeezing into a pair of someone else's too-small shoes, but it had been too enticing to resist.

"I'm sure," Natalie said, in a firm tone.

Thirty minutes later, the cakes were baked and cooling on the racks, and Natalie and Brooke were in Brooke's car, headed downtown. "It's surreal to be together like this," Brooke asked. "Don't you think? After so many years?"

"Sure," Natalie said. "But it's kind of comfortable in a way, too." She looked at Brooke and smiled. "Is that weird?"

"Not at all." Brooke was happy that her sister seemed to feel the same sense of connection as Brooke had earlier, in Natalie's kitchen.

"Well," Natalie said. "When the new space is finished, I may actually need to hire a second pair of hands. At least, I hope I'll be busy enough to need that. I could train you on how to do all my prep work."

"I don't know," Brooke said. "I actually have an interview next week for a new waitressing job." She had spent the last week scouring the ads on Craigslist, applying to as many as she could. Of the many applications she'd filled out, she had received only one call, from a large seafood restaurant on Lake Union, which had advertised for a full-time, fine-dining server. Brooke had left her positions at Applebee's off her résumé; she also slightly exaggerated how much experience she had with higher-end dining experiences. She hoped her knowledge of good wines would help her land the job at the upcoming interview.

Natalie cocked her head to one side. "You're not happy at the bar?"

"It's fine," Brooke said. "I'd just like to work somewhere that's a little more upscale. And that has a better health insurance plan than the one I'm on."

"Ah," Natalie said. "You know, I think there are programs the state offers for new mothers—"

"I'm not taking anything from the state," Brooke said, with a sharp snap behind the words.

"Oh," Natalie said, blinking fast. "Okay."

The two stood in uncomfortable silence for a moment until Brooke finally spoke. "Sorry," she said. "It's just . . . I just can't let my child feel like I did growing up."

"How did you feel?" Natalie asked in a quiet voice.

"Less than," Brooke said, and she felt the muscles in her throat grow thick. She still wasn't accustomed to talking about her past, let alone her feelings about it. She wondered if there'd ever be a time that she could and not end up on the verge of tears.

"I'm sorry," Natalie said. "I wasn't thinking."

"You don't need to apologize," Brooke said. "It's not your fault." And then she looked at Natalie, both women knowing exactly who Brooke did blame for her fractured childhood. The mother Brooke despised, and Natalie still wanted to find.

"That wasn't so bad, was it?" Dr. Travers said, after the amnio was over. Brooke sat on the edge of the exam table with a thin white blanket gathered over her legs, a little freaked out that the tip of a long needle had just punctured her stomach and been so close to her baby. But the test had been painless, and was done in less than a minute.

Natalie sat on the chair in the corner, near where Brooke's head had just been on the pillow. Her younger sister had offered to stay in the waiting room, but Brooke had asked her to come with her. The doctor was a tall, younger woman with pixie-cut brown hair and dark blue eyes. She wore black slacks and a red blouse beneath her white coat. "Your weight's perfect, and so is your blood pressure."

Brooke released an internal sigh of relief. "Are you going to do an ultrasound today?"

"We normally wouldn't," Dr. Travers said. "Your insurance plan only covers so many."

"Oh," Brooke said. "The receptionist mentioned something about being able to find out the sex."

"You can when we get the results of the amnio, which will be in about a week," the doctor said. "Until then, just keep up whatever you've been doing. Get as much sleep as you can, take your prenatal vitamins, and eat well. No raw eggs, undercooked meat, shellfish, or soft cheese, like Brie or Roquefort. Walking is the best exercise."

"I'm a waitress, so that's not a problem," Brooke said. Her job had kept her physically active enough over the years that she'd never even considered joining a gym.

"Perfect," Dr. Travers said. "But be careful lifting anything too heavy. I can write a note for your employer, if you want."

"That's okay," Brooke said, hoping that after her interview with the seafood restaurant, she would have a new place to work.

"Okay, then," Dr. Travers said. "I'll see you in a month." She paused, and then, as though sensing that Brooke needed it, gave Brooke's hand a reassuring squeeze. "Don't worry. You're going to be a great mom."

"She's going to be the best," Natalie agreed, and with her sister's comment, despite all the insecurities that plagued her, something ancient and broken inside of Brooke—something that believed she would be lonely for the rest of her life—stitched back together and she saw herself in a totally different light.

Natalie

Brooke dropped Natalie back at the house a little after three, leaving Natalie more than enough time to finish her dessert order for the party she was catering that night. Katie had asked Henry to come over after school to play with Logan again, and when Natalie realized that she'd gotten the date of the party wrong, she called Ruby's mom and asked if Hailey could play there for a few hours, too. Both women had offered to bring her kids home around six, and Natalie promised herself that she would make it up to them with a box full of decadent treats, as well as at least one date set on the calendar when Natalie would take care of their children. She thought about something she'd often told Hailey and Henry: "You have to be a good friend to have one," and Natalie needed to make sure she practiced what she preached.

"Thanks again for coming with me," Brooke said just as Natalie opened the car door. "It meant a lot."

"Any time," Natalie said, warmly. "Talk to you soon?" Brooke nodded, and Natalie climbed out of the car with a smile on her face. Having a sister was like having a safety net, she thought. It was being one for her, too.

Once inside, Natalie got busy in the kitchen, cutting out perfectly round circles from the sheet pan of sponge cake Brooke had helped mix, topping each of them with a smooth, quarter-inch cylinder of honey caramel and a sprinkle of fleur de sel. Then, she set up twenty boxes on the table with the lids open, and as she began placing individual cakes into them, she thought about Kyle, and the brief spat in the living room before Brooke had reentered the house the previous week. He'd already been asleep when Natalie came to bed that night—or at least he had been pretending to be asleep. The next morning, he left for the office before she woke up. Usually, if he took off that early, he would leave her a note on the dry-erase board that hung in the kitchen, telling her that he loved her or simply to have a good day, but when she went to get her morning coffee that day, the board was blank. They'd spent the last seven days making polite, efficient conversation, each busy enough with work and managing the kids that they didn't acknowledge the tension simmering between them. Natalie wanted to—she knew they needed to—talk, but she dreaded the idea of having the exact same conversation that they'd had before she'd even met Brooke. Her husband was just being cautious, but she felt like he kept applying the pessimistic-lawyer side of his brain to the situation instead of the supportive-husband side she needed from him. Whatever the case, the way he'd spoken to her sister at dinner needed to be addressed. Hoping that they could discuss the issue rationally, she turned around and walked over to the baker's racks by the back door, bringing back a sheet pan full of chocolate mousse tortes layered with hazelnut praline, which she carefully transferred to the remaining boxes.

Twenty minutes later, all of the desserts had been loaded into the back of Natalie's car, and since she didn't need to be at the venue for another hour, she decided to double-check her orders for the upcoming month so she wouldn't have to deal with another event date mix-up. She sat down at the kitchen table with her laptop and booted it up, clicking on the scheduling program she used to keep track of orders as they came in, along with an ongoing list of the supplies she needed.

After verifying that everything was set up correctly and her mistake today was a singular occurrence, Natalie decided to open a search engine. She hadn't mentioned looking for her birth mother earlier in the day with Brooke, and her sister hadn't brought it up, either. Natalie understood Brooke's reason for not wanting to find her, but that hadn't stopped Natalie from digging around on Facebook and other social media sites for women named Jennifer Walker. It hadn't stopped her from registering on several people search websites and a few more online adoption registries, entering as much information into them about herself and her birth mother as she could.

It turned out that Jennifer Walker was an exceedingly common name, and one that Natalie couldn't be sure her birth mother still went by. She could have gotten married; she could have moved anywhere in the world. *She could be dead,* Natalie realized, and the thought sent a shiver up her spine. Poising her fingers over the keyboard, Natalie tried to think of what she could search for next.

And then, not for the first time, she wondered if her parents knew more about her birth mother than what they'd given her in the file. She'd read those pages again and again, searching for some detail, some tiny clue, that she might have missed. There was nothing.

Frustrated, Natalie slammed her laptop shut. She didn't have time for this. She needed to deliver the dessert order. Grabbing her coat and purse, she headed out the door and got into her car, driving toward the Sanctuary at Admiral, where the party was being held. Once she'd unloaded all of the boxes and carried them into the facility's kitchen, she left, and intended to head home, but instead, she found herself driving in the direction of her parents' house. Using the speaker function on her phone, she gave her mom a quick call to make sure it was all right for her to stop by.

"Of course," her mom said. "I'm just getting the auction items ready for the shelter's fund-raiser." One of her mother's charity projects was a local homeless shelter, for which she organized a yearly silent auction right before the winter holidays.

"Great," Natalie said. "See you in a few." At the next stoplight, she sent a text to Kyle, asking him what time he would be home, since that would affect how long she could visit her mom. His reply came quickly: "On my way now."

"Kids should both be home by six. Playdates. Taco makings in the fridge. Going to my parents'."

"OK," he replied, and Natalie set her phone back in her purse, waving as the car behind her honked. The light had already turned green.

Her mother's car was parked in the driveway when Natalie pulled up, but her father's was gone. Likely he was still at work or out to dinner with clients. Natalie shut down her car's engine and made her way to the front door, which her mother opened before Natalie had even knocked.

"Hi," Natalie said, and her mother stepped to the side so Natalie could enter.

"Want something to drink?" her mom asked.

"No, thanks," Natalie said. "I'm good." She followed her mother into the family room, and they sat down on opposite ends of the couch.

"How are things going with Brooke?" Her mother smiled, but the muscles beneath the skin of her face twitched, giving away how much effort the question had demanded of her.

"I like her," Natalie said, trying to choose her words carefully so as not to hurt her mother. "She met Kyle and the kids last week." She considered telling her mother that Brooke was pregnant but then decided against it, not knowing if Brooke would be okay with her talking about it with someone she had yet to meet.

"How was that?"

"Good, for the most part. A little awkward here and there,

which I guess is to be expected." Natalie didn't think her mother needed to hear about Kyle's reservations about Brooke; that was between her and her husband.

Instead, Natalie chose to dive right into why she'd come. "I have to say, Mom, spending time with Brooke is making me think a lot more about my adoption. I just feel like there's something else I need to know. Something you and Dad aren't telling me." Her mother's eyelids fluttered, and she looked away, which convinced Natalie she was on the right track. She pressed on. "Do you know more about my birth mother than you've told me? Do you have more information than that file hidden away somewhere?"

Her mother held a closed fist to her mouth and shook her head, keeping her eyes on the floor.

Natalie fell back against the cushion. "Then what is it? Why are you so against me finding her?" Her mother finally looked up at Natalie, with tears in her eyes. Natalie's frustration softened. "I know you lost a baby before you adopted me," she said. "I know it took away your ability to have a child of your own. I can't even imagine how hard that was for you and Dad to go through. But I've told you a thousand times you're not going to lose me. I'm your daughter. I love you. I love Dad. I just want to know more about the woman who gave me up. Is that so difficult to understand?"

Her mother sniffled, and Natalie reached for a tissue from the box on the coffee table. She handed it to her mother, who took it and dabbed at the corners of her eyes. "I didn't lose just one baby," she said. Her voice was barely above a whisper.

"What?" Natalie gasped. "Oh, Mom—" she said, but her mother cut her off by holding up her hand.

"It wasn't another miscarriage," she said, "if that's what you're thinking." She looked out the window, and then back at Natalie. "It was a year after my hysterectomy, when your father and I first decided to adopt. The agency connected us to a young girl who was seven months along. Back then, most adoptions were closed, but this girl wanted to meet us. We were so anxious to have a child, we did what she asked."

Natalie couldn't believe what she was hearing. How many other secrets had her parents kept from her over the years? She swallowed back the swell of emotion that filled her chest and managed to stay silent, anxious to listen to the rest of the story.

Her mother crossed her long legs, then grabbed a throw pillow, holding it in her lap. "She was eighteen," she said. "And so confident that giving her baby to us was the right thing to do. She wanted to go to college. She wanted to have her own life before being responsible for someone else." She stared out the window again, as though she were watching her memories play out against the dark night sky. "We did everything for her. We paid her medical bills. We gave her money for groceries and maternity clothes. She still lived with her parents, and they seemed so happy to know we were going to be the recipients of their grandchild. We talked about the pictures I'd send them every Christmas. I promised that when our baby was old enough, I would make sure to tell her that she was loved by her birth family, and that she could reach out to them if she wanted to, when she turned eighteen. We did everything right."

Natalie realized she was holding her breath, spellbound as she traveled with her mother into the past. She both dreaded and desired to find out what happened next.

"We were there for the birth," her mother continued, in a detached voice, as though she were describing some dry, mechanical procedure. "She wanted us there, in the room, with her. We stood on either side of her, holding her up, helping her push our baby girl into the world. And when the doctor cut the cord and the nurse started to hand her the baby, she motioned that I should be the first to hold her." She paused, and her chin trembled before she went on. "I'll never forget that moment, Natalie, when I held that child in my arms. I felt like everything I ever wanted was wrapped up in that thin, pink blanket. I knew this little girl was meant to be mine. We all cried, and before we went home, your father and I thanked the birth mother over and over again. She said she wanted to sleep, and our baby girl went to the nursery for the night." Natalie's mom finally looked at Natalie again, her eyes brimming with shiny tears. "Our attorney called us at five in the morning to tell us she'd changed her mind. She wanted to keep the baby. The adoption paperwork hadn't been finalized by the court, so there was nothing we could do. The law was on her side. It was over. We never saw either of them again."

Natalie got up and moved to sit back down next to her mother. "Oh, god, Mom. I'm so sorry. I had no idea . . . I can't imagine."

Her mother nodded her head, once, pressing her lips together.

Natalie removed the pillow from her mother's lap and took her ice-cold hand into her own. So much made sense now. Her mother's reticence about anything related to her birth mom, why she hadn't told Natalie about Brooke. Any piece of the truth she might have relinquished must have seemed like a threat, something that could steal Natalie away. In her mind, her mother did the only thing she could think of to keep from experiencing another devastating loss. She closed the door to the past and never opened it again.

"What was her name?" Natalie asked.

"The mother's?"

"No. The baby's."

"Oh," her mom whispered. "We called her Ashley. Ashley Rose."

And then Natalie felt tears fill her own eyes. Her middle name was Rose, too.

"The whole experience," her mother said, "losing Ashley like that, was the reason why after we found you, your father and I decided we wouldn't adopt again. We were too afraid of going through another painful disappointment. And I was terrified if we had adopted Brooke along with you, your birth mother would be more likely to come along and take you both away from us. I guess I thought if she still had the chance to get your sister back, she'd leave you for us to keep." She let loose a strangled laugh. "Which is completely irrational, I realize, but at the time, it was how I felt. It made sense. All I thought about was protecting you. It's all I can think about now."

Natalie nodded. "I understand, Mom. Thank you for telling me this. For trusting me with it." She squeezed her mother's hand and leaned over to give her a hug.

"I love you so much, Natalie," her mother whispered in her ear. "I'm so sorry if I've hurt you. I never meant . . ."

Natalie pulled away before her mom could continue and used a thumb to wipe away her mother's tears. "It's okay. I love you, too. And I get why you made the decisions you did. But please, you have to know that no one can take me away from you. I'm not going to love you and Dad any less with Brooke in my life. If I meet my birth mother, there's nothing she could say or do to change the fact that you are my mother. I'm not going anywhere with anyone. You couldn't get rid of me if you tried."

Her mother smiled then. "Thank you, honey." She paused. "I wish I did know more about your birth mother, but I don't." She gave Natalie a thoughtful look. "Does Brooke? Has she ever tried to find her?"

"Other than putting her information on the adoption registry that helped me find her, no."

"Did the background check Kyle ran on Brooke tell you anything?"

Natalie froze, staring at her mother in disbelief. "The *what*?"

"Oh," her mom said. Her cheeks flushed and she began blinking fast. "I thought you knew."

"He ran a background check on Brooke?" Natalie said. She clenched her jaw, seething at the thought of what Kyle had done without her knowledge. "When? And how did you know about it?"

"Your father mentioned it," she said. "I'm sure Kyle meant to tell you, honey. Maybe he was just waiting for the results."

"I doubt that," Natalie said. She stood up. "Sorry, Mom, but I need to go."

Her mother stood as well. "Honey, wait. Maybe you should try and calm down first."

"I'll be fine." Natalie kissed her mother on the cheek and walked out the door. She drove home as quickly as she could, gripping the wheel hard enough to turn her knuckles white. How could he do this without telling her? He didn't trust her judgment. He lied to her.

Once she parked in the driveway, Natalie grabbed her purse and headed inside, her arms swinging at her sides. "Mommy!" Henry said, leaping off the couch and racing toward her. He threw himself against her legs and locked on with all four of his limbs.

"Not now, sweetie," Natalie said, bending down to extricate her son's grip. "Where's your dad?"

"We're in the kitchen, Mommy!" Hailey called out. "Guess what? Daddy's trying to cook!"

"Very bad, those smells," Henry said solemnly. He and Natalie walked into the kitchen, where Hailey sat on one of the barstools at the center island with a black olive on the tip of each of her fingers on one hand. She wiggled her fingers at Natalie, who wiggled hers in return. Kyle stood by the stove, stirring something in a pot. An acrid scent filled the air, evidence of something recently burned.

"Hey," Kyle said. "I thought instead of tacos, we'd make homemade pizza, but the cheese on the first one oozed all over the oven and burned." He grimaced. "I cleaned it up, but it still stinks. Sorry."

"That's okay," Natalie said tightly, not wanting to start an argument in front of the kids. "The taco stuff is already done. Let's just have those." She looked at their children. "Why don't you two go wash your hands in the bathroom?"

"We can do it here," Hailey said, jumping down from her seat.

"No," Natalie said. "Mommy needs to talk to Daddy for a minute. In private." The kids waited a moment, and then, seeing that their mother wasn't smiling, left the kitchen and went down the hall to the bathroom.

"What's wrong?" Kyle asked, letting go of the spoon he held and taking a couple of steps toward her.

She gave him a look that stopped him in his tracks. "I know about the background check. My mother told me, accidentally, assuming that you already had."

"Nat, let me explain . . ."

"Not now," she snapped. "Let's just get through dinner and get the kids to bed."

For the next two hours, Natalie spoke politely to her husband, pretending for her children's sake that everything was normal. Once the kitchen had been cleaned up and the kids were bathed and tucked in, Natalie and Kyle returned downstairs, where they stood together in the kitchen, the corner of the house farthest from the kids' rooms. Natalie didn't want them to hear their parents fight.

"Before you say anything," Kyle began, "I want you to know that I was going to tell you about running the report. I just wanted to get the results first."

"And you thought that was a good idea," Natalie said. Her jaw ached from gritting her teeth. "You seriously thought going behind my back was okay?"

"I didn't think about it as going behind your back," he said. "I just thought I'd do the check, and if anything weird came up, I would talk with you about it then."

"It seems more likely that what you were really thinking was that if nothing 'weird' came up you wouldn't *have* to tell me what you did." She paused, watching as Kyle let her statement sink in. "Right?"

He stared at her, unblinking, for a good half minute before speaking. "Fine," he said. "I decided to run the report and not say anything because I knew you'd be pissed. I did it to protect you."

"You lied to me!" Natalie said, trying not to raise her voice, but failing. "After everything we talked about, how important you *knew* finding her was to me . . . after you promised not to judge her—"

"I wasn't judging her!" Kyle said. His light brown eyes clouded with anger. "I was trying to keep you safe! I was looking out for our family. You were so blinded by your excitement—"

"Excuse me, blinded?" Natalie glared at him, her cheeks flushed, her fingernails digging into her palms.

"Yes, blinded. All you could think about was how wonderful it was that you found her. That you finally had the sister you always wanted. I understood that . . . I was even happy for you . . . but you weren't exactly thinking straight. I was just trying to stay rational."

"Because I'm so emotionally driven, I'm incapable of logic? Nice to know you have so much faith in me. Just because I'm not a lawyer anymore doesn't mean I can't think like one, Kyle. You really believe that if there had been any real sign that Brooke was dangerous, I'd ignore it and let her near our children?"

"Of course not! But what if you couldn't see the signs? What if she was good at hiding them? What if there were things in her past she wasn't being honest about? You just took her at her word!" He dropped into one of the kitchen chairs, put his elbows on the table, and tented his fingers on both hands against his forehead. His brown hair was shaggy, growing over the tops of his ears and an inch past his shirt collar. *He needs a haircut,* Natalie thought, and for some reason, noticing this took a slight edge off the anger she felt. They took care of each other. Maybe in running the background check, he had been trying to take care of her and just went about it the wrong way.

"I'm sorry," Kyle said. He dropped his hands to the table, pressing them flat against the wood, staring at her with tenderness. "Okay? There wasn't anything in the report of concern, so I decided you didn't need to know what I'd done. I'm sorry that

I hid what I was doing, but as with everything else in this situation, I meant well. I had your best interests in mind. Our family's best interests. What if it had come back and said that she was a criminal? A con artist or convicted child molester? Would you be okay with the fact that I ran the report without telling you then?"

The question threw Natalie off, softening her anger even more, because Kyle was right. If the report had shown that Brooke was a danger to their family, Natalie knew it wouldn't matter how that information had come to their attention. The only thing that would matter was that Kyle meant to keep them safe.

"Is that why you were late the night we had dinner?" she said, instead of answering his questions. "When you specifically promised me you wouldn't be? Were you waiting for the results?"

Kyle shook his head. "I told you, I got called into a meeting with the DA. You know how it goes. I couldn't leave. I'm sorry, but I swear I didn't do it on purpose. I knew how important the dinner was. Do you really think I chose to be late when I knew how much it would piss you off?"

Natalie hesitated. "No," she admitted. She couldn't think of a time that Kyle had purposely done something he knew would hurt her. That's why it had bothered her so much when she thought he had.

"I'm sorry for how I talked with Brooke," he said. "I honestly didn't realize how I was coming across. She just seemed so guarded, which you know, in my job, usually means someone's hiding something. My defense lawyer senses were tingling."

"She seemed guarded because she was nervous. I told you she doesn't open up easily. And now that I know she's pregnant, it makes even more sense. She's scared, and until now, she's been totally on her own. She needs support, and I'm going to give it to her. I even went to a doctor's appointment with her this afternoon."

"How'd that go?"

"Fine," she said. "But you remember how scared I was when

I got pregnant with Hailey. Just imagine her feeling all of that and not having anyone to talk to. No support. Trying to cope with the idea of having to raise a child completely on her own."

"Yeah, you went a little bit nuts for a while there," he said, clearly teasing. She looked at him from under raised brows, wishing he would stop trying to make light of the situation. He held up his hands in an I-surrender gesture. "I hear what you're saying, Nat. Okay? I promise, I'll do better."

"Can I see it?" Natalie asked. "Do you have it here?" The anger she felt had deflated just as quickly as it had inflamed earlier, sitting on her mother's couch. She tried to focus on her husband's motivation instead of the fact that he'd kept what he was doing from her.

"The report?" Kyle asked, and she nodded. He got up from the table and walked into the living room, returning with a thin folder, which he handed to her. "It came back a couple of days after she came for dinner."

"Thank you," Natalie said quietly. She felt his eyes on her as she sat on one of the stools next to the island and pulled out the few pages in the folder, scanning them. While the background check showed that Brooke had worked for more than ten different employers and lived at eight different addresses since she turned eighteen, she had no criminal record, nor any civil judgments against her. She'd had four tickets for speeding, all of which she contested and had reduced, but paid on time. She'd never been married or filed for bankruptcy. Her record was clean.

"I understand why you did this," Natalie said slowly, as she set the papers down in front of her on the counter.

"I'm glad," Kyle said, with evident relief. He sat on the barstool next to her and put his hand on top of her leg.

"I understand," Natalie repeated, wanting to finish her point before she forgave him completely, "but I still think you should have told me. It's not healthy for us to keep this kind of thing from each other, no matter how pure our motivation might be."

She turned her upper body to face him and searched his face with her eyes. "Can we agree on that?"

"Yes," Kyle said, nodding. "I guess I told myself I was being practical when I really just didn't want you to be mad at me."

"And look how well that worked out," Natalie said, leaning over to rest her forehead against her husband's, the silent signal they'd used over the years to tell each other that everything was okay between them.

"No kidding." Kyle chuckled. He reached for her face, then ran the side of his thumb down her cheek. "I really am sorry, Nat. I've got your back, I promise. I'm here for you . . . for Brooke . . . however you need me to be."

Brooke

Brooke pulled into the parking lot of the Sea to Shore restaurant exactly fifteen minutes before her scheduled interview. After she turned off the engine, she checked her makeup in the rearview mirror, happy with what she saw. In the past week, since the amniocentesis, her skin had never looked better—she assumed this was the "pregnancy glow" she'd read about online. Her black curls were shiny and smooth, and her eyes were clear and bright. Her nausea had all but disappeared. Dr. Travers had called and told her that everything was fine with the baby—there were no discernible problems. But when she asked if Brooke wanted to know the baby's gender, for some reason, Brooke said no. She felt like it wasn't something she wanted to hear alone. Maybe Natalie would come with her to her next appointment, and they could find out the sex together.

Brooke locked her car and walked inside the building, which was right on the edge of Lake Union. It possessed a clean, minimalist décor: teakwood tables—all of which had a view of the sparkling blue lake—brown leather booths, and cream-colored votive candles everywhere she looked. It was three o'clock, two hours before the establishment opened for dinner, and Brooke saw several members of the waitstaff sitting at a table near the kitchen, folding napkins and organizing silverware in preparation for their shift. She'd checked the restaurant website for pictures of what the servers wore, and saw that their uniform was all black, different from the typical white top and black skirt/pants requirements of most places she had worked. She wore a black cardigan and matching skirt so the manager with whom she interviewed might more easily visualize her as part of the staff.

"May I help you?" a man who was standing at the host podium asked. He had blond, slicked-back, short hair and wore a dark blue shirt with a matching tie.

"Yes, thanks," Brooke said. "I'm Brooke Walker. I have an interview with Nick Hudson at three o'clock."

The man smiled and walked around the podium to shake her hand. "I'm Nick," he said. "Nice to meet you."

Brooke felt him appraise her outfit, and she was happy that she'd taken the time to dress appropriately for the interview. "You, too," she said, making sure to stand up straight and look him directly in the eye. Something about interviews made her feel like she was a teenager again, insecure and uncomfortable in her own skin. She reminded herself that she was almost forty years old, likely the same age as the man who was about to interview her. She could do this.

"This way," he said, so Brooke followed him through a maze of tables to a two-top. They both sat down, and Brooke crossed her legs, trying to appear as relaxed as possible. She needed this job. At seventeen weeks, her belly had begun to round, pushing out enough to make it impossible for her to zip up any of her jeans. She needed to get hired before her pregnancy really started to show and no one would want to take her. At a place like this, with an average plate cost of eighty dollars per customer, on any given night, she could make upward of four hundred dollars in tips. She could maybe even afford to move into a small rental house so her child, when he or she was old enough, could have a yard in which to play.

"So," Nick said, interrupting her thoughts. "Tell me a little more about yourself."

"Sure," Brooke said with a smile. She reached into her large bag and pulled out a copy of her résumé, having read on a job-seeker website that it was always a good idea to bring an extra so that the manager didn't have to search through a pile to find the copy you'd already submitted. She handed it to Nick, who glanced at it, then set it on the table within eyeshot. "Well," Brooke began, "I've been waiting tables for almost twenty years. I started as a dishwasher and hostess, but worked my way up." She went on to describe the various places she'd worked, and how much she wanted to move into a permanent position with a stable, well-respected, fine-dining restaurant. "Sea to Shore has the best reputation in Seattle as the go-to place for atmosphere and amazing, farm-fresh menus," she said, paraphrasing what she'd read online. "Your butterfish with a ginger glaze is considered one of the premier seafood dishes on the entire West Coast."

"You've done your homework," Nick said, and Brooke nodded, sensing he was impressed. He spent the next ten minutes asking her questions about wine pairings and different types of cocktails, and Brooke was certain she nailed each of them. He handed her the menu, which she'd already memorized off the restaurant's website, and she recited perfect descriptions of each and every item without having to look down.

When she'd finished, Nick grinned. "Okay," he said. "You're hired."

"Really?" Brooke asked, feeling her chest fill with a fluttering sensation.

"Are you kidding?" Nick said. "I don't think even my most seasoned employee can do what you just did. You're clearly experienced, and I like your enthusiasm." He held out his hand across the table, and Brooke gave it a good, strong shake. "When can you start?"

"Tonight?" Brooke said, with a happy laugh. "Actually, I need to give notice at my current job. I'd like to offer them two weeks, but I'm guessing that once they know I'm leaving, they'll take me off the schedule."

"I understand," Nick said. "Why don't you just give me a call when you have a firm date?"

"Perfect," Brooke said, and was pleased when Nick informed her that the restaurant paid its employees two dollars more than minimum wage per hour, plus tips. A few minutes later, she was in her car, thinking about how much she was looking forward to serving a more upscale clientele—customers who ordered cocktails and champagne to start their meals and a bottle of wine with each course. She felt a little bad that she hadn't told Nick she was pregnant, but her desire to make more money and provide better health insurance coverage for herself and her baby overrode any guilt she might feel. If all went well, she could work right up until the day she delivered, and by that time—according to the job posting—she would be entitled to six weeks of maternity leave. It would be unpaid, but if she budgeted correctly until that point, she and her child would be just fine. When she went back to work, she'd have to find a trustworthy daycare, but she tried not to worry about that right now. With the money she'd be making, she'd be able to afford to pay someone well. She'd never be like her own mother and leave her baby alone.

Brooke was so excited about her new job, she shot a quick text to her sister, asking whether it was okay to stop by. It only took a few minutes for Natalie to respond. "Yes!" her text said. "Come over!" Having someone in her life with whom she could share her good news might have been a small thing, but to Brooke, it felt like everything.

Twenty minutes later, she parked in front of Natalie's house. Brooke knocked, and a second later, Hailey answered the door. "Hi, Aunt Brooke!" she said with a big smile. The little girl gave her a hug, and Brooke felt herself begin to tear up. She thought of herself around Hailey's age, having to return to Hillcrest from Jessica and Scott's house. She remembered the sting of Scott's hand. She remembered crying on Gina's shoulder, wishing with all her might that her own mother would come back.

"Hey," Natalie said as she came up behind Hailey in the entryway. "Come on in."

"Henry and I are playing restaurant!" Hailey announced. "You can play, too, Aunt Brooke, if you want."

"Oh," Brooke said, unsure how to rebuff a child's invitation.

"Brooke and Mommy need a little grown-up time," Natalie said, saving her. "You go on and play with your brother."

"But he burns *everything*," Hailey said. Still, she did as her mother had asked, skipping off through the living room and turning down the hall.

Brooke followed Natalie into the kitchen, which barely resembled the crazy mess of a room that it had been the last time Brooke was there. Everything was clean, and looked to be in its proper place. A stockpot simmered on the stove, filling the air with the scent of what Brooke guessed was some kind of stew. Brooke sat on one of the barstools next to the island, and Natalie poured them each a glass of water from the Brita pitcher on the counter.

"How'd the interview go?" she asked, pushing the glass toward Brooke.

"It was great. I got the job!"

"That's fantastic!" Natalie said with a huge smile. "Congratulations!"

"Thanks. It's such a nice place. I think I'm going to be really happy there."

"When do you start?"

Brooke told her about having to give notice at the bar, realizing that for the first time since their initial brunch, she didn't have a sinking, nervous feeling in her stomach. She felt like she belonged here, in Natalie's kitchen, sharing excitement over the things happening in each other's lives.

"The results of the amnio came back, too. Everything's fine."

"Oh, good! Did you find out the sex?"

Brooke shook her head. "I didn't want to find it out alone." She paused. "Do you want to maybe come to my next appointment, and we can find out then?"

"Absolutely."

"Mommy!" Hailey's high-pitched voice, calling out from another room, cut into the moment. "I need you! Pleeease?"

Natalie smiled. "She probably wants me to pretend to be another sous chef because she already kicked Henry out of the kitchen." She made a funny face, and Brooke laughed. "Be right back."

Brooke waited in the kitchen for Natalie to return. She thought about the dark bar where she'd spent so many hours the past five years. It was where she'd met Ryan, where she realized she might be pregnant with his child. But now, she felt more than ready to move on to bigger and better things. Meeting her sister and landing a new job might only be the beginning of a brand-new life.

She reached for her glass, but instead of grabbing it, she accidentally knocked it over, spilling water all over the granite-topped island. "Shit," she muttered, hopping down from the barstool and stepping over to the sink, where there was a roll of paper towels. She pulled off a handful and quickly returned to the island, mopping up the liquid. Some of it had spread to a stack of papers that sat on the corner of the island, so she reached to lift them from the counter. When she'd finished drying everything off, she set the stack of papers back down, glad that only the edges were damp, and then noticed that there was a manila folder in the middle of the stack. The tab was labeled with her name, written in blue ink.

What the hell? She pulled out the folder, holding it in her right hand, wondering whether or not she should open it. But her curiosity immediately got the better of her, and she reasoned that since her name was on it, she had every right to see the contents.

As she scanned the documents, Brooke's face flamed red and

her stomach twisted. Natalie had run a background check on her. She'd encouraged Brooke to trust her . . . to open up . . . and the entire time she secretly thought Brooke might be a criminal.

"Brooke?" Her sister's voice snapped Brooke out of her thoughts. "Is everything okay?" Natalie glance at Brooke's hands, then Brooke saw her sister's eyes go wide.

"Wait," Natalie said. "I can explain."

"There's nothing to explain." Brooke slapped the papers down onto the counter and held her arms rigid at her sides.

"Yes, there is," Natalie said. "It wasn't me. Kyle was just being overprotective."

"Which explains how he treated me," Brooke said. She had thought it was a good thing that Kyle was protective, but it didn't occur to her that he would have taken it this far. That while he and Natalie smiled at her and made polite conversation, they were digging around in her past. Brooke felt dirty and ashamed, even though she had done nothing to deserve it. She couldn't believe this was happening. Her chest ached as though her ribs had been kicked. "So much for me being family." Her voice was splintered by tears.

"Brooke, please," Natalie said, with a touch of desperation. Her chin trembled. "I'm so sorry. It was a mistake. It never should have happened. He didn't tell me he was doing it. I didn't know, or I would have stopped him. He's sorry, too."

Brooke shot her younger sister an icy glare. "I don't believe you."

Natalie didn't move. She simply stared at Brooke, helplessly, with tears running down her cheeks. Brooke stared back at her. She should have known better than to let Natalie in so quickly. Brooke couldn't believe she'd been foolish enough to make this mistake.

Without thinking, she spun around and strode through the living room and out the front door to her car. Ink-black clouds had moved in from over the gray waters of Puget Sound. Fat droplets of rain fell from the sky, splattering on the pavement, turning it dark, too. *Fuck her,* Brooke thought. *Fuck her and her so-called good intentions.*

"Brooke, wait!" Natalie said, following her outside.

Ignoring her, Brooke yanked open the trunk of her car. She lifted the brown box out of the spot where she'd placed it the morning she met Natalie for brunch. She'd kept it there ever since, unsure if she was ready to share it with her sister. She'd felt possessive, a little greedy, wanting to keep Natalie all to herself. But now that Natalie was showing her true colors, it was time for Brooke to show hers, too. She shut the trunk and jogged back to the front porch, holding out the box to her sister. Thunder clapped in the sky, and a moment later, lightning flashed, raising the hairs on Brooke's skin.

"Here," she said. "Take it. I don't want it anymore." Natalie looked at the box and then back to Brooke, confused. Brooke narrowed her eyes as she spoke again. "I know where our mother is. She lives up north, in Mt. Vernon, with her husband. She's a veterinarian. Her last name is Richmond. She's been there for over twenty years, since she got out of the Skagit Valley Women's correctional facility. She spent seven years in prison for child endangerment and attempted kidnapping of a child. She doesn't have any other children. She trains service animals for people with special needs. She's a real saint." Brooke sneered as she spoke those last words, watching as Natalie's mouth dropped open.

"How?" Natalie asked, nodding toward the box, which she had yet to take from Brooke's hand.

"One of my customers was a detective." Chuck Baker was a hard-edged older man who had been a regular at a bar where Brooke had worked ten years ago. He liked to chat about his job when she served him his nightly pint of stout, telling her stories about how he tracked down suspects using the databases that only law enforcement had access to, and after several months, Brooke worked up the courage to ask him to use his connections to find her birth mother. He liked her well enough to bend the rules, as long as Brooke promised never to use his name in connection with how she got the information.

Natalie's chin trembled. "But . . . I don't understand . . . why didn't you tell me about this before? Why did you let me think you didn't know where she was?"

"I guess I didn't trust you yet," Brooke said. Her voice was hard. Unyielding. "And now I know why."

Natalie closed her eyes, briefly, as though she'd been slapped. "Brooke, please," she said. "I'm sorry. I'm so, so sorry."

"I don't care," Brooke said. Natalie finally took the box, looking as though she might say something else, but before she could, Brooke spun around again and descended the steps. A gust of wind threw icy pinpricks of rain against her face.

"Wait," Natalie called out. "Did you meet her?"

"No," Brooke said, not bothering to look back. "She's all yours." What Brooke didn't say was how she'd driven to their mother's vet clinic and parked across the street, trying to work up the courage to go inside. She didn't say that she'd seen the house their mother lived in with her husband, Evan, and the four dogs that played in the front yard. Somehow, seeing all of this, knowing that the woman who'd abandoned them had moved on and built a life without ever trying to find the daughters she'd once had, filled Brooke with bitter, twisted grief. She never wanted to see her mother again.

They can have each other, she thought as she climbed into her car and slammed the door. Her mother and her sister would probably get along just fine. Natalie didn't have the memories that Brooke carried; she didn't feel like a piece of the woman's discarded trash. The two of them would probably have some irritating, Hallmark-moment family reunion, and Brooke would be where she always ended up. Completely on her own.

Natalie

Dazed, Natalie turned around and reentered the house, gripping the box her sister had been hiding from her for weeks. Her regret that Brooke had seen the background check Kyle had run was overwhelmed by her shock that her sister had known where their birth mother was all this time and never said a word. She understood that Brooke was still in pain about their mother's decision to give them up, but had she really not trusted Natalie to the point of keeping her whereabouts from her? Natalie had asked her, point-blank, if Brooke knew where their mother was, and her sister had said no. What else had Brooke said to her that was a lie? Were the more tender moments they'd shared simply an act on her older sister's part? Natalie had no way to know. All she knew was that suddenly, the relationship she'd hoped to have with Brooke seemed to be over before it had truly had a chance to begin.

Back in the kitchen, Natalie made a cup of coffee and then sat down at the table with the box in front of her. She wondered if she should wait to go through its contents until later, so Kyle would be there for moral support, but decided that she'd waited long enough.

She pulled the thick stack of papers from the box, her eyes immediately landing on several pages of Child Protective Services reports, all of which detailed instances of Jennifer Walker's errant behavior. Natalie read how her birth mother had left her two-year-old daughter, Brooke, alone in a car, then failed to show up for the parenting skills classes that were required of her. She read the description of the night their mother was arrested at a grocery store for petty theft and for child endangerment and neglect. She read through Gina Ortiz's reports of her meetings with Jennifer, whom she characterized as an emotionally unstable young woman with no family or friend support system to help her in raising her two young girls. She discovered that her biological grandmother wanted nothing to do with Jennifer or her two girls. She saw her birth mother's shaky, black signature on the papers that signed away her rights as their mother. She pored over the accounts of her birth mother's first year in prison, written by someone named Myer; she began to cry when, to her horror, she found the police reports describing how, only a week after she'd been released from her initial sentence, her birth mother had snatched a little girl from a playground and run away with her into the woods. She read the judge's decision to send Jennifer Walker back to prison, this time for a decade, and how, when she was there, she began an antirecidivism work-release program that allowed her to train service dogs and eventually earn her GED and a degree as a veterinary technician. There was a prison medical form, detailing how her birth mother had suffered through a severe beating by another inmate, as well as the parole board hearing notes that had allowed her to be released three years early, after the glowing testimony of her employer, Randy Stewart, and several other employees with whom she worked.

After going through all of the official paperwork, Natalie found a page of handwritten notes made on yellow legal paper—jotted down by Brooke, Natalie assumed—listing three addresses in Mt. Vernon, one that appeared to be the clinic where her birth mother worked. The notes also included the name of a college from which Jennifer Richmond had earned her doctorate in veterinary medicine, as well as the location of her husband Evan's automotive repair business.

The last scrap in the file was a newspaper article dated almost twelve years ago that described how Dr. Richmond was responsible for enlarging the same work-release program in which she'd participated, bringing on three other veterinarian clinics so that several female inmates could participate at a time. "I was a broken person when I landed back in prison," her birth mom was quoted as saying. "The opportunity I was given to get out of myself and learn how to care for something other than what I wanted was the most important gift of my life. If it's possible for me pass that gift on to other women who are suffering the same way I did, then that's what I'm going to do."

Natalie finished reading the article and leaned back against her chair, closing her eyes. She wondered how Brooke could have read all of this and not wanted to talk with their mother about everything she'd been through. What Natalie saw in learning about their birth mom was a woman who'd fought her way through some extremely difficult, painful experiences and found a way to channel all of that into contributing something good to the world. She imagined it was possible that their birth mom's guilt over giving up her daughters may have prevented her from looking for them—that she didn't want to disrupt their lives. There was a copy of her marriage certificate in the file, but no birth certificates, so Natalie assumed that what Brooke had said was correct—Jennifer Richmond had had no other children. She had turned fifty-five years old last June.

"Mom?" Hailey's voice snapped Natalie out of her daze. Her daughter had entered the kitchen unnoticed.

"What is it, honey?" Natalie said. She sniffed and used a paper napkin to wipe the dampness from her cheeks.

Hailey gave her a puckered, doubtful look. "How come you're crying?"

"Oh, it's complicated, sweet pea. Just grown-up stuff." She closed the box and pushed the paperwork to the side. Hailey climbed into Natalie's lap, and Natalie wrapped her arms around her daughter and hugged her close. She put her face in Hailey's curls, breathed in the strawberry scent of her shampoo, and wondered how many times her birth mother had held her like this before she let her go. "Where's Henry?"

"In the playroom, still. I made him wash the dishes." She paused. "Is Aunt Brooke gone?"

Natalie frowned, feeling a fresh round of tears gathering behind her eyes. "She is," she told Hailey in a quiet voice. *Maybe for good,* she thought as she sat in her kitchen holding her daughter, wishing she knew how to fix what had gone wrong—hoping that she hadn't found her sister only to lose her all over again.

"It's my fault," Kyle said when he got home that night and heard the details of the fight Natalie and Brooke had had. "Should I go talk with her? Explain that you had nothing to do with it?"

Natalie could have blamed him for what happened—for running the report in the first place—but hearing the ragged edge in her husband's voice, she knew just how sorry he was. And it was Natalie who had forgotten that the file was on the kitchen counter—she'd meant to shred it but kept getting distracted by the kids and work—so the fact that Brooke had stumbled across it was just as much Natalie's fault as it was Kyle's. "I don't think so," she said. "'But thanks for offering."

"Are you sure?" he said. "Maybe it would help."

"I wish it could," Natalie said. She'd sent Brooke a text before Kyle had come home from work, in which she apologized again, and asked her sister for another chance. She didn't receive a reply.

A month passed without a word from Brooke. The plumber finally arrived—four weeks after he'd promised he would. He completed his task in a couple of days, and then Alex and his crew got back to work, managing to finish the job a week before Christmas. The holiday was quiet, and Natalie couldn't help but wish that Brooke had been there, too. Natalie had yet to contact her birth mother. It was strange, how deeply she'd longed to connect with the woman, but now that she knew where she was, Natalie was hesitant to reach out. Terrified, in fact.

Kyle's murder case finally closed after the first of the year—his client was found not guilty—and after that, he made it a point to work from home as much as he could, taking the kids to the trampoline park or swimming on the weekends to give Natalie enough time to do her job without interruption. Natalie had both Logan and Ruby over to her house for a playdate, and invited Katie out for a cup of coffee when she came to pick her son up.

Now, the second week of January, Natalie glanced at her watch and wondered when her mother, who had offered to pick up the kids so Natalie could work, would arrive. A few minutes later, Hailey came bursting through the front door, Henry trailing behind.

"Hi, Mom!" she said as she raced inside. "Gramma said to tell you that she didn't come in because she and Grampa have to go to a fancy dinner tonight and she has to get ready."

"Okay," Natalie said, as Henry launched himself against her legs, causing her to stagger backward. "Careful there, buddy. You're so strong, you almost knocked me over!" She reached down and ruffled his soft hair. He giggled, and let her go, dropping his bag on the floor.

"Hang that up, please," Natalie said automatically, watching as both of her kids put their jackets and backpacks on the hooks by the front door. "How was your day?" she asked as they walked together toward the kitchen.

"Good," Hailey said. "But Chase said my hair looks like Medusa. Like snakes!" She frowned and crossed her arms over her chest. "He's such a butt."

"Such a butt! Such a butt!" Henry chanted.

Natalie had to work hard to restrain herself from laughing. "Hailey, you know it's not okay to call people names."

"But he called me Medusa!" her daughter protested. "It's not fair!"

"I know," Natalie said. "But we can't control how other people act. We can only control ourselves. I know it's hard, but the best thing to do is treat Chase how you want to be treated. If you don't react to his teasing you, eventually he'll stop."

Hailey sighed. "I don't think so. He's just not normal."

Again, Natalie had to bite the inside of her cheek to keep her amusement in check. "Want to help me make the cookies for the bake sale?" she asked. She'd volunteered to provide eight dozen chocolate chip cookies for the PTA fund-raiser at Hailey's school, which would happen the next day.

"I want to help, too!" Henry said.

"You can't," Hailey informed him in a haughty voice. "It's not for your school."

"Sure he can," Natalie said. "We have to make a lot, so there's plenty for both of you to do. Why don't you both wash your hands while I get the ingredients out?"

Her children made their way to the sink, vying to be the first to use the soap and get their hands under the water. "Don't *push*!" Henry said as the two stood together on the footstool.

"I'm *not*!" Hailey replied, and Natalie watched as her daughter shifted her weight away from her brother, as though to prove her point. But her motion tilted the stool, and before Natalie could stop it, Henry lost his footing and fell to the floor. He landed on his side on the hard wood, and Natalie saw his head bounce when he hit. He was quiet a moment, likely stunned, trying to register what had just happened, and then began to wail. She rushed over, dropping the bag of chocolate chips she'd taken from the pantry onto the counter.

"Hailey!" she said in a sharp voice. "You have to be more careful!" She knelt down next to Henry and gathered him into her arms. "It's okay, baby," she murmured. She ran her hand over his entire head, checking for blood, but found only a bump above his right ear, about the size of a quarter. He cried on her chest, rubbing his wet face against her.

"I'm sorry!" Hailey said, and Natalie realized that her daughter was crying, too. "I didn't mean to, Mommy! It was a accident!"

"It's okay," Natalie said, feeling panicked. She could feel her heartbeat hammering inside her skull. She stood up, still holding Henry, grabbed her cell phone from the counter, and quickly found the number for the nurse line at their pediatrician's office. "Hey, Susan," she said, when the nurse answered. Over Henry's now-whimpering cries, she explained what had happened. "Do I need to bring him in?"

"Probably not," Susan told her. "Just watch him, and make sure he doesn't seem too drowsy or disoriented. If he does, or if he vomits, you can take him to the ER to have him checked for a concussion. Otherwise, it's probably just an old-fashioned bump on the head. Put some ice on it, and give him a little children's Tylenol if he's hurting."

Natalie thanked her and hung up, turning to see that Hailey had gone upstairs to her brother's bedroom, coming back with his favorite blue fleece blanket. She held it out, and Natalie couldn't help but think of Brooke and her lavender "soft side," and the muscles in her throat thickened. Henry snatched the blanket from her, no longer crying but still snuggled tightly against Natalie.

"That was very nice of you," Natalie told Hailey, whose bottom lip stuck out and was still trembling.

"It was a accident," she said again, sniffling, and Natalie nodded.

"I know, baby," she said. She sat down at the table with Henry in her lap and her daughter pressed up to her side. Natalie put her free arm around Hailey. "I'm sorry if I snapped at you. I was just scared when I saw your brother fall. You didn't do it on purpose. You don't need to feel bad."

Hailey nodded, but in that same moment, Natalie thought about Brooke. She wondered if her sister would ever be able to get over seeing the background check—if she would believe that Natalie never meant to hurt her. But Natalie feared that the damage was done. Whether a window is shattered by accident or by a deliberate strike, its jagged pieces cut just as deep. The injured party still bleeds.

Brooke

Before Brooke left for her dinner shift at Sea to Shore, her cell phone buzzed. She glanced at the text message, having guessed correctly that it was from Natalie. Over the past month, since the day of their argument in Natalie's kitchen, her sister had left messages and sent her multiple texts, begging Brooke to please call her. "I'm so sorry," Natalie said in her last voicemail. "I can only hope you can find it in your heart to forgive me. Please. Can we just talk?"

Too little, too late, Brooke thought as she climbed into her car and began her short drive to work. She was doing well at her new job. Nick was happy with how quickly she'd caught on to the way the restaurant functioned, and her fellow employees seemed to like her.

Ryan had sent her a few texts as well. "I'm not just going to disappear," he told her, and even though she didn't respond, she didn't block his number, either. If she had, he might simply show up at her apartment again, and she wasn't sure how she'd handle that. After what had happened with Natalie, Brooke was less inclined than ever to take Ryan up on his offer of help. Other than her baby, she wasn't going to let anyone close to her, ever again.

Still, she thought about Natalie every time she delivered a beautiful dessert to one of her tables at work, but she decided it would be easier at this point if she pretended that she never had a sister at all.

Today, once she parked and entered the restaurant through the back door, Brooke punched in, then went to the bathroom to check her appearance and scrub her hands. She had purchased several work-appropriate outfits at a local thrift store, making sure all of her skirts had elastic waistbands and her tops were loose and comfortable. She wore her curls up in a twist with a few black tendrils down around her face and bought several pairs of supportive shoes so her back wouldn't hurt so much at the end of her shift. According to the obstetrician at the clinic, her pregnancy was progressing well, but she still hadn't found out the sex of the baby.

Now that she was twenty-three weeks, the biggest struggle she faced was how to hide her pregnancy under empire-waist tops. Nick hadn't mentioned it, so Brooke decided to wait until closer to her due date to discuss the short maternity leave she would need to take. Until then, she would focus on being indispensable and saving up as much money as she possibly could. She'd been right about the flow of tips—on her weekend shifts, she was making up to five hundred dollars a night. Over the holidays, the restaurant had been so busy, Brooke couldn't believe the amount of money she was bringing home. For the first time in her life, Brooke felt truly competent, grateful to be compensated so generously for the work she was doing. She decided she'd stay in her tiny apartment until the final weeks before the baby came, but she had begun looking on Craigslist for rental houses.

Now, Brooke made her way into the dining room to join the rest of the staff at a table so the chef could describe and let them taste the specials they would be serving that evening. A little while later, she took her first table of the night, a six-top that immediately ordered several cocktails, then asked to speak to the sommelier for assistance with picking out wines to accompany their meal. After putting in the order for their appetizers, Brooke found herself wondering if Natalie had already gone to meet their mother in Mt. Vernon; she imagined the two of them sitting together, clucking about how unfortunate it was that Brooke was too dysfunctional to forgive them both. The thought of this made her feel a little bit dizzy. In fact, she had to grab the edge of the counter by the pass to the kitchen to keep from stumbling.

"You okay?" another server, named Frank, asked. He was a bit older than Brooke, had been working at Sea to Shore for over ten years, and was responsible for training new employees like her.

"Yeah," she said, trying to shake off the feeling. She wondered if she hadn't eaten enough that day. She grabbed a roll from the warmer under the counter and took a bite. "Just hungry, I think," she said to Frank, who nodded, lifted his diners' plates from the window, and carried them out to the floor.

Brooke washed down the roll with a glass of water just as the hostess approached her and said that she had seated two more tables in her section. "Going to be a busy night," the younger woman added. "Two hundred reservations on the books."

"Wow," Brooke said, still waiting for the food she'd eaten to make her feel better. As she made her way out to her section, she walked as straight as she could. She couldn't get sick now, she thought. She needed to show Nick that he could count on her, no matter what.

She smiled at her new customers as best she could as she welcomed them and took their cocktail orders. Weaving her way through the tables back to the servers' station, she quickly punched in their drinks and then grabbed her first table's drink orders from the bar and set them on a large tray. She hiked it up on her right shoulder and carried a tray jack in her left hand, carefully balancing both. Beads of sweat popped out on her forehead, but with her hands full, she couldn't wipe them away.

She was halfway across the restaurant, back toward the

six-top, when a sharp spike of pain shot through her abdomen and down her leg, causing her knees to buckle. She fell hard onto the wood floor, and the tray she carried went flying. Luckily, there were no customers seated nearby.

"Oh, god," she grunted as her muscles continued to spasm. A second later, she felt a rush of something liquid between her legs. Was her water breaking? Brooke thought in a panic. Was the baby coming early? She curled fetal on the floor, bringing her knees up to her chest, waiting for the pain to pass.

"Brooke!" she heard Nick say. "Are you all right? What happened?"

She shook her head, too scared to speak. The pain was excruciating, shooting through her belly into her hips. She was terrified to move, for fear of making things worse.

"Did you trip?" he asked, and again she shook her head, then spoke, her voice wound tight.

"I'm pregnant," she gasped. "Something is wrong."

"Call 911," Nick directed, though to whom, Brooke didn't know. She couldn't open her eyes. All she could think about was her baby.

Nick rested a hand on her back. "It's going to be okay," he said. "Just stay still. Help is on its way."

She nodded as the pain in her uterus squeezed again, and she felt as though she might be sick. She wanted to know if she was bleeding or if her water had broken, but she was in too much agony to check. "I'm sorry," she whispered to Nick. "I meant to tell you . . ."

"Hey," Nick said. "It's okay. I thought you might be, but I didn't want to be the asshole who asks and gets punched in the face for being wrong." He paused. "Don't worry. Everything's going to be fine."

Brooke finally managed to crack open her eyes, only to see a circle of employees and customers with concerned looks on their faces. But she didn't have time to be embarrassed, with only a few words running through her head: *Please, God. Let my baby be okay.*

The paramedics came ten minutes later, pushing all the other people away. Before Brooke knew it, they had lifted her onto the gurney and she was wheeled out of the building and slid into the back of an ambulance. They checked her vitals, and she told them how far along she was. "I think I might be bleeding," she said, unable to fight back her tears. "Or my water broke. I'm not sure."

"Okay," the medic who had stayed in the back with her said. She was a blond woman who looked to be in her late twenties. "I'm going to check on that, then. Is that all right?"

Brooke's jaw and bottom lip quivered, but she bobbed her head. The medic lifted the blanket they'd placed over her in the restaurant and gently pushed Brooke's thighs apart. When she returned her brown eyes to Brooke's, they were unreadable. "There's some blood," the medic said.

"Oh, god!" Brooke cried out, rolling her head to one side, unable to look at the medic a moment longer. She was losing this baby . . . just like she'd lost everyone else. Her tears came in earnest then, and painful, heavy sobs took her over. The ache in her uterus hadn't gone away.

The medic placed a reassuring hand on Brooke's arm. "Hold on now. That could mean any number of things. Let's get you to the ER and the doctors will figure out exactly what's going on. No matter what, they'll take care of you, I promise. They'll do everything they can."

Brooke was crying too hard to respond. The medic held Brooke's hand as she spoke over a radio to the ER, describing Brooke's symptoms. When they wheeled her through the automatic sliding glass doors, Brooke was rushed into an exam room, where the medics left her and two nurses took over.

"I'm Gemma," the older one with silver hair said. "And this is Mark." She gestured to the short, stocky bald man in blue scrubs who was setting up an IV. "We'll be taking care of you today. I understand that you're pregnant?"

"Twenty-three weeks," Brooke said, trying to ignore the biting ache in her gut. "Am I going to lose it?" Her voice shook, and she pressed a hand across her mouth to keep the sobs from taking back over.

"I don't know," Gemma said. "We have to run some blood tests and do an ultrasound before we know for sure what's going on."

"We'll get you started on fluids and check for a fetal heartbeat," Mark said. "The obstetrician is on her way."

"Is there anyone we can call for you?" Gemma asked. "The baby's father?"

Brooke dropped her hand back to her abdomen and considered what would happen if she asked the nurse to contact Ryan. So far, he'd done as she'd asked and stayed away, and she didn't want to call him now and make him think she'd changed her mind about accepting his help.

"He's not involved," Brooke said, rubbing her hand over the pain in her belly. Her hip joints ached like nothing she'd ever felt before.

"Anyone else?" Mark said. "Your mother, maybe, or a friend?"

"No," Brooke said, her eyes filling again. She realized that the one person she wanted to be there was Natalie. She knew her sister would hold her hand; she would push her hair back from her face and tell her everything was going to be okay.

"All right," Gemma said, and several minutes later, the door swung open and to Brooke's surprise, Natalie rushed into the room.

"Your manager called me. You listed me as your emergency contact on your application," she said, answering the question she likely saw on Brooke's face. Natalie's cheeks were red and she was breathing fast. "I came right away."

"And you are?" Mark asked, poising his fingers over the keyboard attached to the computer next to the bed.

"She's my sister," Brooke said, and then Natalie stepped over and grabbed her hand, the two of them waiting for the doctor to come.

"There we go," Dr. Patel said as she pushed the ultrasound wand along Brooke's belly and the familiar, comforting *whoosh, whoosh* of the baby's heartbeat filled the room.

"Oh, thank god," Brooke said through her tears. Natalie still held her hand and now gave it a hard squeeze. "What happened? Where did the pain come from? Why was I bleeding?"

"My guess is the pain was from your ligaments stretching and your hips beginning to expand. For some women, especially first-time mothers, this can hurt quite a lot." Dr. Patel, an attractive East Indian woman who spoke with a musical lilt, kept her eyes on the screen as she continued to move the wand on Brooke's stomach.

"What about the bleeding?" Natalie asked.

"It wasn't much," Dr. Patel said, "even though I'm sure it felt like it was. We don't always know what causes it. Possibly too much exertion, or it could be for no real reason at all. The good news is that it stopped, and it didn't contain any kind of tissue. The baby looks wonderful." She finally glanced back at Brooke. "How's your pain?"

Brooke shifted a bit in the hospital bed, trying to gauge her answer. "I'm still a bit achy, but the shooting pains went away." Her baby looked wonderful, she thought.

"Excellent," Dr. Patel said. "We'd like to keep you overnight, just to monitor both you and the baby. If all remains well, you can go home tomorrow."

"But everything is still okay, right?" Brooke asked, anxiously. "The baby's fine?"

"Yes," Dr. Patel said. "She looks perfect."

"She?" Brooke froze. "I'm having a girl?"

"You're having a girl!" Natalie said, and her brown eyes lit up.

"My apologies," Dr. Patel said. "I assumed you already knew. I do hope you didn't want it to be a surprise."

"No," Brooke said, and a happy, fluttering feeling filled her chest. "It's fine. I wanted to know." She looked at Natalie, unable to deny that she was thrilled to have her sister with her as she received this news.

Dr. Patel stood. "The nurse will be back in a bit to finish the admit process, and I'll update your regular obstetrician. Congratulations!"

Brooke thanked her, and after she'd left, Natalie finally let go of her sister's hand and sat down in the chair next to the bed. They were both quiet, not looking at each other. Brooke wasn't sure that she forgave Natalie completely, but she did know that she'd never been as happy to see anyone in her life as she was when her sister showed up. That had to count for something.

The only sounds in the room were the steady beeps coming from the monitors to which Brooke was attached. She wished she knew exactly what to say, how to express the crazy mix of emotions rushing through her. Foremost she was relieved, but she also felt wary, unsure of how to navigate a conversation about finding the background check in her sister's kitchen that day. But having met Natalie, having spent just a few precious weeks with her, Brooke knew she needed to find a way to work things out— she couldn't deprive her daughter of the same thing Brooke had been denied. She couldn't allow a single argument to ruin the one chance at having a family she'd ever had.

"Thanks for coming," Brooke finally said, in a soft voice. She looked at her sister, searching her face for some clue to whether Natalie was here out of a sense of duty or because she truly wanted to come.

"I thought you'd be pissed," Natalie said, and the tension in her face visibly relaxed.

"But you came anyway." Brooke paused, and gave her sister a wry smile. "We're both stubborn. So there's that."

Natalie's eyes filled with tears. "I'm so sorry, Brooke. I can't apologize enough for hurting you. I never meant—"

"It's okay," Brooke said, holding up her hand to stop Natalie from saying more. "I get it. Kyle ran the report without telling you, and I understand why he did. If I was him, I probably would have done the same thing. Let's just leave it at that."

Natalie eyed her for a moment, looking as though she were trying to decipher whether or not to take Brooke at her word. "Okay," she said.

And then Brooke asked the question that had been in the back of her mind since the last day they'd seen each other. The day she'd given Natalie the box filled with the details of their birth mother's life. "Have you seen her yet?"

The look on Natalie's face told Brooke her sister knew to whom she referred, and Natalie shook her head.

Brooke's eyebrows both rose. "Why not?"

"I'm not sure. I guess I'm afraid."

"That she'll reject you?" Brooke asked. Her voice was barely above a whisper. This was another reason why Brooke had stayed in her car when she drove to her mother's clinic—she could never work up the courage to face the possibility that the mother who had let her go over three decades ago would simply turn her away.

"Yeah. I think that's probably it."

"Me, too," Brooke admitted. And then she spoke again, before she could change her mind. "Maybe it would be easier if we saw her together."

Natalie looked at her. "Really? Are you sure?"

"No," Brooke said, wondering if she would regret what she'd just offered to do. "But it has to be better than either one of us going alone."

Jennifer

I raced down the hall from my office to the front of the building, where I'd been summoned the moment a woman entered the reception area, cradling her bleeding dog in her arms.

"Where are they?" I asked Chandi, who sat at her desk by the door, typing something into her computer. Like me, she was in her midfifties, and at this point, we'd worked together for more than thirty years. She was my business manager, my accountant, and, besides Evan, my closest friend. When Randy had retired and sold me his practice, one of the first things I did was make sure Chandi knew I couldn't run the clinic without her.

"Room three," she said, nodding in that direction. "Paula is with them." Paula was one of the inmates I'd worked with for the past six years, a woman convicted of check-writing fraud. As I had, she earned her vet tech degree while still incarcerated, and when she was released, I gave her a full-time job. She was a short, heavyset woman with a big smile and sparkling green eyes; since joining my team, she'd met and married her husband, and given birth to a little boy named Joseph. Not all of the women from the prison took to the service-dog training program—some quit,

some ended up committing other crimes and returning to jail—
but Paula was one of my success stories.

"Dr. Richmond," Paula said as I entered the exam room. She
wore light blue scrubs, and her auburn hair was pulled into a ponytail on top of her head. The dog lay on the paper-lined table, its
white fur bloody along its side, its breathing pattern staggered and
irregular. I looked at the owner, a woman I recognized as someone new to the clinic—I'd seen her and her dog only a handful of
times, so I had a hard time recalling her name. "This is Gretchen,"
Paula continued. "And her pup, Wiley."

I stepped over to the table and rested a gentle hand on the
dog's head. "It's okay, boy," I said in a soothing voice. He had a
deep, six-inch laceration along his rib cage that I immediately
knew would require stitches. But first, we'd need to get him into
X-ray to make sure he didn't have any broken bones, and then
perform an ultrasound to find any possible internal bleeding. I
raised my eyes to Gretchen, a thin blond woman who was trying not to cry. She appeared to be in her mid- to late thirties.
The same age as my girls. I blinked a few times, attempting to
push down this thought. Even now, more than three decades
after I'd last seen them, they were always lurking in the dark
corners of my mind, ready to take me back to the moment in
which I lost them. I still wrote each of my daughters a letter
on her birthday, filing them away in the same box where I kept
the notebooks I'd written in while in prison. I told them about
my marriage to Evan, my growing vet practice, and the volunteer work I did with other incarcerated women. I told them that
after I'd reached out to my mother several times over the years,
her husband finally called me and said that she'd had a sudden
heart attack when she was fifty-seven and died. I told them how
deeply I grieved the fact that she and I never were able to resolve
our differences, and that I hoped their relationships with their
new families were healthy and strong. I told them that I thought
about them every single day.

"What happened?" I asked Gretchen, forcing myself to focus on the situation right in front of me.

"I was at the grocery store," she said. "I opened the hatch to put the bags inside and he just took off across the parking lot, into the street. A car's brakes screeched and tried to stop, but it still hit him." She shook her head and squeezed her eyes shut, remembering. "The sound he made was so horrible . . . like he was screaming. It sounded human."

I nodded, carefully moving my hand down Wiley's neck to check his pulse. It was fast, but still strong. *A good sign.* "Dogs can do that when they're in pain or scared," I said. I glanced toward Paula and looked down at Wiley's head. She stepped over and held it steady, as she understood I needed her to do in case Wiley decided to try to bite one of us. His dark eyes were glassy, and he seemed to be in shock; from his earlier appointments with me, I remembered him being a sweet, gentle boy, but an injured dog was an unpredictable creature..

"Is he going to be okay?" Gretchen asked in a shaky voice.

"We're going to do everything we can to make sure he will be," I said. "He's conscious, which is a good thing, and it doesn't look like he's had any trauma to his head." I paused, feeling my way carefully down Wiley's sides to check for broken ribs. "He'll need stitches, but my biggest concern is that he might have broken bones and/or internal bleeding, so Paula and I are going to take him in the back for a bit and run some tests, okay? You can stay right here. One of us will be out to talk with you as soon as we can."

Gretchen nodded, Paula lifted Wiley into her arms, and we both made our way to the lab, where we quickly performed the necessary procedures. The ultrasound was negative for bleeding, but the X-ray did show a hairline fracture of his proximal tibia on his left hind leg, so Paula prepped the operating room, and I administered Wiley a strong sedative. Once the anesthesia had kicked in, I had Paula go and update Gretchen. When she returned, she assisted in setting the break and stitching up his wound.

"I take it Chandi rescheduled the last few appointments I had this afternoon?" I asked as Paula handed me the sterile bandage to set on top of Wiley's newly shaven side. The cut was deep, but not so much that I was concerned about its ability to properly heal.

"She did," Paula said. "Once you're finished here, you're done for the day. She also said to tell you that that Natalie woman called again."

The muscles in my gut spasmed. That would be the second call in a week—the second time a woman named Natalie Clark had left only her phone number, never saying what it was that she needed to speak with me about. It wasn't the first time over the years that I'd encountered a woman with the same first name as one of my daughters, but something about the fact that this woman wasn't one of my clients and that she refused to tell Chandi why she was calling set me on edge.

"She's probably just trying to sell me something," I said to Paula. But even as I spoke, I knew this wasn't true. The phone number Natalie Clark had left had a 206 area code, which meant she lived in Seattle. *Could it be her?* I wondered. *Could it be my younger girl has come to find me?* The thought filled me with terror; it shook me to my core. The girl I'd been when I gave my children up didn't exist anymore—she seemed like another person's ghost. I'd worked so hard to forget her, to focus on everything I'd managed to gain instead of all I'd lost. To become a successful, stable, happy woman. For the most part, the life I'd built with Evan and our dogs was so peaceful, so perfect, the idea of disrupting it made me feel wobbly and loose, as though the ground beneath me might melt away.

"Probably," Paula said.

I gave her a quick smile before carefully detaching the face mask from Wiley's muzzle. His eyes were closed and his heartbeat was slow and steady, but before I asked Paula to move him to the large cage we used for dogs recovering from surgery, I shot a strong dose of painkiller into his IV.

"Time for the cone of shame," Paula said, and I chuckled. We put a soft plastic device around his neck, which was meant to prevent Wiley from chewing at the stitches I'd just put in his side.

An hour later, after I'd reassured Gretchen that Wiley would live to chase another cat and made sure that he came out of anesthesia without vomiting or suffering a seizure, I returned to my office to go over my schedule. This was something I always did before I went home—to mentally prepare for my next day's appointments, and make sure I left room for any emergencies that might come through the door.

I sat down at my desk, which like everything else in my life, I kept as tidy as possible. I glanced down at the small stack of messages Chandi had taken for me while I was in surgery with Wiley, and the one from Natalie Clark was right on top. I ran my finger over the phone number, wondering if I should plug it into an online reverse directory and see if I could find out more about the woman who had called. Giving the wireless mouse next to my computer a little shake to bring the screen out of hibernation mode, I opened up a search engine and typed the number in. But before I hit return, my head began to spin.

Oh, god, I thought. *Not again.* The last time I'd had a serious panic attack was when Trixie died. She'd lived to be sixteen, well past the life expectancy for a dog her size, and had drifted off in her sleep in the middle of a warm August night. When I found her, cold and unmoving on her bed the next morning, I'd dropped to my knees and begun to wail, even as my lungs seemed to shrink and my breath became something I had to pursue.

"Babe," Evan had said, jumping up from his side of the bed and racing over to where I knelt. "What's wrong?"

I couldn't speak. I only slid my arms beneath Trixie's limp body and pulled her to my chest. I buried my face in her fur, sobbing so hard it felt as though my rib cage might shatter.

Evan dropped down beside us and took us both into his tight embrace. We'd gone through the loss of Scout five years before, and while I'd come to love my husband's dog, too, there was something special about Trixie. She'd been with me longer than anyone ever had been before. She protected me and loved me without condition. From the moment I scratched her belly in that kennel, she'd gone on to heal something deep and broken inside my soul. We'd healed each other.

And then she was gone. A dark sorrow rose inside me as I curled up on the carpet in my bedroom, holding Trixie while I cried. My insides felt itchy and wild; my skin felt as though it might crack right off of my body. I flashed back to the day I'd said good-bye to my children—the grief I'd felt so intense, I worried it might break me apart. I knew that loss was a part of life; it was a regular requirement of my job to administer euthanasia and help my clients say good-bye to their pets. But losing Trixie was different. It was the end of something I was afraid I'd never find again.

Evan curled up right behind me, holding me and Trixie both. He didn't speak, he didn't try to tell me everything would be okay. He was simply there, serving as an anchor, making sure I knew I wasn't alone.

It took me over a year to fully grieve Trixie's death—a year to get through a day without choking up when I thought of her. But after that, as I continued to train more dogs in need of a home, Evan and I decided it was time to adopt a few for ourselves. We ended up taking four pups from a litter that had been abandoned with their ill mother by the side of the road, two girls and two boys, who brought as much joy and unconditional love into our lives as both Scout and Trixie had.

But now, as I sat at my desk, staring at Natalie Clark's phone number on my computer screen, I felt a panic rise in my body too similar to the one I'd experienced when Trixie died, threatening me just like the one I'd had that day when I snatched the little girl from the playground and ran away into the woods. Looking into who this woman might be was emotionally dangerous—it was a game I decided I couldn't afford to play.

Instead, I deleted the number and put this message, like the other, into the shredder next to the filing cabinet. Tomorrow, I'd tell Chandi to stop giving them to me, knowing she was a good enough employee—a good enough friend—not to ask why. If I didn't call Natalie Clark back, perhaps she'd give up and go away.

Grabbing my coat, I locked my office for the night and headed out to my car. It was already dark outside, a cold and clear late January evening. A few other businesses around the clinic still had their twinkling white lights from the holidays.

On the short drive home, I pondered whether or not to tell Evan about the calls from Natalie Clark. Knowing him as well as I did, I knew he would encourage me to call her back, if only to alleviate my fears about whom she might be. But the idea that she was my younger daughter was too frightening a prospect for me to decide to share the calls with my husband. This felt a bit like a betrayal of Evan, since we tended toward telling each other everything, but the anxiety I'd felt in my office and only barely managed to ward off still simmered in my belly. I was willing to do whatever I could to keep it at bay.

When I pulled into our long driveway, I saw a car I didn't recognize. It was a silver SUV, and there was no one inside it. Evan often had customers mistake our driveway as the one for his business, so I simply parked in my usual spot before making my way to the front porch. "Hey, babe," I called out as I entered the house. I'd barely taken off my coat and set my purse on the table by the door when I looked up and saw two women sitting on our couch. Evan and the dogs weren't in the room.

"Oh, god," I said, feeling a wash of icy cold work its way through my body as I took the women in. I grabbed the edge of the table with one hand and put the other over my mouth. *It's them. It has to be them.* Both were petite, like me, and one could have been me fifteen years ago, when I'd turned forty. *It's Brooke.* She had my pale skin, dark curls, and violet eyes—eyes that were staring at me so intently I feared they might burn a hole in my skin. She was a little heavy—her face was slightly round and full, but her cheeks were healthy and pink. She wore black leggings and a blue top with an empire waist.

The other woman, who wore jeans and a green sweater, was a pixie-faced blonde with big brown eyes; at least, I thought they were brown—she was blinking so fast I could barely see the color. *Natalie. My baby girl.* Tears blinded me.

The two women both stood. "Hi . . . Jennifer," the blond woman said. "We're sorry to just barge in on you like this. I called you earlier, at your office . . ."

It's her, it's her, it's her. Natalie Clark is my daughter. I shook my head frantically. My jaw clenched together hard enough for my molars to squeak. The room began to spin, and I closed my eyes, wondering if I was simply imagining that they were here. Had I managed to conjure their presence with the panic I'd felt back in my office? Was I hearing things, the same way I'd heard Brooke's voice that day so many years ago in the park?

"Jen." Evan's voice called to me through the fuzzy cloud that clogged my head. I felt his strong, warm hand on my cheek. "It's okay. They showed me the paperwork. It's definitely them."

I shook my head again, keeping my eyes shut. I was too afraid to find out what might happen if I opened them. How did they have paperwork? Gina had told me all the records were sealed, that the state would only open them in case of an emergency. *What if this is an emergency? What if one of my daughters is sick?*

This was not what I'd imagined would have happened if I ever saw my girls again. Even with all the letters I wrote them, I had never let myself believe this moment would ever come about. It was too terrifying, too overwhelming to even consider as a possibility. I'd let them go, for their sakes. And for my own. I clung to Evan, worried I might pass out.

"Let's just go," I heard Brooke say. At least I assumed it was Brooke because her voice sounded different from that of Natalie, who had spoken before. "She doesn't want us here."

"Wait," Natalie said. "We've just shocked the hell out of her. Let's give her a minute."

"Evan," I whispered. "I can't do this. Please."

He leaned over and pressed his cheek against mine. His lips were next to my ear. "Yes, you can." He hugged me, rubbing a soothing circle on my back. "They only want to talk. To ask you a few questions. You can do that for them, can't you? It might be good for you. For them, too."

I forced myself to turn my head, open my eyes, and look at my daughters. My heart fluttered inside my chest as I pulled back from Evan's embrace and slowly reached out a hand, thinking I needed to touch them to believe that they were actually here. But at the last second, I jerked my arm back to my side, unable to go through with it. What did they want to say to me? What would I say to them? How could I explain the decisions I'd made, the pain of letting them go, which had torn me apart in ways that seeing them here, in my living room, made me realize just how delicately I'd been sewn together all of these years. All the progress I'd made, the confidence I thought I'd earned, now vanished, and I felt like I was right back in that room where I'd last held them—fragile, uncertain, full of soul-scorching regret. My seams once again threatening to burst.

"Jennifer," Natalie said. "I'm so sorry if we've upset you, just showing up like this. We'll go, if you want us to." She'd taken a few steps closer to me, and Evan stood to the side. I could see the shadows of the baby I'd held around her edges, the shape of her eyes, and the soft curve of her smile. Brooke stood with her arms crossed over her chest, still so much the defiant little girl I remembered, the girl who pretended to be brave when she was riddled with fear. It shocked me, how easily I recognized them. All of those faces I'd searched for in crowds—the ones I thought might be my daughters—were nowhere close to being my girls.

These were my girls, standing right in front of me, asking me to talk. And no matter how hard it might be, telling them the truth about their past was the very least I could do.

The four of us sat down, Brooke and Natalie on the larger couch, and Evan and I across from them on the love seat. "Where are the dogs?" I asked Evan. I was accustomed to our pups' welcoming presence the moment I came home from work. It was odd not to have them lying at my feet.

"They're outside," he said. He held my left hand in both of his, and I was pressed up tight against him. Evan was my touchstone, my security, the place I felt most safe. If I was going to do this, if I was going to talk with my daughters, I needed him there with me.

I nodded, keeping my eyes on the floor. We were all quiet, but I could feel my girls' gazes upon me, waiting for me to begin. "How did you find me?" I finally asked.

"A friend of Brooke's," Natalie said. "A detective."

"And your adoptive family," I said. The words came out staggered—I felt as though I were in a foreign country, speaking an entirely new language. "Do they know you're here?"

"Mine does," Natalie said.

"I was never adopted," Brooke said. Her tone was clipped. "I grew up in foster homes and a facility run by the state."

I snapped my eyes up from the floor to look at my older daughter. "You weren't raised together?"

Brooke shook her head. "We only just found each other in October. Up until then, Natalie didn't know I existed. We were separated about a month after you gave us up."

"Oh my god," I said. My lungs felt shriveled; I couldn't get enough air. "I'm so sorry . . . I assumed . . . I never thought . . ." I let my words trail off, not having any idea what to say to them. My heart pounded an erratic rhythm behind my rib cage. I couldn't believe that Natalie hadn't even known she had an older sister. The only comfort I'd had over the years was in the knowledge that the two of them had each other after they'd lost me. Discovering this belief was false made me feel as though I'd been shoved off a cliff.

"You didn't know," Natalie said, kindly. "It's just . . . the way things turned out." She paused, fiddling with the strap of the black leather purse resting at her side. When she spoke again, she kept her eyes on my face. "We only know a little about your decision to give up custody. We were hoping . . . wondering, really, if you could tell us a little about what led you to make it. We know you were young, and that things had to be tough for you, having the both of us."

"But people do it," I said, my voice barely above a whisper. "Young, single mothers manage to raise babies all of the time. You want to know why I didn't."

"Yes," Brooke said. "Were we that terrible? That hard to handle?" Her violet eyes flashed, filled with what looked like years of inflamed fury and pent-up grief, both of which I knew I was responsible for.

I glanced at Evan, who had been sitting quietly next to me, and he gave my hand a reassuring squeeze. "You weren't anywhere close to terrible," I said, unable to keep my voice from wavering. "You were both beautiful. I loved you so much. My decision . . . what I did . . . it didn't have anything to do with you. It was about me. I was a mess . . . so insecure and scared. I was doing an awful job as a mother . . . having to beg for money . . . living with you both in my car." I looked back and forth between my daughters. *My daughters.* I still couldn't believe they were here. "I was terrified of things getting worse. I was afraid if I raised you, I'd do a horrible job of it. That I couldn't take care of you properly and you'd end up as screwed up as I was. I wanted you to have a better life than the one I could give you. I'd made so many mistakes . . . so many wrong decisions. I was going to jail. Giving you both a chance to start over without me seemed like the only right choice to make."

"I can see that," Natalie said. She looked at her sister, whose chin trembled. Brooke was almost forty and yet, in this moment, still four, looking every bit the wounded little girl I remembered leaving alone in the car with her sister that night at the store.

"Brooke, I'm so sorry—" I began, but then she cut me off.

"I thought you were going to come back for me," Brooke said. "Did you know that? I cried every night, waiting for you. I thought I'd done something wrong. That I made you leave. Did you think about me at all?"

"I thought about you always," I said. Tears rolled down my cheeks and I didn't bother to wipe them away. "Both of you. Every minute of every day for the longest time. I was sick over how much I worried about you both. So much, it made me feel like I was going insane." Again, I looked at Evan, who gave me an encouraging nod. When I looked at my daughters again, they both stared at me, expectantly. "If you found me through the police," I said, "I assume you know the reason I went to prison the second time? For attempted kidnapping?" They nodded, and so I continued. "That day in the park . . . the little girl I picked up and took into the woods . . . I thought it was you, Brooke."

My elder daughter's expression didn't falter. "That doesn't make any sense."

"No," I said, "it doesn't. I felt crazy. I wasn't stable. It was like I was in the middle of a flashback to the moment Gina and that other woman came to take you away from me. Giving you girls up . . ." My throat closed around these words and I had to cough before I could go on. "The day I said good-bye to you both broke something in me. Finding my way back from that . . . finding a way to live with myself for letting you both go hasn't been easy. There have been moments it's been downright impossible. If it wasn't for Evan"—here I gave my husband a grateful look—"and my work, I'm not sure I would have survived the guilt."

We were all silent for a few moments after I finished speaking. I struggled not to give myself over to hysterics.

"I'm sorry you've gone through so much," Natalie said. "But we're together now. Maybe we can find a way to get to know each other."

I thought about this as I kept my eyes on my daughters,

amazed that these two gorgeous women were the babies I'd brought into this world. But in the very next moment, panic overtook that sense of awe, and before I knew what I was doing, I had let go of Evan's hand and stood up. "I'm sorry," I said. I was done; I'd given them all that I could. "I can't."

"Can't what?" Natalie asked, but instead of responding, I did the only thing I could think of. I raced out of the living room and disappeared through the back door, into the dark night.

Natalie

"Did she really just walk out on us?" Brooke asked as soon as we heard the back door slam shut.

"Brooke," Natalie said, her voice full of warning. "I know you're angry—"

"You're goddamn right I'm angry! Thirty-five years later and 'I can't' is the only thing she has to say?"

"I'm sorry," Evan said. He raked thick fingers through his salt-and-pepper hair. He glanced toward the kitchen, then back at Natalie and Brooke. "I didn't realize she'd react like this."

Brooke didn't say a word. Her jaw was set and her eyes were locked in the direction their mother had gone. Natalie looked away for only a split second, but that was all it took for Brooke to get up and head toward the back door. "Brooke, wait!" Natalie said, but when her sister didn't respond, both Natalie and Evan stood up and followed her onto the deck.

Despite the cold, Jennifer sat without a coat on a cushioned couch, surrounded by her four dogs, who lay by her feet. Brooke stood in front of her with her hands on her hips. "Is that all we get?" she demanded. "Your story? Don't you want to know anything about us? Don't you care?"

Natalie strode over and grabbed Brooke's arm, but her sister jerked away. "Brooke, stop," Natalie said. "Let's just go."

"Natalie has children," Brooke continued, as though her sister hadn't spoken at all. "Her daughter's name is Hailey, and she's seven years old. She's really into cooking shows. And Henry is five, obsessed with Buzz Lightyear."

Jennifer looked up from the ground, the glow from the porch light reflecting in her eyes. Her shoulders curled forward, and she seemed so small, a little like an animal, stuck in a trap. In her face, Natalie could picture the young, frightened girl she had been when she chose to let them go. Their birth mother was an accomplished professional, but she also seemed brittle, as though she might shatter from a simple touch or misspoken word. Evan stepped over and sat down next to his wife again, but he stayed silent.

"That's right," Brooke said, clearly fighting back her own tears. "You're a grandmother." She ran her right hand over her burgeoning belly, tucking the fabric of her blouse around it so the fact that she was pregnant was impossible to miss. "And you'll be one again in April. I'm having a girl, too, but I haven't decided on a name yet. I'm single, like you were, but I'm going to raise her on my own." Her shoulders began to shake. "Don't you want to know them?" Brooke asked. "Don't you want to know us?"

"I'm so sorry," Jennifer said in a wobbling voice, then dropped her eyes back to the ground. She reached down and stroked the silky head of one of her dogs in a repetitive movement, one that reminded Natalie of the way Brooke's fingers had worked the edge of her lavender blanket when Natalie returned it to her the first time they saw each other as adults.

"It's okay," Natalie said. "We understand. We just wanted to see you. To let you know we were okay. We won't bother you again."

"Don't do this!" Brooke cried, staring at their mother. "You have to say something! Please!"

Natalie felt the muscles convulse inside her chest; her sister sounded like a child again. A few tears rolled down her cheeks. She couldn't stand the pain Brooke was in; they both had hoped for such a different reaction than Jennifer had given them. But there was no changing it now. The woman obviously wasn't capable of having a relationship with them. It was time for them to leave.

Natalie took Brooke by the arm again, and this time, her sister didn't pull away. "Thanks for talking with us," Natalie said to Jennifer. "And we're sorry to blindside you like this. I'll leave you my card inside, just in case you ever change your mind. We wish you both the best."

"Take care," Evan said, rising from the couch to briefly shake Natalie's hand. "Let me walk you to your car."

"That's okay," Natalie said. "We're fine."

Evan nodded, and sat back down next to his wife. He put a long arm around her, and she leaned into his chest, closing her eyes. "I'm so sorry," she said again, and then Natalie led Brooke into the house, stopping briefly to drop one of her business cards on the kitchen counter. A moment later, they were inside Natalie's car, backing out of the driveway, pointed south, on the road toward home.

Lost in their own thoughts, the two sisters didn't speak until they were almost halfway back to Seattle. Brooke wept quietly for the first ten minutes or so of the trip, but Natalie kept silent, knowing at this point there were few words she could offer that would provide any comfort. They'd made the decision to show up at Jennifer's house together, but it was Brooke who seemed the most driven to confront their mother. It was she who had the deepest issues to resolve.

"I can't believe she just shut down like that," Brooke finally said as they passed the sign that told them the express lanes were closed heading into Seattle. "Can you believe it?"

"I don't know," Natalie said, carefully. "It kind of makes sense. We sort of sprang ourselves on her. Did you notice how shaky she was?"

"We were all shaky," Brooke said. She stared out the passenger side window. "But she hardly answered our questions before she bolted. She didn't ask us a damn thing about ourselves."

"I think it was too much for her," Natalie said. "She could barely speak when we were out on their deck. Maybe seeing us . . . getting to know us . . . would be too painful. A constant reminder of the things she felt like she did wrong." This wasn't about them, Natalie tried to convince herself. It was about Jennifer.

"She did do things wrong," Brooke said, and Natalie felt her sister's eyes on her. "She went to prison for them."

"Right," Natalie said. "And then she changed her life. She's done a lot of good, too. For other inmates, and for herself. She's built a successful career and what looks like a happy marriage. Maybe she's worried if she let us in, she'd lose all of that. Maybe she's just not wired to handle it." She realized that in saying all of this to Brooke, she was attempting to convince herself of it, too.

"Maybe," Brooke conceded. "But that doesn't make it hurt any less."

"I know," Natalie said. "I had expectations, too. I wanted her to leap up and hug us. I wanted a mushy, emotional reunion. The kind you used to see on *Oprah*." Brooke gave her the shadow of a smile, and then Natalie continued. "But we saw her, right? We did what we said we needed to. Everything that happened after that was out of our control. She can't be who we want her to be, just because we want it. She is who she is. And we have to respect whatever boundaries she sets."

Brooke frowned at her. "How are you being so rational right now? I feel like shit."

Natalie thought a moment before answering, keeping her eyes

on the road ahead of them. "Probably because I don't remember her the way you do. It's easier for me to stay objective."

"I don't really remember much about her," Brooke said, softly. "Not specifically." She shrugged. "What I remember is the feeling of her. Of having her with me. And then . . . not."

Natalie reached over and squeezed Brooke's hand, knowing that no words could ever fully heal the loss her sister had suffered the day their mother decided to let them go. She took the Stewart Street exit off I-5 in order to drop Brooke at her apartment on Capitol Hill.

"You all right?" Natalie asked as she pulled up in front of Brooke's building. "Want me to come in?" It was almost eight thirty, and Kyle had likely already put the kids to bed, so Natalie didn't need to hurry home.

Brooke shook her head. "I'm okay." She paused, as though she were reconsidering her statement. "Sad, but okay."

"I'm sad, too. I wish things had turned out differently. For all of us."

"I'm glad we went together, though." Brooke gave Natalie a grim smile. "I might have really gone off on her if you hadn't dragged me out of there."

"You're welcome," Natalie said.

Brooke laughed and put her hand on the door handle. "Talk with you tomorrow?"

"You bet," Natalie said, watching to make sure her sister was safely inside the building before she drove around the block and headed back toward the freeway. She wondered if it was too late for her to stop by and see her parents. She'd called her mother earlier in the day to let her know that she and Brooke planned to drive up to Mt. Vernon.

"We just want to talk with her," Natalie had said. "To understand why she gave us up."

"Okay," her mother replied, quietly. "Will you at least let me know when you get home? And if you're okay?"

"Of course," Natalie promised, so now, using the voice commands on her cell phone's headset, Natalie called the landline at her parents' house. Her father picked up after only two rings. "Hey, Dad," she said. "Is it okay if I come by? Or are you guys about to turn in?"

"I haven't gone to bed before eleven in forty years," her dad said with an awkward laugh, and Natalie knew that her mother had told him who Natalie had gone to see. "Of course you can come."

Ten minutes later, Natalie parked in their driveway, where she texted Kyle and told him where she was, and that she'd fill him in on everything that had happened as soon as she got home. He quickly texted back, "Are you all right?" and Natalie answered, "Yes," even though she wasn't sure this was the truth. She'd remained oddly calm as the situation with Jennifer unfolded, but now, there was a buzzing ache inside her chest, and the tips of her nerves felt raw and exposed.

Natalie tried to ignore her discomfort as she tucked her phone back inside her purse and made her way to the front door. Her mother opened it before Natalie had a chance to knock. "Hi, honey," her mom said. Her face was pale and her expression pinched, and Natalie knew her mother wouldn't have slept tonight if Natalie didn't tell her how things had gone with Jennifer.

"Hey, Mom," Natalie said as she entered the house. She hugged her mother and held on a moment longer than she usually would. When she pulled back, she took off her coat, set her purse on the entryway table, and looked around. "Where's Dad?"

"In his study," her mother said. But as she spoke, Natalie's father appeared in the long hallway and walked toward them.

"Hello, Nat," he said in his usual low, resonant tone. Natalie greeted him with a hug, too.

"Let's go sit in the living room," her mom suggested. "Can I get you anything?"

"A shot of vodka?" Natalie said as they all made their way to the other room. She was only half-joking. The soothing balm of alcohol might be just what she needed.

"Oh," her mom said. "Okay . . ."

Natalie put her hand on her mother's arm. "I was kidding, Mom. I'm fine."

"I just finished a glass of wine," her mother said. "Would you like one?"

"No, thanks," Natalie said, deciding that a drink wasn't what she needed after all. "I can't stay too long."

The three of them sat down on the large sectional, and her parents stared at her, waiting for Natalie to begin. "So," she said. "Brooke and I went to Jennifer's house tonight, but she wasn't home from work when we got there. Her husband, Evan, invited us in to wait."

"Is he . . . was he your biological father?" Natalie's father asked.

"No," Natalie said. "He's someone she met later." She paused. "He seems to really love her."

"That's good," her mother said as she drew a large pillow into her lap. Her fingers worked at straightening its messy blue fringe. "How was your . . ." She stopped and then started again. "How was Jennifer?"

Natalie wondered how best to explain the way her birth mother had reacted to seeing her daughters, then decided that a succinct description of the afternoon's events was the best route to take. "She was shocked, of course, and more than a little upset. Part of me wishes we hadn't sprung ourselves on her like that." Her parents were silent, their eyes glued to Natalie, waiting for her to go on. "Her husband helped calm her down, though, and we were able to ask her some questions."

"What did you ask?" Natalie's mother said, keeping her voice low, as though she wasn't sure she really wanted Natalie to answer.

Natalie went on to describe the brief conversation, and everything Jennifer had said about loving them when they were babies and wanting nothing but the best life for both of her daughters, knowing that with how screwed up she was, she couldn't give that to them. Her parents listened intently, their spines held straight and their heads high as they waited for the one thing from Natalie she knew they really wanted to hear— now that she had met her birth mother, what would happen next?

"She doesn't want a relationship with us," she told them. "She seemed pretty fragile, actually. I don't think she could handle it. She said it took a lot for her to get over the shame she felt about giving us up, all the mistakes she made, and I guess seeing us now . . . the thought of getting to know us better, or having us in her life at all, was too much for her." The buzzing sensation in her chest grew more intense, and Natalie's eyes grew wet. "Brooke had a harder time hearing this than I did, I think. But still, it was hard."

"Of course it was," her dad said. His tone was solemn, and his words were sincere.

Natalie shrugged, trying to appear more detached than she felt. "It's probably for the best," she said. "But I'm glad I at least got to meet her. I feel like I understand why she did what she did now, and how it affected her, too, so that's good. I got some closure." She looked at her mother, who hadn't yet spoken in response to hearing that Natalie wouldn't have any kind of ongoing relationship with Jennifer. "See, Mom?" she said, powerless to keep the quiver from her voice. "You don't have to worry. She doesn't want anything to do with me."

Her mother's expression melted from its frozen state into one of compassion. "Oh, sweetheart," she said. "I'm so sorry." She got up and came to sit next to Natalie. "She has no idea what's she missing."

There was so much love in those words, so much truth in

her mother's eyes, Natalie's grief rose up from roots so deep she hadn't known they were there. No matter the rationale behind it, no matter how much it made sense, the weight of Jennifer's blatant rejection finally hit her, and she began to cry. Hot tears and jagged sobs racked her body until her mother—the only true mother she'd ever had—held her tight, and Natalie knew that she'd never let her go.

Brooke

As soon as Brooke entered her apartment after Natalie dropped her off, she kicked off her shoes and undressed, taking a moment to stand sideways and naked in front of the full-length mirror that hung on the back of the bathroom door. Her breasts were larger, and her belly was certainly rounded, though not quite as much as she'd thought it would be. At her latest appointment with her obstetrician, a follow-up after her trip to the ER, Brooke had asked if her baby girl was growing at the right rate. "I feel like I don't look big enough," Brooke said, and her doctor smiled.

"Every woman carries her pregnancies differently," she said. "Some show right away, others don't. If you remember I told you, your uterus is tilted toward the back instead of the front. Don't worry. You'll pop out any day now, and suddenly, you won't be able to see your feet."

Brooke thought about this as she ran her hand over the swell of her stomach, wondering if Natalie had shown from the start of her pregnancy with Hailey; she made a mental note to ask her sister about it the next day. And then she thought how happy she was that she had a sister she *could* ask these kinds of things.

Especially after today, seeing their mother, she couldn't imagine a life without Natalie in it.

Throwing on her most comfortable pair of fleece pants and a tank top, Brooke plodded out of the bathroom and climbed into bed. Curling onto her side, she pulled the covers up over her shoulders and under her chin, wondering if Natalie was home yet, and if she had filled Kyle in on what happened at their birth mother's house. However much she tried not to think about it, Brooke couldn't help but go over and over everything Jennifer had said, dissecting it for something that would take away the sting of the fact that she didn't want anything to do with her daughters. Brooke understood that Natalie was right—if their birth mother wasn't capable of handling emotionally charged situations, then it was better if they stayed away from her altogether. Brooke had seen, as much as Natalie had, how skittish Jennifer was when she talked with them.

She said she gave Brooke and Natalie up because she loved them. Because she wanted the best for them. Shouldn't that be enough? Wasn't that what Brooke really needed to know? Still, her heart pounded as she remembered standing in front of her birth mother on that back deck, begging Jennifer for something she clearly didn't have in her to give. But then something dawned on her. Maybe what she and Natalie needed from her was something their mother never had in the first place. *Maybe,* Brooke thought, *in walking away, she gave us the most important gift that she could.*

The next morning, Brooke woke up around nine, not remembering when she'd finally managed to fall asleep. It was Wednesday, and she didn't have to work until the following night. When she rolled over and checked her phone on the nightstand, Brooke saw a text from Natalie. "You doing okay?" it read, and Brooke quickly typed her answer. "I think so. How about you?" A few seconds later, Natalie's response came back: "I bawled my eyes out on my mom's couch last night, which helped. I'm better now." Her words were followed by a long line of Xs and Os, which Brooke copied and sent back. It felt so good to have someone check in on her, someone who knew what she was going through well enough to be concerned.

Once she'd showered and dressed, Brooke took her prenatal vitamins along with a quick breakfast, then decided to get in her car and head toward Northgate Mall. Her head still felt foggy and her chest ached a bit after the tears she'd cried the night before, but the more she replayed what had happened with Jennifer—the more she thought about her birth mother's seemingly inherent inability to parent—the more motivated Brooke felt to do everything she could to prepare for the experience herself. The fact that Jennifer didn't have it in her to be a good mother didn't mean that Brooke was destined to the same fate. There were books she could read, classes she could take. She had her sister to help her along the way.

But today, the best thing she could think of to do—the quickest route she could take toward increasing her confidence that she could raise a child on her own—was to make a list of everything she would need to buy in order to take good care of a baby. She wanted to be prepared.

After finding a parking spot near Target, Brooke entered the store and grabbed a cart, thinking that even on her limited budget, she'd be able to buy a few things for the baby. She headed toward the baby section, a department she'd never spent time in before, determined, at the very least, to find an outfit for her daughter to wear home from the hospital. She imagined a frilly pink dress with white lace edging, white tights, and tiny black patent shoes. *And a matching headband with a bow,* she thought. She wondered if her daughter would have any hair when she was born, or if she'd be bald, like other babies she'd seen. She wondered if she'd recognize Ryan in their daughter's face right away. She thought about the night she'd last seen him, standing next to her car, offering his support, his many texts and voicemails since then, and she suddenly thought how resentful she would have been if *her* father had wanted to help take care of her and Brooke's mother refused him. If he had wanted to be a part of her life and was deliberately shut out. She was being unfair, she realized, and decided that she would call Ryan later that night and talk with him about the role he might play in their daughter's life, not wanting to deny her child what Brooke had been denied herself. She would make it clear that she wasn't interested in resuming the more intimate side of their relationship. For her own peace of mind, she needed to prove to herself that who she was—the life she built on her own—was enough.

On her way to the infant and toddler clothing department, she passed a wall covered with a variety of cribs, changing tables, and car seats, and decided to take a look. She ran her eyes over the many items from which she had to choose, realizing she should have searched the Internet for some kind of baby-readiness checklist before she decided to shop. She really had no idea where to start. She didn't know the difference between a crib and a bassinet. And why would Target carry a bedside Co-Sleeper? Hadn't Brooke read stories about women rolling over and accidentally suffocating their babies in the middle of the night? Maybe that was the reason for a Co-Sleeper, so the baby would be within easy reach but not on the bed with her. Did she need them all? She couldn't believe how expensive some of the cribs were; she'd paid less for her junky, high-mileage first car. Her pulse began to race, and she worried she'd made a massive error in judgment thinking that she could do this on her own. If she couldn't even pick out a crib, how was she going to do everything else? How was she going to change diapers, breast-feed, or figure out how to get her baby to stop crying? How would she choose a daycare or know when her daughter should start eating solid foods?

"When are you due?" a woman's voice asked, jerking Brooke

out of her thoughts. She turned to see a tall, elegant-looking black woman standing next to her. She was pregnant, too, likely further along than Brooke, since her stomach looked as though she'd swallowed a basketball. Her stance was wide, and her right arm was angled so her hand was pressed against her lower back.

"April," Brooke said, trying to sound more confident than she felt. "Toward the end of the month." She glanced down the aisle behind her, shocked by the multitude of products sitting on the shelves. There were bottles and bibs, pacifiers and what appeared to be fifty different kinds of infant socks. How would she ever choose the right ones? She looked back at the woman. "How about you?"

"February sixth," the woman said. "I'm not sure I can hold out until then."

Brooke smiled, uncertain how to respond. Did all pregnant women just strike up conversations with each other? Was this something she'd need to learn to do, too? She was good at chatting with customers for her job, knowing how to charm them to work toward a better tip, but in most situations, Brooke was the one to stand back and wait for others to talk with her.

"Is this your first?" the woman asked, and Brooke nodded. "I thought so," the woman said. "You have a bit of the wide-eyed, what-the-hell-did-I-get-myself-into look." She grinned, and Brooke felt her cheeks flame red, wondering if her ineptitude was really that obvious.

"Excuse me," she said, and she hurried away from the woman, heading into the baby clothing department, where she was confronted with even more choices than what she'd just seen in terms of car seats and cribs. There were overalls and shirts and pairs of tiny jeans. There were things called "onesies" and sleeping sacks and bodysuits. Dresses. She wanted to find her baby a dress. That's all she needed to get today. Everything else, she would figure out later.

Brooke took a couple of steps over to a rack of baby dresses and lifted a hanger off a display. The dress was light pink, and while it didn't have lace edging, it was made out of some kind of luminescent fabric that shimmered under the store's fluorescent lights. Seeing that it was labeled "6 months," she put it back and looked for a newborn size, but when she pulled it out, she couldn't believe how tiny the dress was. It looked like it might fit a plastic baby doll. That couldn't be right. Panic twisted in her belly. She couldn't be responsible for something so fragile and small.

She grabbed her phone, her index finger quickly finding Natalie's contact information. Her sister picked up after only two rings. "Nat?" she said, using the shortened version of her sister's name for the first time. It felt strangely intimate, but comfortable, too, as though she'd been calling her this for years. "I don't think I can do this."

"Do what?" Natalie asked. "What happened? Where are you?"

"I'm at Target in Northgate," Brooke managed to say. "I was shopping for the baby and there were so many cribs and pacifiers and all these things I've never even heard of and now I'm freaking out." She took in and released a choppy breath, hoping this would help calm her down. "Will you help me figure out what kind of crib I need to get? And every other goddamn thing? I can't believe how much crap there is to buy. I'm completely overwhelmed."

"You don't need the half of it," Natalie said, laughing. "But of course I'll help. I actually have a ton of baby stuff in storage that I haven't had the heart to get rid of yet. I meant to tell you that you can use whatever you want."

"Oh, wow," Brooke said. "Thanks." She paused. "All I really wanted to do today was buy a cute outfit for the baby, but the newborn size looked so tiny. Are they really that small?"

"Yep," Natalie said with another laugh. "But don't worry. They grow faster than you think. And I've seen you with my kids. You're going to be a wonderful mom."

Hearing this, something inside of Brooke that had been staring downward for years finally looked up. It struck her that while she might always bear the scars of growing up without a mother, she didn't need to be defined by them. Everyone has wounds—we all carry around ghosts from the past. But who she was as a person, the choices she made, the kind of mother she'd be, was totally up to her. Her life and all her relationships were hers to create.

Still, she spoke to her sister again. "You really think so?" she asked.

"I do," Natalie said.

And then Brooke's eyes filled with tears for an entirely different reason than grief. "Hey, Nat," she said, but before she could finish, her sister interrupted, apparently sensing what Brooke was going to ask without her needing to say a word.

"Let me grab my purse," she said. "I'll be right there."

Two hours later, Brooke and Natalie sat across from each other in an Italian restaurant next to the mall, having just ordered lunch. Once her sister had joined her at the store, Brooke was able to ignore the anxiety she felt and enjoy the experience of picking out her daughter's first outfit.

"You probably don't want to go with a fancy dress for her to wear home from the hospital," Natalie advised. "The lace will itch and she'll more than likely spit up on it. Or worse."

"Oh," Brooke said. "I hadn't thought of that." Instead, she chose a light gray pair of buttery-soft pajamas covered in a pattern of pink ballet slippers. She also bought a few packages of onesies, which Natalie said the baby would live in most of the time for the first few months, along with a selection of tiny socks, and a few other pairs of pajamas she hadn't been able to resist. Natalie again reassured her that she had most of what Brooke would need in storage.

"Feeling better?" Natalie asked now, after their server delivered their meals.

Brooke nodded. "Much. Thanks again for coming."

"No problem." Natalie smiled and took a bite of her salad. When she had finished chewing, she spoke again. "I have to eat quick, though, so I'm not late picking up the kids from school."

"Are you going to tell them about meeting Jennifer?"

"No. I don't see any reason to, really. They have their grand-parents."

Brooke felt a twinge of sadness, realizing that her daughter wouldn't have the same thing. How she felt must have shown on her face because Natalie then said, "I need to introduce you to my parents. When you're ready, of course. I'm sure my mom will love having another baby in the family to spoil."

Brooke was about to respond, to express her gratitude for such a generous offer of inclusion, when she felt a flash of something in her belly—a rippling movement, like the flutter of a butterfly's wings. She gasped, and pressed her hand over it.

Natalie put down her fork. "What's wrong?"

"I don't know," Brooke said. "I . . . felt something."

"The baby's moving?" Natalie asked with a smile. Brooke gave her sister a helpless look, and Natalie tilted her head, slightly. "You haven't felt it before?"

"I don't know," Brooke said. "Maybe. It's a little like bubbles moving around." She paused and then lowered her tone so the tables around them wouldn't hear her next words. "I thought it might just be gas."

Natalie laughed. "I thought the exact same thing. Here," she said, scooting out from her side of the booth to come sit next to Brooke. She held out her hand, hovering over Brooke's belly. "Is it okay if . . . ?"

Brooke nodded, indicating that it was fine for Natalie to touch her, and then her sister set a gentle palm on top of her burgeoning stomach, moving it lightly from one spot to the next.

"There!" Brooke said, when she felt the movement again. She pictured the flash of a silver fish underwater, and imagined her daughter swimming around inside her. She took Natalie's hand

and pressed it on top of where the sensation had been. The two women held their breath—waiting, both of them smiling—and Brooke felt more gratitude than she knew her heart could hold. Even though seeing her mother hadn't ended as she'd hoped it would, along the way she and Natalie had found each other. And the next time her baby moved, Brooke's eyes welled up and she hugged her sister, excited for what the future might bring.

Jennifer

After Brooke and Natalie left, I dissolved into hysterical tears. Evan didn't push me to talk, he only led me inside the house, took off my clothes, and put me to bed. He curled up behind me and murmured into my ear that everything was going to be okay. I pressed myself against his body, trying to feed off of my husband's inherent strength. Eventually, he fell asleep, but even as exhausted as I was, I lay awake into the early hours of morning, staring into the dark, replaying the events of the evening inside my head.

"I think it's the flu," I told Chandi the following morning when I called to tell her I wouldn't be coming in to work. I'd cried so much the night before, my sinuses were plugged and my voice sounded as though I'd gargled rocks; there was no need to fake being ill.

"Oh no," Chandi said. "Poor you. Don't worry about a thing. I'll have Paula and the other techs handle what they can of your appointments and reschedule the rest."

"I might be out a few days," I said. My body ached, feeling as though it had been poisoned.

"I won't put anything on your calendar until Friday," she promised.

I thanked her and then hung up, rolling over to tuck the covers under my chin. Two of our dogs, Gypsy and Cleo, curled against me near my feet, while their brothers, Sammy and Chuck, sat next to the bed, whining a little and wagging their tails, unsure what to do. It was seven o'clock, and typically, both Evan and I were in the kitchen drinking our coffee by now; my staying in bed was far from our normal routine.

Evan stood across the room, already dressed in tan Carhartts, black, steel-toed work boots, and a brown flannel shirt. His brow furrowed, watching me. "Are you sure you don't want me to keep you company?" he asked.

I shook my head. "I just need to sleep."

"Okay," he said, but the word was full of doubt. He took a couple of steps closer and then crouched down so our faces were level. His hair was still wet from the shower; his skin smelled of the woodsy, pine-scented soap he preferred. "Should I take the dogs?"

"No," I said. "Leave them, please. They'll take care of me." As though on cue, both Sammy and Chuck leapt back onto the bed, circled twice, and lay down. Gypsy lifted her head from the mattress and set it on top of my leg. Cleo didn't move. None of our dogs weighed more than twenty pounds, but there was a reason Evan and I had a California king-size bed—we needed the extra room. "See?"

"All right." Evan smiled, then leaned over for a quick kiss. "I'll come and check on you at lunch. You need to eat."

I nodded, despite the fact that the thought of food was enough to turn my stomach.

"Love you," he said, and he left a moment later, after I said I loved him, too. When the front door shut and I heard his car start in the driveway, I closed my eyes, wanting nothing more than to fall asleep. But all I saw was the pained look on Brooke's face when she'd confronted me on the deck—the anger that had flashed in her eyes. All I heard was the way her voice strangled when she spoke. The damage I'd done to her clung to her like a second shadow.

Everything I'd thought about the new life I'd given my children was wrong. Hearing that Natalie hadn't even known about Brooke until a few months ago, and that my elder child had spent her childhood in foster homes, had sucked all the air from my lungs. I pictured my younger daughter standing next to Brooke last night: Natalie's blond hair, petite frame, and large, doe-brown eyes, eyes that must have come from her father, a man whose name I'd blanked from my mind, whose face I couldn't recall. She seemed so capable and strong as she attempted to calm Brooke down. Seeing her like this, I had no doubt that Natalie was a wonderful mother—patient and loving—something she must have learned from the woman who raised her. She certainly didn't inherit it from me.

I knew in my gut that I couldn't live up to their expectations, and it only took a moment for me to ruin whatever meet-my-birth-mother fantasies they might have had. I wasn't strong enough to be their mother when they were babies, when they needed it most, and after my response to seeing them last night, it was clear I couldn't be strong for them now. What they sought, I couldn't give them. The truth was, no matter how far I'd come, how much I'd accomplished, a huge part of me was still that young woman who fell apart when she gave up custody of her children. I was still the troubled, unstable girl who thought she heard her daughter's voice that day in the park. Having them in my life now would only magnify that girl, bring her to the surface again, after I'd worked so hard to keep her contained.

This was how I spent the next forty-eight hours, remembering, crying, and sleeping, burrowing beneath the covers, replaying every moment of the short time my daughters stood in front of me, reliving every one of my past mistakes. As he promised he would, Evan checked on me throughout the day, bringing me water and bits of food.

On the third day, he entered our bedroom about noon, bringing with him half of a turkey sandwich and a glass of ice water, which he set on the night table. He called the dogs off the bed, ordering them outside, then sat down on the edge of the mattress.

I righted myself and leaned against the headboard. He grabbed the water and gave it to me. Obediently, I drank almost half of it and then took two bites of the sandwich before I set it back on the plate. He waited while I got up and walked to the bathroom and then watched as I washed my hands and climbed back in bed.

"You aren't going to get up?" he asked. "Maybe move to the living room?"

"I'm fine here," I said. I looked at him with wide, glassy eyes.

"You know you can't do this forever," he said.

"I know," I snapped, and then, regretting my tone, I reached out and grabbed one of his rough-skinned workman's hands. No matter how well he scrubbed, his cuticles were always slightly darkened by engine grease. "I know," I said again, softly. "I just need a little more time."

He stared at me, then squeezed my fingers in return, but didn't say anything more.

After a moment of silence, I spoke again. "Do you think I did the right thing?" My heart banged inside my rib cage, waiting for his reply.

"That's not up to me to decide," he said.

Frustrated by the neutrality of his response, I let go of his hand and pulled my own hands back into my lap, curling them into fists. "Tell me what you think, Evan. Please. I need to hear it. They came here looking for a relationship with me . . . with their mother . . . and I just . . . freaked out. I disappointed them. I hurt them, even more than I already had. I'm a horrible person, right?"

Go ahead, I thought. *Say it. Confirm everything I already know. All the trained dogs in the world can't make up for the fact that I abandoned my children. Twice.*

Evan ran his fingers through his shaggy silver-brown hair. "No," he said, and I could tell from his tone he was a little frustrated with me, too. "You're not. You thought you'd never see them again, but now you have, and this is what happened. You went with exactly how you felt in the moment. It was a genuine reaction. A real one. You were overwhelmed, and scared. You realized you couldn't handle it. That doesn't make you a bad person. It just makes you honest."

"But—" I said, and my voice cracked before I could go on.

"But, nothing," Evan said. "You are so many things to so many people, baby. To me, to Randy and Lisa, to Chandi and to Paula, and all your other employees. To the women you work with through the prison. Not to mention the animals you take care of every day. I feel like you don't see any of how much you mean to us. How good you are. How loved. You can't keep letting one decision define the whole of who you are. Whether it was right or wrong, you have to forgive yourself. You have to accept that it's healthy to know your limits." He leaned toward me and cupped my face in his large hands, locking his hazel eyes on mine. "You gave your girls their best chance. Even if their lives didn't work out the way you hoped, you can choose to be happy they found each other now. And I'm telling you that what you need . . . your best chance . . . is to forgive yourself. You need to find a way to be okay with your decision. Really, truly, deep-down okay."

I stared at my husband through teary eyes, blinking fast, trying to digest all he had said. "You don't think I'm weak?"

"No," he said, dropping his hands from my face. "I don't." He leaned forward and kissed both of my cheeks, then my lips, and I tasted the salt of my own tears. "I think you're one of the strongest women I've ever known," he continued. "Other people who've been through just one of the struggles you've faced might have been crushed. But not you. You kept going. You didn't give up. No matter what, no matter how much pain you were in, you pushed ahead and kept trying to do the right things, make better choices, and live a good life." He paused. "You wouldn't be who you are or where you are without your faults, Jenny. And who you are is amazing."

"Thank you," I whispered. His words felt like balloons, lifting a leaden weight off my chest. *I am more than my mistakes,* I thought. *I am stronger than I know.* Evan was right—everything good in my life had only happened because of the things I'd done wrong. Everything was connected, linked to the moment I got pregnant with Brooke, and then that night when I left the girls alone in the car. Getting caught led me to prison, which ultimately led me to Randy and working with dogs. Working with dogs led me to Evan, a successful career, and eventually, being able to give back to others like me. Yes, I was a woman who couldn't raise her own children, but as a result, I had become so much more than that. The kind of hurt my daughters had suffered—and were surely suffering through right now—was part of their lesson, just as my pain was a part of mine.

Still, I wished I could do something to make up for the damage I'd done. I remembered how easy it used to be to comfort Brooke with just the touch of her "soft side" blanket, and then later, how she gave it to her baby sister so Natalie could be comforted, too. Even if I couldn't be in their lives, I wished for a way I could offer both of my daughters that kind of comfort now.

A thought struck me then, and I knew what I had to do. Without a word, I threw back the covers and scrambled out of bed.

Evan stood up, startled. "Where are you going?"

"The garage." The air outside of the warm bed nipped at my skin; for three days, I'd only worn one of Evan's white T-shirts, so I quickly dug through one of my drawers for a pair of sweats to replace it.

"Now?" he said, squinting at me.

"Yep," I said as I changed my clothes. "Now." I shoved my feet into a pair of his slippers.

"Jenny . . ." he began, but before he could finish, I opened the bedroom door and rushed down the hallway, through the living room, and into the garage. Glancing around at the shelves that lined two of the walls, I searched for the clear plastic box I opened only twice a year, finally spotting it on the highest shelf, next to the red and green Rubbermaid boxes that held our holiday decorations.

"What are you looking for?" Evan said as he walked up behind me.

"That," I said, pointing toward the box.

His eyes followed the direction of my finger. "Our Christmas stuff?"

"No," I said. I took the two steps down to the cement floor and pointed again. "The other box, next to those. The clear one."

This time, he saw what I meant. "Your letters to the girls," he said slowly, and I nodded.

"Are you sure reading them is a good idea right now?" he asked. "You've already had a rough couple of days."

"I don't want to read them," I said, and my voice quavered. "I want to send them to my daughters."

A look of understanding passed over Evan's face, and he came down the steps to join me. He put one long, strong arm around my shoulders and squeezed. "I'll get them down."

I crossed my arms over my chest, shifting my weight from one foot to the other as I watched him take a six-foot ladder and set it up next to the appropriate shelf, retrieving what I needed. A moment later, Evan carried the box through the house and put it on the kitchen table. I followed him inside, then stood next to the table and removed the snapped-on lid.

"I can stay and help," he offered. "If you want."

"Thank you," I said, giving him a grateful smile. "For doing this"—here, I motioned toward the box—"and everything you said to me in the bedroom. You're so good to me. But I think this is something I need to do on my own. You should get back to work anyway."

He looked at me a moment longer, then nodded. "The card Natalie left with her contact information is on the fridge, under the blue magnet. In case you end up going to the post office. There are some smaller boxes in the hall closet that might work."

"Okay." I took a couple of steps over so I could hug him. "I love you so much."

"Love you more," he said, and then he left through the back door. The dogs made a ruckus when he joined them outside, and he called them to follow him, which I appreciated. They'd distract me if he'd let them stay home.

After he was gone, I stood in the silence, unmoving, contemplating what I was about to do. I stared at the stack of notebooks inside the box, the earlier pages filled with one or two sentences, couplets of my thoughts about the girls when they were young; the later containing the letters I'd written to each of them on her birthday each year. I wondered if they would sit down and read everything together. Or if each of them would take a turn, poring over every one of my words on their own before coming back together and talking about the things they'd learned about me—the things they'd learned about their past.

It was daunting to imagine them peeling open these pages and seeing into the depths of me, into the record of the things I'd wished for them, their dreams I hoped had come true. I hoped that in my passing all of this on, both of my girls would better understand what I'd been through, why I made the decisions that affected them both so much. I hoped they would laugh a little when they came across the stories of the funny things they did when they were babies; I hoped their hearts would be warmed by my words. I hoped these notebooks would help them to forgive the woman who'd brought them into the world—the woman who ended up leaving them to the find their way through it without her.

Just like my mom did to me, I thought, and I felt an ache in the pit of my stomach, recalling the day I stood on her front porch and she turned me away. *Am I like her?* At the time, and over the many years since, I couldn't fathom how she could just cut off a relationship with her only child. How she could see me needing her, asking for help, and still she closed the door. Yet here I was, under different circumstances, basically having done the same thing to Natalie and Brooke.

I sat down at the table and, with shaking hands, began removing the notebooks from the box. A voice in my head warned me that I'd probably be better off forgetting the whole idea— that I should just put the box back up high on the shelf. What if getting this package from me only made things worse? What if now, after I'd rejected them, my daughters couldn't care less about my thoughts, or what memories I had of the time together we'd shared? What if the package came back, marked RETURN TO SENDER?

But then another thought struck me. This decision wasn't about me, or how I felt. It was about Natalie and Brooke, about giving them something they needed. I wanted to give them answers, which was more than my mother had given to me. I'd never know why my mom made the decisions she did, but if I went through with mailing the package, Natalie and Brooke wouldn't suffer the same fate. Sending them my notes and letters was about giving them an explanation—giving them the truth, as imperfect and ugly and unfair as it could sometimes be. It was giving them everything I could.

Half an hour later, I had filled a brown cardboard shipping box with the stack of notebooks. Then came the hardest part—writing one final note to my girls. I grabbed a blank sheet of paper from the printer in the den, then returned to the kitchen, where I sat back down at the table and began to write.

Dear Brooke and Natalie,

I know I hurt you both, and for that, I can never say "I'm sorry" enough. I spent so many years trying to convince myself that you were better off without me that I don't know how to believe anything else is true. If I were a different person, I might be able to handle the weight of your pain, but as it turns out, I've had a hard enough time managing my own. I don't offer this as an excuse, only as explanation for my inability to become the addition to your lives that you might have hoped.

What I hope now is that the contents of this box give you at least some of what you came looking for from me. I hope they give you some answers, some important pieces in the puzzle of your history. I hope you get a sense of the scared, messed-up girl I was when I had you and just how much I missed and loved you over the years. No matter the distance between us, the two of you will always be the biggest part of my heart.

I signed my name, and then sealed up the box, resting my palms flat upon it as though I were granting it a blessing. I glanced at the clock on the kitchen wall, noting that I still had plenty of time to get to the post office. All I needed was Natalie's address from the card on the fridge, along with my wallet and my car keys, and I'd be on my way. I'd take the short drive downtown and send the package off. I'd say a little prayer to wish it well— to wish my daughters happiness and peace—and I'd then come home to my husband, to the life I'd built in spite of my many messy but necessary mistakes. Mistakes, as Evan had said, that helped shape me. And while there was no guarantee I wouldn't make more as time went on, one thing was clear—one thing I knew somewhere down deep in the cells of my body. Whether or not my daughters forgave me, sending them this package might be the only way for me to forgive myself. It was time for me to move on.

I'd finally found a way to let go of the past.

Acknowledgments

As so often happens in my writing life, the idea for this story began in the smallest of ways, after my cousin told me how one of the young boys he was fostering reacted upon seeing a fully stocked pantry in their home. This profound image stuck with me, and without my knowing, a seed was planted and this book began to grow. So first and foremost, I must thank Shane Minden, a man with more patience and heart than anyone I've ever known, for the act of sharing a raw, and too often unheard, truth.

Thanks also to the fabulous and formidable Victoria Sanders, my agent and dear friend, for knowing when to comfort me and when to kick me in the ass. Her loyal support and fierce savvy is unwavering, as is her team's—Diane Dickensheid, Bernadette Baker-Baughman, Chris Kepner, and Tony Gabriel. (I know that the toffee-crack I make and send your way isn't the only reason you work so hard on my behalf, but I tell myself that it helps.)

There are few words I can find to express the depth of my gratitude for the relationship I have with my developmental editor, Greer Hendricks. As always, her wisdom and understanding of what my heart was trying to say gave me perfect insight on how to whip this story into shape. She is—to use an idiom she surely would make me strike from the page—one in a million.

Thanks to Sarah Cantin, another gifted editor with whom I have the privilege to work, for her unstoppable enthusiasm and advocacy for my books. Her thoughtful expertise helped put a finished polish on these pages, and I am so very lucky to have her on my side.

Thanks to the amazing professionals at Atria Books—Judith Curr, Suzanne Donahue, Paul Olsewski, Lisa Sciambra, Andrea Smith, Arielle Kane, Jin Yu, Haley Weaver, and Isolde Sauer. This list could go on and on. To every member of the sales team, the art department (especially Janet Perr for designing this beautiful cover!), and marketing—to anyone who touches my books—I cannot tell you how deeply I appreciate you all.

How different my life as a writer became with the dawn of social media! The wonderful people I have met there, the fun we have, the lovely notes you have written me . . . what an amazing sense of community, all founded on the love of the books. I wish I could hug every single one of you for your enthusiasm and support.

Thanks to my best friend, Tina Skilton, for always listening, and with a shrewd eye, helping me to brainstorm my way out of the rough spots. Thanks to my tribe: Kristie Miller, Jenifer Groh, Sally Cote, Sherrie Stockland, Loretta Bellman, Rachael Brownell, and, honestly, too many others to name. You know who you are, and you know how much I need and love you all.

Thanks to my family: my mother, Claudia Weisz, for always listening, my goofy and brilliant children, Scarlett, Miles, and my bonus daughter, Anna, for making me laugh. And finally, thanks to Stephan, not for being perfect, but for being the perfect one for me.

somewhere
out there

AMY HATVANY

A Readers Club Guide

Questions and Topics for Discussion

1. When Jennifer gives up custody of her children, she is told she is giving them their best chance, and she later comforts herself that she did the right thing for both her girls and herself. In what ways does the book support or refute this idea? Does it ultimately seem that this decision was the best choice for all three women? Why or why not?

2. The novel is told through the alternating perspectives of three characters: Jennifer, Brooke, and Natalie. Jennifer's is the only one told in the first person. What is the effect of this style of narration? Whose voice did you most identify with? Are there other characters whose points of view you would have liked to see? How might the story look differently through their eyes?

3. Natalie's parents keep Brooke a secret from Natalie well into her adult life. What were their motivations in withholding this information? Did you feel this decision was justified?

4. Maternal figures play significant roles throughout the novel, including Brooke as an expecting mom. Brooke is terrified she might be a "bad" mother. In your opinion, what makes a good or bad mother, and in which category would you place the various mothers in the novel? Consider Jennifer, Jennifer's mom, Natalie, Natalie's adoptive mother, and Brooke's former roommate Zora. Did reading *Somewhere Out There* change any of your perceptions of what makes a good mother?

5. If Jennifer had not been chosen for the veterinary antirecidivism program when she was released a second time, she might have been in the same difficult position looking for employment as she was after her first incarceration. If she had taken the job offered by her fellow inmate O'Brien—working for a drug dealer—would you see her character differently? How do you think Brooke or Natalie would have responded when they found her?

6. Natalie observes: "[K]ids seem to be who they'll grow up to be pretty early in life. . . . Kyle and I have helped teach them how to make good choices between what's right and what's wrong, but their personalities have been with them from the get-go." When Jennifer meets Natalie and Brooke, she is shocked at how easily she recognizes them. To what extent do Brooke's and Natalie's personalities seem intrinsic, and how much seems to be a result of their upbringing? To what degree has Jennifer's personality changed at the end of the novel, when she's fifty-five, compared to the beginning, when she's a teenager?

7. Discuss the way Brooke approached decisions related to her pregnancy. Did you agree with her initial instinct to keep Ryan, the father, out of the child's life? Or her choice to keep the baby? What would you have done in her shoes? What are the considerations—logistical and philosophical—that affect these kinds of decisions, and how do these considerations play out when Brooke and Jennifer face tough choices?

8. Brooke and Natalie have drastically different childhoods, but once reunited, they find common ground in the shared experience of separation from their birth mother. What other similarities between them mark them as sisters? Ultimately, do you think nature trumps nurture, or vice versa?

9. Throughout the novel, various characters note how technology and popular opinions about adoption influence their actions, from their decisions about whether to tell children that they are adopted to the use of the internet to track down family members. How would this story have been different in an earlier time period?

10. The importance of familial support is emphasized throughout the book, whether it comes from a sibling, parent, or spouse. How are the consequences of a lack of familial support depicted within the book? Discuss which relationships in *Somewhere Out There* seem more or less nurturing, and their direct and indirect effects on the characters involved.

Enhance Your Book Club

1. When Jennifer is in prison, she is able to reach a real turning point in her life as a result of an antirecidivism program. Prison book programs are also shown to reduce recidivism. Consider volunteering or donating books as a group to one that serves prisoners in your area, or learn more at prisonbookprogram .org.

2. Consider reading another novel that tackles the issue of adoption, such as *Little Beauties* by Kim Addonizio, *The Mothers* by Jennifer Gilmore, or *The Comfort of Lies* by Randy Susan Meyers. How is this issue treated differently in those novels compared with *Somewhere Out There*, and how does perspective affect the story being told?

3. For Jennifer, the dogs she works with become not only a way of helping others, but also a source of personal comfort and pride in her ability to take care of something other than herself. How have animals in your life influenced you? Has a pet ever protected you or helped you get past a difficulty? Discuss as a group. To learn more about service animals, read more at pawswithacause.org.